THE CANARY THIEF

When an anonymous tip-off brings Police Constable Lawson to an empty house he finds the body of a murdered prostitute, a pet rabbit and a rucksack with the name Jacob Palmer in it. The police already know about Jacob — a young runaway who seems to be behind a spate of stolen canaries. Is he also the mysterious caller who alerted them to the dead woman's presence? To discover the truth the police are forced to set up surveillance on the house . . .

Kate Stacey lives in Southampton with her two children and a variety of pets. She has been writing for several years. She has attended Arvon and has won a 'Most Promising Novel' award from The National Association of Writers' Groups. Currently she is also doing a media degree. Her hobbies include walking and line dancing and she has a curious fascination for the Seventies' detectives.

KATE STACEY

◆

THE CANARY THIEF

Complete and Unabridged

ULVERSCROFT
Leicester

First published in Great Britain in 2000 by
Judy Piatkus (Publishers) Limited
London

First Large Print Edition
published 2002
by arrangement with
Judy Piatkus (Publishers) Limited
London

British Library CIP Data

Stacey, Kate
    The canary thief.—Large print ed.—
Ulverscroft large print series: mystery
    1. Detective and mystery stories
    2. Large type books
    I. Title
    823.9'2 [F]

    ISBN 0–7089–4658–5

Published by
F. A. Thorpe (Publishing)
Anstey, Leicestershire

Set by Words & Graphics Ltd.
Anstey, Leicestershire
Printed and bound in Great Britain by
T. J. International Ltd., Padstow, Cornwall

This book is printed on acid-free paper

This book is for Mum and Dad
Ben and Emily
for their support and belief.

Acknowledgements

Where to begin? Along this journey there have been obvious 'stepping stones' — places and people who have offered helpful advice, a boost to my ego, or just plain sympathy — and all with unwavering enthusiasm. These people have suffered my homicidal experimentation (literarily not literally!) unflinchingly. The list that follows, compiled in no particular order, signifies the thanks and appreciation I feel for you all.

Val McDermid. Chaz Brenchley. Frances Fyfield. Martin Corrick. Ken and Doreen Le Huquet. Beryl Hughes. Joan Wedge. Ann Matthews. Marion Jones. Karen Meredith. Barbara Godwin. Peter Cooper. Peter Fowler. Peter Morice. Jean and Roy Romsey. Veronique Sandiford. Juanita Nadal. Mary Clarke. Elizabeth Clarke-Melville.

Jo, for the optimism and the bottles of wine — and for denying that my printer kept you awake next door at two in the morning when I'm sure it did.

The Cougall Society.
The Arvon Foundation.
Southampton University.

Kay Smith and the Southampton branch of the WEA.

The National Association of Writers' Groups.

Barbara Large and The Winchester Writers' Conference.

All my family and friends.

And especially Gillian Green for making a dream come true.

Prologue

The boy gently curled his fingers around the canary's slim body. The black eyes darted fearfully, the beak ripped sharply at the boy's flesh.

'Easy!' he whispered, gingerly taking the bird from its cage. 'Easy!'

To stop it flying he wrapped it in the small hand towel he'd taken from a washing line that morning. Then, with the bird's head at eye-level, he gently stroked it and made encouraging clucking noises.

He'd never had a canary like this. The other two had been plain yellow, boring really. This one had a circle of brown feathers crowning its head which, Jacob thought, made it look like a monk.

He could feel the little heart fluttering rapidly beneath his fingertips. Birds were such bony things, feathers adding fraudulent bulk.

'See, it's not so bad.'

A bright black eye looked back into his blue ones, defiant now. The beak had stopped nipping and now began a loud, chirruping alarm call.

'Now don't do that.' Jacob changed the bird into his other hand, 'We don't want anyone hearing us.' In this derelict place no one would, but Jacob, so used to being accused of things he hadn't done, feared the repercussions for something he had.

But what had he done really? Saved the old folk in that home was all. Already they'd been staring at walls or rocking and moaning or spitting when they talked. All he'd done was reach through an open window and unhook the bird cage. No one had shouted or pursued him as he walked quietly away. They must have known he was helping them.

The bird started pecking again, struggled to be free.

'Steady now,' soothed Jacob. 'Soon be over.' He took the penknife from the windowsill, watched his fingers caress the silver blade before tightening around the tortoise-shell haft. 'Here we go.' He tilted the brown-capped head back to reveal a downy throat covered in buttermilk feathers. The blade, looking incongruous against such fragility, slid effortlessly through the flesh. Turning the breast and the edge of the towel with his fingers, Jacob watched the red bleed down, the shade of death.

1

The house was called Storm Mount. Its white stucco walls were draped in Virginia Creeper wearing its autumnal palate — gold through orange through poinsettia. Its pantiled roof glowed dull tan in the sunlight save for the confetti left by fantailed doves perching on the chimney in the centre. Each end was gabled; beneath the right-hand gable, an integral garage, empty but for a rusting bike, and mice.

The river had kept its distance since the last owner left. Now, though, it lapped at the wicket gate at the bottom of the garden, beyond the small orchard, in the highest tide for five years. As the sun sank to its four o'clock level, the upper windows of the house blazed as though the interior was suddenly alight. A dove, returning to its fellows on the roof, was gilded in its rays.

A magpie, mocking loudly, flew for the oak tree beyond the wicket gate. Landing on a branch already winter-bare, it turned its glossy head to peer at the shadow gingerly treading the narrowing line between water and hedgerow. Startled by the magpie, Jacob slipped, grabbed the hawthorn, pulled away a thorn-punctured finger with a loud hiss. Muttering crossly, he reached the gate and clung tightly to it with one hand, his rucksack swinging from the other.

He snuck through the orchard, sneakers soggy from the waterlogged riverbank. Every four or five paces he paused to heave his rucksack higher onto his left shoulder. His face was frozen in concentration, his cheeks and blond hair striped with mud. Where orchard became garden he stopped and knelt on the wet grass to take from his rucksack a parcel neatly wrapped in a carrier bag, and a tablespoon. Tongue between his lips he dug a small hole beside two tiny mounds with lolly stick crosses at their heads. Soon satisfied with the depth of the hole, he opened the parcel, stroked the dead canary perfunctorily and laid it to rest. With a silent promise to God to put a cross on the bird's grave as soon as he'd found two lolly sticks — a task made harder in the winter due to fewer people consuming lollies — and no backward glance, he made for the ramshackle outhouses at the back of the house.

A Dutch rabbit, in a hutch tucked beneath a blackberry bush at the end of the outhouses, hopped eagerly to the wire as Jacob approached.

'Now then Odd-Job,' Jacob spoke in his best Sean Connery accent. 'I see you remain well.' He plucked at the yellowing grass, pulled the screwdriver from the latch to release the door and stroked the rabbit. 'Your ears are cold. Mustn't have the captives complaining about their quarters, I'll bring you some more hay next time I come.' Closing the door and checking the water bottle, Jacob left his rucksack on top of the hutch.

Along the front of the outhouses were two doors. Jacob ignored the first one. Solid wood, it was locked and the key had been missing for years. The door had swollen too big for the frame and so, unless he needed to get inside, he didn't force it open. He made out the comforting shape of his sleeping bag piled against the back wall. He'd been coming here for six months now, since Tina.

He listened, edged towards the back door. He'd not been inside the house since July, before the trouble. Nobody had fixed the window he'd broken last time. He'd done it on purpose to test whether anyone was keeping an eye on the place. Obviously not. Sliding a hand between jagged glass and hardened putty, he turned the snib and pushed open the door. Back flattened against the wall, hands moulded into the shape of a gun, he waited as the door slammed back against the wall. No one there.

Take it steady now, James Bond's voice said in his head. *Remember what I've taught you.*

Gingerly he stepped forward, carefully avoiding the grit on the green-stained lino that crunched underfoot like sand. Gun at arm's length, he stopped in the centre of the kitchen, swivelled 360°. The carcass that had once been a kitchen, with cabinets the infrastructure, was shabby. Tiles had fallen randomly from the wall, lying broken on the floor. A wire hung from the wall, disconnected from a long-gone gas cooker. Jacob paused under the striplight; no bad guys in here. Whistling softly under his breath, he made for the hall, flattening against the wall at the door once more until satisfied no one was waiting to pounce.

Well done, came Bond's approving tones.

The staircase was uncarpeted, rotten. Two of the treads on adjacent stairs halfway up had gone through and the resultant three-stair stretch was difficult for Jacob's twelve-year-old legs. He kept meaning to put planks down but nicking planks was a heavier business than he was used to. As he leant over the banister, slipping feet into alternate gaps between the spindles, he fancied he saw a

6

movement in the lounge below him. He froze, cursed silently. James Bond would have ensured the ground level was secure before attempting to go upstairs. He really must tighten up his technique. He stood for several moments, each one punctuated by his thudding heart, but saw nothing more.

'But this is my house,' he told himself firmly at the top of the stairs. 'Surely even James Bond can go into his bedroom without checking every other room first.' But deep down he knew that probably wasn't true, when you were a top agent the enemy didn't respect the fact that you needed to bathe, eat or sleep. Neither did adults when you were a runaway boy.

Great plans he had for this house. One day, when he was rich, he'd have it back in all its glory. For now though, he did a little here and there and drew plans and designs in notebooks he stole from WH Smith. He'd chosen the back bedroom for his own. It ran the entire width of the house, save for the corner taken by the bathroom, and looked out across the garden with its canary graveyard to the orchard and river beyond. One day last summer, he'd seen a kingfisher, watched it dive, turquoise blue, into the shady water. That decided him. This room had the best view. He was having it for himself.

No one cared about Storm Mount just like no one cared about him. Made for each other they were. He knew that. And, one day, so would his dad, and Tina, and the nosey old bag across the road who, if she saw him, told him off for trespassing and threatened to call the police if 'he didn't clear off out of it'.

The sky had become twilight grey and now it was difficult to separate water from sky. Jacob turned his back on the window and, hands on hips, surveyed his handiwork. The wallpaper, once rose pink, now hung in faded strips. Mice had helped themselves to bits from the corners and snails had made a meal of the bit under the window.

'Shit!' Jacob peered over his shoulder towards Odd-Job's hutch. He'd got slug pellets in his rucksack. He'd fetch them later.

The pale blue he'd painted the chimney breast was streaky in places where the white and blue paints hadn't been mixed properly. Mould was still spreading in the top left-hand corner. He sighed. He'd have to paint that again. Still, it was taking shape. It was going to be yellow and green — Norwich City colours — and he'd have a matching duvet. After he'd got a bed, that was.

He pulled at a strip of wallpaper close to his right hand. It came away easily and he carried on, humming the James Bond theme quietly to himself. He made a gun shape again, pulled a stance at the door then at each of the corners before, satisfied, blowing the end of the barrel and putting it away. He'd be James Bond one day, the snazzy suit, the vodka martini — shaken not stirred, the fancy cars — he fancied a Maserati — and the girls. Sean Connery was James Bond. Pierce Brosnan an acceptable stand-in. And Jacob had started to practise ridding the world of evil, even though it was just canaries. But at least he'd got the hang of keeping things prisoner, thanks to Odd-Job.

We all have to start somewhere.

Still humming quietly, he made his way downstairs. Heading for the lounge, his stomach jumped uneasily. Had there been something moving in there? He wrinkled his freckled nose at the smell. Not musty, not damp, more sort of — metallic. He'd never noticed that before. He edged slowly into the doorway.

An inglenook fireplace dominated the far wall. Placed direct centre, it was flanked by mahogany shelves some six feet wide, covered in dust and mice droppings and mould. One day he'd have a roaring fire there with a rocking chair in front of it and a collection of books by Charles Dickens because he'd written Oliver Twist and Jacob felt akin to him.

The smell was stronger. He stopped just inside the doorway, the hairs on the back of his neck standing up.

'Hello?' He didn't like the way his voice shook. Clearing his throat and repositioning his gun he called out again. 'Hello?' He held his breath, ready to run should anyone answer. No one did. He breathed again.

His heart was thudding for the second time in recent minutes. He couldn't work that out. Nothing frightened Jacob Palmer, not even his dad taking his belt to him. He pushed the door back with his right leg, keeping his imaginary gun firmly pointed into the room. Eighteen inches from the wall, the door met resistance. Cocking his head around the door, he looked, screamed, stepped back.

He'd seen a naked woman before — most of Dad's girlfriends slept and paraded around the house that way. He'd never seen a dead body though. And this one was obviously not sleeping. Her silver-streaked hair was long and half-obscured her face and neck. Fingers shaking, Jacob leant down to gently pull it back. She looked vaguely familiar but with her eye a vicious purple it was difficult to remember whether he knew her or not.

He touched her face, jumping when his

fingertips made contact, then, when she didn't react, stroked her cheek. He hummed the Beatles tune Dad played over and over, 'Blackbird'. He was fascinated by her breasts, floppy and full. Gently he stroked those too. He let his fingers carry on down the swell of her belly to the triangle of hair between her legs, occasionally glancing at her wide open eyes as if to make sure she didn't mind.

Having finished his exploration he sat back on his heels and, motionless, watched her. A necklace of bruises around her neck was all, save the black eye, that disfigured her appearance. She was old, he guessed, older than Dad's girlfriends, older than thirty. Very old. And cold, he now realised as his hand brushed her arm, so cold.

'Hang on,' he whispered. Backing out of the room he headed though the kitchen to the back door.

This was an emergency, he needed to get into the outhouse. The door was so stiff it absolutely refused to budge today. Grabbing a brick, Jacob smashed the grimy window, hoisted himself through the small space. The sleeping bag was damp, slightly smelly, and forcing it back through the window took time Jacob suddenly didn't want to sacrifice.

Arriving, breathless, by the body, he draped it over her. Arranging the hand nearest to him

11

beneath the blue quilting, he found a chain clenched in her palm. He prised it free. A heart-shaped pendant hung on it, one that shone several shades of blue when tilted this way and that. Pushing it hurriedly into his pocket he whispered a crude prayer, and ran.

The phone box was at the end of Amber Close, opposite the church. Jacob thought he'd never run so fast, in fact later, when no one had caught him, he congratulated himself in running faster than the speed of light.

Making that phone call was the hardest thing he'd ever had to make himself do. He knew it was right — Sean Connery would have done it.

It *is* the right thing to do.

But he couldn't shake his Dad's face frowning at him, his voice shouting unrecognisable words, though Jacob got the gist, the usual stuff about 'pigs' and 'bastards'. The officer asked for his name, he slammed the phone down. Enough was enough. He'd told them what he'd found and where, anything else they'd have to find out for themselves. Wasn't that what they were supposed to do?

Exhausted, he pressed himself against the phone box. The cold from the glass seeped through his thin jacket and sweatshirt before the sound of a distant siren galvanised him into action. Time to vacate. Eyes checking right and left, he caught a fleeting glance of the nosy old bag's face peering at him round her net curtain.

Which was all he needed.

He urged his stiff legs across Church Lane and over the church wall. Dodging through the gravestones he could hear the vicar's nightly recital in full swing. From five o'clock for 45 minutes every evening, the vicar practised on the organ. The door was unlocked and, if he was quick enough, Jacob knew he could be through the door, along the side of the church and through the velvet curtain to the left of the pulpit without being spotted.

As he made his way to the tower the vicar began to play 'Onward Christian Soldiers'. So enthusiastic was the rendition that a herd of elephants could have made it up the squeaky spiral staircase without the vicar being any the wiser.

It was dark in the cupboard-like space at the top of the tower, and cold. Jacob suddenly wished he'd not given his sleeping bag to a corpse.

2

PC Sebastian Lawson attended the body at 5.22 pm on Thursday, 21 October. An anonymous call to the nick almost an hour earlier had sent him off on this errand. A fool's errand he'd thought, like that false alarm a fortnight ago when he'd chased a young mother down the High Street after someone had reported her stealing the pram and infant from outside Cashsave. This, he was sure, was another such set-up; another reason for his leg to be pulled in the canteen.

He was wrong.

Very.

The back door was ajar. Cautiously he stepped through, involuntarily shuddering at the state of the place. The mystery caller hadn't detailed which room the body could be found in and so, heart in throat, Lawson made for the lounge. He knew before he stepped through the door. Barely had he tweaked back the sleeping bag before the urge to vomit overcame him. Miraculously he made it to the front door; miraculously it was unlocked. He threw up over the most convenient rose.

Death was something he'd been assured he would get used to. He wasn't so optimistic. To him, getting used to the horror of losing someone the way his father had died meant the death of compassion — and what little of that he had, he intended to hang on to. He hunkered down in the hallway and peered through the crack in the door. This woman was someone's daughter, friend, possibly wife, possibly mother. What had she done to end up here dead? Possibly nothing more than be in the wrong place at the wrong time. Then he remembered the look in her eyes. No. She'd known this was coming and she'd resigned herself to it.

He straightened himself up, wishing he smoked, and headed for the front door checking his watch like a fractious parent. Where were the others? He considered another phone call to the station. No, he'd wait until the hands on the Norman church tower overshadowing the close reached quarter to. That gave them three minutes.

They made it in two.

DI Dungannon was first to burst out of the collection of Fords now filling Amber Close.

'You do that?' He wrinkled his nose at the vomit decorating the rose bush.

Sullenly, Lawson nodded. He studied his superior's face for signs of an imminent

15

bollocking but saw only the usual lines, as if he were on a video and the tracking needed adjusting, and the bushy black eyebrows that crept across his forehead like poisonous caterpillars as he shouted instructions. He was as tall as Lawson's six feet-one, but as round as Lawson was slim. His head was a small circle with ever larger ones forming his body. Not waiting for a reply, Dungannon marched into the house.

'What we got?'

Lawson followed Dungannon inside, filling him in. He waited in the hall, not risking that he may throw up again. Dungannon studied the body briefly, returned to the hall.

'Dotty Spangle. No great surprise. Should've placed a bet — expected her to cop it this year. Could've retired on the payout.' He cocked a brief smile at Lawson. 'Where'd the sleeping bag come from?'

Lawson shrugged. 'That's how I found her.'

'Someone must've thought she'd be cold.'

A rumble of unsure laughter came from the other officers now crammed into the hall.

'Buggered the crime scene up though.' Dungannon shook free a cigarette, lit it. 'Or maybe they wanted her decent — though the last time I reckon our Dotty was decent was the day she was christened.'

16

'Sir . . . ' Lawson frowned.

'What?' Dungannon dragged deep on his cigarette. 'Where's my sense of respect? Lawson, do you know who we're dealing with?' Lawson shook his head. 'Potty Dotty Spangle, local tart with a heart. She was the first to admit she'd fallen off the straight and narrow a long time ago.'

Lawson's head was pounding. Speaking ill of the dead was not something he'd considered decent though killing a certain DI was becoming more acceptable by the minute.

'SOCO on their way?' Dungannon made for the front door.

'Yes.' Lawson followed him.

'Good. Let's hope they find more than foreign fibres and someone else's fucking dandruff.' He turned to Lawson. 'That's me done. You're with Rogers. I expect your report on my desk ASAP.' And, in a curl of tobacco smoke, he was gone.

Lawson wished it was as simple as that.

'Take no notice.'

Lawson turned at the quiet voice. A petite redhead stood before him.

'He always winds up new officers. I'm Kate Rogers.' She held out a hand. Lawson shook it. 'He's not a particularly sensitive man. Especially,' she paused, flushed. 'With coloured people.'

17

'Black,' Lawson corrected her smoothly. 'And then I'm not completely. Mixed race. I guess that makes it worse.'

'How so?'

Lawson shrugged. 'It just seems to. Something to do with a white woman being contaminated.'

'Oh,' she said, hurriedly looking away. 'Let's see what's in those outhouses.'

It took them five minutes to find the black and white rabbit and the rucksack. WPC Rogers, hands carefully gloved, checked inside. 'J. Palmer.' She squinted. 'There's something else . . . 8R W.'

'Class number?'

'Possibly. Could be year eight, make him or her eleven, twelve? That cuts our options down to three schools. Shouldn't take long to trace.'

'You think that's who reported the body?'

'Control said it sounded like a youngster.' She frowned. 'Palmer. That name rings a bell.' She shook her head. 'But right now, I can't think why.'

'Strange,' Lawson had crouched in front of the cage and was busy feeding grass through the mesh. 'To find a pet rabbit at an empty house. He's well looked after — been cleaned out recently, plenty of food and water. Most odd.'

18

'Maybe we ought to notify the RSPCA?'

Lawson shook his head. 'I think we'd be better to leave it here. If it belongs to J. Palmer, chances are he or she will come back to feed it.'

'Right on, new boy. So, we'll leave Bugs here then?'

'Yeah. Though what Dungannon'll say when he finds out we're staking out a rabbit, God only knows.'

'I shan't tell him.' Rogers laughed. 'Do you think you ought to get back to the nick? Dungannon'll have your guts for garters if his report is delayed. I'll finish up here.'

'Cheers.' Lawson looked glum.

He dithered in front of the house wishing he'd asked her out, wondering if he dare go back. Had she looked as though she were expecting him to ask? Was she one of these new women who would have asked if she'd wanted to go out? Shaking his head in frustration he decided to ask, she could only say no. Turning back he caught sight of movement in his eye corner. Just the barest twitch, but he knew a nosey neighbour when he saw one. They had been known to turn up trumps in investigations such as these. WPC Rogers forgotten, Lawson crossed the road.

He knew she was watching his uncertain progress up her path. Strategically placed black bags forced him to slalom his way down a course that would fox a burglar on a dark night. Unable to find a bell, he knocked. It echoed like a train going through a tunnel. Nothing. He knocked again. Then he rattled the letterbox. Finally, as he bent down to call through it, the door opened. A wizened woman breathlessly clutching a zimmer frame frowned at him.

'This about the boy at Storm Mount?'

'Boy? I . . . er . . . yes.'

'You'd better come in. I'm Eleanor James.'

'PC Lawson. Can I help you?' He asked, feeling guilty as she struggled back along the hall.

'No thanks. I'm better bullying this thing meself. Now,' she turned into the lounge. 'Don't think me inhospitable but I'm not going to offer you a cuppa.'

Lawson, surveying the clutter and grime of the room, was not sure he wanted one anyway. An unmade sofa bed ran along the wall behind the door; a black and white portable TV sat perilously on an orange box in one alcove on the opposite wall; by the other sat a rail with three or four nylon nighties in various garish shades on it and a small heap of undistinguishable clothes beneath.

'Takes me so long see. And I had one 'bout

half an hour ago. Mind you, that could still be drinkable,' she cupped her hands around a stained teapot on a table under the window. 'Nah, too cold I reckon, but if you want me to pour one anyway?'

'I'm fine, really.' Lawson wondered if he'd been overeager with his refusal.

'So, you saw a boy then?'

'Always seeing him, little sod. Never seems to be in school. Loitering 'round that house.'

'And you saw him today?'

'Came out looking like he'd got the devil himself on his heels. Went in the phone box.'

'What time was this?'

'Let me see,' she closed her eyes while she thought. Lawson studied her face. A moustache of coarse grey hairs adorned her upper lip. The front of her hair was nicotine yellow as was, he noticed, the index finger of her right hand. '*Fifteen to One* had just finished. 'Bout half four.'

So that was who raised the alarm then.

'You don't happen to know the boy's name?'

She shook her head. 'What's going on in there then? You don't have swarms of coppers for nothing. Is it a body?'

Lawson hesitated. Ladies of this vintage reminded him of his Gran and he remembered her panic if a drunk had swayed into

21

her hedge late at night. He didn't want this old lady worrying unnecessarily.

'It is, isn't it? Oh, how exciting! Is it anybody I know?' Her dark blue eyes danced behind her bifocals.

'Er, identification's not complete yet.' He paused. 'You can't tell me any more, I suppose?'

She shook her head sorrowfully. 'No.'

'Does anyone else live here?' He asked the question fully expecting her to say no. Why else would she live in a pigsty like this unless she couldn't do the housework?

'Only my son.' She looked at him cautiously. 'Danny.'

'Danny James?'

'Yes.' There was a pause as if she was waiting for him to say something then a gush of words when he didn't. 'He's not around much — that's why the place is in such a state. Doesn't always live here — comes and goes.'

'But he's here now?'

'No,' she looked worried.

'No, I mean, he's living with you at present?'

'Oh, yes.' She closed her eyes again. 'He sometimes fishes in the river.'

'Danny?'

'The boy who was at Storm Mount today.

22

Comes in fine weather. Off down the tow path like Red Rum if anyone approaches him.'

'You don't know where he lives?'

'Aside from kipping in Storm Mount from time to time, I haven't a clue.' She suddenly looked tired. 'Now, if that's all officer, I think that's all I can tell you today. Would you mind seeing yourself out?'

PC Lawson left 1 Amber Close thinking exactly what Eleanor James expected — that she was a past-it old busybody with nothing better to do than drop other people in it.

'Penny for them?'

Lawson jumped. Night had fallen already and with it, a frosty bite to the air.

In the shadows by the gate, he'd not noticed WPC Rogers.

'Sorry. Did I startle you?' She laughed. 'I thought you'd be long gone.'

'I suddenly remembered why the name Palmer was so familiar.'

'Astound me.'

'A runaway was reported yesterday, his name was Jacob Palmer. Here's his address.'

'You don't fancy checking it out with me now?'

'Sorry can't,' she started walking away as she spoke. 'Mustn't be late home.'

Watching her go, Lawson concluded that if

she would stand him up on official business, she wouldn't accept a social date. She probably wouldn't want to be seen with a black man anyway. By not asking, he'd only saved himself another rejection.

3

Jacob watched his rucksack being carried to a police car. Shit! Now they'd know he'd been around again. Now *Dad* would know he'd been around again. No way was he going home tonight. No way. Huddled, knees to chin, in the church tower, he watched the tableau unfold below. Couldn't hear anything but could guess what was being said. Learn the lingo at training school these coppers, he thought, a sudden gust ruffling his hair.

He peered up at the bell. It looked like a black hole in the dark, like everything he knew and understood had just vanished into it. A faint yellow glow from a streetlight looked like a crater on its surface — or maybe a lagoon shimmering, giving life to alien beings. Tina was an alien being. He'd told Dad that after she'd gone home that first 'introduction' meal — fish and chips from Emie's. Got a wallop for his trouble.

She reminded him of Sigourney Weaver in that her hair was shortish and dark and curly. Tina wasn't American but Essex born and bred; she wasn't tall and slim but short and lumpy. With hindsight she was nothing like

Sigourney Weaver at all, more like one of the bit players — the ones who had aliens bursting out of their stomachs. Jacob liked those bits best. Tina's teeth were pointy — all of them, not just her incisors, and they kind of snarled when she laughed. That's when she reminded him of the Queen Alien — The Bitch.

'She looks like The Bitch,' he'd said to Dad as Tina, still waving, tottered away, stilettos bending alarmingly beneath her weight. He'd meant it as a compliment. Unfortunately Dad wasn't so highly educated in the horror movie department. The terrible pain down the left side of his face was the next thing he recalled, that and the sleepless night, the thumping head. He wanted Mum then, more than he could ever recall wanting her before. But Mum didn't care. She'd gone and left him. Gone to Spain with a bus conductor, Dad said. Jacob had no reason to doubt him.

After that, Jacob was instructed to stay in the kitchen when Tina came. Dad didn't want him saying the wrong thing in front of her. But he wouldn't have. If she'd never seen *Alien* he wouldn't have taken it any further.

He shivered as another gust of wind whistled through the unglazed window. Pity he'd sacrificed his sleeping bag. Maybe the coppers would have left it when they took the body away. He didn't think so though.

He was hungry too. How long was it since that McDonald's? At least seven hours. He trawled his pockets; an empty chewing gum wrapper, a torch battery, two safety pins, a fifty-pence piece and an ancient Locket which had gone soft, leaked through its wrapping and acquired a fluffy coat from the inside of his pocket. At least he hoped it was only fluff. Picking off the worst of it, he stuck it in his mouth, rolling it around his tongue to smooth the surface then sucking it slowly in an effort to make it last.

Tina was a good cook. Not that Jacob spent much time at home since she'd moved in. It happened around the same time Gran died so Dad had said Jacob had to move into Gran's house — something, Dad said, to do with keeping his name on the rent book — she'd popped in occasionally when Dad suddenly had to go away. She said she was 'keeping an eye' but Jacob thought she was missing Dad. Jacob tolerated her 'cos he felt sorry for her. Her house, she said, was about to be pulled down and she'd got nowhere else to go. That was all she talked about when she came round anyway.

Jacob was pretty handy with the microwave and toaster so starving was out of the question, but Tina was nifty with all kinds of exotic creations — spaghetti Bolognese, chilli, curry — all the stuff he vaguely remembered Mum making once upon a long ago. Tina had frozen portions, written down instructions and left him with only the defrosting and microwaving to do.

She hadn't looked like an alien then, more a friend's mum. The kind who asked you politely if you've had a good day while hugging their own child. And he liked the pale blue top she wore — it went with her creamy skin and grey eyes — until he remembered seeing one just like it in Mum's wardrobe. The next time he was round Dad's, he checked. Mum's had gone. So he was right, she was a bitch. He threw all her meals in the bin, made himself beans on toast.

The Locket finished, he turned his attention back to the ground. Still the policemen were hanging around. Dungannon was back, Jacob could hear the coarse voice. Bastard. Dungannon was often sniffing around home, asking where Dad had acquired the computer, the car, the leather jackets, the videos. Weren't none of his fucking business. Jacob knew that 'cos that's what Dad always said as soon as Dungannon had left.

Dungannon disappeared into Storm Mount. Jacob glanced down at Nosy

Parker's house. The front window was in darkness. Anyone else would think she'd retired for the evening. Not Jacob. He knew that while this was going on she'd be watching. His belief was rewarded moments later when the orange glow from a cigarette showed itself through the mouldy net curtains.

It was going to be a long night. Jacob zipped up his jacket and pulled it over his knees. That might keep some of the draught out. Then he wriggled back into the corner, formed a pillow by folding his arms over his knees and dropped his head onto it. Exhausted, he dozed.

★ ★ ★

Brushing black curls from her face with a rubber-gloved hand, Tina Harker peered out of the window. Where the bloody hell was Jacob? It was raining outside, peeing down. If he was out in this he'd get soaked — or worse. She winced as her bruised ribs complained about moving. That's what she'd got last night for bothering about her boyfriend's son. Not, apparently, this child's father.

This wasn't how she'd imagined life with Dave was going to be. From the outside it had seemed romantic, bringing up a mother-less son, supporting its father and basking in the glow of appreciation. 'Pah!' She spat, violently enough to distort the Fairy Liquid bubbles clinging to the sides of the washing up bowl. 'Bloody pah!'

She took a tea towel from the oven door where it warmed through each evening when she cooked the meal, started drying. Dave would soon be in. She threw a quick glance at the clock above the back door. Ten minutes, she guessed. But he'd be pissed. She expected no less. He reckoned it was his privilege. She agreed with whatever kept the punches at bay.

The fist on the window came from nowhere. She screamed, bit her lip, tasted blood. Dave. Pissed. Shit.

'Open the fuckin' door.' Fists pummelling the door, Dave launched into a string of expletives.

'Hang on,' she struggled with the key, turned the handle. 'Sorry,' she said to the red-faced man whose thinning hair was plastered to his scalp by the rain. 'God you're soaked. Here, use this.' She handed him a towel.

He swiped it away. 'If you hadn't taken so fucking long to open that fucking door, I wouldn't have got wet.'

She nodded glumly, no point arguing. The

slap caught her unawares, sent her crashing against the oven door. Still hot, it made her jump. She managed not to call out. Slap again. This time the other cheek. This time she was ready and held her ground.

'Who the fuck you been talking to?' His eyes were bloodshot she noticed, bad sign. 'Well?'

'No one.'

'Liar. Fuckin' lying bitch! Whore! Dropping me in it with Danny. Seen what he did?'

Through throbbing eyes she peered, couldn't see anything, nodded anyway.

'That's your doing.' The hand was raised again, held shakily in mid-air, slowly lowered. 'You fuckin' bitch.' Lurching unsteadily, Dave left the kitchen, one hand steadying himself against the counter.

Tina looked at the muddy footprints on her Flash-clean floor.

Happy families.

The doorbell rang. Wiping face with palm, she went to answer it. The policeman stepped back when he saw her. He'd obviously not been expecting that then, Bride of Frankenstein opening the door.

'This about Jacob?' Lawson nodded. 'You'd better come in.'

He'd not been expecting this. Somehow to Lawson a house that looked so run-down and neglected from the outside should have a similar interior. This hadn't. OK, so it wasn't *Homes and Gardens* — the furniture was too shabby for that, the carpets too threadbare — but it was clean. Spotless. And he was ashamed of himself for expecting anything less.

'He ain't here.' Tina glared defiantly from her bruised face.

'No.'

'Don't know where he is.'

'I see. How long is it since you did know where he was?'

There was a long silence during which they stared at each other, lions trying to outstare the enemy to end the battle before blood had to be shed. Tina dropped her eyes.

'I've not seen him for a couple of weeks.'

'He's not been home for two weeks — and he was only reported missing yesterday?' Lawson was incredulous.

'Sssh!' Tina glanced nervously at the ceiling. She continued *sotto voce*. 'It's not quite as bad as it sounds. *I've* not seen him for a fortnight — I don't know about his Dad. Thing is, it was me what reported him missing — and I ain't told Dave yet. Like as not he'd kill me.'

Yes, thought Lawson, like as not he would.

'So, you've been away for a fortnight.'

Lawson pulled her back on track.

She shook her head. 'I ain't been nowhere.'

'But you've not seen Jacob?'

'He avoids me if he can.'

Lawson shook his head. 'We seem to be talking at cross purposes. Can we start again?'

She frowned. 'Nothing more to say.'

Lawson mentally counted to ten. 'Let's back track. Where's his mother?'

'Ran off with someone else.'

'Does he ever see her?'

She shook her head.

'And you've known him . . . how long?'

She shrugged. 'Long enough.'

'To get to know Jacob?'

She shook her head. 'Like I said, he avoids me.'

'Avoids — or doesn't bother coming home at all?'

She shrugged again. 'Sometimes he stays at his Gran's house — keeps him out of my way.'

Lawson shook his head as though trying to jiggle the information into place.

'And this house is . . . where?'

'Round the corner. Only I reckon he ain't been there for a while now. That's why I rang the police.'

'Tina?' A loud voice came from upstairs. 'Who you talking to?'

'Er, no one Dave. It's just the TV. I'll turn it down. Look,' she turned back to Lawson. 'You'd better go. He's in no fit state to be rational, he'll think you and I are up to something.'

Lawson, not relishing an argument — or worse — agreed: but he hadn't quite finished. 'Last night . . . where was Dave?'

She considered for a long moment. 'Here. He was here with me all night.'

★   ★   ★

A loud voice jerked Jacob from his semi-conscious state. Had they found him? Heart thumping, he peered forward. All looked as before on the ground. The voice again, shouting — no, singing — and coming from the direction of the town centre.

A figure stumbled into view, tripped over the kerb, swore. His sneakered feet made no sound, his coat, undone, flapped in the breeze. Danny! Jacob drew back as though he might be spotted. Suddenly he was cold with fear. Since when was Danny James back in town? Shit! He should have guessed, as soon as he found the body, that Danny wouldn't be far away.

34

4

Lawson turned the key to his bedsit, pushed the door gingerly open. It squeaked like the lid of Dracula's coffin. Shit! He stopped, waited for the inevitable footsteps in the bedsit opposite. He folded his arms, took a deep breath. The chains and bolts were drawn across. Lawson arranged his feet squarely on the threadbare carpet. The door opened. Maggie Taylor, all curlers and nylon babydoll, stood ready for battle.

'How many times do I have to tell you to oil that bloody door? Some of us are trying to catch up on our well-deserved — ' or desperately needed, thought Lawson ' — beauty sleep you know!' The door slammed before Lawson could attempt an apology. He took off his coat, closed his door behind him.

The place still smelled of last night's dinner. Fish and chips. His stomach rumbled. When had he last eaten? If he'd still been in Sheffield his mother would, right now, be flitting from oven to table with an array of lovingly home-cooked fayre. But she wasn't, so it was down to him. A Pot

Noodle was the order of the day.

Waiting for the kettle to boil, he flicked on the answering machine.

'It's Mum. This is the third time I've called. Didn't leave a message the other two times. It's ten thirty. Thought you'd be in sooner than this. Ring me when you get in if it's before midnight. Hope you're looking after yourself properly.'

Lawson checked his watch — 1:20 am. No point ringing her now though he doubted if she'd be sleeping; she'd taken his leaving badly. Being an only child was rarely disadvantageous but sometimes, like now, he wished there was someone else for her to worry about too. It wore him out bearing the brunt of her anxiety but not feeling he could retaliate.

Guilt hit first. Then pity. Being robbed of a life-partner in such a violent way was something Sebastian Lawson could only imagine. The fact that the deceased was also his father still didn't seem to have sunk in at the deepest level. In his line of work, life-partners were short on the ground — particularly when the only female you were likely to come across was a dead one.

His mother had been shattered by the death of his father, something he would empathise with eventually. Right now he was

36

still in angry mode. He'd been there three years and showed no sign of changing gear. Whoever had killed his father outside the chippy that night in a fit of temper or prejudice or God knew what, was still roaming free.

He mixed the Pot Noodle, stomach churning at the smell of artificial additives. Had he not seen Dungannon attack others, Lawson would have assumed the malice thrown at him to be because of his skin colour, not white, not black, a mixture of the two. He was used to it. At school he'd been taunted. He'd learnt to deal with the worst of it with his fists; later with a sharp tongue developed after thousands of detentions and the threat of expulsion. No way was he going to let his mum and dad down like that.

Mum had suffered too. Shopping, even at the supermarket three miles from their local community had generated stares, whispers and occasionally comments like 'black man's whore'. It had never stopped her going out. Not once had he seen her blanche in public. Head high, small chin defiant, she would ignore the detractors. Once home she would lock herself in her bedroom for up to an hour, appearing eventually with swollen eyes and red nose. Ironically it was the same people who rallied when Dad was killed. Not out of malice but genuine concern. Or guilt.

Headphones on so as not to disturb any of the neighbours, flicking through the channels, he munched and recapped on the day. Dungannon was a bastard. Didn't care who thought it either. Still, Dungannon's hostility had brought Kate Rogers on side — always a silver lining! He'd have to suss her out though, the fact that she was nipping off smartish tonight could mean there was a fella on the scene. He didn't want to be stepping on anyone's toes and making a fool of himself.

Break over, Lawson got ready for his night shift.

* * *

This was turning out to be one of his less good ideas. Watching a rabbit was a mind-numbing, body-numbing exercise. Lawson struggled to massage a cramped hamstring. Next time he had a bright idea like this he'd bury it immediately. He yawned. The air was so cold he was surprised his breath hadn't frozen. Surprised he hadn't frozen, period.

Walking up and down and beating his arms around his body seemed the best way of keeping warm, but it would warn Jacob Palmer of his existence, and that would defeat the whole object of him being here. But would his target turn up at — he checked his watch — 3:10 am? Probably not. Even SOCO had clocked off for the night, leaving Storm Mount neatly packaged in blue and white tape. They hadn't seemed to find it odd that he wasn't leaving when they were. Just as long as they didn't tell Dungannon. Spending the rest of his life in a straitjacket was not what he had in mind.

How many times had that rabbit hopped up and down? Like counting sheep, watching a rabbit. Yawn-inducing stuff. At this rate he'd be discovered frozen behind this bush in the morning. He'd give it another half hour and then he'd go home — he needed to be bright-eyed and bushy-tailed for work in the morning.

To keep himself entertained and to prevent his brain from seizing up like his body appeared to be doing, he mentally started a list of things to do tomorrow. Dotty's clothes hadn't shown up during the search of the house. The net would have to be widened. Could they have been thrown into the river, he wondered. Would it have carried them far enough quickly enough to get them out of the way forever? Doubtful, the amount of shopping trolleys that found their way into the murky water — bound to get caught up somewhere along the way. It would be helpful to know what she'd been wearing.

The rabbit thumped its back feet, froze, ears radaring. Lawson froze too, listened, hoped that no one came now 'cos he didn't think his legs were capable of responding. There was a rustling somewhere to Lawson's right, further down the garden. It came closer. The rabbit thumped again. Lawson tried to persuade his feet to perform. He managed to position himself in a crouch. The rustling came closer. A snuffling sound. Then silence, followed by a skull-shattering howl that sent the rabbit scurrying into the bedroom compartment of its hutch and Lawson six feet into the air with a startled yelp. He rounded the bush in time to see a fox disappearing back towards the tow path.

Bloody hell!

He remained standing. At least this way he could jiggle about and try to keep his circulation going. He checked his watch, three thirty three. Surely he could go home now? A few more minutes, he decided.

He'd have to start checking on the list of the deceased's last known contacts. This was where the hard work started. Lawson knew he was going to be kept busy trying to trace Dotty's clients and the other prostitutes she hung around with for a start.

The rabbit hopped from one side of its hutch to the other. Again. This was like being at Wimbledon — only colder. Lawson peered around into the gloom, couldn't see anything much but, as far as he could tell, nothing was moving. Except the rabbit. Didn't it ever go to sleep? Maybe it would die of hypothermia if it stopped hopping about. He knew the feeling. He'd made up his mind to go, and started extracting himself from the bush, when he heard something coming from the other direction, from around the side of the house. He crouched, melting back into the shadows.

There were footsteps making unsteady progress towards him. He held his breath. Should he stay quiet and hope they passed? Or should he leap out and hope that in the few seconds of ensuing chaos, he could grab them? Discreetly he tested his limbs. Too cold, bit dodgy. He'd stay quiet.

The footsteps stopped. Someone coughed quietly. 'Lawson?' Came a whisper. 'Are you here?'

'Kate?' He went to step forward, stumbling as his legs gave way.

'Lawson! You OK?'

'Yeah. Just freezing solid.'

'That's why I came. Brought you a thermos of coffee.'

He laughed. He couldn't help it. Pent up emotion poured from him as he convulsed. 'God, you sound like my mother!' He managed at last. 'But it's very thoughtful of you.'

'I'm not sure that's a compliment,' he could hear the smile in her voice. 'But I'm glad I thought of saving your life anyway. How much longer were you planning on being here?'

'Well, actually . . . '

' . . . you were just going.'

They met by the back door. Only the whites of eyes and teeth showed up in the gloom.

'Yeah.' He smiled. 'But I'll have a coffee with you. Shame to waste your journey.'

'OK. It's sugared, not how I normally take it, but I'll bear it. I thought you'd be bound to take sugar — being a man.'

Wrong — he didn't — but he wasn't going to blow it. 'Thanks.'

'One other slight problem.'

'And that is?'

'There's only one cup so we'll have to drink in shifts.'

'I can live with that.'

'Any joy here tonight?' She poured the coffee. Its warmth and strong smell suddenly made the monochrome night seem 3D.

'Nah! Fox damn nearly frightened me to death but no other excitement.'

'Jacob Palmer's probably giving this place a wide berth for now. Maybe there'll be more success tomorrow night.'

'I don't think I can survive another night of this. Anyway, surveillance should be twenty four hour — we don't know what his movements are at all.'

'So you're going to chat Dungannon up are you? Ask him for the team to be on overtime to keep an eye on a rabbit?'

'I was rather hoping — '

'Oh no! I know when to keep my big mouth shut!'

They'd been walking as they talked, passing the cup between them until the coffee was gone. They reached the pavement outside Storm Mount.

'Thank you,' Lawson stopped, half turned. 'That made things more bearable. It was actually quite romantic, didn't you think?'

A pause. A sharp intake of breath. 'If you like that kind of thing. Now, if you'll excuse me, I'd better be getting back.'

Whoops, he cursed silently, pushed the wrong button there. Women were temperamental creatures. If he was going to keep Kate on side he'd have to be careful where he trod.

Yawning, he headed bedwards. He would need the last three remaining hours of night to sharpen his wits for the visit to Dotty Spangle's last known address first thing. He was starting to feel like a one man band.

5

Rattan Towers dammed the ever-sprawling centre of Righton from its old-walled epidermis. It had been built in the sixties when planners decided humans should start living like shoes, each pair in a box balanced somewhat precariously on another. Somehow incongruous, the highrise nevertheless added kitsch to the area, bridging the old part of the town from the Arndale Centre and its surrounding new housing estates and, beyond that, the industrial estates.

Lawson stretched as he got out of the car, breathing in the sharp, early morning air. A sea mist was rolling slowly away from the cobbled streets around the harbour, revealing a slipway, partly mud-covered, and a handful of boats bobbing on the ebbing tide. There must, he decided, be a cracking view from the top of the tower block. Pity he wasn't going far enough up to see.

Even on the fourth floor, he discovered, the view was good enough to see the ruined castle on the opposite point of the natural harbour some four miles distant. Or so Gus Chandler told him. The mist was still thick

45

out to sea, revealing nothing. Lawson sat opposite Gus on a white moulded plastic chair hastily plucked from the balcony on his arrival.

'Better than the bean bags,' said Gus promptly dropping into one. 'So, what's she been up to this time? I'm right in thinking Dot's in trouble? She down the nick?'

Lawson was surprised by the cultured accent coming from behind the thick grey beard. Gus Chandler was a big man with big red hands and piercing blue eyes. He wore a striped towelling dressing gown, revealing thick white chest hair in the V that almost reached his navel. His forehead creased slightly as Lawson cleared his throat and started to speak hesitantly.

'I'm afraid it's slightly worse than that.' Lawson noticed suddenly that his shoes needed polishing, that the rug on which they squirmed was threadbare.

'I see.' Gus folded his arms, nodded for Lawson to go on.

'She . . . '

'Is hurt? Dead?' Gus's voice was calm, hypnotising Lawson.

'The latter I'm afraid.' Lawson looked up sharply, observing the other man's reaction.

'I see.' Gus closed his eyes, nodded again. 'I see.'

'I'm very sorry . . . '

'I'm sure you are,' Gus opened his eyes, smiled slightly. 'But we knew it was a possibility. Hoped it would never happen, but . . . ' Tears started to slide down his cheeks, irrigate his beard.

Lawson looked away, embarrassed by the show of grief. 'You supported her work?'

Gus gave him a sharp look. 'As in pimp?'

The stare made Lawson squirm.

'I wasn't her pimp,' Gus spoke quietly. 'I didn't approve of her making her living the way she did. But I loved her. Are you in love?'

Lawson shook his head.

'Thought not. There's a peaceful aura around those of us who are truly in love; those who accept and are accepted for who they are, not for what others expect them to be. Dot did what she did because that's what she had to do. End of story. I loved the person she was, not the job she did. But we always knew the risk. We talked about it occasionally.' Gus levered himself out of the bean bag, started pacing the strangely bare room. 'When a prostitute got beaten up — or murdered — she'd say, 'I'll give up, Chuck' — she always called me Chuck. Like Cilla Black. Guess I won't be watching *Blind Date* for a while.' The smile he tried slid from his face as he dissolved into silent convulsive sobs. After a moment or two he waved a hand toward one of only two pieces of furniture in the room, the sideboard. Lawson registered the box of tissues, passed them. Gus mopped up, blew his nose, crumpled the soggy tissue in his palm. 'Sorry.'

'It's OK.'

'But she couldn't give up. It was like a drug. She'd try, but three evenings of Coronation Street and Eastenders and she'd be climbing the walls.'

'Aren't we all?'

Gus smiled briefly. 'She had a regular crowd, always said she'd not pick up strays, that way she'd be safe. Always stood outside CashSave. Do you know why?'

'No.'

'Because of the security men. She figured that if there was any trouble she'd only have to holler and someone would come running.'

'Do you happen to know who her regulars were?'

Gus nodded. 'There's a calendar in the bedroom. Hang on.' He disappeared briefly through a bead curtain in the corner. 'Here.' He handed Lawson a 'Cute Pets' appointment calendar, innocent puppies and kittens adorning its pages. Marked on each night Monday to Saturday were names, mainly only one a night but

Tuesday and Thursday sported two.

'And do you know all these men?'

'Most of them,' Gus smiled. 'I know you think that's odd, coming across your partner's clients while shopping.'

'Bizarre.'

Gus nodded. 'She was different with them, don't you see? All tarted up. I saw the quiet, more cultured side of her.'

Lawson couldn't imagine this side to the painted mannequin he'd seen at Storm Mount. He studied Gus. Could this really be right? Did he have no feelings of jealousy? There was no doubt in Lawson's mind that he couldn't have been so benevolent had he found himself in the same position. Not that he'd find himself in that position in the first place.

'Did Dotty have a code? Some of these names don't seem quite . . . complete.' Lawson looked hopefully at Gus.

'Like shorthand, do you mean?' He thought momentarily. Nodded. 'I guess you could say that.'

'So you could identify these men?'

Gus looked. 'Most of them.'

'And do you know their addresses?' Lawson flipped over the page of his notebook.

He shrugged. 'Ditto.'

49

Again Lawson was amazed at the nonchalance. Wouldn't Gus be wanting to kill them, accuse at least one of them of being capable of killing Dotty? Or maybe Gus had killed Dotty himself to put himself out of her misery.

'I suppose you'll be wanting to know my whereabouts on . . . Wednesday night?'

Lawson squinted, nodded.

'I do Italian at night school. I'm home about nine-thirty, although it was nearer ten fifteen last week — popped into the Joiner's for a swift half on my way home.'

'And after that?'

'I was home alone.' Gus barked a laugh. 'Although I did get a phone call from my brother in New York. Does that count? I guess you'll want his number.'

'Please,' said Lawson, scribbling grimly. 'Did you not think it odd when she didn't come home?'

Gus shrugged. 'It happened sometimes. If a client was especially eager, or if they were both pissed or high.'

'And where would they go on such occasions?'

'Either to the client's home or to Storm Mount, the empty house by the river.'

So it all tied in. Lawson stood. 'Thank you. Before I go, I think there's just two more things — and I'm afraid you may find them rather upsetting. The first is: do you have a current photo of Dotty? And the second . . . ' Lawson cleared his throat. 'Erm . . . Unfortunately, when Dotty was discovered, there were no clothes in evidence — I wonder if you can remember what she was wearing?'

Gus went to the sideboard, started fiddling in the top drawer. 'There's some photos here somewhere that I took of her last year — we had a week in Ilfracombe, you know. Wearing?' he fell silent for a moment. Lawson was thankful he could only see Gus's backview, he could tell by the man's shaking shoulders, that he was crying again. 'Psychedelic leggings — her favourite — and a sexy lace top with a plunging neckline in a sort of metallic pink.'

Lawson left numb. Dealing with this kind of thing conjured any number of ghosts. The only thing he noticed as he got into his car was that the castle was beginning to show through the mist.

★ ★ ★

'Did he show no emotion?' Dungannon, turning away from the blind, frowned. 'Did you get the impression he already knew?'

'No to the second question, I'd say.'

51

Lawson wriggled uncomfortably on the plastic moulded chair designed to force admissions from even the most innocent of suspects. 'He got upset when I told him she was dead.'

'Mmm,' he crossed to the desk, his forty-year-plus stomach undulating gently with the effort. He peered thunder-faced at Lawson. 'You know he's been done for GBH?'

'Gus Chandler?' Lawson's surprise was no act. The ageing hippy hadn't appeared to be able to define violence never mind demonstrate it.

'Mm. Twenty-odd years ago, granted. Some quarrel over magic mushrooms, I believe.'

Lawson sniggered, caught Dungannon's homicidal glare, realised it wasn't a joke, straightened his face.

'This is no wind-up, Constable. It is fact. A fact which proves this chap, so seemingly sweet and innocent, is as capable of breaking the law as the rest of society. And, what is more, he is capable of violence, which is something we can't all take credit for. Add to that the fact that we haven't yet confirmed his alibi for the time of the murder and we could be cooking with gas.'

'And we could be in for a tough ride if

we're wrong — he won't take it lightly if we accuse him and then it turned out he wasn't guilty.'

'Neither would anyone else. Anyway, he could've paid someone to do the deed for him, arranged for his brother to call. Maybe it was a regular Wednesday evening thing. Check it out, will you?' Dungannon looked pointedly at the clock on the wall. 'Ten twenty-two am and we can honestly say he has to be our main suspect.'

'It does seem odd that he knew all of her clients, knew where they lived, passed the time of day with them. Most bizarre.' Lawson shook his head. 'But I can't help thinking that he would have picked *them* off one by one rather than kill the woman he loved.'

'Professed to love. Maybe she defied him. Maybe there was a client Gus couldn't abide, maybe they rubbed his nose in the fact they were sleeping with his girlfriend. Maybe they wound him up so much that Gus had Dotty killed just so he would no longer have to put up with the piss-taking.'

Lawson shrugged. 'Possible I guess.'

'OK,' Dungannon wiped a weary hand over his face, straddled the chair opposite Lawson. 'The other thing that strikes me here is that we've got our runaway hovering on the periphery. Am I not right in assuming that the youngster who informed the police of the body is one Jacob Palmer, reported missing three days ago?'

'It would seem that way, sir.'

'And he's . . . where exactly.'

Lawson looked abashed. 'We're not entirely sure, sir. According to a resident of Amber Close, one Eleanor James, our Jacob is a regular visitor to Storm Mount — sometimes sleeping over.'

'I see: And can you deduce any particular reason for that?'

'Define 'dad'.'

Dungannon frowned. 'I'm in no mood for mind games.'

'This is no game. I'm just curious to know whether I'm the only person on the planet who carries a certain image in their head.'

Dungannon sighed. 'OK.' He closed his eyes, steepled his fingers in front of his nose. 'Someone who takes you fishing or to the footy; someone who gives you a couple of quid when your mother says you've spent all your pocket money and you can't have any more; someone who stands behind the door and clips your ear when you come in later than agreed.'

'Good.' Lawson smiled. 'I'm not alone on the planet then.' He accepted Dungannon's offer of coffee, watched while he crossed the room to the permanently bubbling pot and poured it. 'Thanks. Jacob's dad, Dave Palmer, seems to think it's the exact opposite of the above.'

'Maybe prospective parents should take an exam to see if they're suitable material.'

Lawson shrugged. 'Maybe the cracks don't show until it's too late. Certainly Dave Palmer, so I hear, wouldn't notice the world had stopped turning until he ran out of beer.'

'Bad as that, huh?' Dungannon curled his lip in a passable Elvis impersonation then cleared his throat and straightened his tie as though remembering who he was fooling around in front of.

'Believe me,' Lawson ignored his superior's discomfort. 'That man shouldn't be allowed to keep a cockroach.'

'So, where's the missus?' Dungannon drained his cup, checked his watch.

'God knows. Probably ate her. There's a woman around, little more than a girl, covered in bruises. More tits than brains, I'd say. In fact, he must have given her a lobotomy to make her stay.'

'So the kid's better off out of it?'

Lawson nodded thoughtfully. He had a certain empathy for the lad. He could remember reaching the point, on several occasions, where the only answer seemed to be to run away. Only his idea of running away was to head to Ghana, to his grandmother. Once, he got as far as London. His father came to fetch him from King's Cross with thunderous face and harsh words; not because Lawson had left but because he'd chosen that particular Wednesday afternoon to do it. Reverend Lawson had planned to visit a very sick parishioner in hospital, had promised the elderly lady that he'd be there. She died while he was still on his way back to Sheffield. Lawson was made to carry the guilt of that episode for a long time. In fact, if he allowed himself to probe deep enough, he could still find traces of it in his stomach.

Dungannon checked his watch again, stood. 'Look, I'm going to have to fly. Can you check with the school, see if there's any other known address for Jacob? And can you get in touch with Social Services and find out which social worker is on his case? If it's a dragon called Sophie Sullivan I'd rather you didn't let her pollute the atmosphere in the nick. Meet her and greet her on her territory.' He paused briefly. 'No coincidence her initials are 'SS'. And then I'd like you to look into a syndicate calling themselves 'The Fairweather Organisation'. They are the current owners of Storm Mount and one of that syndicate is . . . would you like to hazard a guess?'

Maybe it was the word hazard that encouraged Lawson to try a wildcard. 'Dotty Spangle?'

'Got it in one. Check out the other members — WPC Rogers has the list,' Dungannon registered the smile that formed on Lawson's face. 'See if any of the others have managed to get themselves killed recently. If they haven't we can conclude that Dotty was either a one-off or is the start of an epidemic.'

'Will do.' With an uneasy feeling, Lawson watched Dungannon leave. Why was Dungannon being nice to him? Was it, maybe, that Dungannon was really one of those strange sets of twins who only inhabit the world of Walt Disney, where one is of ill humour, the other of good and they take it in turns to do the same job?

'He's like that sometimes,' WPC Rogers entered the office, placed a sheet of paper on the desk. 'Rarely. This is the list of members of The Fairweather Organisation.'

Lawson pulled it towards him.

'Can I suggest,' she picked up the paper, started for the door. 'That we study it outside of his office? I don't want to take his good humour for granted.'

'Maybe he hasn't had a row with his missus this morning. Is he married?' Lawson closed the door behind them.

'Don't have a clue.'

'Look, I'm sorry if I said — or did — something wrong before. I'd like us to be friends.'

'Sure. I've got some phone calls to catch up on. OK if I leave this with you for now?'

'Of course.' Lawson watched her go with the feeling that, once more, he'd hit a nerve.

6

Tabbi Sparrow kissed her baby's forehead before placing him in his battered buggy at the bottom of the steps. Looking back at the front door she could see, through the frosted glass of the top half, the landlord coming down the hall. She ran to the road, feet skittering through soggy, unraked leaves, and then along the pavement until she reached the church. If necessary she'd go in and beg asylum. She looked back. No one was following.

She'd run out of money. Not a crime; inconvenient. You are a victim, she told herself firmly, of the social security system. If they paid a decent whack she wouldn't have sunk like this as soon as the babysitter let her down and she had to miss a few nights' work. A lot of women in her situation would, she knew, have left the child alone and carried on working. Whatever else Tabbi Sparrow was, she wasn't a bad mother. And, in the words of her late grandmother during her scarce moments of lucidity, she would not be a victim.

She ducked into a shop doorway, poking a

foot beneath the buggy's wheel to stop it rolling onto the road (its brake had ceased working long before she had acquired it) and rummaged carefully in the string bag stretched across the handles. One kettle, stolen from her bedsit; two eggs, ditto and still fortunately intact; Blue's bottle and spare dummy, wrapped in a small towel; and three disposable nappies. Her stuff, save for the mobile phone in her coat pocket, had had to be sacrificed in their bid for freedom. She should have been better prepared, she told herself: she knew it was rent day — and that the landlord was far from tolerant of his lodgers' problems.

The overnight rain had stopped but a keen northerly wind had got up, chasing leaves and litter across the pavement and getting between the buttons of her showerproof jacket. Nearly lunchtime, according to the clock over the jewellers; God knew what she'd be able to offer Blue. Briefly she considered writing a note, attaching it to his coat and leaving him outside a police station or hospital, rather like Paddington Bear — 'Please look after this baby. Thank you.' Only she couldn't.

Passing a greengrocer's on the High Street she reached out, almost lazily, and removed a banana from the display outside. An elderly lady, struggling with a shopping trolley, eyed her suspiciously, opened her mouth, then a gust of wind tugged at her plastic rain hat and sidetracked her. Tabbi gritted her teeth with a silent 'Yes!' At least she'd got something to offer Blue when he awoke. The next thing was to get out of the wind.

At the end of the High Street a cobbled lane with a slight downward slope snuck away to the right. She paused. The cobbles would shake the buggy and probably wake Blue. She decided to chance it. The lane got steeper and, the nearer she got to the sea, the denser became the shops selling shells and candy-floss; postcards and 'kiss me quick' hats. Many of these were now shut for the winter.

She'd been down here not long after Blue was born. Walking helped her to keep things in perspective, to try and come to terms with the cruellest twist life had thrown her. She'd known Steve two months when she discov-ered she was pregnant. He denied he could ever be the father. Her mother, coldly disapproving, had ordered her to leave the house before the bump began to show. And so dissolved her chances of starting art school that autumn. It had never crossed her mind to have an abortion; no one had discussed that option with her.

At the bottom of the hill on the right was

an expensive sailing clothes shop; opposite that, where the cobbles gave way to the car park, was Jim's café, housed in a small, white-walled, black-beamed building. She'd spent many hours here recently, the food was cheap, the décor cheerful and usually a radio chattered behind the counter.

The windows were steamed up today, rivulets of water meeting eye-level net curtains. She pushed open the door, ready to smile a greeting at Jim when he turned towards the clanking bell. It was the clanking bell, too, that did what the cobbles had not. Jerking awake, Blue sat momentarily, arms outstretched, before opening his mouth and wailing like the seagulls they'd left outside.

'Young 'un be hungry.' Jim came over wiping butcher's hands on a blue and white apron. He pulled a chair away from a table in a corner nearest the counter. 'Make your-selves comfortable. I'll fix up some grub.'

Tabbi smiled, released Blue from his buggy and took the banana from her pocket. Peeling it and breaking off a small piece she mashed it between her fingers before squeezing it between Blue's suddenly vice-like lips. By the time Jim returned with a brimming platter, Blue was back in his buggy contentedly sucking his dummy. It wasn't until Tabbi's hunger had been sated that she thought, once more, about her finances. She'd enough to pay for the meal — but affording a roof over their heads tonight was quite a different matter.

★ ★ ★

He hadn't known how to bear it just before dawn. Shaking so much he thought he'd fall to pieces, Jacob took to stomping up and down the stairs, not caring how much noise he made or whether anyone turned up to arrest him. At that moment, he would have been grateful if they had. He could be waiting in a warm cell eating a cooked breakfast while someone rang the social services. He knew. He'd been there before.

From his lookout now he saw no one moving in Amber Close. The clock peeling eight in his ears, he headed downstairs for the door. Breath hanging in the air, he cocked his head so the plumes wouldn't be seen from the street. A movement across the way. Jacob ducked back into the doorway. Danny, insulated like an Eskimo on a fishing trip, was leaving his house. Over the back wall.

Staying close to the side of the church, Jacob followed him as far as the end of the churchyard. Danny paused to light a cigarette by the gate. As he pulled his lighter from his pocket something silver fell and slid beneath the gate to land on the flint path of the churchyard. Danny didn't notice. With a brief glance left and right, he carried on his way.

The holly, abundant by the side gate, was pricklier than ever with the frost. Jacob was stabbed on the side of his face as he knelt to find the key Danny had discarded. He yelped, slapped a hand across his mouth, peered after Danny. Nothing. So muffled up was he that he wouldn't notice a nuclear bomb going off if it were in his underpants.

'What are you doing here?' The voice was well-spoken, polite. Jacob looked up. Shit, the vicar!

'Erm . . . Mum thought she'd dropped something down here when she came to visit Dad's grave,' Jacob improvised, quite successfully, he thought. 'I said I'd come first thing to look for it.' His fingers discovered what he sought, and closed over it.

'Very noble, I'm sure. Tell me, when exactly did your dad die?'

Jacob followed the vicar's gaze. All the graves were green, their lettering now smooth in places — and not one of them was dated after 1874.

'I think you'd better be on your way, don't you?'

With a nod and a scuffle, Jacob was off.

Not knowing where to go — the tower was out of the question and he daren't risk Storm Mount yet — he headed towards the old part of town. With no conscious decision he found himself heading for the quay, little more than a muddy puddle these days, but with enough history to attract tourists in the summer. His decision not to stop before had been fuelled by the sight on every corner, or so it seemed to him, of a police car, bike or man.

A weak sun dyed damp cobbles ochre; the dampness making them slippery under sneakers. By an ancient slipway, Jim's café vented saliva-jerking smells. Jacob fished in his pocket. Still got fifty pence. Soon have to do something about his finances. The steam and warmth hit him as he pushed open the door.

The tables were square, covered in red and white cloth and mainly uninhabited. Save two. One by a geezer, looked like Father Time's grandad, the other by a young girl with a white face, black, black hair and a baby beside her in a buggy. Keeping his eyes on the floor he headed for the counter. Jim, he realised, had been watching him since he entered, forearms, like hams, folded across his chest.

'What can I do for you?' Built like Fred Flintstone, he had a smiley face and a soft spot for the underdog.

Jacob slid the coin across the counter. 'What will this buy?'

'Depends how hungry you are.' Jim half-turned, indicated the price list behind him. 'Full English, sausage sarnie, egg on toast, beans on toast — any variation you care to mention.' He frowned slightly, put a finger to his lips as though in deep thought. 'You look to me as though you could manage a Full English with extra toast and a pot of tea. Would I be right?'

Jacob nodded — although he'd rather have had an extra sausage rather than toast, and orange rather than the tea, he wasn't going to look a gift horse in the mouth.

'Go sit down. I'll bring it over when it's ready.'

Jacob headed for a table away from the other inhabitants. Just about to sit down, he was halted by a loud 'Pssst!' He turned. The white-faced girl with black, black hair was beckoning wildly. He went over.

'Sit down! Sit down!' She lisped in a loud whisper. 'I want to talk to you.' He obeyed. 'I couldn't help but overhear your conversation at the counter. If it's money you need, I can help you. Nothing illegal. Interested?'

Look interested. Give nothing away.

Jacob nodded. Fascinated by her lisp and

by the way her polished fingers worried a paper napkin until it gave up the battle and collapsed into dust, he let her talk until Jim brought his breakfast over.

'What I wants is a babysitter see. For when I'm working. Only my job is a bit specialised and I work unsocial hours — well, unsocial for some but not for me. Very social my hours is. Anyway . . . ' she lit a cigarette. Jacob looked at the bold 'No Smoking' notice above her head. She followed his glance and smiled. 'Jim's OK, long as there's no one much in. Anyway, like I was saying, I needs a babysitter and you needs some money. So what you say?'

'I can't do unsocial hours — me Dad'll kill me.'

'Don't think so — met guys like you before. Reckon he'd kill you more if he knew you was bunking school.'

Jacob nodded, she reckoned right. 'Anyway,' he continued. 'Don't know nuthin' about babies.' And he really didn't want to, but he had to be polite; going now would just leave a big hole in his belly. But the money bit was interesting. He furrowed his brow in what he considered to be an adult expression. 'How much would I get?'

The girl laughed, her mouth shaped like an 'O', a stream of smoke pouring from it. 'A man after my own heart. Fiver a night?'

'A night?' She nodded. 'What all night?'

'Yep. Can you manage that?'

Jacob shrugged. 'Cash up front?'

'Cash after your shift.'

'And where would I do this babysitting?'

She paused. 'I'm in the process of sorting out some digs. I'll let you know later on.'

Jim brought Jacob's breakfast, stood over him while he started shovelling it into his face.

'And how long is it since you saw a square meal?' Jacob shrugged, squirted tomato ketchup on the sausages. 'There's no need to tell you to hurry up is there? But I will anyway. The missus is due to arrive in about half an hour — and she'll have me in the oven if she knows I've been feeding the poor again.'

Several moments passed before Jacob looked at the girl again, but his mind had not been idle. If all he had to do was look after a sleeping baby he'd be earning money for nothing wouldn't he? Doddle. He started speaking hesitantly. 'I might know of somewhere you could stay. I'm moving in there myself. Be easy then to babysit . . . '

'Blue.'

'I meant the baby's name.'

'Blue.'

'I . . . oh. Anyway, you could go and do whatever you had to and I'd be there anyway.'

'Like we were married.'

Jacob choked. He hadn't quite meant that. 'I don't even know your name.'

'Tabbi.'

He frowned, egg yolk dripping down his chin. 'Like the cat?'

'With an 'i' instead of a 'y' — short for Tabitha. Mum had some sort of class complex. Maybe she thought it would make her seem posher, me having a posh name, or maybe she thought if I'd got an upmarket name it'd buy me an upmarket life. That's a laugh isn't it? That kind of thing don't happen to people like me.'

'How old are you?'

'A gentleman isn't supposed to ask a lady's age.'

'I never pretended to be no gentleman. I'm twelve if it helps.'

'I'm fifteen.'

'But you've got a baby.'

'And you've left home and don't go to school.'

'But you've got a job too. Isn't that illegal?'

Tabbi frowned, leaned forward, caught his wrist and whispered with a snarl. 'I told you — nothing's illegal. You do what you're told and everything will be fine. Now, are you going to show me this gaff or aren't you?'

'Erm . . . ' he had to stall for time. Dad's girlfriends were like this, fine one minute, going ballistic the next. How could he have forgotten what it was like to live with a female he wasn't related to? 'Well, at the moment there's quite a lot going on there.' He didn't want to mention the police presence. Somehow he sussed that Tabbi wouldn't be interested if he let on and he'd grown rather partial to the thought of easy money. 'Maybe,' he added hastily, seeing a shadow cross her face. 'I could go back and see and I could meet you later somewhere. Give you a chance to do whatever else you've got planned today.'

Her face cleared, the smile almost reached her eyes. 'That's not a bad idea. OK, let me see.' She looked at her watch, checked it against the clock ticking loudly above a fruit machine next to a flight of stairs with a chain across and 'Private' written in thick black felt-tip on a piece of card. 'Do you know Drumboli's Lane?' Jacob nodded. 'Good. I'll meet you down there by the Chinese Herbal Shop at four o'clock. If anything changes ring me on my mobile phone.' She scribbled down the number on the back of a bus ticket she plucked from the vinyl flooring.

Blue whimpered as she tucked the blanket around him. She left with a wave to Jim, not

70

saying goodbye or looking back at Jacob. After a moment, he followed. He too waved at Jim before leaving the café and turning right. Tabbi had gone left. He didn't want to run into her again too soon. He'd check Storm Mount out but already he was having doubts about this venture. Did he really want to share his house with Tabbi and her baby? Did he really want to play happy families when he knew such a thing didn't exist?

He started walking back the way he'd come an hour before. Strange how life can turn in so short a space of time. He remembered that Wednesday he'd been sent to the corner shop to get a loaf of bread. Gone ten minutes he was, because there'd been a queue, normally he'd have been no more than five. When he got home his mother had gone to Spain. Gone. Upped and left and never even said goodbye. And his Dad had clipped his ear and said if Jacob ever mentioned her name in the house again he'd end up in an orphanage. Sometimes Jacob wished he'd taken that option.

The sun had managed to scramble higher in the sky and he found himself blinking into it as he stared across the water from the quay. Away in the distance a horizon divided his life from his dreams. If he could just find a way of crossing this great divide, life would be completely different. He watched an old salt, who he suddenly recognised as the geezer from the café, step into a small rowing boat clutching a fishing rod and a thermos, untie it and set off at a gentle pace across the water. Maybe that was all he had to do, row a boat to the horizon and plop over the other side into his dream life. What would James Bond do? Well he certainly wouldn't cry. Jacob wiped away the tears sliding, without permission, from his eyes. No, James Bond would straighten his jacket, square his shoulders and thrust himself back into battle.

That's right lad, pull yourself together.

Feeling better, Jacob headed back to the town centre. Optimism returning, he told himself that Tabbi couldn't get hold of him. She knew his name sure, but she didn't know the address of Storm Mount — and she didn't have a phone number to contact him. He was in the clear. He didn't have to play mummies and daddies; he didn't have to share his house.

He wouldn't be earning any easy money. He'd have to find some other way. His fingers closed over the key in his pocket. What secrets did that hold? Had Danny realised he'd dropped it? Jacob didn't think so. And Danny didn't know Jacob had picked it up. If only he, Jacob, could find out what the key was for, he might find out something useful, something he could hold over Danny. That would be good. Easiest place to start was at the beginning — at Danny's home.

One thing at a time.

'Eh?'

Tabbi today, Danny tomorrow. Patience.

'S'pose.'

Good lad, focus is the key.

7

Lawson had chosen to ignore Dungannon's requests for the moment and familiarise himself with Dave Palmer's record: obviously trying for a world record for being arrested for petty theft, petty this, petty that; nothing major had ever been pinned on him, somehow he just managed to slip justice. Lawson sighed, he'd come across guys like this before, experts in passing the buck.

Something interesting though. Dave Palmer was very well acquainted with Danny James. They'd been linked on several of the 'petty' cases — and Palmer, although never convicted, had appeared to be on the periphery of a pornography case Danny was involved in.

Lawson thought back to his first visit to Mrs James; the way she'd hesitated when she'd mentioned her son's name, as though waiting for him to recognise it. She'd been in that position before — the police arriving on her doorstep — and she'd been expecting Danny to be towed away in connection with Dotty's murder. Was that because she knew something? Or because that was what usually happened when a crime was committed around her? First stop Danny James, just in case it was him? In that case, why hadn't one of the other officers put Lawson in the picture? Easy answer there, most of them were still at the 'good morning' stage if they thought they really had to speak to him. Anything he needed to know he was having to find out the hard way.

Coffee, he decided, before he got onto Dungannon's list. Anything to put off going down the lists he seemed to be acquiring. That was 'new boy' syndrome — getting to do all the donkey work. It did have its advantages though; he was getting the groundwork on some of the local villains. Always a silver lining . . .

A quick phone call after his coffee, revealed that the social worker assigned to Jacob Palmer at the time his mother left was, indeed, one Sophie Sullivan. Lawson recalled the dread in Dungannon's voice when he said her name. Lawson wasn't up to dealing with a dragon at the moment. Fortunately, at that moment, Kate Rogers put in an appearance.

'No chance of a favour, I suppose?'

'What makes you think you deserve one?' She shot him a sly glance.

'Nothing. I just thought — '

'You'd try your luck. Just like every other man around here.' She walked past him to a filing cabinet in the corner.

'I'm sorry.' He looked down, embarrassed. 'I didn't mean to upset you.'

'You didn't,' she headed back towards him. 'I'm winding you up. What is it you want?'

Sheepishly, he handed her the social worker's phone number. 'You couldn't call her for me? Ask about Jacob?'

'Sophie Sullivan? Sure. What are you going to do?'

'Have a chat with Dungannon.'

★ ★ ★

'What we need is a motive,' Lawson faced Dungannon across the mahogany desk.

'Strikes me,' Dungannon leered. 'There's as many motives as there are suspects.'

'Admittedly,' Lawson nodded. 'It's going to be harder to pinpoint one — it could easily be jealousy . . . '

'We've ascertained that already.'

'Money — presumably she'd earned some that night.'

'We may never know.'

'It could simply be a sex game that went wrong.'

'You're firing on all cylinders today.' Dungannon scratched his belly idly. 'You do any good on that list of clients?'

76

Lawson pulled his notebook from his pocket. 'Got most of their addresses from Gus, got their phone numbers from the phone book — '

'Amazing piece of detection.'

'Most accounted for. Two mysteries: first, the person she saw the night of her death — a regular booking in the name of B.B. Roache; second, again fairly regular, on the Thursday night, the initials S.M.'

'Someone was in for a heavy session that night then.' Dungannon smirked.

'Not necessarily. I wondered if S.M. stood for Storm Mount. After all, Gus said she went there from time to time.' Lawson looked square at Dungannon. 'Had she arranged to meet someone there?'

'Or was it a morbid case of déjà vu?' Dungannon frowned. 'In my day, now I know that was in the dark ages but, we went out onto the street and we asked people questions. Maybe you should try that. Never know, you might do some good.'

'I'm going,' Lawson scraped back the chair, a defiant gesture.

'Don't you want to know about finger-prints *et cetera* at the scene?'

'Yeah.'

'Crap. Fingerprints are a complete mish-mash. Someone completely decimated the crime scene before we got there.'

'Deliberate?'

Dungannon stretched, yawned. 'No idea. Now, Sherlock. Time to hit the beat.'

'Yeah. Oh . . . ' he paused at the door. 'Jacob's social worker *is* Sophie Sullivan. Kate's trying to get hold of her now.' Seeing Dungannon's expression slide was completely satisfying, Lawson left the office with a smirk on his lips.

★ ★ ★

Flick was her name, she told Lawson defiantly, and yes, she'd known Dotty. A little. Lawson grabbed this straw with both hands; all the other working girls had made hurried exits when they saw him approaching.

'Ain't got nothin' to hide,' Flick tossed bottle blonde hair, sucked on a spliff. 'You ain't gonna arrest me if I'm helping, are you?'

'Probably not — today at any rate.'

CashSave was relatively quiet. He was attracting very few stares, he was relieved to notice, from the harassed shoppers. He shuddered to think how old Flick was — and how long she'd been doing this. But he was thankful that whatever it was she was smoking had loosened her tongue enough to want to talk to him.

'She didn't pick up much casual trade, our Dotty. Had her regulars. Met 'em here then bogged off.'

'Where?'

'Dunno. Never bothered to ask.'

'Did she go off with her clients in their cars?'

Flick shrugged. 'Sometimes.'

'What about Wednesday night? She go off with anyone then?'

Flick sucked on her spliff again, concentrating hard. 'Can't remember.'

'What was she wearing?'

'Look love,' Flick ground the finished spliff under her heel, put her hand on a bone-thin hip. 'It ain't *The Clothes Show* down here. We're here for business, not for the catwalk. She weren't doing so bad Wednesday — had a few hundred quid on her.'

'Dotty?'

'Ain't that who we're talking about?'

'How can you be sure it was Wednesday?'

'First day I was down here. Had a cold. Only time I seen Dotty this week.'

'She showed you this money?'

'Yeah. I was behind on me rent 'cos I'd been ill, and she said if I needed it she'd lend me some.'

'And did she?'

'What?'

'Lend you some?'

Flick shook her head. 'Nah. Told her I didn't need no handouts from Mr Posh to get me through my life.'

'Who's Mr Posh?'

'Geezer who used to pick her up — think that was on a Wednesday.'

'Can you describe him?'

'Nah.'

'Why did you call him Mr Posh?'

'Because he drove a big posh car.'

That was it. Sum total. Lawson thanked her, told her she'd been a great help and left her to it. With a description like that he couldn't fail to haul in the suspect. Not.

8

The Fairweather Organisation had six members. Lawson ran a thumb down the names. Three of them were dead. Admittedly it seemed only Dotty's death was deliberate. Of the other two, one had suffered a heart attack and the other, a long fight with cancer. Some sort of curse, decided Lawson, must be attached to the membership. Odds-on that the other three had less than even chances of living their full lifespan. Lawson decided to visit them.

★ ★ ★

Margaret Dubois was tall, slim, elegant. Her black hair had a silver streak reminiscent of Cruella Deville, the image completed by red talons and mink coat. Lawson decided it wasn't fake on the basis that the six bedroomed house and the Merc weren't.

'I'm just going out. Is this important?' She peered snootily down at him from the lofty heights of her doorstep.

'Oh, I think so, Madam. May I come in?'

'Didn't you hear me? I'm just going out.

Oh, damn! Come on quickly, get in. Quickly!' She grabbed his sleeve, pulled him into the hall, slammed the door shut. 'The cleaner from number three,' she explained in a hushed voice. 'If she sees you here I'll be gossiped about for the next fortnight.'

'I'm here about The Fairweather Organisation,' Lawson watched her face, it remained impassive. 'I believe you are a member.'

She leant against the banister, carefully arranging one foot on the bottom stair. 'I'm at a loss as to why you need to know anything about the organisation.'

'I'm investigating the death of a member.'

'Dotty?'

'Yes. How well did you know her?'

She struggled to make her eyes hold his gaze. 'I ... er ... didn't know her at all really. We'd all meet annually for lunch. I saw her then. That was all.'

'What about the other members?' He tried to stop staring at the delicate gold crucifix which dangled temptingly in her freckled cleavage. It was then he realised that her natural hair colour was not likely to be black. Or did black-haired people have freckles too? He would run that one past Kate. Not that he considered it to be important to the case, he was just curious.

Margaret Dubois produced a packet of

cigarettes from the pocket of the mink now draped over the banister. She took one out, lit it, replaced the packet, watching Lawson all the time as if daring him to ask for one. Twice now he'd been subjected to such prejudice, if it continued he'd be getting a complex.

'No,' she exhaled, eyes closing in satisfaction. Silence. Lawson waited. Eventually she spoke. 'I'm not really very sociable.'

'Do the other members keep in touch?'

'I really think you should be asking them.'

'I intend to, I just — '

'Thought you'd cut a few corners. Not with me you don't. Now, if you don't mind . . . ' She shook out the mink, draped it over the shoulders of her black wool sweater.

'Just one more thing. Where do you meet for your annual lunch?'

'Pantiles.'

'Thank you Ms Dubois, I shall hold you up no longer.'

She watched him until he'd turned right at the end of the road, a frown on her face. She'd had doubts recently about remaining with The Fairweather Organisation. Now she wished she'd followed her gut feeling and got out. She didn't need her past delving into.

Lawson drove to the last name on his list with a feeling of defeat. The second name — Betty Harker — had not been home.

83

Peering through uncurtained windows he ascertained the place was empty. Betty had vacated.

Better luck with Stan Rawlings.

The bungalow, like the garden, was tidy, if slightly shabby. Rawlings, a big man with a thatch of white hair, a drinkers' nose and a pair of red and yellow striped braces over a canary yellow shirt, was a soft-spoken Yorkshireman. After a firm handshake, he led Lawson down a blue-carpeted hall with a small table on the left holding a collection of unopened mail and into the living room.

'Sit down, I'll put the kettle on.'

Lawson opened his mouth to protest. Dungannon would be watching the minutes tick and was likely to penalise Lawson severely if he was back later than reasonably expected. While he waited he studied the group of silver-framed photos on a dusty baby grand piano. Mostly black and white, some sepia, nearly all of a woman with a cheerful no-nonsense face, and a girl.

'The Fairweather Organisation?' Stan strained the tea. 'Long time since I've heard that name. Not since . . . ' his voice wobbled and he glanced across at the photos. As did Lawson. Rawlings cleared his throat and tried again. 'Not since Nora died. Seven months it is now. They reckon time is a great healer — but I don't reckon I'll live that long.'

'I'm sorry. You discussed it with your wife then, did you?' Lawson, dunking his Morning Coffee, cursed silently as he misjudged the length of time submerged, and it slid to the bottom of his cup.

'No, she discussed it with me a time or two when things hit a sticky patch and she didn't know whether or not to stay with it.'

'But you were a member?'

'No, she was,' he leant towards Lawson's list, pointed it out with a broad thumbnail. 'Mrs S. Rawlings — must've rubbed the 's' off Mrs at some point.'

Lawson sighed. Rawlings was right, at some point over the years Mrs must have mutated to Mr. 'So, what is the organisation about?'

'Preserving the rights of ancient women.' Rawlings thought for a moment. 'No, that's not right — preserving the ancient rights of women. That sounds better doesn't it?'

Lawson was not so sure. 'Could you elaborate?'

'No.' Rawlings shook his head. 'That's all I ever really knew. Some secret women's thing. Believe me son, when women create a coven there's no point asking questions. Only ends in trouble. Like I said, she'd only mention it if things weren't going well.'

'Anything recently? I mean, before she died? Any trouble then?'

'The last thing I recall was some rum do over a prostitute joining. She'd bought out someone else. Nora wasn't too happy about that — not that the prostitute had joined but that the members hadn't been called together to discuss it.'

'I see,' said Lawson scribbling furiously. 'When would that have been?'

'Beginning of the year, January or February, I guess. More tea?'

'No thanks.' Lawson continued. 'Did you know any of the guys on the periphery of The Fairweather Organisation?'

'Men? I've already said — '

'I mean men like you — husbands, partners — '

'No,' Stan shook his jowls.

'Ever heard of Dave Palmer?'

Stan hesitated, thinking. 'No, don't reckon I have.'

'OK. What do you know about Margaret Dubois?'

'Audrey Dubois.' He stopped, bit his lip. 'No, you're right, it was Margaret. Yes, I've heard of her, yes.'

Inwardly Lawson groaned. He shook his wrist, at this rate he'd be pensioned off with something as life-threatening as RSI.

'Margaret Dubois,' Stan nodded, rolling the name around his mouth as though he hadn't said it for a long time. 'Always kept herself busy keeping herself out of trouble, that one.'

'Did she indeed? Any particular incident you can think of? Anyone in particular she didn't want to be linked to?'

Stan's expression blanked as his face closed down. 'I don't know. I'm an old man.' He stood with difficulty. 'And my mind fancies it remembers all kinds of things — then I recognise things I thought *I'd* said and done in the black and white re-runs on the telly. I can't tell you any more son. Best all round if you leave.'

'Sure.' Lawson closed his notebook with the feeling he'd pressed the wrong button somewhere, seemed to be making a habit of that. 'I'll see myself out. If you remember anything . . . '

But he knew as he closed the door that Stan's mind was conveniently, permanently blank. And, what was more, he now knew that four members of The Fairweather Organisation were dead, and one unaccounted for.

9

Acquiring money was harder than Jacob could ever have imagined. One shopkeeper had laughed in his face when he offered his services; he'd scuttled out red-faced and determined not to try any more. He'd have to take Tabbi's money. Babysitting — how hard could that be? After all, he looked after Odd-Job, didn't he? Which reminded him, he must feed him later. Blue was just another pet really. Tabbi's pet. That was what connected them. They both had something that relied on them to survive. A powerful feeling, but one that needed security to survive. Jacob could provide Tabbi with the security of a roof over her head; she could provide him with the security of money. Whichever way he looked at it, this venture was bound to succeed.

Drumboli's Lane was heaving with people. Unknown to Jacob it was four o'clock each day when the shops and stalls knocked their perishable goods down to get shot of them. Weaving through the throng, he made for the Chinese Herbal shop. No Tabbi. Wheeling through three hundred and sixty degrees on the heels of his battered sneakers revealed nothing. Shit! Perching on a concrete bollard, he scoured the faces around him. All kinds of people of every race, but no Tabbi. He asked a carrier-laden woman the time. She frowned, put down some of her baggage, checked: 4:45 p.m. No wonder Tabbi wasn't here. He wouldn't have waited forty five minutes either. A sudden idea brought him sharply to his feet. He'd ring her, that way he'd find her.

He waited patiently outside the phone box by the car park until its occupant had finished. Scrabbling in his pocket for change he found her mobile phone number, picked up the receiver. Realising he'd got no money he put it down again. What to do? A memory stirred, of him and his mother late home from the cinema; they'd been to see 'The Jungle Book'. She'd made a call without any money. How had she done that? Screwing up his face he forced his memory to reveal its secrets. She'd rung the operator, he decided, and asked for help. Something like that any way.

Worth a try. He could always make out it was an emergency and that Tabbi was his mum. He picked up the receiver again.

Tabbi's voice, initially languid, was soon incensed. 'How dare you let me down! And . . . ' she paused for breath then continued at greater volume ' . . . how dare you reverse the charges!'

Jacob kept a sullen silence.

'So, what do you want?'

'To meet you, like I said. I'm at Drumboli's Lane. I'm sorry I'm late — it took longer than I thought to check the house was all clear.' A lie; he'd been nowhere near the house.

'I see. Now look, I don't appreciate being stood up. I ain't prepared to be fucked about by anybody.' She sighed. 'Oh, what the hell. OK, I'll be there. Give me twenty minutes. We'll finish arguing then — at least it's cheaper face to face!'

Jacob thought there was the trace of a smile in her voice.

She took forty minutes.

Moving stiffly, she made her way down the now almost empty Drumboli's Lane. As she came closer, Jacob noticed black rings under her eyes he'd not seen before. She walked straight past him.

'Come on, it's nearly Blue's tea-time. Don't want him screaming all the way down the street.'

They walked in near silence. The wind was biting and their breath hung before them. Occasionally Blue snuffled. Once Jacob started to say something, changed his mind, fell silent again.

The kitchen light was on and, as they

turned into Amber Close, it attracted like a siren on a stormy night. He led Tabbi to the back door, helping her negotiate the buggy round the tight bend by the rockery.

'Who's is it?' Tabbi spoke in reverent tones, her eyes wide as she looked around.

'Dunno. Mine now. One day,' Jacob, warming to his subject, straightened his shoulders and flung his arms wide. 'I'll have this place looking like it used to — all posh and that.'

'Just as well 'cos it's a dump at the moment.'

Jacob was stung into silence.

'It won't take that much cleaning up.' He watched her eyes cruising the kitchen. Letting go of the police tape, he closed the door. 'Go straight through to the lounge.'

She did. It was dark, the glow from a street light throwing shadows across the floor.

'It's spooky in here, turn on the light.'

'It doesn't work.' He threw the switch to show her, was proved wrong. 'Oh! The police must have changed it.'

'Like they taped up the back door? Why were they here? I . . . Oh shit!' Tabbi started backing toward the door. 'Someone died in here. There's a fucking body down there! No wonder the place feels spooky!'

Jacob followed her gaze. The chalkline of a

human figure decorated the floor. 'The body's gone now. Anyway, she seemed nice.'

'She? Did you know her then? Alive?'

Jacob shook his head. 'Don't think so, but she seemed nice dead.'

Tabbi backed into the hall. 'Do you seriously think I'm going to let my baby live in a house where a woman was killed? 'Nice' or not?'

Jacob, suddenly tired of this whole thing, shrugged. 'Do what you like. You won't find anywhere else to sleep tonight. Look at it this way, even if she's turned into a ghost she won't be after us. We didn't kill her.' He turned cold inside. She might haunt him after what he'd done to her before he gave her his sleeping bag. He shuddered. Of course she wouldn't. She'd know he was only being friendly.

Tabbi came slowly back into the room, Blue now in her arms. 'OK, you win. But if I have any trouble with her, I'm off!'

'Right, if you're stopping I'd better show you your bedroom.'

She followed him up the stairs, handing Blue up to him while she negotiated the missing stairs. 'How long have you lived here?'

'Six months, off and on.'

'And nobody's moved you on?'

92

'Nosey cow across the road calls the police every time she sees me, but they can't do nowt if my folks don't want me.'

'You're not old enough to be on your own. They can set Social Services on you.'

'They've tried that — Sophie Sullivan her name is. Give her the slip every time she comes — got to catch me first, see.' Jacob allowed his face to twist into a lop-sided grin, the one he practised in front of the mirror to impress the girls. He thought it made him look older. And cool. 'Anyway, I've got squatter's rights.' He led her to the front bedroom.

'Mm. Not sure if they count if you're underage. Now me . . . '

'You're underage too.'

'Yeah, but I've got a baby. They've a tough job proving I'm not old enough — 'ticularly when they don't know me proper name.'

Jacob watched her prowl the room. He'd only been in here twice before. He didn't like to admit it but the low eaves and the way the wind whistled through them scared him. A double bed stood against the chimney breast. Its mattress was bare and there were two stained pillows, one leaking feathers. Tabbi bounced enthusiastically on it making the springs groan protestingly before going to the fitted wardrobes running the entire length of the partition wall and opening each door in turn. Hangers. Wire mainly. Some wooden ones removed from hotels. Behind the last door, a shelf with a selection of blankets.

'Bingo!' Tabbi pulled them all down before sifting through them. Two she rejected for being too holey. Two more she handed to Jacob. 'For your bed. Blue and I will have the others.'

'Blue?' Somehow he'd expected the baby to remain in his buggy.

'He needs somewhere to sleep too. What did you think I was going to do with him?' She didn't wait for an answer. Fishing in her cleavage she pulled out a nurse's watch. 'Soon I'm going to have to go to work. Better have some dinner.'

Now Jacob was really confused. They'd got no food. What did she mean? He followed her back downstairs.

'Tomorrow we'll get bulbs for the whole of this house,' Tabbi was saying as she moved the buggy nearer the front door, removing the bag from its handles, Blue balanced expertly on her hip. 'Amazing the electricity has been left on. Usually have to fiddle it somehow.' She took the kettle from the bag, filled it with water, then took out the two eggs and placed them carefully inside. To Jacob's absolute amazement, she plugged the kettle in. 'These won't take long.' She started snooping through the cupboards.

'Not a lot,' she placed two chipped bowls and two different sized plates on the worktop. 'But it'll do. These'll do for a cuppa.' She'd found a handful of stale teabags. 'No milk. Just have to close your eyes and imagine.'

The kettle started to vibrate. Tabbi peered in. 'Nearly ready for lift-off. See if there's any spoons, the smaller the better.'

No spoons. A fork, a rusty knife, but no spoons.

'OK. We'll just have to dunk the bread.' Fishing eggs from the kettle she broke their shells with the end of the fork. Three slices of bread each and dinner was ready.

They sat in the lounge. It was cold, slightly damp and Jacob thought he could smell perfume. Worriedly he kept checking the spot where the dead woman had lain as though expecting to see a puddle of it. Nothing. Thank God. He'd not seen any blood. She'd not died messily. If you didn't know, well you wouldn't know. He wished Tabbi didn't know.

You shouldn't have brought her here. Shouldn't have got her involved.

'Right.' Tabbi pushed a last piece of soggy bread into Blue's mouth. Jacob noticed she'd barely had any of the meal herself. She stood, handed her plate and Blue to Jacob. 'I'm going to have to leave you to do the washing up.'

He frowned. That was what Dad said to Tina when he was going out to get pissed. That was what he always said the nights Tina got the beatings. 'You mean you're going out? I'm babysitting?'

'That's the agreement.' Tabbi started undressing. Jacob shut his eyes. Opened one just to peek. Undressing no. Just reducing her garb. Beneath her flowing ethnic skirt she wore a black one that barely covered her bum. Beneath the misshapen sweater she wore a lacy bra. From her bag she fished a pair of stilettos and a man's black jacket.

'OK. Do I look set?'

Jacob nodded grimly.

'Good. I'll be in just after midnight — unless I get a better offer! Blue'll want a feed about ten. There's half a banana in the bag and give him some of the water out of the kettle. It'll be cool by then. There's a spare nappy too. He can sleep in the clothes he's wearing.'

'Nappy?'

'You've never changed a nappy before?' Tabbi's eyebrows arched in amusement.

'No.'

'Dead easy. Just take note, when you take that one off, of which way it goes and you'll

96

be fine. When you take off the dirty nappy, wipe off as much crap with it as you can, use a wipe to clean off the rest and shove the clean nappy on. Easy. Make sure you grip his ankles tight to keep him on his back. Little sod has started to twist over and crawl away.' She kissed Blue's cheek and left the room.

Jacob heard the back door close with a heavy feeling in his stomach.

★ ★ ★

Lawson picked his way carefully to the back of the house. Should be in bed by rights, catching up on the sleep he'd missed this week. But he was on surveillance. The courage to ask had failed, denying him the luxury of having anyone else on the rota. Keeping an eye on Bugs was something he was having to do in his spare time.

'Some hobby!' he muttered to himself, squatting beside the rabbit hutch. 'Now then mate,' the rabbit hopped towards him. 'Not so cold tonight, is it? Hungry?' He pulled up some dandelions from around the cage. He pushed them through the wire. 'That'll keep you going for a bit.'

Close by, a door opened, closed; footsteps sounded, heels clacking off into the distance. Was it Storm Mount's door he'd heard? He thought about it. Unlikely. Since when would a twelve year old lad be out in heels? Nah, probably next door.

There was no moon tonight. Very inconsiderate. Proud of being a city lad, Lawson had a problem with foliage, when it wasn't in a vase that is. Too much of the stuff and he started to feel claustrophobic. He was starting to feel that way now. It was so dark and cold that only someone absolutely desperate to be here would arrive now. And Lawson didn't think that very likely. Had the lad been here today to feed the rabbit, he was obviously long gone. Lawson nodded, endorsing his decision. Time to go home.

★　★　★

Time went so slow without a telly. The church clock had just struck nine. Seemed more than ninety minutes since Tabbi left. Blue seemed to think so too. He wriggled when Jacob tried to put him in his buggy; grizzled when Jacob tried sitting down and bouncing him on his knee. All he was happy doing was staring out of the window at the rain which was now streaming down the pane. Jacob hoped Nosey Parker wasn't looking. Occasionally Blue would reach out a pudgy hand to try and touch the rivulets, but mainly he gurgled and farted. Jacob wrinkled up his nose. He hoped there wasn't going to be a dirty nappy to deal with. He wasn't overly confident about the whole nappy thing and would rather Tabbi was there to take charge.

His arms were aching, his back had seized into a position similar to Quasimodo. He tried, once more, to sit down. Blue dissolved into hysterical tears. It was then that it occurred to Jacob the real reason for Blue wanting to stay at the window. Had he, Jacob, not taken up residence on the windowsill when his mother left? Had he not watched everybody who moved on the street below in case it was her? Had he not been terrified to go to the bathroom in case he missed her while he was in there? Indeed he had. That was why he'd spent three nights huddled in his quilt in the corner of the windowsill so as not to fall off if he fell asleep; and three days playing hookey from school and refusing to go downstairs for meals.

'It's OK Blue, she'll be back tomorrow. You're ever so lucky to have a mum to care like that. I know this place isn't much, but your mum's doing her best for you. I know I'm not the best — but I'll try. She knows that, else she wouldn't have left you with me. We'll be OK, you and me. Maybe we could pretend to be brothers or something, maybe that'll make it easier. I'm not old enough to be your dad.' Blue had stopped whingeing, lulled by Jacob's voice. Slowly, Jacob sat down. 'Anyway, dads can be crap. Not all of them though. Me mate's dad treated him like a prince — took him fishing and everything. My dad gave me a fishing rod once, then told me to piss off and work out how to use it. I wasn't very good. Got it taffled up in a branch that some lads had wedged in the stream. Had to tell Dad someone'd nicked it else he'd have killed me. One day I'll nick you one from that shop by the quay, take you fishing.

'You'd like that, sitting in your buggy on the towpath watching the water and the fish. Sometimes I see a kingfisher or a water vole. I'll take you when the water level goes down.'

Blue smiled. Jacob smiled too. In that moment, two youngsters found a common ground, briefly. Jacob had expected to get 'the feeling' about Blue, particularly when Tabbi started doing her motherly thing, but he hadn't. Tabbi still treated him the same, Blue wasn't taking anything from him. He wouldn't have to kill him.

That's all right then!

Jacob tried to think of a suitable retort for James Bond but Blue suddenly remembered his unease and started grizzling again.

'Shit!' Gathering up the child and heaving himself upright, Jacob made for the kitchen. Forcing Blue into his buggy, he rinsed the plates under the tap. 'Don't tell her I didn't wash them properly. Ain't got no time for farting about like that. Now, you hungry again?' He collected Blue's supper. 'Two minutes and I'll check your nappy.' His stomach churned at the thought. 'If you're not dirty you can stay in that one. Then it's bedtime.'

But Blue had other ideas. Two hours later he was still screaming every time Jacob tried to lie him on the bed. In exasperation, Jacob hauled the buggy upstairs, strapped the baby in, closed the door and left him to yell. He couldn't come to any harm and with any luck he'd exhaust himself.

Downstairs he could still hear him.

He went outside. Stars diamond-bright in the dark sky. He leant against the wall, sighed, watched his smoky breath disappear. He peered down the garden. Funny how trees and bushes seemed to move at night. One was walking there, near to Odd-Job's hutch. Odd-Job! He'd forgotten to feed him. In the bright, full moonlight, Jacob made his careful way along the outhouses. The rabbit didn't come to his call. Odd. He should have been starving, should have come *without* Jacob calling. Hunkering down in front of the cage, he saw the reason why.

Odd-Job had plenty of food. Not just the dry stuff but someone had picked him dandelions. Who? Danny! Who else? Jacob banged the side of the cage with his fist. Danny. Had to be. Who else came down here for God's sake? And it had to be someone who wanted Jacob to know they knew about his rabbit, that they were on his case. Danny.

Well, Jacob's stomach dived, there was only one thing to do when you got found out. Cover your tracks. Which meant ... he opened the hutch door, stroked the rabbit's ears.

Don't get too attached to anyone — they only leave you in the end.

'I'm so sorry Odd-Job,' he whispered through his tears. 'I'm so, so sorry.'

10

Eleanor James, cigarette drooping from mouth corner, watched her home help weave between the black sacks. She waited for the key in the door, the cheery 'Cooee'.

'You're early.' Eleanor didn't get up. She watched Audrey Willis's eyes pan over her grubby nylon nightie, big enough to cover everything save her dirty toes.

'Just a minute or two. Beautiful day for the time of year. Got me up and out.'

'Bully for you.' Eleanor stubbed out her butt on a saucer, plucked a scrap of paper from under yesterday's newspaper. 'Here's me shopping list — give me chance to get sorted while you're out.' She treated Audrey Willis to squint-eyed scrutiny. How come the bloody woman was always so immaculate? Bobbed greying fair hair, long pale pink nails, slim figure still, in her mid-fifties, acceptable in jeans. Didn't look like a cleaner in Eleanor's eyes at all.

'I'll be off then. Be as quick as I can.' And she'd gone, in a whiff of Chanel or Forever. Eleanor had better things to worry about than which perfume was what. Like how she was going to persuade Audrey that she no longer wanted her to work for her.

Time was when Audrey had done as she was told and no more. Lately she'd been treating Eleanor more and more like an invalid, offering to do the jobs that Eleanor prided herself on still being able to cope with; tutting when Eleanor wasn't as neatly turned out as Audrey would have liked. Yes, life with Audrey was becoming more hassled.

It was the Grand National that did it. Mortal Favour had a lot to answer for. Eleanor had never expected to win; she didn't expect Mortal Favour's jockey had either but as it happened most of the experienced horses came to grief one way or the other. Audrey had been despatched to pick up the winnings — and a large bottle of Courvoisier. It transpired, over increasingly generous helpings of the spirit, that they had a lot in common: uncaring, bloody-minded offspring — she a son, Audrey a daughter; both their husbands dead — hers when his natural time was up, Audrey's Seymour crashing into a motorway bridge after visiting his bigamous wife; and the fact that they each held themselves in much higher esteem than any other *homo sapiens* on the planet.

Soon they were as pissed as sailors out of Jamaica. Pissed as proverbial newts. They started swopping stories, each one bolder, dafter, than the last. Eleanor told of leading the riot of '62 on the bus station after the curtailment of the number seventeen to the bullring.

Audrey told of shoplifting Heinz baked beans from the corner shop because her good-for-nothing first husband (who worked at least sixty hours a week as a door-to-door salesman) only earned enough to buy cheap brands.

Eleanor told of leaving Danny in his pram in a church hall while a jumble sale was going on to save her having to pay for a babysitter while she nipped to the cinema to see *Dr Zhivago*. She failed to mention that, because of the length of the film, the jumble sale was over long before she got back to find the church hall closed and a note tied to the drain pipe asking the mother, if she came back, to collect her son from the vicarage. Sometimes she'd cursed her honesty at picking up the child, it would have been so much easier to have left him and let someone else bring him up.

Audrey revealed that she'd set out to snare Seymour soon after his first wife died, finding out, through useful contacts, where he was likely to lunch or swim or play golf, and turning up in a waft of expensive perfume, a swish of elegant scarves and perfect hair-dos, with a surprised 'Fancy seeing you here'; 'Oooh people will talk,' and any other cliché she could think of, each orchestrated with a girlish giggle and a flutter of false eyelashes. She'd planned for the chase to take three months; it took six. 'Always was slow on the uptake,' she said with a sharp laugh.

'No slower than you working out he was already married.'

'I believed him when he said he was a widower. There's got to be trust in a relationship.'

When Eleanor told of the surprising murder her husband Bill had committed, Audrey sat open-mouthed, disguising the fact that her scheming brain was filing away information that may become useful later on.

'Scott Drew was in Danny's year,' Eleanor started, her 's's now 'sh's. 'Not his class, his year. They were good friends, very close, shared interests — football and things. Harmless it seemed at the time. Normal. I should have known though that Danny was far from normal. Scott got into drugs, not just using them but selling them too. I blame his parents — product of the sixties, believing in free love and hallucinations. Danny started using too, although I'd never heard of him selling then.' Shakily she lit a cigarette,

106

dragged deep. 'Scott came to live with us when his parents went to Australia for a year, his father was a professor of some sort and went on sabbatical. All was good until Scott got a letter from his mum saying they'd decided to stay in Sydney and, although they'd love to see him, they'd quite understand if he chose to stay in Righton.

'Looking back, I made a mistake. I should have said, 'Look, it's a shame to split the boys up, why don't you take Danny to Sydney with you?' That would have saved all the aggravation. But after what he considered to be his mother's rejection, Scott became very morose, very argumentative — like he was having hormone trouble, but I didn't think that applied to boys. I stopped being the understanding foster mother — something that never sat well with me — and started treating him the way I did Danny. Instead of improving, things got worse.

'Then Danny started pushing drugs for Scott. Bill caught them one night when he'd gone to the corner shop to get milk. Brought them home he did, by their ears. I'd never seen him so mad. I'd never fancied him quite so much either. He thrashed the pair of them, told them if he ever caught them again he'd do something they would regret.'

'And did he — catch them again?' Audrey

was leaning forward, hands gripping her knees.

Eleanor smiled wanly. 'You have to remember that whatever Danny did, he couldn't help himself. He's not the brightest of lads is our Danny.

'There was an axe in the shed. I didn't know, the shed was Bill's domain, nothing to do with me. He'd kept it sharp and polished in case we ever needed logs chopping, a habit that had come with him from boyhood. He'd been to see the vicar, about what I don't know. Bill sometimes had trouble with a guilty conscience — I wonder if it wasn't that thrashing he gave those lads playing on his mind. He wasn't a violent man, see. Anyway, he was coming back through the churchyard, the quickest route from the vicarage, at gone ten one Friday night when he heard scuffling in the bushes by the wall.

'He didn't look. Them bushes were a well-known haunt for teenagers trying out their bits and Bill didn't want to get involved. He'd got out onto the street before he heard voices he recognised — Danny and Scott — and went back to listen. There were several youngsters in there apparently, all haggling about the price of something. It didn't take Bill long to work out what and, when one of them said they'd tell the police if the price wasn't dropped, Bill waded in, scared off the hangers-on and brought home our two by the scruffs of their necks.'

'I suppose, in those days,' said Audrey, trying to sound empathetic, 'drug abuse was something that was swept under the carpet. No support groups or professional bodies to help parents understand why their child couldn't see that what he was doing was wrong. As I see it, Scott wasn't really your responsibility, and his parents were on the other side of the world. It would be doing our society a favour to punish him.' She smiled. 'I can see where you're coming from.'

Eleanor nodded. 'I was in the kitchen handwashing my smalls. I did it in the dark, something my mother had instilled in me — never do for anyone see you doing stuff like that — so Bill couldn't see me from outside. He sent Danny in but told him to watch from the bedroom window 'cos if he ever caught him again, this was what he'd do to him. Then, still clinging to Scott's pullover, Bill took the axe from the shed.

'Scott laughed when Bill lifted it over his shoulder. I smiled too. The thought of Bill threatening anyone was absurd, he wouldn't even throw water at next door's cat when it used his flower beds as a toilet. Scott was still laughing when the axe caught him just below the jaw. It didn't take his head right off though, just cut through the front so the back acted like a hinge. Closing it wouldn't have stopped the blood though. I've never seen so much, went everywhere it did, even ran down the window like it was raining.

'I think I screamed then. Must have done. Bill suddenly saw me standing at the window. He came into the kitchen still clutching the axe, his face and clothes spattered with blood. He smiled.

'That's done then, our Eleanor,' he said. 'Danny'll be in no more trouble now.'

'How I wish that were true.' She closed her eyes, her face suddenly grave at the memories she'd just recounted. 'But after that, Danny's always been . . . ' she fished around for a word that best described her son's mental state ' . . . different. Became a complete outsider.'

Audrey wriggled forward. 'So what became of the body?'

Eleanor smiled. 'Compost.'

★ ★ ★

The banging on the front door brought her back to herself. Eleanor groaned, she'd not even got dressed while Audrey had been out.

'Here we are,' Mrs Model of Efficiency

1845 entered the room like a geriatric tornado, weighed down by Eleanor's purchases. 'You're not even dressed.' She spoke in the voice of one who regards slovenly pensioners as toddlers. 'Why don't you try and tidy yourself up while I pop the kettle on and make us a nice cup of tea?'

And that, thought Eleanor viciously, was, as far as she was concerned, enough of a reason to rid the world of Audrey Willis.

★ ★ ★

'Look what I've got!' Tabbi, barefoot, waving a sheet in front of her, made Jacob jump.

An old sheet, thought Jacob scowling up at her, judging by the stains and the big hole in its centre. 'What's that for?' He didn't care unless it was for wrapping Blue in while she went to work at night. He looked hopefully for an apple to stuff in the baby's gob.

'Curtain for the front room. Good innit?' She almost skipped through the kitchen. Not, thought Jacob, to dash upstairs and see to her baby, but to rush into the lounge and hold the sheet up in the centre of the room, squinting at the window as though seeing the curtain in its hanging glory.

'Where did it come from?' Jacob followed her in.

'Found it in the Sally Army bin.'

'Them's meant for refugees.'

'That's what we are innit? Refugees?'

'In a way,' consented Jacob. 'And where did you get that from?' He frowned at her shoulder bag then the crysanths she pulled from it. 'And them?'

'Bag came from the Sally Army too. Flowers came from the garage on the corner.'

'Nicked?'

'No!' Tabbi looked hurt. 'I bought them. Got a pay rise last night and anyway, I've more respect for the dead than to nick flowers for them. Sometimes rearrange 'em a bit in the cemetery — make things more even. Y'know, give some to those who haven't got any, but I'd never nick 'em for me own purposes. Found out what her name was too,' she bent to place the flowers in Dotty's chalkline. 'Dotty. All the girls are talking about her.'

'She's fading.' Jacob hunkered down.

'Yeah, I was thinkin' about that last night. Couldn't decide whether to re-do the outline or whether to let her go in peace. Decided in the end, she'd be better off just fading into the sunset. Don't you think that's romantic?'

'Er, — suppose so. Oh,' Jacob stood as Blue's early morning cries came down the stairs. 'Better go and get His Lordship.'

It wasn't until he was halfway down the stairs, babe in arms, that he realised he'd wandered, naively, into Tabbi's role. Should he be doing this?

Blue watched, between fistfuls of dry bread, as his mother tried to fix the sheet against the window.

'Don't know why we need it,' muttered Jacob.

'Because it gives added privacy. People won't know we're here if they can't see us moving about. And anyway, I've had this brilliant idea — if we can rig up some music. This room has a fantastic dance floor. We could have all-night raves — make some money.'

'The whole bloody neighbourhood would know about us then.'

Tabbi shrugged. 'Just an idea.'

And one Jacob would veto as quickly as possible.

'Anyway,' he battled on. 'They'll know someone was here in the first place to put the curtain up.'

'And who's going to notice, Smartarse?'

Nosey Parker for one, thought Jacob, wiping Blue's mouth with a grubby bib.

'Right, he's had enough,' Tabbi waved one end of the sheet at Jacob. 'You're going to have to help me with this. Cop hold of this end . . . that's right . . . and hold it against that end of the window,' she jerked her head toward the fireplace end. 'OK, now a bit higher . . . stretch . . . more than that. Oh God!' She threw her end on the floor. 'You're bloody useless! Ask a man to help and the job takes three times as long.'

'But,' suddenly Jacob was near to tears, she sounded like Tina. 'I'm only a boy. I'm not tall enough to reach even as high as you can.'

Tabbi nodded, ran agitated fingers through her hair, took a deep breath. 'OK, we'll try again. Maybe if you stand on the windowsill,' she moved over to put a finger where she thought he might stand. 'About here, and . . . ' her eyes caught sight of movement across the road. She squinted, gasped, stepped back.

'What is it? Police?' Jacob ducked below the level of the windowsill, pulled himself up high enough to peer out. 'Nah, it's only that woman what goes into Nosey Parker's.'

'You've seen her before?'

'Yeah. Few times. Usually 'bout this time. Stays an hour or two. Why, you know her?'

Tabbi was suddenly aware that Jacob was eyeing her closely, a puzzled frown puckering his face. 'I . . . er . . . no, silly me,' she forced a false laugh. 'Seeing

114

things. Thought it was someone I knew. It wasn't. Now, where were we? Ah yes, you stand about here,' she tapped a purple nail on the peeling paintwork. 'And we'll try again.'

It took them another quarter of an hour to attach the sheet, with drawing pins magically appearing from Tabbi's bag, around the window. Strange, thought Jacob, that Tabbi remained in the gloom of the room, content just to shout orders.

★ ★ ★

'Did you know Dotty?' Jacob came into the room, having made two mugs of tea, to find her sitting beside the chalk figure, a faraway look in her eyes.

'Not as such. Knew of her, got some mutual contacts. Knew enough about her to know there's no family to grieve for her.'

'That's sad,' said Jacob, wondering if he had. 'Have you got any family?'

Tabbi shrugged, stared firmly at the swirling brown liquid before her. 'Used to. Decided I was better off without them. What about you?'

'It was the other way 'round for me — they decided they were better off without me. Or at least Mum did. Buggered off to Spain

115

while I was out getting the bread.'

Tabbi snorted so loud it made Jacob jump. 'Not seriously?' She giggled.

He nodded.

She looked aghast. 'Sorry, shouldn't have laughed. Didn't think anybody could have worse parents than I did. My mum divorced my dad when he went off with another woman; then she marries a pretentious git who thinks that children are for . . . ' her voice faltered. 'Well anyway, he didn't like me. Mum wouldn't listen when I tried to tell her. Said I was making it up 'cos I didn't like him. Well I didn't but not even I would make up things like that. Then I got pregnant and she went ballistic so I decided I'd be better off alone. 'Cept I'm not alone am I, Little Man?' She threw Blue expertly into the air, caught him, blew a raspberry on his tummy. He giggled.

'Don't you ever wish you could see her again?'

Tabbi considered, slowly shook her head. 'Not ever.'

'I wish I could see my mum again. I'm going to save up and go to Spain and find her.'

'How on earth will you find her in a place like that?'

116

'It'll be easy — she speaks English, everyone else will speak Spanish.'

Again Tabbi laughed. 'Oh poor little naïve boy, Spain is heaving with ex-patriots. And even the Spanish speak English. You're in for one heck of a search.' Her face softened as his fell. She reached into her bag, pulled out a fiver. 'Here's your first pay to put towards your air ticket.'

'Thanks,' he crumpled it into his back pocket.

'What about your dad?'

'Arsehole. Hits me, has new girlfriends every week, hits them, they hit me, he hits them, they leave.'

'So you left?'

'Yep.'

'And don't ever want to go back?'

'Nope. This is my home now.'

Tabbi lay on her back, arranged Blue on her stomach, one of his legs on each side of her as though he was riding a horse. 'How did you find this place?'

Jacob looked uncomfortable, scuffed the dusty floor with the toe of his sneaker. 'Promise you won't laugh?'

'Promise,' she quickly killed the smile playing at the corners of her mouth.

'It's about a year ago now, first time I came.' Jacob dropped his head into his hands, spoke to the floor. 'I'd got this canary to bury . . . '

'Why?'

'Because it was dead.'

'Uh-huh.'

'And I was looking for somewhere along the riverbank, only there were a lot of people about — fishing and walking dogs and things — so I couldn't stop to dig a hole, they'd have thought I was up to something strange — '

'Never!'

'Look,' his head snapped up. 'Do you want to know or don't you?'

'Oh, I do, I do.'

'Then shut the fuck up.'

'Touchy.' Tabbi jiggled Blue until he giggled.

'Anyway, I found the gate into the garden. The place looked overgrown so I nipped in.'

'And buried the canary?'

'Yeah. Always bury the canaries here now.'

'Always?' Tabbi pushed herself onto her elbows. 'How many dead canaries have you come across?'

'A few.'

'And in which exotic corner of Righton do you find dead canaries?'

'Any.' He looked at her thoughtfully. 'I murder them.'

'Wha . . . Why?'

118

He sighed. 'It's a long story.'

She smiled. 'Well we've bugger all else to do today.'

It all started with his mother's canary, Norman. Norman was the only thing, in Jacob's mind, that his mother bothered about. The canary was always flapping round the house, always being asked if it wanted its treat of apple, always allowed to sing to the *Coronation Street* theme tune. Life wasn't fair. Jacob decided that if Norman wasn't around, Mum would treat him like that — buy him the sweets he wanted, let *him* sing along with *Top of the Pops*. So he strangled it and buried it in the garden at Storm Mount.

It didn't work.

She became completely withdrawn, sitting in the corner of the lounge all day in her dressing gown. Except on Fridays. Then she'd be up, showered and out of the house by seven in the morning, often not returning until well after dark.

'Where did she go?' Tabbi still couldn't work out whether Jacob spoke the truth or whether this was pure fantasy.

'Never found out. But don't you see? Canaries don't just borrow someone's love, they steal it completely. If the canary is killed, the love that it was shown dies with

119

it, doesn't get passed on to someone else.'

'I see,' Tabbi nodded, disguising the fact that she didn't see at all.

'Mum could lie too. That happened after I killed Norman.'

'And what did she lie about?'

'She said she was expecting a baby and would I like a brother or a sister — '

'Like you get to choose.'

' — And I said I didn't want either 'cos I wanted her to love me.' His eyes had taken on a dreamy look. 'And she said 'Don't you think I'll love you any more?' And I said no.'

'And?'

'Nothing. She just turned and left the room. Never mentioned it again.'

'Mothers have expansive hearts, J,' Tabbi said. 'They don't transfer their love from one child to another; they have enough for as many children as they have.' She suddenly looked uneasy. 'What did you do to the baby?'

'That's where Mum lied — she never got fat, never had a baby. She'd been winding me up.'

Tabbi cast a worried glance at Blue. 'What *would* you have done to the baby?'

'Dunno.'

You've said more than enough. Can it.

120

'OK.' Tabbi hugged Blue to her. 'So you've explained why you killed one canary. What about the others?'

'They both belonged to rest homes. I snuck in the first, grabbed the cage and ran; the second I stole through the window.'

'Why from rest homes?'

'Because of what they do to the old people in there. They're fine when they arrive. Then, weeks, sometimes only days later, they lose their minds — start moaning and spitting and can't remember who they are.'

'And you think it's the canaries do that?'

'Yeah. They suck the intelligence out of you . . . '

'Along with hijacking the love meant for children.'

'That's it. Spot on.'

'Jacob,' Tabbi spoke softly. 'Did you know someone who went into a home?'

'My Granny.' He wiped his eyes with his cuff.

'And she went like that?'

'She didn't know me no more.'

'And there was a canary?'

'No. But it was at the time I was having trouble with Norman — he'd been Granny's before he came to live with us.'

'I see. Jacob, did you love your Granny?'

'Yeah.' He nodded. 'Now she's gone and

121

Mum's gone and there's no one to care about me.'

'I do. And Blue. We'll be fine together, the three of us,' she lifted her mug. 'Here's to the Three Musketeers.'

'To us.' And Jacob, smiling sheepishly, joined in the toast.

11

Jacob envied Blue. Watching the infant snuggled to his mother's breasts beneath the dirty pink blanket, Jacob wanted to cry; to scream; to rip the baby from her arms and lie there himself, warm, loved, safe. Very safe. Jacob took another step into the room, creaked a floorboard, paused as Tabbi moaned softly. She threw a careless arm across the pillow, releasing a nipple from the shelter of the blanket. Jacob stared at it for a very long time, her skin was so white, so flawless, unlike the body downstairs which had been freckled and lined. He fingered the necklace in his pocket. That would look nice against the white skin. He held it at arm's length, squinting as he studied the blue against the swell of perfect skin. He nodded. Lovely. He'd give it to her later.

Anger had replaced the feeling of being sorry for himself. Anger at his mother for leaving, at his dad for not caring, at society for not noticing and at the fucking bastard who had made him murder Odd-Job. Hot tears ran down his cheeks as he ran down the stairs, pausing only to bridge the gap. He had nothing, no one, in the world. No-fucking-one to cuddle up to, to run to when things got tough. Not even Odd-Job. He knew what James Bond would do, he'd avenge the death.

But not by screaming and shouting. Be diplomatic, wait for your chance, for vengeance. Work out who's to blame, let them know you know then deal with them . . . slowly.

Classy, James, very classy.

First task was to bury the body. Lifting Odd-Job from his hutch, Jacob cried some more. The rabbit was cold, wet underneath, smelly. Jacob, in grief, hugged the corpse to his chest and carried it to the graveyard at the bottom of the garden. He lifted his head, focussing as though just realising where he was. How could he bury Odd-Job alongside the victims of his own callousness? It didn't fit. This ground was tainted with the blood of murdered souls. He couldn't lay Odd-Job to rest here. But had the rabbit not been murdered? Yes, he answered himself, but it wasn't the same. He turned away.

Across the garden, where it met the orchard, grew a pear tree, its branches gnarled and twisted as though it had spent all its life fighting with the wind. Beneath it was a clear patch of soil. Here was a fitting place. The ground was hard. Being slightly higher, the river water had drained away. His spoon bent as he dug.

'Bloody useless thing!' He flung it against the trunk, heard the metallic clunk, remembered those same words from his father's mouth when Jacob had broken a dish while washing-up. Only he never said 'thing'. 'Bastard' was his favourite. He'd have to find a spade from somewhere. Gently placing Odd-Job's body in dense vegetation along the side of the garden, Jacob headed for the outhouse.

The door was open. He stood, open-mouthed, in the doorway. It hadn't been open last night. Had Tabbi been here? But if so, why? His reflexes took over. Forming hands into a gun, he backed against the wall, took a deep breath, raised his arms above his head. With an explosive push, he twisted away from the wall, spinning around to stand, once more, in the doorway, gun pointing into the gloom. 'Come out with your hands up!'

No one did which, Jacob silently admitted, was perhaps as well. He took a small step forward, knees bent, feet ready to turn and run. Checking left and right as he went through the doorway, he stopped as a shadow completely enveloped him. There was a strange smell. His stomach turned. The last time he'd smelled a strange smell was when he'd found the body, but this wasn't a dead smell, he was sure of that. Which meant . . .

'Go on then, shoot!'

Jacob didn't stop to discover who owned the voice. Sneakers slipping as he turned, he made for the door. He grasped the jamb, hauled himself through, felt a hand on his collar. His knees sagged as he lost the fight and was pulled back into the lair.

'So, Jacob Palmer. Or should that be — Who? — Jesse James?'

Jacob stared, tightlipped: Danny. James Bond would never stoop so low as to feed a villain's ego.

'Aren't you a little old to be playing cowboys and Indians?'

'Aren't you a little old to be hiding in outhouses?' Jacob wriggled free, leant against the wall. 'Should be out earning, man your age.'

He knew this was dangerous territory. Danny was touchy about his age, he'd spent most of his schooldays struggling to keep up with his classmates; eventually the system had won and he'd spent his last two years at school being moved from class to class refusing to behave or attempt to learn and so had left with nothing but bad memories and a bad report.

'You little shit!'

Jacob ducked the hand that swiped towards him, head-butted. Danny who collapsed into the corner where the sleeping bag had been. Now there was only hard concrete; the impact brought tears to his eyes. Jacob crouched, a safe distance away.

'Did you feed my rabbit?'

Danny continued trying not to cry.

'Because if I found out it was you, I'll have you. I've had to kill him 'cos of you.'

A noise from Danny that could have been a laugh. 'Why don't you ask the filth why they were babysitting him?'

Jacob studied him closely for a moment then shook his head. 'I'm warning you Danny. No one fucks with me.'

'No,' Danny croaked. 'You just fuck with other people.'

'Eh?'

Danny struggled onto his haunches. 'That tart you've got stashed away here. I've seen her. Giving you lessons is she? My guess is you need them. Inexperienced, no doubt, still playing cowboys and Indians.'

Don't let him rile you, smile slightly, or raise your eyebrow. Let him know you don't take him seriously.

Jacob stared at Danny, the stocky shadow now brushing himself down with short, thick fingers attached to muscular arms and heavy shoulders. One on one he didn't stand a chance. Subtlety was the order of the day. He shrugged. 'Maybe you're right.'

'Good man,' Danny pushed Jacob's shoulder hard. 'And who knows, while you're out riding the range, I might teach your tart one or two lessons of my own.'

Danny's leering laughter followed Jacob down the garden. There was no point trying to bury Odd-Job while that lout was around. He'd come back later.

Right now, he'd go for a walk along the riverbank, try and clear his head; maybe see the kingfisher.

★ ★ ★

It wasn't until he'd actually said the words that Danny even considered what he might do to Tabbi. He'd seen her, recognised her for what she was. Prostitutes have a certain smell — and he should know. Not dirty — or cheap come to that — more sort of . . . available. For long moments, he stood outside the outhouse, a smile playing on his lips. Jacob's tart, now there was something worth investigating. Not up to his usual standard, of course, but then no one could match up to Melanie.

She must have been fourteen, Danny three

years older. He'd only seen her from a distance until that Saturday afternoon he'd left his house after another slanging match with his mother. Pouring with rain it was, and cold, and the shirt he was wearing was saturated before he reached the gate. Melanie Croft had spotted him before he saw her, almost as though she was looking for him from the lounge window.

In those days Storm Mount was a family home bulging with a middle-class couple and three children. Melanie was the middle child, and the only girl. Her parents were shopping, she informed him, taking hold of his dripping sleeve and tutting, and her brothers were at the football. Why didn't he come in, dry out, keep her company till her family got back? It was an offer he chose not to decline. He knew what she wanted. The cup of tea she offered, the game of Monopoly, were all part of the build-up. The foreplay. He giggled. She looked up sharply.

'What?'

'Nothing. Just a silly thought.' Not a silly thought, silly word. Foreplay was a word he could use in History and get Miss blushing and the class laughing.

She won Monopoly easily. He'd never played before and anyway, wasn't really interested.

'More tea?' She tossed her blonde hair over her shoulders, smiled a smile that lit up her pretty blue eyes.

'No, thank you. Look,' he stood, placed a hand on her shoulder. Just one, more friendly that way. 'You don't have to pretend with me.' A look — panic? — flashed through her eyes. He let his hand drop away. 'Well, OK, maybe just one more cup.'

It was when his shirt had had time to dry and her mother had rung to say they had been delayed and would be at least another hour that she took him by the hand and led him upstairs, giggling nervously. His heart started pounding — this was more like it. They went into the front bedroom, with its four-poster bed and fancy blinds; its goatskin rug and en-suite bathroom. He bounced on the bed, pulled her down beside him, looked up, saw the mirror and thought he'd just landed in paradise. She looked up, laughed, pulled her mini-skirted body away from him and knelt up.

'Can you reach?' She nodded at the mirror.

'Eh?'

'There's a catch on the right hand side, release it and the mirror comes down, it's on a hinge. There's a hatch behind it, leads into the attic.'

'Oh.' It wasn't what he had in mind but he

complied. It seemed to matter to her that he could reach, as though it were some bizarre macho initiation. Once the hatch was open, a short step ladder could be pulled down. He followed her up.

The attic was boarded out, sectioned into cupboards under the eaves, a multigym in the centre and piles of boxes around the chimney. She threaded her way to the back of the house, to a small round window, like a porthole, looking over the river. It was grimy, with a peephole scrubbed by impatient fingers. There was a red rose in the centre of the stained glass which looked as though it should be in the church, not here.

'Sit down,' she patted the window seat, once rose-pink, long since faded, and a cloud of dust erupted into the dry atmosphere.

He obeyed. Finally he had completed the course, now he would get the glittering prize. He licked his lips, moved closer to Melanie. They kissed briefly before she pulled away.

'You have to know you're not the first,' she began hesitantly.

'I can live with that.' Bravado hid disappointment.

'But I feel I can trust you.' Baby blues fluttered behind the protection of her blonde fringe. 'I see you helping your mother, so I know you're a good person. And I need a good person in my life right now. I've got a problem I could use some help with. It's a bit of a big one.' She smiled apologetically.

He squeezed her hand. 'I'm sure I can cope.'

'That's why I wanted to try it with you too. Just to see. And now I know, so I need you to help me. I mean, it's not as though you're my brother, it's not as though you know my brothers, so it's not likely to get back to them.'

'No.' He knew what she meant. He wasn't like her brothers, he was the man she wanted to be with. He'd often looked at her and thought she'd make a good wife — the right sort of woman to be seen on his arm. He'd make heads turn then; make his mates green.

'I've told my best friend at school, but she said I was too young to know yet.'

In his opinion there was no 'too young to know'. Surely you just knew when the time was right; when the right person had come along? He'd thought, several times, he'd found the 'right one', but they'd all managed to let him down one way or another. He gave her hand another squeeze, smiled. 'Spit it out,' he said and then wondered if that was too vulgar a way of putting it.

Melanie hadn't seemed to notice. Her slender index finger doodled busily in the dust on the windowsill, she wriggled on the window seat, sending up another plume of dust. 'It's just that, well, I think — no, I know now — now that I've spent some time with you . . .'

He smiled.

' . . . that I'm gay.' She sighed, smiled brightly and turned her brilliant eyes towards him.

Brilliant blue is the colour of a traitor, he thought. Brilliant blue needs to be stamped out.

She leaned towards him as though expecting a hug. He stiff-armed her away, got shakily to his feet. 'You bitch!' His voice was low, shaking with anger and frustration. 'You bitch!'

Her smile had gone. Her face paled. She, too, got to her feet, one hand behind her, feeling for the windowframe. 'Danny, I . . . you said you would understand.'

'What? That you're a freak? A pervert? A prick teaser? Did you really create this whole charade just to tell me you don't fancy boys?' His whole body was shaking now, perspiration beading his brow. His fists were clenched by his sides. 'Are you trying to make a fool out of me?' She shook her head, tears running silently down her cheeks. 'Well you've done it — and bloody big-time too. You deserve a kicking for what you've done; for what you'll do to a lot more men — those baby blues of yours sending the wrong messages.' He closed one with a thump. The force sent her head smacking back against the wall. She moaned. The animal sound triggered something in him, he lashed out over and over again until, exhausted, he let her limp body fall to the floor.

The weather had kept the neighbourhood, normally keen Saturday afternoon gardeners, inside; that and the football. No one saw him leave. Save one. The net curtain twitched as he ran up the path, the orange glow from his mother's cigarette glowed brighter as she inhaled.

Melanie survived the attack — just — and the Crofts left Storm Mount shortly after, never to return. No one was ever convicted of the crime.

Danny came to himself, his erection pressed hard against his jeans. Even now, five years later, Melanie was the only girl who could do this to him. Except now, Storm Mount housed another — a prick teaser, a girl who made fools of men. Maybe this was a sign, time to move on; time to do the world a favour.

12

It was the atmosphere that drove Lawson from the station; the stagnant airstream that revolved around Dungannon like an evil shroud. Kate Rogers was out checking the various demises of the members of The Fairweather Organisation to see how many, if any, could be put down to natural causes, and which to murder. Lawson wished he'd had the bottle to suggest he'd gone with her, Gus Chandler's alibi had held up; his brother wasn't a regular caller and since *he'd* rung Gus there couldn't have been any premeditation. That fact had been confirmed by checking with BT — the only phone call across the Atlantic had not come from Gus. Lawson sighed. He needed an alibi himself right now; the phone hadn't stopped ringing and Dungannon, always one to pass the tasks to Lawson, had merely nodded or flicked his pen towards the receiver each time it trilled to be answered. Lawson decided to take a coffee break, and made it halfway to the door before the phone shrilled again. Sighing, he backed up.

'Yeah.' He checked his watch, five hours to knock off.

'Paine, Forensic.'

Lawson smiled. It was the standing joke that the last thing anyone should be feeling in Forensic was pain — it was assumed everybody, including the staff, was beyond that. 'What you got?'

'Dotty Spangle, forensic just in.' A faint Scottish burr still betrayed his roots despite thirty years living at the opposite end of the country.

Lawson pulled paper and pencil towards him. 'Go.'

'Basically not a lot except that it's not the boyfriend what dunnit.'

'Mm. Guessed as much. Very obliging with the samples was our Gus — and his alibi came through for him. So we know who it wasn't. Any idea who it was?'

'As we suspected, her being such a friendly lass an' all,' Paine wheezed slightly as he spoke. Lawson always imagined him to be wizened and white-haired. It could, of course, be nicotine induced. 'She had a selection of samples in various orifices.'

Lawson shuddered, ran splayed fingers through his tight-cropped hair.

'Hazard of the job. Some of these we'll be able to identify when we get samples from her

136

regulars. Always assuming they're forthcoming.'

Lawson nodded. 'They're already queuing at the door as we speak. Busier than the blood donor unit we are today.'

'Methinks you're being a tad sarcastic.'

'Just a tad. But we'll be right onto it, never fear. Any idea when she died?'

'She'd been dead maybe twelve hours when she was found.'

'So chances are the person she'd kept company the previous evening knows something.' Lawson glanced up at Dungannon who was making a poor attempt at some sort of charade.

'Mm, not necessarily. Popular girl like our Dotty? Anyone could've been waiting for her if they knew where to be.'

'Cause of death?'

'She'd been strangled. No other marks save the black eye. Interesting there were no bruises on her forearms. I'd say, if my arm was twisted way up my back, that she'd known her murderer. She was comfortable with whoever it was — no need to be defensive when they started playing rough.'

'So it was likely a punter then?' Dungannon, Lawson noticed, looked to be throttling himself.

'Possibly.'

'Hang on.' Lawson covered the mouthpiece, spoke to Dungannon. 'Is there something you need to tell me, sir?'

'I want to know if it was a man who killed her — or if there was the possibility of it being a woman.'

Lawson relayed the query.

'Almost definitely male. She was only in her thirties — still strong enough to shake off any woman but the strongest.'

Lawson put down the phone, passed on the information to Dungannon who nodded and immediately headed for the canteen. Lawson pulled a face at his disappearing backview — he'd still planned to take his coffee break now. Thoughtfully, he chewed the end of his pencil: what needed to be established was who she was with on Wednesday evening.

He flipped to the page in his notebook where he'd jotted down names from the calendar. Wednesday night was B.B. Roache. There was a phone number alongside it. He stared at the receiver: he'd had enough of phones today. Could he really face another call? The door swung open, letting in a welcome draught of chill air from the corridor — the nearest thing Righton nick had to air-conditioning. Kate Rogers was smiling.

'OK?' He copied the name and phone

number onto another piece of paper.

'Yeah. Didn't find out anything we didn't already know.' She slumped in the chair he'd just vacated.

'I'm off for a wander myself now. Do us a favour and stall Dungannon if he comes looking for my blood.'

'Sure, I'll sacrifice one of the pigeons on the windowsill instead. Anything else?'

'Thank you for asking.' He handed her the piece of paper. 'Follow this up can you?' He pushed the phone towards her, smiled and went to the door, where he paused. 'Oh, Gus Chandler rang earlier wanting to know whether there was a necklace on Dotty's body. Various shades of blue, he said. Ring any bells?'

She shook her head.

'No, that's what I said.' Pulling his collar tightly up around his chin, he headed outside. He'd had enough of that side of the case. Now to try and track down the runaway, Jacob Palmer; the boy also fitting the description of the thief taking canaries from residential homes.

★ ★ ★

Righton Comprehensive was geometrically unimaginative; square buildings with square windows in square metal frames. Grey brick, grey roof — so uninspiring. The students, equally grey-clad, huddled in groups where once gates had hung, smoking, flirting, poking middle fingers at Lawson.

He'd once imagined the uniform would provide some kind of protection; create a forcefield around him, enabling him to do his duty to community and Queen with no outside interference. It was, he had learned, more likely to have the opposite effect. He regarded himself fortunate that no one had yet pelted him with eggs or flour — or worse. It was only a matter of time. Locking the car, he fancied he felt the hostility of maybe twenty pairs of teenage eyes. Turning back to the gate he saw it was no fantasy. Checking he'd locked the car, he crossed grass-framed concrete to glass double doors with 'Reception' written in blue above them.

The receptionist, unofficially at lunch, scowled over reading glasses. He explained the reason for his intrusion and was told the Head, Mr Drewery, was at lunch, would he care to take a seat? No, was the blunt answer. He stood his ground until, tutting, she retreated through a connecting door into another room. She soon reappeared, told him to go through, and returned to scooping cottage cheese from a pot with a selection of crackers.

Mr Drewery was a tall, thin man, grey-haired, grey-suited, grey-skinned. Lawson wondered if grey was something you caught from attending this school. Drewery stooped, didn't smile, paced the office all the time he was talking, slapping one palm against the other as though unable to break the habit the cane once gave him.

'Jacob Palmer, is it?'

'That's right. He's . . . wanted for questioning. Currently he appears not to be staying at his home address. Wondered if you knew of anywhere else he could be hiding out.'

'Jacob Palmer doesn't often grace us with his presence.'

'Aren't you supposed to ensure he does?' Lawson, having arrived determined to be friendly despite his aversion to headmasters, found his good temper slipping.

Drewery pulled his lips back in semblance of a smile. 'There's not much we can do with boys like Jacob.'

'How many like Jacob do you have?'

'Same as any school — half a dozen.'

'And you ignore them?'

'Mr Lawson,' Drewery leaned over the desk, placed long thin fingers, which looked

141

like they'd been grown separately in a dark cupboard then grafted onto his hands later, on top of the blotter. 'For every Jacob in this school we have ten copycats, boys who, given half a chance, would emulate him. We have our work cut out trying to keep them in school. The ones who are already beyond redemption when they get here — '

'Have no hope.'

'Your words, not mine, Mr Lawson.'

Lawson swallowed the bile in his throat. These institutions hadn't changed since he'd been in one. Any sign of trouble, racism, bullying, and the school turned in on itself, dealt only with the majority, those who could manage to behave themselves. Not that Lawson hadn't, but the colour of his skin and his father's position in the community made him a prime target for bullies. He closed his eyes, took a deep breath, forced himself back under control. 'Can you give me a list of names and addresses — including Jacob's — of these boys? In case one of them knows where he may be.'

'Surely — but it'll take a little time.'

Drewery squinted ferrety eyes at Lawson in an attempt at a smile. Lawson pulled himself up to his full height, face remaining expressionless. 'I've got five minutes spare, Mr Drewery, I'll take the list with me.'

'I do hope you're not trying to intimidate me,' Drewery's face slipped into its familiar scowl.

'No more than you are me,' Lawson spoke softly, left the room, banging the door as he went.

The secretary presented him with the list ten minutes or so later. Lawson thanked her and left, knowing that Drewery's eyes were watching his departure.

He stopped outside the school gates, far enough away from the school to avoid the head's prying eyes but near enough to watch the lads as they sauntered back to class. With ties loose and cigarettes hidden in curled palms, they looked a motley bunch. The language, as they passed, was more suited to troopers, thought Lawson, then smiled when he realised he was sounding like his father. On a more serious note, if these delinquents were the best that Righton Comprehensive had to offer, then maybe Drewery had a harder task than Lawson had given him credit for. He checked the list, put them in order — nearest first — and set off to pay calls.

★ ★ ★

No joy.

He'd been to five of the eight addresses.

Either no one was in, they scented his profession and ignored the doorbell, or they didn't know Jacob well. Three thirty. Dungannon would be after his guts if he stayed out much longer. Shifting into gear, he drove away to check the next address.

Primrose Lane had once been *the* place to live. A short, cobbled street, it was flanked on either side by pretty cottages which, had they been thatched, wouldn't have looked out of place on top of a chocolate box. As it was, with moss-covered slates and dislocated gutters, they sat glumly on the east side of town, running parallel with the river, as though praying for a demolition ball to bowl them into obscurity.

Lawson paused by the car to check the number: sixteen, this was it. The gate swung open lopsidedly on its one remaining hinge. He left it resting halfway across the path where it had made a scuff in the cement. The nets were holey. An empty milk bottle, with something green and furry growing inside, sat stubbornly on the doorstep. He rattled the knocker. The noise cannoned through the house, making the windows on the first floor shake. No reply.

Inside he could hear a TV, voices then, eventually, footsteps. An elderly man, maybe seventy, opened the door. He was shorter

144

than Lawson by nearly a foot, and he stooped as though the braces he wore were bending him in half. He tipped his face up towards the policeman, smiled a toothless smile and shuffled back slipper-clad feet to make room for Lawson to enter.

'Police,' somewhat belatedly, Lawson flashed his warrant card.

'So I see. You'll be here about that Jacob lad. Tina said you'd be here sooner or later. Go through. Mam's in the back.'

Lawson led the way down the floorboarded hall to a small room, also bare boards save for a dark green circular rug in front of a TV. The only picture — of a blue-faced Spanish woman — tried, in vain, to disguise a crack in the far wall.

Mam Flint was a woman as fat as her husband was thin, sprawling in an overstuffed chair, watching Channel 4 racing. Beside her right hand, a box of Milk Tray, in her left, a gin and tonic.

'Mam's at the races today,' said the old boy, indicating Lawson should sit on a sit-up-and-beg type dining chair. 'But she'll maybe be available when the adverts come on.'

'Couldn't you tell me?' Lawson crossed his legs, perched uncomfortably.

'Oooooh no. Can't be doing that.'

Lawson declined the offer of a dandelion tea or a dandelion and burdock and watched bemusedly as Valiant Valerie romped home. The adverts came on. Mam was available.

'Jacob? Nice lad.' She'd got foil stuck in her teeth where she'd not peeled a chocolate properly. Or, thought Lawson nastily, where she had not bothered peeling it at all. 'Not seen him for a while, not since that Tina came on the scene.'

'And he used to come here?'

Quite often when Terry was here.' She pulled a piece of paper from the box to reveal the next layer of chocolates.

'And Terry is?'

'Our grandson.' A smile of pride crossed her face.

'But he doesn't live here now?'

'No. He's in Borstal at the moment. On the Isle of Wight. Nice place so I'm told. Said to Father — ' she nodded at her husband ' — be nice to go in the summer and visit. You know, with it being near the seaside and all.'

Lawson tried to mirror her smile. Had she realised how callous that sounded? He thought not. She struck him as being of little — or no — education and had picked up the pleasantries of social speaking without considering what she was really saying.

146

'Did Jacob ever sleep here when he visited Terry?'

'Once or twice.'

'And since Terry . . . er . . . left?'

'No.'

Lawson hesitated, trying to phrase the next question as delicately as possible. 'Does — did — Terry live here permanently?'

'Yes.' Once more pride filled her voice. 'We done our best for him.'

'One last thing,' he cleared his throat. 'You mentioned a Tina. Would that be Tina . . . ' he checked his notebook ' . . . Harker?'

'We don't know no Tina,' Mam's face shuttered.

'But you've both mentioned a Tina since I've been here.'

The Flints exchanged glances. Mam's, thought Lawson, was decidedly homicidal.

'Oh,' she giggled, taking Lawson unawares. 'That Tina! Yes, yes, we know Tina.'

'In what capacity?' He caught her blank expression. 'How?'

'Oh,' Mam hesitated. 'She was my Avon lady for a while. Keeps in touch.'

The adverts were over; so was Lawson's interview.

13

Lawson indicated right; two streets to go. Nearly home. The radio burbled. Sighing, he acknowledged.

'Request you meet Dungannon at one Dave Palmer's address in Water Lane.'

'On my way.' He knew he sounded pissed off. He was glad.

Dungannon was already there, pacing outside the gate like an expectant father. 'What kept you?'

Lawson opened his mouth to defend himself, gave up, closed it, followed Dungannon up the path.

'Domestic going on, according to the neighbour who rang us. Said they didn't usually bother only this one sounds worse than normal.' Dungannon stood on the doorstep, ear cocked towards the door.

'Who the fuck you been talking to?' *Crash*. 'The police?' *Bang*. 'Some boyfriend you've got stashed away?' *Wallop*. 'Well?'

A woman crying was the only response.

'Whoever it was you've dropped me in it with the Social. Good an' proper.' *Smash*. 'You fuckin' bitch.'

'I think that's our cue.' Dungannon rapped sharply on the door. 'Good evening,' he flashed his warrant card at Dave Palmer when he snatched the door open. 'May we come in? We did so enjoy your little cabaret, but I'm not sure the understudy's up to much more.'

'You can do what you fuckin' like,' Palmer turned towards the stairs. 'I'm goin' to bed.'

They watched him stagger up the stairs. Lawson raised an eyebrow. Dungannon shook his head.

'Let him go for now. He's pissed — and angry. Not a good combination. Wait till he's unconscious then we'll tackle him. Now,' he turned to Tina Harker. 'Maybe you'd like to fill us in on what's going on?'

'OK.' She turned towards the kitchen at the end of the hall.

'Don't you want to get cleaned up first?' Lawson thought if Dungannon wasn't going to give her the option, he might at least mention it. She looked even more fragile than the last time he'd seen her. Black leggings made her legs seem beetle-like, the white sweater a shell.

'I'm OK.'

'Dave do that?' Dungannon arranged himself on the corner of the pine table and nodded at her face.

Self-consciously Tina covered her swollen

eye with a lacerated hand, shook her head.

'Don't tell me — the budgie's got a bad case of rabies.' His voice softened. 'You can bring charges you know. Stop him doing that.'

'He'd kill me.'

'He wouldn't. There's all kinds of things you can do.'

'What, go into hiding? Into one of those women's refuges? Behave!' She wiped her face with a dish cloth. 'I've spent all my life dreaming about a house like this, and a family. Now I've got it, I'm not going to let it go.'

Lawson, thumbing through some mail on the dresser, decided his assessment of her from the first time he was here wasn't far wrong — all tits and no brains. He surveyed the kitchen with its grease-stained ceiling, split lino, doorless cupboards and shuddered, swallowed the bile that rose in his throat. 'Any news on Jacob?'

Tina threw him a sidelong glance from her unblackened eye. 'No.'

'You've heard nothing?' Dungannon was incredulous.

'No.' She set her jaw. 'He's . . . difficult sometimes.'

'I see,' Dungannon shifted his weight. The table creaked. 'And Social Services, have they been in touch?'

She paused before slowly nodding her head. 'That's what brought on his temper.'

They'd gathered that from when they were standing outside, thought Lawson, so at least she was telling the truth at this point — or had she reckoned on them hearing what Palmer had said and daren't risk denying it?

'Do they know where Jacob is?' Dungannon idly scratched his nose.

'No.'

'And has Jacob's social worker been here?' Dungannon crossed the kitchen to the sink, leaned idly against the enamel sink to peer at the tableau reflected behind him in the window.

Tina shrugged. 'She knocked. Didn't answer — never had much to do with her.'

Dungannon's face, Lawson noted with glee, was getting paler by the second.

'I see,' he managed to splutter before disappearing into, in Lawson's opinion, a completely fabricated coughing fit. 'What's your relationship like with Jacob?' Lawson, hero that he was, stepped into the breach.

'I . . . er,' Tina spoke first to Lawson then to Dungannon's back. Dungannon smiled to himself, disorientation was a marvellous weapon. 'He doesn't like me.'

'Why?' Lawson dropped his voice, made her turn back towards him.

'Because I'm not his mum? Because he blames me?'

'For what?' Dungannon turned around.

'For *not* being his mum.' She sighed. 'And because I use his mum's things sometimes.' She registered the shock in Lawson's face. 'Well she ain't here is she? And I ain't got nothing, so where's the harm?'

'What about Mr and Mrs Flint?' Lawson stepped towards her. 'How well do you know them?'

'Who?' She was a bloody good actress, Lawson gave her that. 'Flint, you say?' Lawson nodded. 'Never heard of them.'

Lawson frowned. Why would she lie about something like that? What could possibly be so secret about her knowing the elderly couple? 'That's odd, Mrs Flint said you'd been her Avon lady.'

'Oh,' relief relaxed her body. '*That* Mrs Flint. Yeah, that's right.'

'How many Mrs Flints do you know?' Lawson ignored Dungannon's frown.

'Only the one,' she sighed. 'Look, sometimes — 'cos of Dave — I have to forget that I know people. That's all.'

Lawson nodded, hoped it was true.

'Do you know a Danny James?' Dungannon leaned against the sink and shook out a cigarette. Tina refused the offer, nodded approval for Dungannon to smoke.

'Should I?'

'He's been known to hang around with your Dave from time to time. Petty stuff mainly — all that we can prove anyway. Handy with his fists.'

'Is he built like a brick shithouse?'

'That's him.'

'He's been around a time or two.'

'Let me guess,' Dungannon hit the sarcasm button. 'You had to forget you knew him, too.'

Tina flushed, looked at the floor.

'Seen him recently?' Lawson asked.

'Week ago, maybe two.'

'Any idea why?'

She shook her head, winced.

'Look,' Lawson glanced at Dungannon. 'I really think Tina ought to get cleaned up before we ask her any more.'

'Where do you work?' Dungannon ploughed on.

'Joiner's Arms. Pub opposite CashSave. Three nights, I do — injuries permitting.'

Lawson stared. She was young, pretty, maybe not the most intelligent woman he'd met recently, but with enough about her to cope in the real world. Why did she put up with this? If what she truly wanted was a home and family there must be plenty of men wanting to fill the vacancy.

'I love him.' She said it quietly and so completely out of context that Lawson thought she must have read his mind.

Bedsprings groaned overhead, footsteps sounded. Tina paled, crumpled onto a dining chair. Dungannon headed for the hall, Lawson tripping at his heels.

'Dave,' Dungannon called up the stairs. 'So good of you to put in an appearance.'

'What the fuck?' Dave, mid-stumble across the landing, wobbled at the top of the stairs. 'Who are you?' He added, alcohol having erased recent memory.

'Police, Mr Palmer. We'd like to talk to you. Are you coming down or are we coming up?'

The response was a cough, a heave and an explosion of vomit. Dungannon curled his lip in distaste as it splattered the stair carpet. 'I'm afraid, Mr Palmer, we need to speak to all of you — not just your stomach contents.'

'I don't want to speak to you.'

'Fortunately for us, you don't have a choice. Now, we either do it here or . . . ' he turned as Tina lurched from the kitchen ' . . . we do it down at the station.'

Lawson fancied he saw Tina's head nod imperceptibly at the second option. Dungannon must have been aware too because that is what he opted for.

'OK. The station it is. Now, another big choice Dave, are you going to come quietly or are you going to fulfil my fantasy and let me handcuff you to the headrest?'

Palmer, swaying like a sunflower in a force ten gale, went quietly.

'You going to be OK?' Lawson touched Tina's shoulder. 'Is there anyone I can call to sit with you?'

'No.'

The touch burned hot long after Lawson escorted Palmer to the car.

Dungannon turned on the doorstep, smiling Cheshire-cat style. 'We're taking lover boy in — give you chance to get a good night's kip. He'll probably be home around mid-morning — can't think there's much we can hold him on — but it'll give you chance to decide whether or not you still want to be around when he gets back.' He became serious. 'If, however, you do flit, please tell us where you are just in case we need to speak to you again.'

She watched them go from the lounge window, saw Dave's face twist into an evil grin. She knew that was a threat. Golden opportunity, she told herself. Yes or no?

★ ★ ★

155

Finally, thought Lawson, climbing the stairs to his bedsit. He slid the key into the lock, smiled smugly as the door opened silently. Whatever else he'd not achieved today, he'd remembered to oil the hinges. Now he shouldn't disturb . . . the door of the flat opposite opened. He froze. Disobeying every last brain cell that was screaming 'run', he slowly turned. Maggie Taylor, in glorious cerise. She wasn't alone. Beside her, another Maggie, this one in bright turquoise.

'This,' she announced in a voice that could guide the contents of the Bermuda Triangle home, 'is my neighbour, Mr Lawson. He's a policeman.' They giggled conspiratorially. 'And this,' she addressed Lawson, 'is my sister Eunice. We're twins.'

'So I gathered,' Lawson managed to swallow the sarcastic remark about him being a detective and having worked it out for himself. 'Now, if you'll excuse me . . . ' And he fled.

The light on the answerphone was flashing. 'It's mum. Call me when you get in. Don't worry about the time.'

He dialled.

'Do you know what the time is?' she squawked, not even giving him chance to say 'hi'. 'I've been in bed nearly an hour and a half. I was just dropping off — and you know

156

how difficult it is for me to get to sleep these days.'

'Sorry, but — '

'Since you're on the phone you might as well know that I plan to come and visit you. I was going to come tomorrow but, with one thing and another you'll have to manage without me until the next day.'

'No!'

'Pardon?'

'I said 'Oh'. That's really disappointing, Mum, but it's perhaps as well. I don't think it's a very good idea you coming just at the moment. Maybe after Christmas?'

'But that's ages away.'

Exactly.

'Don't you want to see me?' Her voice had taken on its sulky, hurt tone.

'Of course I do,' Lawson soothed. 'Only I'm really busy at the moment — got a lot on at work — '

'I'd gathered that by the fact that you're never there . . . unless there's a girl?'

'No Mother.'

'Oh Sebastian, I worry about you sometimes. At your age you really should be thinking about settling down.'

'I will.' As he talked he flicked through his mail. Junk. All of it.

'She could look after you properly.'

157

'I can look after myself properly.'

'Have you eaten tonight?'

'Er . . . no.'

'And it's nearly midnight. See, you're not looking after yourself. I'll come down the day after tomorrow. There's a train straight through to London then I can pick up one that comes to Righton — I think. But don't worry about me, new experiences are what life's all about and if I get lost I'll have an adventure.'

'Mother, I really don't have time for you to have an adventure at the moment.'

'But I'll do it on my own.' She sounded hurt, like a child being told their mother couldn't spare any more time to play aliens.

'I'm sure that's your intention, but inevitably I'll be summoned to come and retrieve you.'

'I think that's really selfish of you to throw that at me again. It only happened once and I know what to do now.'

'I'm sorry Mum, I just don't have the time at the moment. Look, why don't we arrange it properly — I'll take some leave — that way you'll not be on your own all the time down here.'

'But I'm always on my own anyway.' She sounded close to tears.

'But you do have friends there mum. Here

you know only me, and if I'm not here you'll be more lonely than usual.'

'I'm not lonely!' She retorted. 'And if you don't want me to come and stay, I'll bid you good night.'

Lawson stared at the dead phone in his hand. Upsetting her seemed to be the only way to snap her out of it — whatever 'it' was — but it left him feeling guiltier than ever. Should he ring her back and say OK, she could stay? He studied his reflection in the mirror, shook his head. Nah, couldn't be doing with that.

There was another message. Kate Rogers, sick of not being able to find him at the station, had rung to say that the number for B.B. Roache was disconnected.

★ ★ ★

That supermarkets were now open twenty four hours a day had never struck him as a blessing but tonight, knackered from a hard day — from a hard week — and unable to sleep because of his rumbling stomach, Lawson admitted there may be some sense in it after all. And it gave him the chance to check out Dotty's spot at the time of day she would have used it. The pole on the corner, Gus had said, where punters could get money out of the cash machines.

He slowed down, assessing the number of people about, the number of cars in the car park (a surprising amount), the chances of a prostitute picking up any work. As he watched, a girl (she looked no more than fourteen) stepped out of the gloom behind the pole and rubbed herself suggestively against it as a man pushing a trolley containing no more than six items walked slowly past her. The man backed up, spoke to the girl. They both disappeared back into the gloom.

Voyeurism. What other pastimes could he add to his list? He felt guilty, as though what he'd seen didn't concern him.

But this did. Very much.

How callous, he thought, pulling a reluctant trolley from its line, that another girl had moved in on Dotty's patch before it got cold. He turned back briefly, caught sight of the Joiner's Arms across the road. It afforded a view of Dotty's patch, he was sure of that. Maybe he'd better check that out tomorrow. And also pass on to the beat bobby the fact that the bar lights were on more than an hour after time should have been called.

'Milk,' he muttered to himself, mentally ticking it off the list. 'Cheese — Red Leicester, Cheddar, Stilton?' Unable to

160

decide between them, he took a packet of each. 'Butter, proper stuff, not 'lite' anything.' He continued, idly picking things up and sniffing or squeezing them then returning them to the shelf or putting them in the trolley. His mind was not on his shopping but on the close shave he'd had that evening.

What a relief he'd rung his mother. Couldn't be doing with her arranging his life at the moment. Just hadn't got the energy to be patient with her, that was all, and she wouldn't, couldn't, understand that. But, if he dug down far enough, the pity was still there. She was alone, two hundred miles away — and she worried that he'd come to the same end as his father. She'd told him shortly before he left Sheffield that he was tempting fate — 'dancing with the devil' was her exact expression.

'Scuse me!'

'Wha . . . ? Oh, I'm sorry,' Lawson reversed his trolley out of the front of a guy who was built like a heavyweight wrestler. 'Wasn't looking where I was going.'

'So I noticed.' The tone wasn't friendly. Lawson stood back to let him pass and headed for the checkout. If he didn't get some sleep soon, he'd be leaving here and going straight to work.

14

It wasn't fair. Just wasn't fair. Jacob had spent the night, between bouts of pacifying Blue, staring at the ceiling or pacing the floor. Odd-Job had been his only friend, his family. And now he'd had to dispose of him. Fucking police, couldn't leave anyone alone. He felt sorry for Dad now. He'd never believed Dad before when he'd said they harassed people like that; now he knew it was true. Why were the police watching his rabbit though? Was it to do with the dead lady in the lounge, or could Danny James be involved in some way? Nothing Danny did to get him into trouble would surprise him — Danny was a bad lot. Jacob nodded. He was pretty sure it was Danny. But how to prove it?

There things got more complicated. Danny was bigger, louder, more violent than he; Danny wasn't going to admit to anything he didn't want to. What would James Bond do? Lacing his fingers behind his head, Jacob focussed on the orange circle from a streetlight on the ceiling and considered his options.

Thing was, he was at a disadvantage when it came to trying to emulate James Bond. No Q for a start, and even James Bond wouldn't be James Bond without his gadgets. If he, Jacob, could get hold of a cigarette that shot bullets — like a blow pipe — from a decent range, he could shoot Danny from Storm Mount and no one would suspect him. He could take Danny out in his own bedroom. Mrs James didn't go upstairs, he remembered Danny once telling him centuries ago when they were best buddies, so Danny could be dead for days before anyone ever found out. There was that cleaner woman but she didn't go in every day.

Maybe he'd kneecap Danny, let him linger in pain for what had happened to Odd-Job because of him. Maybe he could castrate him. Jacob giggled. The image of climbing the drain pipe and shooting Danny while he sat on the toilet was very satisfying.

But he didn't have a special blow pipe. Reality stank.

He'd just have to think suave, think subtle. Five minutes passed. Actually, he wasn't sure what suave or subtle meant. He'd have to go to the library and look them up.

★ ★ ★

163

Jacob Palmer. Lawson yawned, cupped his hands around the Styrofoam cup of cappuccino. He hated it when they ran out of china cups. Styrofoam was so — impersonal. He turned his thoughts back to the doodled spider diagram in front of him.

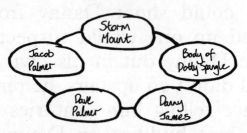

Jacob Palmer. Twelve. Alone in the world save for an uninterested father and a social worker who, according to Kate, had been trying for a long while to get the lad put into care. Seemed Dave Palmer knew the right things to say at the right time and always managed to hang on to the lad. Always managed to lose him immediately afterwards.

Jacob Palmer. Twelve. Fiercely independent. Capable of surviving despite having a father who barely acknowledged his existence. Had to admire the lad. Had to.

Storm Mount. Last known address of the unwanted boy. Deserted itself, it was logical that the lad would go there. Kind of Hollywood. Lawson shook his head. Too little sleep made his brain atrophy — or maybe it was too much caffeine? Since when was the

164

slimy side of Righton akin to Hollywood? Concentrate, he told himself.

Sophie Sullivan. Social worker. According to Kate, efficient, likeable and concerned about Jacob. No sign of the Nazi Dungannon had insinuated. But then, Kate had only spoken to her on the phone, maybe the physical presence betrayed something that the voice did not. And what had she done to Dungannon that made him, socially allergic as he was to most — all — of his colleagues, put up the force field? Maybe he, Lawson, should have a chat with her. Maybe he would dare to meet her face to face.

At least she'd probably be able to fill him in on the sketchy details he had of Jacob's early life. No apparent problems until his mother left, was the way Lawson read it; the way that Sophie, via Kate, told it. No clue that his primary school years had been difficult. In fact, it seemed that no one had ever heard of Jacob Palmer until his mother, his protection, left. Attention, then, was probably a motive enough for the trouble he got into at school. So easy for lads to slip into truancy when parental responsibility ran to only getting noticed when you needed a beating.

Lawson doodled again. Bloody school didn't help. That headmaster was so up himself, writing Jacob off as one of the few 'expected' to rebel. Could anyone blame Jacob for getting out and trying to make sense of life alone? No, decided Lawson, one couldn't. Maybe the lad should be left to get on with it — adult guidance hadn't done him any favours up to now. But see, that wasn't acceptable either. Independent he may be, but he was also too innocent, in a streetwise kind of way, to realise the dangers that people like Danny James posed. Yes, Lawson nodded, a conflab with Sophie Sullivan in the not too distant future was the way to go. He yawned again. Another cappuccino, china or no china, was next on the agenda.

★ ★ ★

It was on the way back from the library that the urge struck. It worried Jacob because it usually only happened near old folks' homes. Blue was happily asleep, a dustbin liner wrapped around him to protect him from the drizzle that had set in mid-morning. In a way though, he was pleased of the urge, it took his mind off the fact that that lazy cow Tabbi hadn't come back this morning to take her shift. Blue, after a restless period at breakfast time, had appeared to accept the situation and had settled down. Jacob was seething.

166

Not only had he not planned to visit the library, he'd not been paid either.

Libraries stank. He was sure the words 'swarve' and 'suttle' existed but could he find them? Could he bollocks. Another wasted journey.

Language.

'Oh piss off.'

Time was when he'd blush when he swore — thought maybe his mum could somehow hear him and be disappointed. Now he didn't care one way or the other. Wasn't surprising, when he thought of it, that the urge had struck again.

Only this time it wasn't to be a rest home. Passing a pet shop, he peered in. These days pets were kept in the back of the shop, not in the window as they had once been. To stop people freeing them, Jacob thought. He knew *he'd* break a window to free caged animals. Didn't care what happened to him either. That *was* very James Bond. Working for the down-trodden, doing what he believed was right, and not considering the consequences. Very heroic.

He went in. Two girls stood at the cash register in the centre of the shop. Neither looked up, both too busy changing the till roll. One of them he recognised, she'd been three years above him at school — the last

167

time he'd been to school. Tilting his chin down he made for the cages at the back of the shop.

Rabbits, but not one like Odd-Job. A tear slid down his cheek. Poor Odd-Job. Should he replace him? Jacob studied the choice. Thing was, when you had had unconditional love like he had had from Odd-Job, it was hard to believe another could provide the same. Anyway, he wasn't going to pay for one. Odd-Job had come from the Children's Farm in the centre of town. Jacob would get another from the same place provided their security hadn't improved. *If* he felt the need of a replacement.

Budgies. He didn't want a budgie, reminded him of his other Granny and that blue thing that used to crap on his head when he visited. He moved along to the far corner. Iguana. He shuddered. No thanks! Above that, a red, blue and yellow parroty thing. Not a Macaw or an African grey but that kind of thing, about as big as a small magpie. He liked that. '£60' said the label on the cage. Sod that for a game of soldiers! He reached up, twanged the bars with his fingernails.

'Hello.' The cage was far too small. 'Are you lonely in there on your own?' A small pair of steps leant against a sack of dog food. Jacob set them up, climbed up to greet the parrot at eye level. It studied him curiously. 'When were you last cleaned out?'

The urge took over. Even as he tried to talk himself out of it, he was taking off his coat and sweatshirt, replacing his coat. The cage wasn't locked. 'They don't deserve to have it then,' Jacob muttered, justifying the theft to himself. He slid his hand, covered by the sweatshirt, into the cage before the bird had the chance to squawk or bite, and wrapped it tightly to stop it flapping. Tying the arms loosely around the package to stop it unravelling, he carefully dropped the bird into the bag swinging on the handle of the buggy. He looked around. The girls were still at the till, no longer fiddling with the till roll but talking about boys or hair or something equally girly. Sticking to the edge of the shop, Jacob headed for the door, pausing only to take a bag of parrot food from the shelf as he passed.

All the way to the corner of the street he kept expecting someone to shout, to chase, to lay a hand on his shoulder. Nothing. He'd never done anything quite as daring as that before but he'd got away with it. Maybe that was an omen. Maybe he *could* take Danny on and win if only he found the right way to go about it. Once he'd turned the corner into the High Street, the only problem he had was to get home before the parrot escaped from the bag. Blue, started from sleep by the bag banging and screeching against the buggy, sat momentarily saucer-eyed before opening his mouth and wailing in harmony.

Jacob stopped. His immediate reaction was to run, to leave these two idiots squawking together and make a quick getaway. It was the strange look he got from a woman at a cashpoint that urged him on. He broke into a trot and arrived at Storm Mount ten minutes later puffing and with his arms aching from trying to keep the buggy, with its rogue wheels, going in a straight line. Cautiously, he let himself into the kitchen, aware that Tabbi would probably be asleep but not wanting to raise any suspicions were she not. The mug he'd left ready for her with a tea bag and just the right amount of milk in it had not been used. He touched the kettle. Not been boiled. Odd. Very. The bag wriggled again, let out an angry screech. Jacob unhooked it, headed up the stairs. Blue, abandoned in the kitchen, fell into stunned silence.

Where to put the parrot hadn't occurred to him at the shop. Only on the trot home had he tried to decide a plan of action. He'd come up with the bathroom. He was sure Tabbi could be made to understand — she only went in there a couple of times a day, in the morning when she came in and before she went out at night. He was sure she could manage to co-bathe with a parrot. As for him, he'd manage in the bushes in the garden most of the time.

The bathroom, shabby and mildewed as it was, was probably the best place for the parrot. It allowed freedom to fly without risk of injury. Perches were available in the shape of a towel rail, a shower curtain, the curtain pole at the window and even the windowsill or the toilet. Provided he kept the window closed and the door wasn't opened very far when access was required, the parrot would be safe. He closed the door behind him and unwrapped the sweatshirt. Bedraggled and disoriented, the parrot gripped his forearm. Jacob convinced it to sit on the wash basin. It watched him put in the plug and run a few inches of water into the bottom.

'Your drink,' Jacob explained. 'And here's some food.' Jacob forced a small hole in the plastic bag and tipped some food onto the windowsill.

'There, you just settle in. I'll be back later.'

He'd have to write a note for Tabbi and leave it on her bed. He didn't want her letting the parrot out when she awoke. 'Parrot in the bathroom. See Jacob.' He'd scribbled it on the back of a CashSave receipt, hoping she'd notice it among the printed writing already there. He tapped softly on her bedroom door. No answer but he wasn't expecting one. He crept in, eyes firmly on the floor looking out for loose boards or things he could trip over. He made it to her bed, lay the note on the edge then stopped. The bed was empty. She wasn't there.

'Tabbi?' he called hopefully. Blue wailing once more was the only sound Jacob could hear. 'Tabbi?' Softer this time. Something hard settled in his gut, twisted as he considered the prospect of being alone with Blue all day.

'Easy,' he muttered, swaggering out of the room with a confidence he didn't feel. 'Double-time, that is. It'll cost her ten pounds a day for me to babysit her fucking brat.' Then he felt guilty. It wasn't Blue who was the fucking brat it was Tabbi. No way would he, Jacob, take out on Blue the fact that he'd a mother who couldn't hack responsibility. Jacob knew what that was like. He'd got one of his own.

★ ★ ★

Jaws. On account of the beak. Jacob nodded, yes, that would do nicely.

Jaws had settled in well. Already nutshells

were dotted on the windowsill, the floor, even the cistern. The make-do perches sported crap on the floor and in the bath beneath them. He wiped the bath clean. If Tabbi came home and found that she'd eat the parrot for supper. Whole. Jacob sat on the loo seat, talking softly to the bird who watched suspiciously from the top of the shower curtain.

'You're OK now. Well, you will be once I've cleared it with Tabbi. She's got Blue so I'm sure she won't mind, not since Odd-Job died. And its not as though you could live in his cage. Totally impractical. She'll be home soon,' he threw a worried glance out of the window at the closing dusk. 'Soon be time for her to go out again.'

Jaws aimed another dollop at the peach ceramic.

'You'll have to stop that. She can be a bit stroppy.' Jacob held up a grimy hand. 'Come and sit on my arm. I won't hurt you. We could be really good friends.'

Jacob was relieved when the parrot remained where it was. It had a certain haughtiness which he read as hostility. Any other bird he would have killed and buried by now. Why was Jaws different? Was it just because of Odd-Job's recent demise that he was being soft, or was it that he felt a certain power was held by the bird? He'd read 'Salem's Lot' recently. OK, so Jaws was no vampire but the supernatural was a funny thing to be playing around with. Tina had said that when she found out what he was reading. Told him to close his bedroom window and be careful who he invited in during the night. He'd thought she was potty but for several nights after that he slept fitfully, leaping awake at any little noise or disturbance. Jaws had that look in his eyes, sort of evil, sort of 'go on, I dare you'. Right now, Jacob daren't.

It must be nearly Blue's tea-time. Right on cue, a wail came from the kitchen. Jacob had left him there when he'd nodded off after lunch so that he was the first thing Tabbi saw when she came through the door. Only she hadn't. Had she, she'd have given him bollocks for letting Blue sleep all afternoon. 'Won't sleep tonight' she'd rant. He'd heard it all before — only yesterday, though it seemed like forever ago. But he didn't care whether Blue slept or not tonight, he was buggered if he was babysitting tonight when he'd been on duty for nearly twenty four hours now. *Language*, the little voice whispered. Piss off, he told it once more.

Cold baked beans and banana flavoured milkshake, that was Blue's dinner. Who cared what happened in his nappy after that, it wouldn't be Jacob dealing with it. He was out tonight, even if it meant sitting in the graveyard all night. 'Salem's Lot' insinuated itself back into his mind. Maybe not the graveyard; maybe he'd go down to the quay.

Banana flavoured milk didn't agree with Blue. He brought most of it back up all over Jacob's cleanest shirt. 'Little sod,' Jacob turned away to hide the tears standing in his eyes. Where had they come from? 'How's about I do the same to you when I come in pissed tonight?' He'd had a brainwave. When Tabbi came in and relieved him he'd nip home. Dad wouldn't be in. Tina probably would but she weren't nothing worth bothering about. Dad kept three or four bottles of whisky in the kitchen on top of the unit by the window. Dad didn't know he knew. He'd once taken one to school and sold it. Dad had found it missing and half killed Tina. She had her uses, thought Jacob. He'd take advantage again.

He stopped cold. Never before had he compared himself to Dad. And yet here he was, planning on getting drunk and coming home to make his presence known, albeit by throwing up all over the baby, but that was what Dad did — not throw up but demand attention by clouting the missus. Shit! it was

175

kids what did it — turned men into drunken gits. Jacob shuddered, maybe the graveyard was a better idea after all.

* * *

By nine o'clock Tabbi obviously wasn't coming. Blue had worked that out too and, despite having slept all afternoon and despite the poisonous whiffs coming from his nappy, he was sleeping deeply, looked set for the night. Jacob was pacing; stir crazy, Dad would call it. And Dad should know. Jacob pulled back the sheet at the lounge window, once more peered into the Close where a powdering of snow had gently caressed the surfaces, natural and man-made alike. What to do? Sleep was nigh impossible. No TV. Not even a book. Right now, he'd kill for something to read. He smiled grimly, imagining the expression on his English teacher's face had he ever willingly wanted to read something before. Always a first time.

He'd talk to Jaws, that's what he'd do. Maybe the parrot could talk already. If not, he'd plenty of time to teach him. The church clock had just struck midnight when he heard the back door open. 'Tabbi's here,' he told Jaws. 'You stay here and keep quiet until I've had time to explain you.'

His anger had gone. Relief instead. He realised how frightened he'd been that she'd gone for good, left him to deal with a snotty-nosed, crappy-arsed infant. He'd forgive her anything so long as she promised not to do it again and paid him double money. He'd even forego sitting in the graveyard.

He paused at the top of the stairs, listened. Didn't sound like Tabbi's footsteps. Too loud, too heavy. Clumsy steps came through the kitchen, stopped in the hall. Jacob backed away from the stairs. Who was it? The footsteps made their unsteady way to the bottom of the stairs. Jacob craned forward, saw the top of a broad head, balding slightly at the crown, a thick red neck joining it to broad shoulders. Danny!

Thinking fast, Jacob slid into the back bedroom. Something had made him put Blue in here tonight rather than in the room he usually shared with his mum. Huddling in the far corner beside the buggy, hand poised above Blue's mouth to silence him should he cry out, Jacob listened. Danny came slowly up the stairs. At the gap where the stairs were missing he paused, grunted, cursed loudly, continued to climb.

Jacob held his breath, terrified of what he may be forced to do should Danny come in. He didn't. To Jacob's great relief the footsteps didn't even hesitate outside the door. Instead, they headed straight for the front bedroom. Jacob heard the door open then close. He heard the light go on, the bed springs creak. Then a noise like a door being opened. Jacob frowned. What was that? The wardrobe? Then something that sounded like furniture being moved. Maybe Danny was wedging something up against the door, but it didn't sound to be coming from the right part of the room. More heaving and grunting as though Danny were going up stairs again; more furniture removing; footsteps in the distance. Silence.

Minutes passed.

No more noises.

Jacob carefully stretched cramped limbs before crossing slowly to the door, edging it open, peering out. When nothing, no Danny, no vampire, got him, he stepped onto the landing. Fingers held in gun-pose, back against the wall, Jacob, eyebrow raised, moved slowly for Tabbi's bedroom door. He listened at it. Nothing. He put his 'gun' away, took hold of the door handle. Still nothing. Carefully turned the handle, opened the door an inch, stepped back. Nothing. Urged the door open further, reformed his gun, stepped into the shadows of the room. Nothing. No Danny. Nothing.

He'd seen enough. Had he ever needed

proof, this was it. Danny was as evil as any vampire he was likely to come across. Maybe he'd turned into a bat and flown out of the window or up the chimney; maybe he'd possessed Jaws by some intricate means of ESP; maybe Jaws was Danny's familiar — and he, Jacob, had invited the bird in. Fatal that, with vampires. False bravado filling his chest, Jacob left the bedroom for the bathroom, ready to deal with the forces of darkness.

15

''Nother bird gone missing.' Dungannon slapped a file into Lawson's palm. 'Parrot this time. Me laddo's goin' up in the world.' He studied Lawson thoughtfully. 'Looks like you spent too much time with the birds last night — or was it the dawn chorus disturbed you?'

Lawson ignored him, read the notes. 'Jacob?'

Dungannon nodded. 'ID'd by one of the assistants. Went to the same school apparently.'

'Why didn't she stop him?'

'Didn't notice. Said they were having trouble with the till — nail polish wasn't dry is my guess. Only found the bird missing when they were getting ready to close. Recognised Jacob on the CCTV. We've got a still from the film. At least we know what the little sod looks like now.'

'Good.' How many parents, thought Lawson, don't have photos of their children? Then again, how many parents are like Dave Palmer? His face cleared. 'So we're now on the trail of a stolen parrot.'

Dungannon shook his head. 'I've just

passed the buck. This one's yours.'

'But ... ' Lawson watched him go. Smiled. Two could play at that game. He went into the squadroom. Kate Rogers was sitting on a desk in the corner, speaking into the telephone. She waved when she saw him. He went over, waited for her to finish, handed her the file. 'Missing parrot. You couldn't — '

'Look into it, sure.'

'You don't mind?'

'Of course not. What you on?'

'Dropping into the Joiner's.'

'Drinking on duty — be careful you don't steal Dungannon's title.' She laughed at his frown. 'Police officer still able to stand upright after sinking five pints in half an hour — and that's just at lunchtime.'

'Oh.'

'You OK?' She reached out to touch his arm. As though receiving an electric shock, he pulled it away.

'Yeah ... not really. Domestic problems.' He looked at her, laughed. 'Hark at me! All that's really the matter is that I need a good fry-up. Coming to the canteen before you hit the parrot trail?'

'No, don't think so. The steak and kidney pie's excellent at the Joiner's though. Might meet you there lunchtime.'

Lawson grinned. The day had just got better.

★ ★ ★

The Joiner's Arms was a small pub with dirty bricks and empty troughs outside. Not the accepted idea of an office. And yet both Danny James and Dotty Spangle (deceased) were purported to have worked from here. Not your accepted clientele either.

Flat-capped pensioners played cribbage and dominoes in a corner between the gents' loo and a grimy bay window; a gaggle of shop assistants, forsaking CashSave's staff canteen, giggled loudly and balanced precariously on stools at the bar. Add to that a couple of tables filled with Darby and Joan types, carrier bags stuffed with the day's specials at their feet, and a crowd of check-shirted, blue-jeaned youths at the dart board. That was Dotty's range of regulars. Lawson wondered how she'd kept herself in pantyhose.

The sight of his uniform brought hostile silence.

As usual.

He removed his cap, smiled cautiously. The flat-capped brigade went back to their games; one of the youths made a smart Alec comment that Lawson chose to ignore. Briefly, he caught a glimpse of Tina Harker, sporting a black eye, in the kitchen. He approached the landlord, a weaselly chap of about five foot six, immaculately turned out in three-piece suit and red silk tie. From previous visits he knew his name to be Toby Strait.

'Who is it you need to be seeing?' The man's perfectly manicured moustache twitched nervously.

Lawson had thought about this before entering. Asking about the clients of a dead prostitute was likely to freeze the already stone cold trail solid. He decided to go the other route. 'Anyone who knows Danny James.' Prime suspect in a case with a dismal lack of evidence.

'He ain't here.' One of the youths had swaggered from the dart board to stand next to Lawson.

'So you know him?'

'Yep.'

'Any idea where he is?'

'Nope. And if I did I wouldn't be telling.' He spoke with bravado, cocking an eyebrow at his mates in the corner. Raucous laughter, egging him on. The rest of the punters had started talking again, albeit in hushed whispers, eyes fixed on Lawson.

'Now that's a shame,' Lawson turned to the landlord. 'Could I have an orange juice and the menu please?' He spoke again to the youth. 'Because I might have some information that might make him a rich man. Imagine what he would do to you if he ever found out you'd prevented that.' He hoped this lad was in awe of Danny, hoped this bluff was going to work.

'He's not here.'

'We've already established that.'

'I mean, he's not at home. That's all I know.' The lad was backing towards his mates, losing interest in this game.

'You any idea, Toby? I'll have the steak and kidney, by the way.' It looked like he was eating alone, Kate hadn't appeared.

'Saw him a day or two ago. Never spoke to him. He's not really due some money is he? What is it, PR with Joe Public?'

Lawson shrugged. 'If they think we don't only come with bad news, they might give us a break from time to time.'

'Dream on. He have anything to do with Dotty's death?'

Lawson frowned. 'Possibly.'

'Repeat offender.'

'Explain.'

'Before your time this. A lassie living at Storm Mount got attacked at home. Swore it

184

was him, then buttoned up just before testifying. Danny got off. She committed suicide six months later. Turned out he'd been blackmailing her over some lesbian thing. No proof, of course. And he didn't *actually* murder, mind.'

And why wasn't that nugget of information on Danny's records?

'Good as. Did he know Dotty well?'

'Yeah. They was teenage sweethearts — or at least, he was a teenager, she was a good ten years older. Caused all kinds of aggro with his mother.'

'I can imagine. So what happened?'

'Far as I can work out, Mrs James went to war — wasn't so disabled in those days — damn near drummed Dotty out of town.'

'Off the planet, more like.' The steak and kidney was transported from the kitchen by Toby's voluptuous wife Gina. Side by side they looked like Mr and Mrs Jack Sprat.

'Without being indiscreet, could you point out any of Dotty's punters here?' He looked up from salting his lunch to find Toby convulsed in silent mirth.

'Give me a break. If Dotty'd had her way with this lot I'd have to close down, she'd have given them all heart attacks,' he explained to a bemused Lawson. 'Nah, she greeted her punters at CashSave. This was her . . . observatory. That window over there,' he pointed to a small window behind the door. 'Gave her the best view, she said. They knew to look over here if it was cold or wet. If she was in the window, business was on. If not, they had to make other arrangements. Bit like a red lamp without the red lamp if you get my drift.'

'I think so. Did you see her with anyone but her 'usuals' on Wednesday night?'

Toby's face clouded. 'Maybe. But if I tell you, you didn't hear it from me. Got it?'

'Yep.' Lawson sighed. So much drama in the daftest situations.

'OK.' Pulling a small notebook towards him, he tore off a page, scribbled down a name, folded the page and handed it to Lawson. 'Don't you dare mention my name.'

Back outside after lunch Lawson would unfold the paper. Interesting but not surprising. And conveniently awaiting questioning. Some days the job felt good.

He allowed himself the luxury of a stretch before sliding back into his car. Across the road something caught his eye. A posh car. Parked on its own by a trolley park. What was it Flick had said? Dotty used to talk to a guy with a posh car? Lawson, closing his car door again, jogged across the road, circled the car.

A Bentley. So black it shone blue, like a raven's plumage. Immaculate interior. Leather and walnut. One cool car. On the back seat was a traditional, expensive-looking car rug, jazzy yellow and red tartan. That, he decided later, should have been a clue. But it wasn't the rug that immediately took his attention; it was the piece of fabric poking out from beneath it.

'Mr Lawrence, isn't it?'

'Lawson,' Lawson corrected automatically, turning to face the Bentley's owner.

'Admiring the view?' Stan Rawlings nodded towards the car.

'Absolutely.' Lawson smiled as Rawlings stroked the bonnet. 'Curious too.'

'About what?' Rawlings heaved three carrier bags into the boot of the car. 'How I could afford it? Easy,' he continued without waiting for a response. 'I invested the money I inherited from my mother in it, years and years ago. It's my one luxury. I think we're all allowed one, don't you?'

'Indeed.' Lawson joined him at the rear of the car. 'But that wasn't what I was curious about.' He pointed through the side window to the back seat. 'What is that piece of fabric poking out from beneath the rug?'

Rawlings frowned. 'Don't know. Can't say I recognise it. Probably something that's been used as a duster and I've forgotten to take it out. What say we have a look?'

Psychedelic leggings. Lawson recognised them immediately as the ones last seen on Dotty Spangle. As did Stan Rawlings.

'Oh my God!' He gasped. His usually florid face suddenly washed of colour. 'These were Dotty's.' He nodded, repeated more quietly. 'These were Dotty's.'

'You recognise them?'

'Of course.'

'Was this what she was wearing the last time you saw her?'

Rawlings thought for a moment. 'Yes, yes I do believe it was.' Panic flashed across his face. 'Oh no! You think it's me, don't you? You think I killed her! I didn't. I would never hurt Dotty. It wasn't me.'

'Mr Rawlings,' Lawson took a step closer to him. 'I haven't said anything.'

'You don't need to, son, I know how it works, incriminating evidence and all that. Guilty until proved innocent.' Lawson opened his mouth to protest. 'Save it son,' Rawlings shook his head sadly. 'Even if justice claims it to be the other way around, society immediately hands out the sackcloth and ashes — and even if you are proved innocent you get tarnished.'

Lawson frowned. 'Have you ever been

subjected to that then?'

'No son. But I read the papers, watch the telly, same as everyone else. Propaganda the whole bloody lot of it.'

'Any idea how these leggings,' with gloved hands, Lawson carefully folded them and placed them in a plastic bag. 'Came to be on the back seat of your car?'

'None.' Rawlings shook his head. 'Believe me son, if I had any clue I'd tell you.'

Lawson nodded. He was relieved to see that the colour was returning to Rawlings' face. 'All the same — '

'You'd like me to come down to the station. Of course. When?'

'ASAP.'

'Now? I can follow you down there — if you trust me not to drive off in the opposite direction. Always fancied myself as Steve McQueen.'

Lawson smiled. 'Don't think the Bentley's quite up to the *Bullitt* treatment.'

'Probably not. I'll see you there.'

Lawson had just made the kerb when he heard a strangled gasp. He turned. Stan Rawlings, white once more, had collapsed beside the Bentley.

16

Kate had planned to join Lawson at the pub. Arriving at Storm Mount, slightly out of breath after striding into the wind, all had seemed quiet. The back door was ajar. She stood outside for a moment listening, watching, looking down the garden for any hint of movement that might be human-made. Nothing. A bird singing in a tree close by. The river running by out of sight. She pushed the door open, stepped slowly out of the daylight.

The kitchen looked pretty much as it had that first night, save for the kettle, teabags, carton of milk and half loaf of bread. Signs of habitation. She paused to touch the kettle. Cold. Stopping again at the doorway to listen, she moved slowly forward when satisfied, walking on tiptoe so as not to alert anyone on the first floor.

She shouldn't have come alone. She knew that now. She should have asked Lawson to come with her. He would have, had he known she'd planned this little caper. It just seemed the obvious place to find Jacob at this point.

The lounge was empty. A curtain, now

draped across the window, cut out the view across the street, gave the room a surreal light. She stood in the centre of the room having first checked no one was waiting to pounce from behind the door. Very little sign of occupancy here. The chalk outline had almost disappeared and, bizarrely, there was a bunch of dying flowers in its centre. A shiver ran up her spine, the act of tenderness so incongruous here.

Well, she steeled herself. No one down here. Better try upstairs. She mounted the stairs as quietly as possible, taking her time over the gap, not wanting to be startled by anyone and thrown off balance. Silence greeted her. Then a scrabbling. She froze. God, how many horror movies had she seen? Wasn't this how they started? The empty house, the noises? What would the conclusion be — something ghostly or horrendous flying at her when she opened a door?

'Get a grip,' she told herself firmly. 'This is ordinary, every day life.' The scrabbling had stopped. 'See,' she said more loudly. 'Just the product of your imagination.'

Bypassing the closed door ahead of her, she went into the back bedroom. Obviously been slept in, grubby blankets on the floor. No one here now. The front bedroom door was ajar. Same scenario. Which left the closed door.

She knocked. Wasn't it only polite? No response. 'Jacob?' She called in as steady a voice as she could muster. 'Are you in there?' When silence still reigned, she gripped the handle, opened the door, slowly pushed it all the way back.

What flew at her convinced her this was a horror movie, something from Hitchcock. Multi coloured, huge and so very, very loud, the monster threw itself at her face. Too late she put her hands up for protection, too late she lashed out. Her thrashings though, caught it, knocked it off balance, drove it past her and away. A dreadful flapping and shrieking in her ears and it disappeared downstairs. Heart banging, forcing breath in and out, she leant against the door jamb. Taking her hands from her face she saw blood. Gently she explored her left cheek with her fingertips. More blood — but nothing life-threatening. She stepped into the bathroom looking for a mirror; found a cracked, mouldy one on the windowsill behind the curtain. A couple of scratches. The fiend had scratched her but now, thankfully, gone.

'Are you OK?'

Kate stopped. Was she hearing things?

'Is anyone up there?' Came the woman's voice again.

'Erm . . . yeah. Hang on.' Hastily brushing

down her uniform, she went to the tap to wash her face. It was then she noticed the bird food, the droppings, and laughed. The parrot, she'd found the parrot!

'I found the parrot,' she explained minutes later to the blonde-haired woman who stood, nodding attentively, in the hall.

'Of course you did dear. Is that what happened to your face?'

Kate nodded.

'Well, I'm sure it'll soon heal.'

'Who are you?' One good thing about the uniform, Kate didn't need to explain herself at this point.

'Sophie Sullivan, social worker.' She held out a confident hand.

'Ah.' Kate accepted the vice-like shake with barely a wince. 'So we finally meet. Kate Rogers.'

'Pleased to meet you in the flesh. Is it Jacob you're looking for?'

'Mm.'

'And you found the parrot.'

'Yes.' Kate touched her cheek, laughed ruefully. 'Didn't keep hold of it though. Shan't be flavour of the month at the station or the pet shop.'

'But no sign of Jacob?'

'No.'

'Pity,' Sophie took a notebook from her

193

handbag, ticked an item off a list. 'Just about run out of places to look. So, you're looking for him too. Maybe we could have a chat?'

'Sure. When?'

Sophie checked her watch. 'It's lunchtime. Now?'

Kate nodded, hoped Lawson would understand, this *was* work after all.

★ ★ ★

The coffee house, as it called itself, was tiny. In the summer it would open up its front and spill aluminium tables and its young professional clientele onto the pavement; Drumboli's Lane in winter, however, was best spent indoors.

Kate Rogers and Sophie Sullivan studied each other across the table in a corner housing a collection of plants which, decided Kate, could easily rival those at Kew. Fronds descended over the condiments in the centre of the table, threatening to divest themselves of any insects, indirectly, into the customers' food.

Sophie Sullivan, a large, angular woman, with large-knuckled hands and a 'jolly hockey-sticks' type of voice, was, nonetheless attractive and curiously feminine in her discreetly expensive suit. What Dungannon had against her, Kate couldn't *quite* fathom. Professional, intelligent, interested, surely none of these attributes made her the enemy?

'Quite a little Houdini, our Jacob, isn't he?' Sophie raised her eyebrows, unbuttoned her jacket.

'It would seem so, though I expect you know more about him than I do.'

Sophie nodded. 'Poor little sod. Some children get moved from pillar to post when one parent goes walkabout and the one left behind can't cope. Jacob just got . . . left.'

'Have you never tried fostering him?' Kate caught the look in Sophie's eyes. 'Oh, sorry. I'm not here to try and tell you your job.'

'Don't worry, I won't let you. Yes, is the simple answer. Unfortunately, Jacob doesn't understand the word 'simple'. He decided to leave the family we put him with — three times. When we finally got through to him that it was there or nothing, he set about wrecking the place. Therefore arming himself with a reputation which nobody but those regarding themselves as saints were prepared to take on. And, believe me,' she smiled bitterly. 'There's not many saints out there.'

'But if he didn't want to be with them where did he want to be?'

'At home.'

'With Dad?'

'No,' Sophie took a cigarette packet from her crocodile-skin handbag, offered one to Kate who declined. 'He wanted to be there for when his Mum came home.'

'That's sad.' Kate signalled for their coffee cups to be refilled. 'Is she likely to return?'

'Who knows? We don't know for sure that she ever *did* go to Spain.'

'So, if he's not at Storm Mount, where is he?'

'I don't know,' Sophie admitted with a small sigh. 'But I don't think he'll be far away. This area is all he's ever known. Add to that the fact that he's still hoping his mum'll appear. One thing I will say though, is that if you find him before I do, the first thing he'll do is insist on having me attendant at the interview — he knows his rights, that young man. He's as sharp as that parrot's claws. Maybe you ought to get that scratch looked at – never know what diseases these creatures arry.'

And Kate, reminded of the attack and the robbing in her cheek, nodded.

★ ★ ★

ck at the ranch, Lawson, sipping hot 'puccino, checked Dotty's file. Someone ʰ researched her life pretty well. He whistled. No wonder women turn to prostitution if they could expect earnings like these. But it hadn't always been so, he checked back. The money had started to increase at approximately the same time as Dotty became a member of The Fairweather Organisation. According to her bank statements, an extra two thousand pounds a month was paid in cash on the first of the month. A retainer? Interest?

He intended to talk to Tina Harker about Dotty ASAP. To his regret, Tina had decided that leaving Dave was one thing but leaving the house quite something else and so had changed the locks and refused Dave entry. Which lasted all of ten minutes while he fetched a sledgehammer from the shed. Dave was currently enjoying another secondment in the cells. Which reminded Lawson, if he didn't get on and question him soon, he'd have lost his chance.

The phone rang. 'Sebastian?' A shrill voice asked before he'd even said hello.

'Mum?'

'I'm just ringing to apologise.'

'Mum — '

'It's just that I worry about you.'

'Mum,' he paused, waiting for the chance to interrupt. There was none. 'I'm sorry, I can't talk right now. I really wish you wouldn't phone me at work unless it's important.'

'Well I thought this was important,' she huffed. The phone went dead.

Lawson sighed. Again he'd have to make peace with his mother when he got home. Again. Distracted, he put the phone down, forgot about Palmer in the cells.

Dotty Spangle — or Dorothy Smith as she was known before her 'showbiz' career — had started working life as a secretary. According to friends (Lawson had tracked down two who remembered her before prostitution clawed its way into her life) she was a plain, round, mousy girl who never had a boyfriend and always went to Sunday School. She'd left school at sixteen, got a job in a typing pool and continued, for several years, to live her nondescript life.

Then Danny Jones began to show an interest in her. 'Like he'd suddenly decided she was Ursula Andress in that Bond movie,' said one. The other friend was less complimentary, something about a dog on heat. The question was why. Lawson had urged both parties to check their memories for clues but neither could remember. One thing they were agreed on was that it wasn't just that he'd suddenly fallen in love with her.

'Penny for them.'

Lawson looked up. DC Tim Stewart stood over him, clutching a cup of tea.

'Don't know that they're worth that much.'

'Dotty?'

'Yep.'

'Me too.' Stewart sat opposite Lawson, moving an ashtray onto another table. 'Oh, sorry, did you need that?'

'Nah, don't smoke.' But privately, Lawson smiled. This was the first time anyone around here had bothered to enquire. 'What have you found out?'

'Not as much as Dungannon'd like. Been talking to her regulars — at least the few I could find.'

'How few?'

'Half a dozen. Most of the names on her calendar are fiction — including the B.B. Roache WPC Rogers was trying to trace — the punter Dotty was supposed to be with when she died.'

'There's an update on him,' said Lawson, remembering a document Forensic had found in the Bentley's glove compartment while giving the car the once over. Real name Stan Rawlings. Don't know why he needed the alias. Don't think he's responsible for Dotty's death. Can't prove it though.'

'Yet.' Stewart added this information to his notebook.

'I don't suppose you've seen her?'

'Dotty?' Stewart sugared his tea.

'WPC Rogers.'

'Not since this morning.'

'Me too.' Lawson chased the last bit of chocolate-topped froth around his cup with a spoon. 'Why would she invent punters?'

'Maybe she didn't. Maybe they just didn't give their real names. Or maybe she *did* invent them to give her a reason to go out.'

'A cover?' Lawson eyed him keenly, nodded slowly. 'Do you know, you could be right. Maybe she was meeting someone, just not the person in her diary.'

'It could be the person in the diary; maybe they concocted the name B.B. Roache between them to hide the identity.'

'So she could have been having an affair with Stan Rawlings?' Lawson laughed with disbelief.

Stewart raised his eyebrows. 'You ask me, that's what she was doing every night anyway.'

'But,' Lawson nodded thoughtfully. 'That doesn't really help, just brings us back full circle.'

'Yeah. Maybe B.B. — Stan — was pandering to her fantasy.'

'Maybe, but unfortunately he's currently in intensive care — heart attack — so he can't comment. Talking of fantasies, what would a lad, considerably younger than Dotty, be doing falling for her illicit charm?'

'Danny James?' Stewart sipped his tea.

'The one and only.'

'Looking for a mother-figure? Screwing the only woman who'll let him get his rocks off? God knows. There's as many explanations as there are perverts. Anyway,' Stewart smoothed out the paper in front of him. 'Back to my list. None of them remember seeing her since Wednesday last week.'

'That's ten days ago.' Lawson nodded at the girl who came to clear their table. Stewart watched morosely as she whipped away his half-full cup.

'Hey! I'm not fini — !' Too late. He turned his attention back to Lawson. 'Caring lot aren't they? None of them even admitted to spotting her outside CashSave when they went shopping. Guess that's because their other halves would have been with them and they don't want us going around asking questions.'

'Any of them make a financial commitment to her? A regular payment?'

'Direct debit, you mean?' Stewart laughed. 'Shouldn't think so. None of them look as though they've enough cash for a jump at Christmas.'

'Any idea what she charged?'

Stewart shook his head. 'But I can tell you, she was no Spice Girl.'

'Which makes it odder. Why was she getting more — considerably more — money at the end of a rather lacklustre career than she was at the beginning?'

Stewart shrugged. 'Is there anyone who's not been questioned yet?'

Lawson jumped. 'Shit! Dave Palmer is downstairs. Forgot all about him.'

'Not any more he's not. Released twenty minutes ago. Watched him strut away myself.'

'Shit!' Lawson stood. 'Guess I'd better get myself over to his.'

'You sure he'll go home?'

Lawson smiled bleakly. 'Oh yes, he's got a stronger homing instinct than a pigeon.'

'There's one more thing.'

Lawson paused at the door.

'Have you come across Margaret Dubois?'

Lawson nodded.

'Seems she's been getting mystery payments too.'

Lawson walked two steps back from the door. 'How much?'

'Two, three thousand a month. Started eight months ago.'

'So not when she joined The Fairweather

Organisation?' Lawson circled behind Stewart, read over his shoulder.

'No, but worth a question or two don't you think?' Lawson nodded. 'Good.' Stewart stood. 'Let's go before Grumpy gets back from the quack's.'

'If I ever find you were referring to me, I'll chop you into small pieces and eat you on toast.'

Lawson cringed as Dungannon's voice boomed across the canteen.

'Wouldn't think of it sir. Think far too much of you sir.' Stewart grabbed Lawson's sleeve and pulled.

'I should think so.' Dungannon stepped forward to intercept. 'Have we got a lead?'

'Nothing as strong as that, sir. A coincidence is a better description. Got to fly.' Stewart hauled Lawson from the room, called back over his shoulder, 'Got to act quick, she's a slippery fish, don't want her getting away.'

17

There'd been no one at Dave Palmer's, not even Tina so it was with a certain amount of frustration and self-recrimination Lawson drove to Margaret Dubois'. He'd timed it to perfection. Leaving the car as the cleaner turned the corner, Lawson and Stewart made for the front door. It opened before he knocked.

'Was that deliberate?' Margaret Dubois, cigarette holder in hand, frowned.

'Good morning,' he dodged the issue, stepped as bidden into the hall with Stewart close on his heels. 'Just a couple more questions if you don't mind.'

'And if I do?' She swept a diamond decked hand towards the lounge. 'Go in. I'm just making coffee.'

More relaxed this time, thought Lawson, more together. Had time to set up an alibi? Get her story straight in her mind? He sat on a cream leather chair opposite a yellow portable TV. Another chair and a two seater sofa matched the chair he sat in, a cream carpet dotted with ethnic rugs. A wall-hanging depicting an African sunset hung over the fireplace. He was admiring it when she brought in the coffee. Stewart, who'd remained in the hall, followed her in.

'You like?' She set down the tray on a small table next to her chair.

'Mm. Is it original?'

'Yes. I did a lot of travelling once upon a time. Picked all sorts of things up. Coffee?'

'Thanks.' He took the mug. Had she really smiled? 'If you don't mind me saying so, you seem a lot happier today.'

'I did tell you I was on my way out last time,' she crossed her elegantly trousered legs. 'Anyway, I'm curious to know what you've found out about me.'

Lawson cringed. He'd not come to talk about her. 'Dotty Spangle,' he said, getting back on track. 'I think you knew her better than you let me believe before.'

'And how well do you think I knew her?'

'I think you had business dealings.' He watched her closely. Her eyes gave nothing away.

'Business? You do know what Dotty did for a living?' He nodded. 'And you think I was part of that? Well . . . '

'Maybe she used your contacts? Your property?'

Margaret Dubois laughed. 'Are you seriously telling me Dotty Spangle had enough money to suggest she worked for the higher echelons of our society?' Her face froze as Lawson nodded.

'Helped along by large amounts being deposited monthly into her account.' Stewart chipped in.

'Funny that, isn't it?' Lawson stood, using his height advantage as a mute threat. 'Funny too, that she was found dead in Storm Mount, a house owned by The Fairweather Organisation — or should I say Margaret Dubois? What is it, some kind of plc set up for tax purposes?'

For a moment Lawson thought she looked frightened, then she straightened her shoulders. 'No,' she said quietly.

'Would you like to explain it?'

She shook her head, not in refusal but bewilderment. 'How can this come down to me? I've done nothing. I've nothing to do with Dotty's death.'

'Then you've nothing to fear by telling the truth.' Lawson leant against the windowsill, waiting for her to begin. He was bemused by what he heard.

Margaret Dubois, eyes firmly set on her nails drumming on the chair arm, started to speak in a voice not much louder than a whisper. The Fairweather Organisation, soon to celebrate its centenary, had been set up as a sort of co-operative for working women. All very admirable, though slightly unusual when it turned out the 'working women' were 'ladies of the night', a phrase seeming more glamorous with Margaret Dubois' husky tones and inflections.

'It was worse for them then than it is now — rape, violence, murder — all more prevalent then. They suffered more than any of us could ever imagine. So a distant relative of mine, Doris Fairweather, set up a hostel for these women to recover. She was lucky enough to have inherited a house so a few regulars financed her life.'

Stewart sniggered, tried to disguise it as a sneeze. Doris Fairweather was hardly the kind of name he expected a prostitute to sport.

'And it's carried on?' Lawson frowned at Stewart.

'Mm. She left strict guidelines for those who inherited the organisation, for that is what it is, an inheritance. It went to the oldest girl in the next generation which meant that nieces often picked up the burden.'

'That's how you got it?'

She nodded. 'Membership is strictly limited to six in the elite circle. If any of those members choose to help individuals outside of that it is entirely down to them.'

'And Dotty was a member?'

'Yes.'

'How long had she been one?'

'Ten years, nearly.'

'Any idea who might want to kill her? No jealousy? No punter-swopping? No one so desperate to join they created a vacancy?'

She shook her head. 'I really don't think so. You can't imagine how many sleepless nights I've had since Dotty died, trying to work it out.'

'So you think the organisation is involved in some way?'

She spoke carefully, picking her words. 'I think there is a possibility, yes.'

'So why didn't you speak out before?'

'I wasn't sure.'

'But I came here before and you said you knew nothing. Had you even given me a few pointers we could have reached this point in our enquiries a lot sooner, maybe arrested the murderer by now and made the streets safe for your other members. How many other members still operate?'

She cleared her throat, was suddenly fascinated by her scarlet talons. 'We're . . . er . . . experiencing a fallow period at present.' Getting a grip, she leant forward, elbows on knees, and looked him in the eye. 'You have to understand that these ladies are members for life, unless they wish to revoke their membership. Some do but most keep it because they can use it to help others. This means, in the cycle of things, since most women are similar ages when they start, they're similar ages when they finish — '

'Die,' intoned Stewart.

Margaret and Lawson ignored him. 'Currently we're going through a period of regrowth, that is — '

'The old ones have pegged it and the new ones aren't in place yet.' Stewart suggested.

'If you wish to be so blunt, yes.'

'I see,' Lawson pondered. 'And is there a waiting list, or do you pick the lucky girls yourself?'

'Word of mouth usually. You know, someone knows so-and-so who needs this, that or the other. We assess their needs and whether or not we can help them.'

'Are there any girls currently being assessed?'

Silence. Lawson was suddenly aware of a dip in the temperature.

'I'm not at liberty to answer that question.'

'Very well, although you may not have any choice at a later date. Tell me, when you inherit the organisation, do you inherit the mantle of 'lady of the night'?'

Her head shot up. 'I hope you're not insinuating that I was ever a prostitute! I've made my money legally and above board.'

'That's interesting,' said Lawson. 'Our friendly computer tells us you were charged with soliciting several times, using a different name, naturally.'

'Never!' She paled to the colour of the carpet. 'This is outrageous! If you don't apologise and leave at once, I shall get in touch with the Chief Constable, he's a very good friend of mine.'

'Oh, I'm sure he is.' Stewart took up the reins. 'And the computer's a very good friend of ours. Do you like riddles Ms Dubois?'

She looked understandably puzzled.

'What do a computer and a camera have in common?' He paused, tapping his pencil on his notebook. 'Shall I tell you? They never lie, Ms Dubois. Your lovely face adorns a certain file in our computer's memory. So you see, you can call the Chief Constable but it'll only prolong what could be a very messy investigation.'

Myriad emotions crossed her face but her voice, when at last she spoke, was tightly controlled. 'I think it's time you left.'

'Of course,' Lawson, all smiles, got up. 'Wouldn't want to outstay our welcome.' He led the way to the front door, paused. 'One last thing: have you, in all your dealings with the public, ever come across a Danny James?'

This time there was no doubt of her reaction. She started, took a pace back. 'No.' Her voice trembled.

And this time he knew she was lying.

★ ★ ★

Number three was a mirror-image of Margaret Dubois' house. Stewart having gone back to the car to radio in, Lawson went round the back of number three, hoping to gain the attention of the cleaner and not the owner. The cleaner was in the kitchen. He tapped on the window. Startled, she nonetheless opened the door. 'Hello?'

He flashed his ID. 'I wonder if I may have a quick word with you?'

'Why?' Panic crossed her elegant features. 'What has happened?'

'Nothing, nothing,' he soothed. 'I just wondered if you could help me.'

'I could try — but maybe you're confusing me for the owner of the property, I'm not, you know, I'm just the cleaner.'

'I know that — I don't know your name though.'

'Audrey Willis. I'd invite you in,' she said apologetically. 'Only I'm not sure it's the done thing with a house that's not my own.'

'I understand totally. All I want to know,'

211

he took Dotty's photo from his pocket. 'Is whether you recognise this woman. And, if so, where you know her from.'

She studied the photo for a long moment — too long, thought Lawson, for it to be genuine.

'No. Sorry, never seen her before.'

Liar.

'Oh well, worth a try. I just thought, with you being a regular visitor and all, that you might have seen her around this neighbourhood. Has a friend lives round here by all accounts.'

'No, I'm sorry but I've not seen her here. Maybe she's not around when I'm here.'

'Maybe.' But Lawson didn't need to see her pink-tinged cheeks to tell she wasn't being wholly honest with him. 'Well, I'll not keep you from your chores any longer. Nice to have talked to you.'

He was halfway to the car when he remembered Stan Rawlings' slip the first time he'd questioned him — he'd exchanged Audrey's name for Margaret's, though he did correct himself immediately. That made him even more certain there was some sort of conspiracy going on at the heart of this.

'Unfortunately,' he said to Stewart as he explained his theory on the way back. 'The one person we really need to speak to right now is lying in a coma. The connection between Rawlings and these two women may remain a mystery forever.'

'Eternal triangle?'

Lawson shook his head. 'Shouldn't think so, too bloody obvious for that lot.'

An unprofitable session, he told himself later, not only had the trail gone cold on Dotty, he'd mislaid Dave Palmer and Tina Harker. Careless.

Very.

18

Jaws had gone. Jacob couldn't decide if he was relieved or angry — or worried. Relieved that he didn't have to deal with it; angry that someone, probably Danny, had come into *his* house and let out *his* bird; worried that, had it been someone else, they knew he was around and may arrest him for stealing the bird in the first place. But there was something else. Had he, inadvertently, released some kind of evil into Righton? He stopped in his tracks. It was a vampire, that's how it had got out, by becoming smoke and squeezing through the key hole.

If it was going to do that, it would have done it the first night. Vampires aren't active during daylight hours.

Jacob relaxed. James was right. So it had to be human intervention that had released the bird and not something supernatural.

There was another problem.

Tabbi still wasn't home. The selfish reason for wanting her here had gone. Now there was only worry and fear. The worry of her whereabouts; the fear that he may be left to deal with Blue forever. Not even his mother had taken on that challenge.

Lunch had been a dismal affair. Blue no longer smiled when Jacob made an aeroplane from the eggy soldier; he lay motionless as Jacob changed his nappy. He was missing his mum. The lack of language was no barrier here, Jacob could read the signs in the fearful eyes, the downturned mouth, the desperation oozing from the pores.

'She won't be long.' He threw Blue up towards the ceiling, caught him expertly, pulled a face. The baby regarded him solemnly, burst into tears. 'Don't cry. Please don't cry, I'd show you the parrot only someone's let it go. Anyway, it's p'raps as well. Bloody thing was the devil in disguise.' He looked at Blue. 'You're not are you, some sort of incubus, I mean? I'm not the only one here who doesn't come from the dark side?' Jacob froze. Noises from upstairs.

Wasn't the parrot, that much was definite. Anyway whatever it was was making too much noise. Something moving, something big. What? He listened to sounds like furniture being moved, something sliding, then footsteps. Thanking God he'd packed Blue's bag as soon as they'd come downstairs, Jacob strapped the baby in his buggy and wheeled him out of the house. Whoever — or whatever — was roaming

Storm Mount could have the rest of the afternoon to vacate.

★ ★ ★

He came to the riverbank whenever his mind was disturbed. If he saw a kingfisher everything would be all right. He scoured the willows, the gnarled branches that twisted over the water's surface, dappling the slow-moving, mud-coloured liquid with ominous shadows. No kingfishers today. Which meant . . . Jacob shook his head. He didn't even want to think about it. Blue tipped his head back and smiled hopefully up at him. A good omen. It was the first time Blue had smiled today. Jacob came round to the front of the buggy, hunkered down, poked Blue playfully in the stomach.

'That's better! Thought you'd gone off me . . . ' his voice trailed away as he caught sight of something — someone — familiar. He stood.

Suddenly everything was silent. Wrong. Blood pounded in his ears in an ancient rhythm of fear. Fear whispered through the grass as he walked, slow motion, away from the buggy. The birds weren't singing, the day had gone from colour to black and white, and all the time the pounding in his ears. No! No!

No! His feet marched in time with the voice screaming in his brain. No!

The lightning tree.

The lightning tree and . . .

He didn't want to think about it, didn't want to see, closed his eyes, moved slowly onwards.

The lightning tree and . . .

The tree had stood for years, its trunk split into a V by the lightning bolt that had killed it. Local children knew the left arm was safe to climb and swing from; the right arm was not. There was no one playing on it now.

Someone was sleeping against the trunk. The sleep of another world. So beaten and bloody was her face that he wouldn't have recognised it out of context. He closed his eyes, maybe he was wrong; prayed he was wrong. He opened his eyes. No, the clothes gave it away. Mini-skirt — no longer covering her bum; black bra, worn now as a necklace; the black jacket was nowhere in sight.

Selfishly, his first thought was not for Tabbi but for himself. However was he going to cope with Blue? He hunkered down, took hold of her wrist. A pointless exercise he knew but one that created a brief spasm of hope within his chest. Then the tears came. This time exclusively for the pretty girl-woman he'd come to admire and the

217

eight-month-old infant cooing gently in the buggy completely unaware that, six feet behind him, his mother lay dead.

It was Blue's stomach that dictated the crossover from fantasy to reality. Had he been alone, Jacob would have sat with Tabbi until someone else had discovered them, called for help, taken over the arrangements. Blue had other ideas. There is very little else more demanding to an infant than its need to take in calories — unless it is expelling the residue from the other end. Still in a state of shock, Jacob tried to put his thoughts in order as he dragged vegetation from the riverbank to cover Tabbi with.

The police would have to know. He could always make another anonymous call. Another! How many bodies did most people discover in a lifetime? None? One? He'd found two within days of each other — and he was only twelve! And how sympathetic would the police be if they ever found out it was him both times? It had been easy fooling them first time (or so he'd thought!) but another? He thought that less likely. He'd think about it.

'Goodbye Tabbi,' he gently stroked her hand, noticed the necklace around her neck. He'd better remove that. So, with more of the déjà vu, he once more found himself taking the abalone necklace from a corpse. Maybe that alone had sealed her death warrant. He shuddered. He'd have to be careful who he gave it to in future.

Blue had got steam up now and was wailing fit to bust. No more thoughts of police or bodies or the devil for now, Jacob pocketed the necklace and, backing Blue out so he wouldn't see his mother, headed for Jim's Café.

★ ★ ★

Jim's strength as a café owner was his knowledge of people. Certain expressions on faces required certain questions or responses. He'd got many required sentences down pat — 'You look like you've won the pools' or 'Mr Right finally showed his ugly mug then,' — simple stuff like that. Commiserations were less often required purely because the people who needed them often stayed home until they needed them no longer. Sadness and grief require a dark corner and lots of silence. So when Jacob blundered through the door, smashing the buggy so hard against it that Jim thought the glass would break (and damn nearly told him so in no uncertain terms), with his shoulders hunched, and his face looking as though expression had been sucked from it deep into the inner machinations of the brain, Jim stopped singing along with 'Carrie Ann' and watched.

The baby was gurgling happily, ripping to shreds the foil from a KitKat. Jacob arranged the buggy, handles against the wall, between two tables, then rounded the one nearest the counter and sat with his back to Jim.

'Food, young 'un?'

Jacob didn't respond. His head was down over his hands and now, Jim noticed, his shoulders were shaking. Wiping enormous hands on his apron, Jim switched off the radio, went to the boy's side.

'Problem?'

Jacob shrugged.

'Come on. Can't be that bad.' Jacob turned red-rimmed eyes to Jim, who stepped back. Never had he seen such — what? Fear? Despair? He was about to add 'in a boy' but he stopped. Not ever, he decided, had he seen that expression in *anyone's* eyes. He moved forward again, rested a hand on Jacob's shoulder. 'What is it? Anything I can do?'

'No.' A dark undertone.

'Shall I get the police? Is it that serious?'

Jacob shrugged. Yes, he wanted to shout, yes, it's as serious as it gets, you old fool. But I don't want no cops around me again, asking questions, taking Blue. This is a mess, the biggest fucking mess you can imagine and right now I don't know what to do. Leave me alone. 'Leave me alone.'

Jim nodded. 'Yeah.' He stepped back, paused. 'Anything to eat? Drink? For the little 'un mebbe?'

'We're fine. I just need to sit.' And Jacob realised that was true. The fry-up he'd been promising himself, probably in an asinine way of convincing his brain that everything was normal, now turned his stomach when he thought of it. Had it materialised in front of him he knew damn well it would never have got half way down his gullet before he spewed it up again. He dropped his head into his hands once more. This was a fucking mess. Who would want Tabbi dead? He hadn't known her long admittedly, but he'd seen enough to know that she was a good mother and, having had a bad one, he recognised gold-card status in that department.

First Odd-Job now Tabbi. It made no sense. The people he'd been closest to most recently in his life were dead and he'd been left to bring up an eight-month-old boy. Not that the authorities would let him — but they had to find him, had to find Blue. If he holed up at Storm Mount, he could keep Blue. Few more improvements and the house would be

221

home. Except for the noises like furniture removing and footsteps in the attic. Suddenly Storm Mount wasn't such a comfortable option.

Life had been fine until he'd spotted Danny James. Always a bad omen. Danny was guilty of causing Odd-Job's death, Jacob had already decided that, but would he have killed Tabbi, for her death was obviously no accident? He recalled his run-in with Danny. What had he said? 'I might teach your tart one or two lessons of my own.' Surely that wasn't a murder threat? Surely that was the testosterone talking? Mentally Jacob shrugged, he wasn't experienced enough in that department to know. And anyway, Danny James was the only person Jacob knew who was capable of killing someone, and he was the only other person to know she was staying at Storm Mount.

Had to be him.

Had to be.

The anger surged briefly but, when it hit the dampness at the back of his throat, it died, came out as a sob. Stuffing his cuff into his mouth, Jacob sobbed silently onto the formica, not noticing when the door opened bringing with it a blast of fresh air and a familiar stranger.

★ ★ ★

'Drop me at the quay, will you?' Lawson banged a fist on the dashboard. 'Need some air. I'll walk back to the nick from there.'

After several moments silence, Stewart asked. 'What do you make of Ms Dubois?'

'Dunno. Hiding something, tart with a heart of pure lead. Wouldn't want to meet her in a dark alley.'

Stewart laughed. 'Know what you mean. Here do?'

'Fine.' Lawson got out. 'See you in a bit.'

A piercing drizzle was driving shoppers home early. Lawson moved against the flow, down the cobbles to the quay. Not a mist this time disguising the castle but drizzle and spray. Seagulls, obscured by the cloud, cried mournfully, adding to the supernatural atmosphere. Like, thought Lawson, some ghost ship is going to mysteriously appear through the mist and infect the town with rampant paranoia and bloodthirsty vampires. He shuddered inwardly at the creepy image.

Daylight dimming and the seagulls suddenly quiet, Lawson looked around. All the shops were closed save the café. Winter, no holidaymakers for kiss-me-quick hats and candyfloss. He'd never been to the seaside in the winter before. As a child there'd been snatched days out in Cleethorpes — two or three hours on the train for the same amount of time on the sandy beach. Mum would take a picnic — ham sandwiches usually. After lunch he'd have a donkey ride and an ice cream and then it would be time to get the train home. The miracle was, he'd never once known it to rain on the days his mother planned a beach day. He checked his watch. Time for a quick cuppa.

He ordered tea and a toasted tea cake from the huge man behind the counter. He ignored the look the man had given him. He used to think it was because he was a policeman — someone had once told him that even in plain clothes he was obviously a policeman — but childhood paranoia is hard to shake and deep down he still believed it was his colour. Particularly around here where different-coloured skins stuck out like bananas in a potato sack.

He looked across at the only other customer, a boy out with his brother or sister in a pushchair. Nice that, giving mum a break. Not many kids would do that. He acknowledged his tea with a nod, settled down to think about Margaret Dubois. As cool as they come — until Danny James was mentioned. Who was this ignominious Mr James? Time, maybe to find out. Son of the irascible Eleanor, that much he knew, but something told Lawson that Danny was not a chip off the old block. Had he been, Lawson had no doubt that low-level gopher was not where Danny would have stayed for long had he ever wanted to climb off that particular rung. Tough lady Eleanor, so unlike Mum.

Guilt. Again. Mum, alone now, worrying about him; him not having apologised for the last little faux pas. He must ring her tonight. Was that why he was dallying, delaying going back to the station to delay making out his report to delay going home? He felt deep into the pit of his stomach. Yes, he discovered sadly, it was.

A chair scraping across the lino brought him out of his daydream. The boy had got up from the table and was busy rearranging a scarf around the baby's neck. Releasing the brake, he pushed the buggy towards the door.

'Mind how you go,' the man behind the counter called. 'Keep your chin up.'

Lawson smiled, the guy was obviously doing his fatherly bit. Chin . . . he glanced at the boy. Familiar somehow. He'd seen him before, and recently. Realisation struck. He pulled the CCTV photo from his pocket, unfolded it, slapped it against his palm. He'd just come face to face with The Canary Thief.

19

Money.

Jacob turned out his pockets. Nothing. Had he been thinking straight two hours before he'd have fed Blue at Jim's Café. Jim wouldn't have charged when he realised what shit the lad was in. Mind, he'd had to leave a bit smartish when he remembered seeing the guy who'd come in with Dungannon before. A copper! Last thing he needed right now was to be sussed.

'Shut up!' Jacob hissed at the screaming baby. 'I can't think while you're making that racket.' Blue, squirming like a purple maggot in his all-in-one, refused to co-operate. By the time they reached the corner of the High Street, Blue's face was almost the same colour as his outfit.

Night was drawing in. Shops, although still brightly lit, were long closed. Except ... Jacob squinted at the shop on the opposite corner. Still open. 'Open All Hours' boasted the peeling legend across the top of the window with its faded postcards and pocket-money toys. Not true. Jacob had come more than once in the past to find the place shut even earlier than this. He'd shoplifted from here before; knew that the father couldn't stagger round the counter fast enough to catch him but the son would be upon him before he reached the door. Which was only part of the problem. A screaming baby was hardly undercover material. He'd have to stash him somewhere.

Further along the block, an empty shop, once an off-licence, stood alone. Of the houses either side, one was derelict, the other was in darkness. Pretty safe bet the owners weren't in. Jacob knew (from having slept here occasionally) that a loose plank afforded entry to the yard behind the off-licence and that here a lean-to, still containing the original loo, provided shelter.

Squeezing the buggy through a one-plank gap wasn't on. He removed Blue and took him through first, placing him in the centre of the yard and praying he wouldn't disappear in the next thirty seconds. Next he folded the buggy, brought that through, opened it up and retrieved Blue. Moments later, having strapped Blue back in and wedged the buggy between the loo and the wall, he was off across the street.

A girl came out, hugging a baby about the same age as Blue. Jacob stopped, startled by the emotions welling up inside him. He'd known Tabbi for a few days was all; a few days too long. And now he was feeling this sadness. Maybe Dad was right, he was too soft. Where did that come from? Why think of Dad now? And Tabbi? Blue was who he should be thinking of, that was why he was here. He armed away the tears pricking at his eyes, opened the shop door. As the bell dinged, he turned away from the counter opposite, scoured the shop, targeted the corner he needed, ran.

Ignoring the two shoppers and the shop assistant (the father, he noted) he grabbed a bag of nappies, three jars of baby food and a dummy. Then he was off. The shop assistant had hollered as soon as he grabbed the nappies. Jacob risked a glance back, the son was skirting the counter, heading for the door to cut him off. Shit! Jacob dodged a tackle by a white-haired gent in crest-emblazoned blazer, raced for the door, knocking a young girl into a display of baked beans. The son had reached the door, filled the frame. Jacob slithered to a halt, dropped one of the jars. It rolled towards the man's foot, he stopped it with a DM, at least size ten. A hand came at Jacob's throat, he ducked, twisted away, shot beneath the guy's arm. Freedom.

'Stop!'

Fuck off! He wanted to shout but couldn't

spare the breath. He was off down the alley behind the shop. Lead them away from Blue, he told himself, fiddling about with the buggy will only slow you down. He'd find somewhere to hide down here until the furore died down. Footsteps behind him. He reached the T-junction, six foot fences flanked each option. What to do?

Right. Turn right.

He didn't stop to question Bond.

The alleyway curved to the right, giving him the briefest cover in which to disappear. To his left the fence had been smashed down revealing wasteland. Eyes flashing desperately, he looked for cover. No hiding place. And no chance of sprinting over the overgrown ground. The footsteps were so close now they pounded in his head, dictated the rhythm of his pumping heart. Dizzy. He dropped flat. And waited.

The footsteps left concrete, hit grass. Unable to hear them, he waited for discovery. Inevitable. Pressing his face into ground that smelled of dog crap, he held his breath, as much to stem the smell as listen. He daren't look up. The nappies, he knew, were the most likely thing to give him away. The white plastic shining like a beacon — 'Here I am. Come and get me.' He should have thrown them. Thrown the scent; bought himself a

229

moment maybe two.

A branch snapped under someone's foot. Size ten? Jacob suddenly realised he was crying. Silent hot tears were dripping into the ground under his face. At least he'd not wet himself. He'd got some nappies should that eventuality happen. The bizarreness of this thought made him want to laugh; to lay on his back, kick his legs in the air and laugh. He controlled himself. He listened.

Someone grunted. Not as close as the branch snapping. Or was that his imagination? He was dying to peek; dying to know. He couldn't. He couldn't.

'Shit!' A voice now. Further away still. This time he was sure. He'd done it! Yes! Keep your head, he told himself, don't go blowing it now. Five more minutes. It started to spot with rain. Enough for the guy to decide to return to the shop. Jacob waited until the footsteps hit concrete, slowly disappeared. Cautiously he raised his head, pushed his weight onto one elbow, peered above the empty husks of Dead Man's Finger, buddleia, nettles. All clear. Good.

Blue.

For the first time, the possibility of leaving the baby crept into Jacob's mind. After all, who would know? No one could accuse him of dumping the child for no one knew he'd been looking after him. Except maybe Jim — and he'd be easy to fob off. No one (not even Jim) knew the child's mother was dead (or so he believed. Half an hour previously, while he'd been securing Blue in the outside loo, a fisherman, out for a quiet night's sport, had discovered the body and rung the police.) Maybe no one knew of the child's existence. He could walk away from all this, from Righton, and never be held responsible.

But therein lay the problem.

Whatever his father's difficulty with responsibility, it hadn't been passed down through Jacob's genes. Nurturing was part of his make-up (always assuming you weren't a canary). Maybe the very fact that he so much wanted something to care for stemmed from the fact that he didn't want to emulate his father. The brief tussle with the thought of freedom over, Jacob scuttled out of the mouth of the alley, past the corner shop and back to the off-licence.

Silence.

The cold hand of fear grabbed his heart. Someone had found Blue. Even now they were waiting in the shadows for the person guilty of such a heinous crime to return. That copper! The one who'd come into Jim's Café. The one who'd clocked him and tried to follow. He'd found him! He was waiting to pounce!

Don't be stupid! As if they'd wait if they found a child. Chances are someone's handed him in to the police.

A shaky relief began to flood Jacob's body. Maybe someone *had* found Blue, *had* handed him over to the authorities. And if that's what had happened there was nothing for him to feel guilty about. Smiling now, Jacob slid through the fence. The yard was in deeper shadow than before but, even so, he could make out the wheel of the buggy glinting like a winking eye in the gloom. His spirits dipped. The buggy was still there. He got closer. Blue was there, asleep.

★   ★   ★

Ranjit Patel flashed angry eyes at Lawson. 'They think they can just come in here and help themselves! It's not as if they're all kids either.' He led the way through a box-laden passage to a sitting room at the back of the shop.

'But this one was? This was a boy of . . . ?'

'Eleven? Twelve? Small, finely built, blond hair, shabby clothes.' Ranjit's accent gave no clue to his Asian background. Educated at local schools, he was a product of Righton

232

through and through.

'This him?' Lawson unfolded the CCTV photo.

Ranjit nodded. 'Definitely.'

'And he stole baby products?'

'Yes.'

'Did he have a baby with him?'

'No.' Ranjit was positive. 'I chased him down the alleyway. No, there was no baby.'

'OK.' He must be living within spitting distance — or else it belonged to someone and he was babysitting it. But that didn't make sense if he was stealing for it. 'What exactly did he take?'

'A packet of nappies, a dummy and two jars of this,' Ranjit held up the jar Jacob had dropped. Lawson took it and shoved it in his pocket.

'Have you seen him before?'

'Yes. He's been hanging round for a few weeks, off and on.'

'Ever seen him with anyone else?'

'No,' Ranjit shook his head, a fine furrow running vertically between his brows. 'Hang on — yes! A day or two ago. I looked out. He was crouching down as though he was tying a dog to the rings outside the shop — especially for our customers with dogs.'

Lawson nodded. He'd noticed the 'Dog Park' on the way in. 'Very commendable.'

Ranjit looked pleased. 'He didn't have a dog though, must have been casing the joint, but he was with someone — a girl, bit older than him. And,' Ranjit smiled triumphantly. 'She had a pushchair.'

'And a baby?'

'Presumably.'

So there were two of them. He didn't have to be living desperately close then. Like as not she was babysitting while he went out to capture provisions. Sort of, 'Cry Baby Bunting, Daddy's gone a-hunting'. But surely he wasn't the father.

'OK.' Lawson pulled the conversation back to the events of the evening. 'Where did he go when he left here?'

'I've already said — down the alley at the back. It's fenced a short way down on both sides but then one side has fallen down. There's an expanse of wasteland, I figured he'd make for there. There's no place to hide. I'd see him. That'd be that. But he'd gone. I looked for a while.' He shrugged. 'I don't know.'

'Ranjit?' Both men turned to face the white-haired gentleman who had appeared silently in the doorway.

'Mr Lawson, this is my father.'

Lawson shook hands, made polite reference to the 'ugly business of the evening'. Mr

Patel Snr gave a tired smile. 'It is happening too often,' he said and turned to his son. 'I have closed the shop for the evening. I keep seeing shadows helping themselves to our profits. If you'll excuse me gentlemen,' he backed away from the door towards some stairs halfway along the passage. 'I'm going to turn in.'

Lawson waited until Ranjit's attention was fully on him again before he spoke once more. 'This girl you saw, have you seen her before?'

'Not before she helped herself to a loaf of bread, no.'

'You didn't catch her name?'

'Ah!' Ranjit waved a slender index finger in the air. 'Am I supposed to ask customer's names as they enter my shop in case they intend to leave without paying?'

'No. Why didn't you report that incident?'

'Because it happens. It's one of the hazards of being a shopkeeper — anyone will tell you that. Police come, shrug their shoulders, say there's nothing they can do except advise us about prevention. What kind of crap is that?' The young man's voice had risen to a shout. His words hung on the air. He sighed. 'I'm sorry, I shouldn't have said that. I know you're only trying to help, but it gets so frustrating. And then there's the colour thing.' He looked Lawson up and down. 'I can't help feeling that the fact we're from Asian extraction makes our case that much harder to plead. People assume we're making a fortune — and stealing their birthright. It's not the case. But I don't suppose I need convince you of how hard that can be.' His expression was conspiratorial.

'No.' But Lawson wasn't going to embroider. Wasn't going to admit to lying awake at night wondering whether there'd be graffiti sprayed on the front door, dog shit through the letter box, or worse, a lit firework. All three had happened on occasion when he'd been a child. And if these things happened to the house of a man of God, how must it be for regular citizens?

'I want him caught. I want a spectacle made of him. I want someone to start taking us seriously.' Ranjit stood. 'And if that's all, I really ought to be doing my evening rounds — making sure everything's secure for the night.'

'Sure.' Lawson pocketed his notebook. 'We'll do all we can,' he was bleakly aware of how hollow the words sounded. 'And if you remember anything else . . . '

'Yes, surely.'

He headed for the alley. Might as well walk that way while he was here. He came to the wasteland sooner than he'd expected, stood for several minutes looking. No hiding place — but plenty of cover. That lad could easily have dropped flat and not been seen. Anywhere. No point looking for clues, he'd be here all night. Without a backward glance he headed back to his car, remembering as he reached the streetlight outside the shop that he still hadn't rung Mum. Shit! He really must, exhausting though it was, train his mind to remember to ring Mum before the middle of the night. Tightlipped, he drove away, ready to face the music.

20

Blue was angry. Jacob glanced back one more time before leaving the bedroom and going downstairs. Blue was livid. Never had Jacob seen a baby so distraught. He'd tried everything he could think of; singing — he didn't know any nursery rhymes but had tried a couple of rugby songs his dad had taught him. Then he rocked the child; threatened him; even smacked him lightly on the bulk of his nappy. Nothing had worked. Leaving him to scream himself to sleep was probably best. Maybe some sixth sense was telling him that his mother was lying dead on the riverbank. Maybe she'd just visited him, a ghostly vision in the bedroom. Jacob shuddered, looked down at Dotty's fading chalkline on the lounge floor. One ghost was more than enough for Storm Mount.

Danny had killed Tabbi. That much Jacob was certain of. Proving it and making the police believe him was going to be quite a task. He still hadn't reported Tabbi's death. Hugging his knees and rocking backwards and forwards on the dusty floorboards, he asked himself why. And he couldn't answer.

Not truly. One brush with the law had been enough — when he'd rung to report Dotty's death. Maybe they had some kind of scanner that recognised voices. He'd be incriminated purely because he'd been the one to find both bodies. How would he prove he'd not done the dirty deeds? Best to keep quiet. Didn't want to be locked away for something he hadn't done. Knew about all that, Dad was always going on about stuff like that. Mind you, Dad's innocence was dubious at the best of times.

He listened. Still Blue bawled. Jacob hadn't dared risk putting him in Tabbi's bed. Two reasons. One, he was frightened the baby would roll out and hurt himself. Two, Jacob hadn't dared enter Tabbi's room since he'd heard those strange noises. Now he wondered if they'd been made by Tabbi's ghost coming back to rest here. He shuddered. No, Blue would stay strapped in his buggy. Best place for him.

What would James Bond do in a situation like this? Jacob pondered. It was all supposition. Never had James Bond come up against the forces of the supernatural. His enemies were human — or superhuman — but they could be killed in normal ways. No need for a silver bullet or a crucifix, stake or garlic. And how did you kill a ghost anyway? Escapism or something, he remembered vaguely, something a vicar did. He thought briefly of the vicar in the church but decided against asking him. Vicars so set in routine as he was probably weren't open-minded enough to understand about malevolent ghosts.

With tears running down his face, Jacob went upstairs to retrieve Blue. He touched his hands. Ice. 'What the fuck do you want?' He demanded of the distraught child. 'Are you hungry? Is that it? Well, I've got nothing for you. If you'd gone to sleep when you was supposed to you'd not know whether you were hungry or not. Daft git. Stop it. *Stop it!*' Squeezing Blue to him, he headed back to the lounge.

Suddenly he was aware of a *whup, whup, whup* above his head, then a light, brighter than daylight, flooded the room. With a cry of terror, he curled up on the floor. This was it! Armageddon! The noise had either drowned out or silenced Blue's wails. Maybe he'd been beamed up. For the second time that evening Jacob found himself quietly hoping the child was no longer his responsibility.

When the light remained static and the whupping noise moved slightly away from the house, he crawled towards the back window, keeping tight into the shadows at the edge of the room. Staying below the windowsill, he scrunched up his eyes, and his courage, and peered into the garden. He ducked back down before registering anything. When, after furtive pats, he discovered his head was still in one piece, he risked another, longer look.

Lights. White and blue. Some flashing, some not. Some twitching left to right, right to left. Uniforms. Voices. Six-foot shadows with size ten boots. They'd found Tabbi. Police were searching, a helicopter flattening grass, swirling water, creating daylight. Relief, then. He'd not had to do anything this time. No one need know that he knew her.

★ ★ ★

Three hours later they were still there. Jacob had spent most of that time watching and listening, having gone up to the back bedroom for a better view. After becoming used to the first wave of noise (or maybe because Blue's shouts had become louder) Jacob had sat, crosslegged, on the bedroom floor, rocking Blue, rigid with fear, backwards and forwards.

Twice he'd shaken him, only gently, to try and underline the message that this behaviour was really pissing him off. Blue obviously didn't understand. He'd smacked him once

241

again on the nappy, not wanting to hurt, merely get his point across but his point must have got lost somewhere in the padding. Then, somewhere around four, Jacob had taken to prowling the house, Blue hanging over first one shoulder then the other.

'Shut up! Shut up! Shut up!' Jacob hissed, quietly at first, in time with his footsteps. 'Shut up! Shut up! *Shut up!*'

He dropped the baby onto the lounge windowsill. Not far to fall, particularly when landing on the padding of his nappy, but far enough to jolt him into peering silently at Jacob through eyes swollen from crying for hours. Jacob dropped to his knees, put supportive hands on Blue's waist. 'Please stop. Please. I don't know what to do with you.' Blue regarded him silently for a moment before resuming his wailing.

Jacob joined him. Silent tears dripped from his chin to the floor. What was he going to do? He armed them away, blinked furiously to focus on Blue. Maybe he should just take him to the police station, leave him on the doorstep. Maybe he could leave him at the hospital, that was nearer. A movement caught his eye, way across the road. He stopped crying, watched. An orange circle, the glow from a cigarette was swaying gently in Nosey Parker's house. Maybe she was watching the police activity, although she'd not be able to see much except the helicopter hovering over Storm Mount. Maybe she was watching him, although Tabbi's sheet was still up at the window, covering all but a few inches at each side.

He had an idea. She was a mother, wasn't she? Only to Danny James, admittedly, so she couldn't have got it all right — but she must know what to do in these circumstances. Gathering Blue in his arms, he left Storm Mount via the front door and walked across the road, looking for all the world like he'd just rescued him from a hostage situation, the light from the helicopter creating a spectacular backdrop.

He knew she was watching him. Knew she was smiling her self-satisfied smile.

Come into my parlour said the spider to the fly.

He tripped over a black sack, nearly lost his purchase on Blue, managed to hold them both upright by going down onto his knees. He yelped in pain. The porch light went on. Blue, fearfully silent now, didn't take his eyes from Jacob's face. The front door opened moments after he knocked.

'Yes?' Eleanor James leaned over her zimmer frame, cigarette dangling from the side of her mouth.

'Please.' To his embarrassment he started crying again. 'Please missus. Can you help me?'

She looked at the lad's frightened eyes, the baby's mucus-covered face. Nodded. Bogeymen like these she could deal with.

'What is it, young 'un playing up?'

'Yes.'

'His Ma not around?' Her eyes slitted suspiciously.

'No.'

Blue, silent since Eleanor had started talking, now began yelling with fresh impetus.

'And why do you think I may be able to help you?'

'Because you're a mother.'

She nodded again, apparently satisfied with his answer. 'Right you are, bring him in.'

Jacob followed her down the dark, dusty hallway, Blue struggling in his arms. The room he'd assumed was the lounge had in it a bed and, in one alcove beside the fireplace, a rail of clothes. The other alcove boasted a portable black and white TV perched on an orange box.

'Oh, is this your bedroom?' Jacob started edging backwards through the door.

Eleanor snorted. 'This is my everything room. Can't get up the stairs — haven't been able to for nigh on twelve years. God only knows what it looks like up there. Danny's the only one ever sees it these days — oh, and the cleaner goes up there sometimes.'

At the mention of Danny's name, Jacob glanced around wide-eyed. 'Is Danny here?'

'Nah.' Eleanor snorted again. 'Dunno where he is. Last seen him three days ago proper. Ducked in once or twice since,' she leant forward conspiratorially. 'But see, he takes advantage of the fact I'm not so nimble. Up and down them bloody stairs like a shadow, he is. And me calling after him like a demented fishwife.'

'I hope you don't mind me coming. I . . . I didn't know what else to do.' He forced a smile. 'Thank you.'

'Don't thank me yet — been a long time since I had to do anything like this,' she nodded at Blue. 'But I suppose it's like riding a bike — not that I ever have. Go and put the kettle on. If the little one's hungry I'm afraid he'll have to deal with cow's milk. Is that what he has anyway?'

'Dunno.'

'Not to worry, a bit won't hurt. Just enough to soothe him.'

'Right,' she continued when Jacob came back through. 'Make a bed on that chair,' she pointed to the one that had been Bill's. 'Use a blanket from the bed in the front bedroom and put those two cushions at the front to stop him rolling off.'

Jacob did as he was told.

'What's his name by the way?' She watched him arrange the cushions at Blue's feet.

'Blue.'

'Blue? What kind of name is that for a baby?'

Jacob shrugged.

'And where did you get him from?'

'I'm minding him for a friend. She's been . . . delayed.'

'That the girl I saw in Storm Mount?'

Jacob shrugged.

'That helicopter and racket something to do with her is it?'

Jacob shrugged again, kept his eyes firmly on the threadbare carpet.

'Or is it 'cos of you?' She poked his shoulder with a stubby finger.

Slowly he shook his head. Suddenly this didn't seem like such a good idea. This interrogation was making him twitchy. He edged towards Blue. 'Maybe I shouldn't have come.'

'Rubbish.' Eleanor collapsed into her armchair. A fallout of dust headed for the ceiling. 'It's an omen you coming here. You need a home, I need a lodger. Couldn't be better. There's two spare bedrooms upstairs

— Danny's is the front one but the two back rooms are free. My advice would be to take the one on the left at the top of the stairs — it's got an outside wall. Less chance of the neighbours finding out about the baby.' She poked a nicotine-yellowed finger into Blue's midriff. 'Blue.' She snorted. 'What kind of name is that?'

'It's his name. Different, but kind of nice when you get used to it.'

'I'm too old to get used to anything different now.'

Jacob studied her briefly: the white hair, the lined face, the faded clothes. Yes, he decided, she probably was. He couldn't remember knowing anyone as old as this before. Terry Flint's grandparents were old, of course, but he wasn't sure they were over eighty. If he'd had to bet on it, he'd have said that Eleanor James must be well on her way to receiving a telegram from the Queen. Had Eleanor known that, like as not she'd have ejected him from her house by one of his pink-tipped ears.

'What can I call you?'

'Mrs James.'

'But that doesn't sound very . . . friendly. Can I call you Mrs J?'

'If you like. I might not answer. Right,' Eleanor folded flabby arms over her pot belly.

'You'd better get the little sod fed. Just warm the milk with a little hot water. Is he on solids?'

'Eh?'

'What's he eating?'

'Oh.' Jacob ran the list past her.

Her face remained impassive. 'You'll maybe find some Weetabix in the kitchen. That'll have to do for now.' She saw Jacob's hesitation, held out her arms. 'Give me the babby. Give us a chance to get to know one another while you're busy.'

21

Pouring the last cup of tea from the pot, Audrey Willis carried her trophy back to her chair. She'd make the most of this cuppa. At eight o'clock she'd shower and prepare for her day. Mrs J first call, then she'd nip to CashSave for a few bits. The headlines were as usual: African unrest, train drivers threatening industrial action, teachers likewise, mortgage rates to go up. Audrey sighed feeling the lightness of the beginning of the new day already hardening into reality. She didn't take much in over the next few pages, scanning only headlines until something caught her eye, then reading a few lines to see what was what. On page thirteen her eyes froze, glazed over, her mouth opened in a tidy 'O' and a small gasp slipped out: 'GIRL FOUND MURDERED. Last night the body of a young woman was discovered on the riverbank, close to the new supermarket. As yet she has not been identified.'

Audrey read the remaining few lines, her eyes widening as she did so. The hand that replaced the cup on its saucer was trembling. It shook even more as it covered the mouth.

It became wet from the tears waterfalling through dyed lashes. Audrey slumped back in her chair, the outside world forgotten. She had tunnel vision now, with a hideous image at the end of the tunnel, not a light. The girl hasn't been identified, she told herself firmly.

But you know who it is. Who else's description could it be?

And Audrey Willis, not one for listening to voices in her head or being taken by whimsical notions, nodded. She knew. Like any mother would. Some deep animal sense told her that this girl, dead by the water, was her beautiful child. Her precious child, her only, had met a violent death on waterlogged ground beneath a tree.

Rationality peeped in for a moment. That girl could be anyone. Until there's a name, you can't be sure. It can't be her. Can't be her. Can't be.

Of course it's her. Who else could it be?

Violent death is something that strikes in a millisecond; it causes a lifetime of angst for the people close to the victim. 'Why?' Audrey looked heavenward. 'What did I do?' She slid to her knees, her pale pink dressing gown riding up her thighs. Unconsciously, she clasped her hands together, closed her eyes, whispered a prayer. Then again she asked what she'd done.

It might not be her daughter. But she was damn sure it was. Nervous energy suddenly hit, driving her to her feet, whirlwinding her out to the kitchen to deposit her cup on the draining board, upstairs to take a shower. If she went to work, this would go away. Normality would make this all a nightmare. By the time she came home, this morning would never have happened. Putting on foundation, powder blusher, eyeshadow (brown or rose?), mascara and lipstick, she knew this not to be true. It would still be here tonight. Maybe by then they'd have confirmed that this was her daughter. Not once did it occur to her to go forward, offer to identify. If she let things be, chances were it would turn out to be a fantasy. Anyway, it was best nobody knew; best for all concerned if she kept quiet and suffered silently.

By the time she was ready for the outside world, she could no longer face it. Thoughts like dervishes had stripped her of her excess energy; now she was numb. Like an automaton, she stepped into the cold day.

The cold light of day!

'Shut up!' she told the voice sharply, ignoring the stares of people in a bus queue.

Audrey Willis was the kind of person who pooh-poohed the idea of being in a daze, who couldn't believe that emotion could stand in

251

the way of rationality. Today she was going to be put sorely to the test. By evening she would realise that she was as fallible as the best (or worse) of them. It was in the aforementioned daze that she weaved her way to Mrs J's, back poker-straight, legs marching to an unheard regimental band, chin high, eyes unseeing. As if by radar, she manoeuvred around the black sacks in Mrs J's driveway. It was only now she realised she'd left the door key hanging on its nail beside her own front door. She rang the bell.

She knocked.

She rattled the letterbox.

She coo-eed through its mouth into the empty hallway.

No one in?

No chance.

Mrs J hadn't left the house in six years. She always said the only way she'd leave was in a box . . .

No!

Not again! Hope surged. It was Mrs J's body that had been discovered. Her daughter was alive.

Since when was Mrs J described as a girl? Worn out old crone is closer.

'Shut up!' she wiped sweating palms over her face, mushing carefully applied make-up into a contemporary painting. Her stomach, she noticed, was close to her Adam's apple, her knees felt as though they were in twenty feet of water. This had to be a nightmare — all of it. If she could only get back home, back to bed, to sleep, this whole thing would go away. None of it would have happened when she awoke. She could start the day again. Get it right next time.

She stepped back, stumbled over the step, put her hand out to steady herself, her eyes down to study the terrain. 'Audrey' — on a bit of paper poking from a milkbottle. She plucked it out. 'No longer require your services.'

Not even signed. Audrey tutted, folded the paper, put it in her handbag. She'd go to CashSave now, back to normal, then think things over when she got home. If, after everything else that had happened today, there hadn't been a tornado that had whisked it away. Surreal. That was how today had started, like she'd woken up in a Dennis Potter play. Bizarre. Maybe a cup of coffee in the café and a browse in the washing powder aisle would put everything back in order.

Had she looked up when she turned back to latch the gate, she'd have noticed the net curtain twitch, the orange glow from a cigarette, maybe even the frowning countenance of her erstwhile employer.

It hadn't worked. Despite half an hour checking out powders, tablets and liquids in the washing powder aisle, Audrey still had the feeling of being in a parallel universe. *If* the body on the riverbank was that of her daughter, shouldn't she do something about it? At least show some concern? Thing was, she hadn't reported the girl missing when she'd gone. Admittedly she'd been underage but Audrey had pretty much told the girl to beat it. The pregnancy had been the straw to cripple that particular camel. It wouldn't do, Audrey guiltily remembered saying, for the neighbours to know about the baby. What would they think? Bugger them, had been her daughter's reply, which pretty much summed things up for Audrey. Her precious child had been taken over by some irresponsible demon and, likely as not, was nurturing an incubus. Anyway, it wasn't as though the girl had run away. Underage or not, she'd gone by mutual consent. That was the way Audrey liked to remember it, anyway.

A man was hovering at the end of the aisle. The security guard. He'd spoken to her once already. She fixed a smile on her face, dredged her brain for a polite response, turned to face him.

It wasn't the security guard.

'Danny James.' She spoke in a voice loaded with wary surprise. 'Is your mother ill?'

'Dunno.' She thought he looked faintly abashed. 'Not seen her for a day or two.'

'Oh. I thought you'd moved back in.'

'Nah. Just passing through. Got a place of me own now.'

'Oh.' The first flush of conversation over, Audrey shuffled, turned over subjects in her mind that they both may be able to talk about. Like doing fractions; search for the common denominator. 'You're looking well.' She didn't mean it and he knew it.

'Er, thanks.' He edged backwards. 'I'd better be off. Thought it was you. Just checking.' And he was gone.

Just checking? Audrey made her way to the till, her meeting with Danny unsettling her. Strange thing to say, 'Just checking.' Acceptable if she'd caught him off guard, she supposed, but he'd come to her; he'd searched her out. Just checking what? The question kept her mind occupied as she paid for the paltry items in her basket. When it came to it, she'd not been able to concentrate on her list, finding that her appetite, never more than a sparrow's, had deserted her. She'd ended up picking up one or two things she 'might fancy later'. So involved was she in how she was going to keep her mind busy for the remainder of the day (maybe she'd dead-head the roses which bloomed consistently until Christmas) that she didn't notice Danny sitting on the bench at the entrance to the shop.

But he saw her. Smiled.

Frowned.

Jacob Palmer was heading his way. Alone. Danny watched him enter the supermarket. After a quick count of twenty he followed him in, ducking behind an elderly couple trying to steer an unobliging trolley. He didn't want to be spotted. Jacob was busy in the babyfood aisle. Danny frowned again. The lad was taking this surrogate fatherhood very seriously. Maybe he should take steps to separate them; leave the infant on a doorstep in swaddling clothes. He followed Jacob to the cake aisle, watched him pick out a ginger slab cake. His mother's favourite. Curiouser and curiouser . . . Maybe he wouldn't separate them; a lever could be useful if it came to blackmail.

Also . . .

It was a long time since Danny had been involved in snuff movies. The last one had gone wrong. Very. He'd ended up putting the poor sod out of his misery. Not such a problem when it's a dog or cat but when it's a fourteen-year-old boy, things get a bit messy. And he'd had to keep his nose clean for a very long while. In Britain at least. Holland had provided a base for the last year or two but now the heat was on him there too. Hence the sudden desire to reacquaint himself with his mother.

There were strings attached to coming back though. Danny's life had been one long string of attachments. Stan was good at attachments, never forgot when Danny owed him a favour. Now he needed a favour. Now he needed a star for his next movie. Maybe Jacob could be Danny's prodigy; the Oliver to his Fagin. Maybe he could finally make an attachment work in his favour. He was smiling as he followed Jacob from the shop. Better keep his fortune in sight. Where was he going now? He was headed for the quay. The closer they got, the stronger the tang of the sea came, the louder the cries of the gulls which swirled and wheeled over an abandoned bag of chips by the slipway.

Clutching the carrier close to his chest, Jacob ducked into Jim's Café. Danny, damp and cold, cursed. He didn't want to be hiding in a doorway in this weather. Deciding the trail had gone cold, he turned for home. The lad would soon put in an appearance anyway, what with him leaving the baby in Amber

Close. Danny smiled; from his vantage point in Storm Mount there wasn't much was going to get past him.

* * *

The café was, as usual, warm. Condensation ran down the wall behind the counter, the windows were steamed up. Jacob made for the table near the counter, tucked himself tight by the wall. Unconsciously, he'd made the decision to run, to leave Blue at Mrs James's and set off alone to start again somewhere else.

'So, what's it to be?' the red-haired waitress, who was in on Tuesdays and Fridays as a rule, smiled. 'Usual?'

Jacob nodded. Too tired to think or speak, he was glad of the familiarity of the place. He just wished . . . but that was no use. Tabbi was dead.

'You OK son?' Jim, hands full of cases of baked beans, entered through the front door. 'Your friend not with you today?'

'Friend?'

'The girl — the one with the baby?' Jim looked amazed as Jacob burst into tears. 'Whatever is the matter?'

'Nothing.'

'My arse.' He grunted as he dumped the

baked beans on the counter. 'Just been to the cash and carry — anything to keep the missus off my back. Just let me take these through the back and we'll have a little chat. Shan't be a mo.'

Jacob didn't care whether he was a mo or a decade, he didn't want to talk, to be comforted, or worse, to have to face the police and have to be reminded of Tabbi and what had happened. He was scared, confused, unsure of what to do now. His urge was to go home, to fall into his mother's arms and let her deal with everything. Only he hadn't got a mother — and he hadn't got a home. The only person he could turn to was Mrs J — and she was about as much use as a mermaid in the desert. His fingers curled around Tabbi's diary, which he'd found wrapped in her 'day' clothes, in his pocket. Next to it was her mobile phone. Fascinating things, mobile phones. An invention which caused individuals, whilst conducting private conversations, to scream, in body language, 'Look at me, I've got friends; I'm important enough for people to want to ring me 24–7.'

Tabbi had always huddled in corners with hers, talking in a hushed monotone which ceased the moment she thought he was within hearing. He was never close enough to identify a word, never mind who she was talking to. Now though, he'd be able to play with it himself. She'd explained to him about having to buy a token to buy air time but he thought it was nearly fully charged. He'd check it out later when he got back to Mrs J's. Unconsciously, it seemed, he'd decided to go back.

Jim put a plate of food before him. He nodded his thanks, realised suddenly how hungry he was.

'I've just been listening to the radio while I was frying your egg.' Jim's face, Jacob noticed, looked tired and grey. 'A body's been found by the river. It's not your friend is it?'

Jacob shrugged.

'I know they've not officially identified her yet, but she fits the description. Maybe you didn't know . . . ?' Jim let the question, the get-out clause, hang in the air before continuing. 'I lost my best pal when I was about your age, maybe a bit older. Fell off a railway bridge right under the 11:15. Fooling about we were, whole gang of us. One minute he was there, next minute he was splattered on the track. Shut it away, never talked about it to no one — thought it would make me a sissy. It doesn't though. Talking about things is the best way to deal with them, I reckon. Stops your brain getting bogged down with the weight of it all if you share it with someone.'

Jacob, vigorously dissecting a sausage, ignored him.

'Of course, *when* you talk is quite up to you. Grief is a personal thing.' Jim remembered an article he'd read in one of his wife's magazines. 'Everybody deals with different things at different rates. If it helps, I understand what you're going through. If you need someone to talk to, I'll be honoured to supply the ear — and as much fried bread as you can eat.' It was meant to lighten the atmosphere but the boy had closed down completely, his face blank, his eyes staring at the hole he'd made in his fried egg.

Jim got to his feet, took up his place behind the counter. From time to time he glanced at the boy, but not once did Jacob return the favour. As soon as he'd finished his meal, Jacob left without a word and, although Jim didn't know it then, it would be the last time Jacob graced Jim's Café with his presence.

How could anyone else understand? The tears flowed freely now as he ran along the quay, kicking an empty can viciously several times before it disappeared into the water. He, Jacob, was twelve and he was responsible for a baby. Not occasionally, like had been originally agreed, but all the time. Since Tabbi had gone and got killed,

261

Blue had belonged to him.

How dare you think of abandoning Blue! That was Tabbi's voice. Jacob stopped.

You'd better get back before the old witch claims him for her own.

'Tabbi, how could you?' Jacob screamed into the wind, startling a man beneath an umbrella, fishing. 'Why did you do it? Why did you leave me?' Sobbing noisily now, he ran back towards the town, tears blurring his view so that he knocked people, clonked lamp-posts with his carrier bag, stumbled across roads. She'd done what his mum had done — promised to be there and then gone to another place. For all he knew, they were in the same place, Mum and Tabbi. A small part of him couldn't believe that his mum wouldn't have tried to get in touch with him. She must be dead.

Your Dad got to her letters when they landed on the mat. Tore them up, he did. She thought you didn't care and stopped writing.

Jacob ignored the voice. He didn't know what to believe any more.

Riverside View. He stopped. The name of the street had popped so clearly in his mind that he might have read it on a signpost. Where had it come from? His fingers tightened around Tabbi's diary. It was there, under 'Mum'. Maybe he should go there, see Tabbi's mum, explain what had happened.

Blue will have to go and live there — and then what will you do? You'll have nobody then, nobody in this big, wide world that you can call a friend.

'It wouldn't be like that,' Jacob slowed to a walk, holding his sides to limit the pain a stitch was giving him. He was nearly back at Mrs J's. Another moment or two and he'd have to think of an explanation as to why he'd been so long.

You might even get the blame for keeping Blue away from his real family; you might go to prison.

That decided it — prison was not somewhere he ever wanted to go. He'd heard enough tales about prison life from Dad to know that it was no picnic. (The only thing, his maternal grandmother would have said, that his wretched father ever did to help him grow up with any sense of responsibility at all.) No, for the time being at least, he had to keep Blue at Mrs J's. Soon, if he could get rid of the ghost, Storm Mount would be ready for its new family. Soon he'd be in control of his destiny.

22

Guilt.

Lawson watched the dawn breaking over the skyline. To his left, the monoliths masquerading as tower blocks, to his right, the hospital chimney that always made him think of the death camps. What did they use it for? Imagination already ripe due to lack of sleep — or maybe Jack Daniel's — he changed his view. Having already tried to cajole his mother since he got home — and failed — he'd hit the bottle.

Guilt.

He'd tried to explain that he'd been called to a body before he'd managed to get home; that the shock had jolted the necessity to ring his mother clean from his mind. Once upon a time she would have humoured him, at least; listened to his carefully constructed excuses before blowing her top. Tonight she'd hardly given him chance to open his mouth. And all he could do was scream at her that another woman was dead — this one no more than a girl; that she'd died, alone and frightened and in agony, and he'd listened to his mother crumple as she relived the night the same

264

thing had happened to her husband, his father.

Guilt.

He tried not to think of his father's death. He tried not to consider the fear, the panic that must have surged through the six-foot black man's frame when faced with death. Murder. The man who'd earned respect, had met his maker in the most violent of ways — stabbed by a gang of youths that were probably the offspring of his parishioners.

Yet the respect his father had won was not shared by his mother. She'd had years of not knowing what people were going to say to her. 'Hello, how's the Rev. Lawson?' or 'How's the black man's bit of stuff?' And worse. Yet it had been as hard for him. Schoolyards are not the easiest of places to be when you're a different colour to almost everyone else, taller than everyone else — and a vicar's son to boot. It taught him to be hard. It taught him to believe in himself. It taught him to view himself as a vigilante, someone to stand alone and put the world to rights. That was before his father's death. Since then, he'd realised that no one man could make a stand against evil; he had to have company. Hence his transfer to the police force from a promising career in accountancy. And it was trust in himself that had led him through the jeers he got during training — and not all from fellow cadets. Once more, his colour made him stand out. He emptied the glass. Take tonight: some smartarse comment from one of the officers. Instead of bristling, of standing to be counted, he'd laughed along with the rest of them, glad that darkness hid the fury in his eyes.

Time was when something like that would push the paranoia button and he'd spend the night rewinding conversations, meetings with the persons concerned; was this a personal dig? He poured another Jack Daniel's, downed it in one. Guilt now, not paranoia. Guilt that he was denying his birthright to make himself more acceptable. At school his peers were always asking what his dad did, nobody asked any more. That was a sign of age. Once you reached the end of your teens you became a person in your own right, not judged by the job your parents did or by who they were in society. No, you had to take responsibility for your own life.

And your mother's.

He stared glumly at his front door. Should he ring her again? Plead forgiveness, apologise profusely? No, he didn't think so. In the long run it would only make things worse. He'd better leave her. He contemplated bed.

Nah. Less than four hours before he had to brown-nose to Dungannon again. Best thing he could do was sober up. With the Rolling Stones playing quietly in the background, he went through to the kitchen to perc some coffee.

★   ★   ★

'You've been a long time.' Eleanor eyed Jacob suspiciously. 'Take Blue up there once you've unpacked the stuff you need to leave down here.' She followed him through to the kitchen, grunting and tutting with each item he took from the carrier. 'Disposable nappies!' She exploded as he lifted out the last thing. 'Disposable nappies! In my day we had no such thing — proper terry towelling, lets the baby's bottom breathe — not like tying it up in a plastic bag. What good's that to anyone?'

Jacob didn't care as long as it kept the gooey stuff under control but he didn't want to say anything.

'Jars of food?' She shuffled across the kitchen, slippers sticking to the greasy tiles like flies on flypaper. 'In my day babbies ate what we did, just mashed it up was all. Better for them — none of these additives they're all allergic to now. Them things what make 'em bounce up and down all night. That's probably what's the matter with little 'un, you've been feeding him processed crap. Good wholesome food is what he needs.'

Probably, thought Jacob, but there wasn't much evidence of that in *this* kitchen.

'And I bet they're expensive, these jars. Everything is so expensive these days if you don't make it yourself. You're not to buy any more jars, Blue can have what we eat. And as for disposable nappies — you can use that packet and then we'll think again.'

Jacob nodded, stepped back towards the hall. 'Back bedroom, did you say?'

'Yes. It has a window that opens. You can take me lad's buggy up there and let him sleep by it in an afternoon. That way, no one need know he's here. That room used to be Danny's. Loved it. Grew rosy apples in his cheeks. Didn't give me a moment's worry then.'

Jacob stepped back another step. Mrs J slammed a cup down on the work surface, making him jump.

'You *were* a long time. Are you sure you only went to CashSave?'

'Ye-es. It was busy. I had to wait ages to pay.' Jacob hoped his face wasn't colouring. He didn't want her to think he was lying. He was reluctant to reveal all his secrets to this woman. Already he was regretting involving her.

'It's like that sometimes.' She followed him slowly into the lounge where Blue was sprawled on the faded yellow candlewick bedspread covering the sofa bed. 'Look at him.' Without turning, Jacob heard the smile in her voice. 'Look so cute, don't they? Like they're never going to be a moment's trouble. I can remember Danny coming in from school . . . '

Jacob sighed. He'd heard enough about Danny.

' . . . bag flying behind him, knees filthy, dirty from playing football. Boys wore shorts then, didn't grow up too fast.' She glared disapprovingly at Jacob's holey Reeboks. 'You remind me of him a bit, before he went wrong. Now I've been given another chance — and you won't go wrong.'

Jacob, intent on picking up Blue without waking him, wasn't really listening to what she was saying. Even had he been he probably wouldn't have understood her mumblings. 'Where's Danny now?' He asked brightly, thinking she was easier to bear when talking about her son rather than moaning at him.

'Gone away. To . . . Portugal I think he said. Somewhere exotic anyway. For all the bad things he got up to, he managed to turn his life around. Knows people all over the world. Goes to stay with them when . . . things get too much for him. Pressure of work,' she added hastily, seeing the question in Jacob's eyes.

Something wasn't ringing true. Suddenly Jacob was sure he'd made the wrong move in coming here. Somehow he had to reverse it.

'Maybe it would be better if Blue and I went home. After all, it's a lot to expect you to put up with — a crying baby when you're used to this place to yourself. He seems to have settled now. I'm sure he'll be OK if I take him back across the road.'

A shadow crossed her face. 'It's no trouble, really.'

'But . . . ' Suddenly he'd had enough of this place. He wished that policeman, the dark-skinned one, the one with the nice face, would come back. Never in his life before had he wished to see a policeman. *Too soft.* He heard his father's voice. *Too fucking soft.*

'Across the road? But this is your home now.'

'No. Storm Mount is my — our — home.'

'But you can't stay there. You're not old enough.'

Ominous recollections of this same conversation with Tabbi. 'It never bothered you before.'

'There wasn't a young baby there before. Anyway, I used to ring the police.'

'But only 'cos you thought I was going to break in here. Now you know I won't you can let me go back.'

'How do I know it? I don't. Anyway, I have my duty to do, bring you up properly. It's what Bill would have wanted.'

Jacob looked around, this was getting really scary. 'Who's Bill?'

Eleanor didn't get the chance to answer. Blue chose that moment to open his mouth and proclaim loud and long that he was hungry.

'I'll go.' She turned with surprising nimbleness, adding to Jacob's discomfort that all was not as it seemed, and headed for the kitchen. She appeared moments later, a jar and a spoon on the tray in front of her zimmer.

Unscrewing the lid, Jacob sniffed it, pulled a face, loaded the spoon and eased it into the child's wide-open mouth. Blue, he decided, watching the child guzzle it, must have no sense of smell and a stomach lined with tin. Still, he was eating well. With any luck he'd catch up on the sleep he'd lost last night, give Jacob a chance to think things through and try and find a way out of this situation.

Eleanor grabbed the half-empty jar when

271

Blue was sated. 'I'm not having any more of this poison in my house. Do you understand? From here on in he has wholesome food, lovingly prepared. That's how babies thrive.' With a fearsome glance at Jacob, she manoeuvred her zimmer down the hall, opened the front door and threw the jar in the general direction of the black sacks. It crashed with the sickening crunch of broken glass. 'You can clear that up when you've finished with Blue.'

Like bloody hell I will. Jacob sniffed delicately at Blue's nappy.

'And if you run away, I shall ring the police and tell them you stole a baby.' Eleanor, as though reading his thoughts, shuffled back into the room, a sheen of perspiration on her forehead at the effort.

Now he was really fucked. Jacob sighed. It would take a phenomenal plan to get out of this. Blue, choosing that moment to fill his nappy, seemed to agree.

★ ★ ★

The room was basically furnished — a single bed, a chest of drawers, plenty of dust and cobwebs. Grunting with distaste, Jacob set to work making the bed safe for Blue; he didn't want him falling out. He tapped his pocket;

272

there was something he needed to do as soon as Blue was asleep.

Danny's bedroom was furnished better — it had a wardrobe. Jacob crept in, closed the door slowly, listening for any sounds other than his pounding heart. He had to be quick; didn't trust Mrs J for a moment. For all he knew that zimmer of hers turned into a broomstick when she needed to fly upstairs.

A quick peek beneath the bed revealed nothing but dust; the chest of drawers was empty save for half a dozen pairs of elderly Y-fronts and four and a half pairs of socks. The wardrobe, then. He gingerly crossed the bare floorboards, not wanting to advertise his presence in Danny's room to anyone listening below. The wardrobe door was stiff. He yanked it. It opened with a jerk that sent him two steps back into the centre of the room. He froze, listened. The noise he'd made should have woken the dead; apparently the quick downstairs had other things on their minds.

Two pairs of tatty jeans and three faded shirts hung in the wardrobe along with a faded blue anorak so old its quilting was leaking through the seams. On the floor of the wardrobe was a pair of trainers that looked old enough to be the first pair ever to be invented and, pushed right to the back corner, a metal cash box.

Jacob trawled his pockets, produced the key Danny had dropped in the churchyard the other morning. Holding his breath, he introduced the key to the lock, smiling grimly as it fitted and turned. The box wasn't holding any money. That was the first shock. Jacob had always assumed that something called a 'cash box' would automatically be used for holding cash. The other shock was what he actually *did* find; photos. And not your regular holiday snaps. Pictures of children mainly, some women; all of them naked; most (to Jacob's young eyes) in unnatural, even painful positions. He slammed the lid down, turned the key, started to push the box back. Stopped. Shaking as he was, something told him that what he'd discovered could be important.

Always capitalise on your opportunities.

Unlocking the box once more, he took a handful of the photos, leaving just enough, he hoped, to fool a cursory glance should Danny come looking. He headed to his room, painfully aware that he was taking longer than he'd planned. Mrs J would be after him soon.

Just as long as it's no one else.

The first hiding place he thought of, under his mattress, he discounted as being too obvious if Danny came looking. He settled, for now, on stuffing them at the bottom of Blue's bag. Danny wasn't likely to risk hunting in there and coming across a dirty nappy. Then, smugly satisfied with his work, he went back downstairs.

23

'In my office in five minutes, Sonny Jim.'

Lawson groaned. Dungannon's office in five was bad enough, being called by a diminutive meant that the boss was trying to seem nice; which was always a worrying sign. Time to grab an extra-strong black coffee from the canteen. As he entered, trying to ignore the smell of fried breakfasts to stop his stomach somersaulting, he noticed Kate Rogers at a table under the window engrossed in a conversation with a dark-haired DI who was laughing just that little bit too loudly.

'Bastard!' Lawson muttered under his breath, grabbed a coffee and left at a run.

'Seb?'

Kate.

Pretend you haven't heard her.

'Seb?' This time a tap on his shoulder.

'Oh . . . hi.'

'I called before — '

'Yes, I didn't hear you. That is . . . ' he stopped, dropped his shoulders. 'Look, I'm in a hurry. Can we talk later?'

She frowned. 'Sure. I'm on my way to the

big D's office, maybe I could walk along with you.'

'Big D?'

'Dungannon.' She laughed, an angel in the vestry of Hell. 'Don't tell me you've not heard that.'

'Dungannon?'

'Yeah, you know, big, hairy, Yeti-like creature only known to hunt when he smells rotting martyr.'

Lawson laughed briefly. 'I've got to see him too.'

'I know dummy, it's a conflab about the hoo-ha last night.'

'What, with everyone?'

'Yes.'

'Not just me?'

'No. Why?'

'Nothing.' He let out a long sigh. 'It's just that I couldn't decide whether to use my arsenic ampoule in my coffee now or ask for another cup later as my final request.'

Kate studied him, a frown flickering across her forehead. She shook her head. 'You're quite mad, Sebastian. Quite mad.'

'Runs in the family.'

'Along with the paranoia?'

He hesitated. 'That obvious huh?'

'Yep.' They reached the office, Kate held the door open for him to pass with his coffee.

As he did so she whispered. 'Jolly Tar, eight o'clock.' Deciphering his frown she explained. 'You said you wanted to talk later.'

He stopped, watched her become engulfed in the mob of policemen. Suddenly time seemed to have stopped.

'Lawson,' Dungannon appeared in his vision. 'Are you joining us — or will you be requiring transfer to the job of doorman?'

'Er . . . sorry sir.' Suitably abashed, Lawson slunk to the back of the room, cradling his styrofoam cup.

'What we have here,' Dungannon, satisfied that all attention was on him, waved a shirt-sleeved arm towards the white board centre front of the room. 'Are the details of the body found on the riverbank last night. Coincidentally the body is female, was not far from the house Storm Mount where Dotty Spangle's body was found. Footprints around last night's so-far-unidentified body seem to be those of a young teenager, maybe the same one who raised the alarm over Dotty?'

'Is that the killer then, sir?' Came a voice from the back.

'Very unlikely — but there seems to be a connection between this person and the dead women nonetheless — and the sooner we trace him or her — '

'Him.'

Dungannon frowned. 'Yes Lawson, we all know who it *probably* is.'

'I don't.' The same voice from the back.

'Just returned from Mars, have we?' Dungannon was now snarling. 'We think this person is probably one Jacob Palmer, truant, canary thief, regular troublemaker — '

'At the grand old age of twelve.'

'Would you like to exchange places, Lawson?' Lawson shook his head. Dungannon cleared his throat, continued. 'Unfortunately we cannot locate Jacob. Unless . . . WPC Rogers, you were looking into that. Any joy?'

'No sir,' Kate shook her head. 'I'm liaising with his social worker, she'll inform me if she finds him.'

'I see. Good. Early ideas . . . '

Lawson spoke, he couldn't resist this. 'What was the name of Jacob's social worker again?'

'Sophie Sullivan,' supplied Kate.

'Thank you.' Lawson watched with satisfaction as Dungannon's face went pale at the name once more.

'Early ideas . . . ' continued Dungannon, looking at neither Lawson or Kate ' . . . seem to agree that this girl, too, was a prostitute. M.O. appears to be the same — strangulation,' he squinted towards the back of the room. 'For those of you who have just returned to this uninspiring planet, then, slight differences: the age, for one. This girl was just that — a girl. Sixteen tops, though conservative guesses make her less than that.

'Also, she has borne a child in the not-too-distant past. Whether that child remained with her or found its way to pastures new we'll, hopefully, discover at a later date.' He paused, checked his congregation. Satisfied they were still all wide awake, he continued. 'Now the good bit, boys and girls: door to door. Amber Close seems a good place to start. Some of you have already done that stretch. If you *did* go that route following Dotty's death, I would appreciate you calling on the same houses, with the same partner . . . '

Kate Rogers looked across, winked at Lawson. His shoes suddenly became totally fascinating.

' . . . the savages tend to respond better if they recognise the copper they shat on the night before.' He stretched, tucked his shirt back in. 'And, as the saying goes, take care out there — I can't be doing with any lawsuits 'cos you goons can't stick to the speed limit or control your handcuffs. Any questions?'

'How's Stan Rawlings?' Lawson said. 'Have you heard?'

'No change. Still in a coma.' He looked around. 'That it?' Nods and numbles. Dungannon made for the door, paused. 'Lawson?'

'Sir?'

'Accompany me along the corridor, will you?'

'Sir.' His stomach dived for the floor.

Kate Rogers brushed against him. 'I guess now's the time for the arsenic.' She laughed at his panic-stricken face. 'Be positive. It'll be fine.'

It wasn't.

'What are you doing tonight Lawson?' Dungannon was half a stride ahead, his broad shoulders denying Lawson the glory of walking at his side.

'I'm busy actually sir,' he said, thanking the Lord for Kate.

'Nothing you couldn't put off? Only I think it would be advantageous for the two of us to socialise, get to know each other a bit.'

'Look,' Lawson stopped, expecting Dungannon to do the same. He didn't. Lawson trotted to catch up. 'I've promised to take my mother out tonight. You know how delicate things can be . . . Maybe another time?'

'Very well. Let me know when it's convenient.'

Lawson watched the disappearing back of

his boss, a cold finger of unease climbing his spine. He'd lied! He'd lied to his boss!

It was only a white lie, but a lie nonetheless.

★ ★ ★

Number one Amber Close sat like a grieving partner at the side of a grave. Curtains half-drawn, nets half-clean, gate swinging open, black bags spilt and spewing trash across the drive. It looked for all the world like the desire to keep itself decent had quietly left with the dawn.

'Oh dear,' Kate Rogers paused at the gate.

'Looks worse in daylight, doesn't it?'

'Most of us do.' She threw him a sidelong glance, giggled at his unsure smile. 'Particularly when we're vampires.'

'And you call me mad.' He pushed the gate right back, propped a half-brick against it and made his way carefully up the path.

'Foxes?' WPC Rogers eyed the mess.

'Probably.' Lawson answered quietly. He'd spotted something amongst the rubbish that had set his mind wondering. He rang the doorbell. To his surprise, the door was promptly opened.

'You again. Come in. Bring the other one with you if you like.' Eleanor James, resplendent in cigarette-burnt nightie and lavender-coloured shower cap, turned the zimmer and headed back down the hall. Blue veins traversed the layers of cellulite not covered by the nightie. Lawson tried not to look. 'I was just having a wash. You don't mind if I finish up, do you?'

'Go right ahead.' Lawson watched her disappear into the kitchen. She would have done no matter what he'd said.

'Had a bad night. I'm all behind this morning,' she explained through the closed kitchen door. Lawson and Rogers, hovering in the hall, exchanged glances.

'Anything in particular?' Lawson asked as she finally reappeared.

She wasn't going to be conned so easily. 'Why do you say that? What's happened to bring you slathering at my doorstep again?'

'Another woman was found murdered last night.' Lawson wished she was sitting down, he didn't fancy his chances of holding onto her should she collapse in shock.

'Oh, that. Oh yes, I'd worked that out.'

'Had you? How?' WPC Rogers stepped forward.

'I'm not daft, missy. Coppers all over. Helicopter overhead. Dogs barking. Any wonder we had a disturbed night.'

'We?' Lawson jumped on the slip.

'I mean I . . . I was forgetting Danny wasn't here.' The fact that she couldn't hold onto his gaze told him otherwise.

'Easy mistake to make.' Lawson barely hid the sarcasm. 'Did you hear or see anything unusual before the police arrived last night?'

'No. Never notice anything once I've closed the curtains for the night.'

And that, Lawson knew, was total crap.

A creak overhead.

'Is Danny home?' Lawson peered up the stairs.

'No!' She shuffled forward in an attempt to get between him and the staircase should he decide to leap up them. 'No. Must just be the house waking up. You know how they creak and sigh. Actually,' she laughed self-consciously. 'I *did* see someone yesterday — or maybe it was the day before: young girl — dark hair and a pretty grey-blue top. Very attractive she was. At first I thought it was the girl at Storm Mount but now, thinking about it, I'm not so sure.'

'I see. But this dark-haired girl *could* have been the one at Storm Mount? Do you mean there's someone *living* there?'

'No. Just seen her around.'

'I see. And it's likely it was that girl and not another one?'

'Probably.'

'OK. So where's Danny now then?'

'Somewhere hot. He's gone on holiday. That's all I know.'

'When's he due back?' Lawson smiled. 'Oh, sorry, I forgot. He doesn't even know when he's getting out of prison, does he?'

Rogers jabbed him in the ribs with her elbow. Eleanor James's eyes filled with tears. She rubbed them away, jutted her jaw. 'That was harassment. I'll be in touch with your superior if you continue in that tone.'

And Lawson, although he'd picked up that particular interview technique from Dungannon, knew damn well that his boss would interpret his squirms and apologies the same way Hannibal Lector does an invitation to dinner.

'I'm very sorry, Mrs James. I too had a bad night and I seem to have left my best manners at home with the shirt I took off at three-ish this morning.'

Maybe it was the common connection, the bad night that hit her conscience. She nodded. 'I accept your apology. I realise it must be very difficult for you, these murders and no suspect in sight.'

'Just one more question, Mrs James — '

'Actually,' WPC Rogers tapped his elbow. 'I really think we ought to be going now.'

'But — '

'Goodbye, Mrs James. Thank you for your co-operation.'

'But — '

'Shut up,' she hissed, grabbing his elbow and shoving him out into the freezing daylight.

'Why did you do that?' He was breathless having followed her, at a run, across the Close and down the side of Storm Mount to the riverbank behind the white house.

'There was someone there.'

'Mrs J.'

'No, someone else.' She turned a flushed face towards him. 'There was someone upstairs. I heard them moving about.'

'Danny?'

Rogers shrugged. 'Who knows. But she certainly wasn't alone in there; though she was certainly keen to make out she was.'

'Was it a child . . . baby?'

She looked at him askance. 'I heard pressure on a floorboard. Unfortunately today I left my gadget at home that tells me the age and specifications of the footsteps.'

'No need for sarcasm. It was a perfectly legitimate question.'

'If you're Mr Spock, yes.'

'Live long and prosper.'

'We'll not be doing that if Big D catches us dragging our heels.'

'One more legitimate question before we get back to the trail. If you were so sure there was someone upstairs why didn't you ask to go up instead of dragging me out? We've got to gain entry again now.'

'Because I knew that's what you'd want to do. Don't you see? She's dealt with the law before. She'd have us hung, drawn and quartered if we tried to do anything without a search warrant. What?' She noticed Lawson's puzzled face.

'There's a light on over there,' he jerked his head towards Storm Mount.

'So? Someone left it on is all.'

Lawson shrugged. 'Maybe. Except it's an empty house. All known residents are members of the Twilight Zone.'

'There you are then.'

'How many ghosts do you know need electric lights to see their way around?' He started up the garden towards the back door.

Rogers, memories of her brush with the parrot still fresh in her mind, kept a respectful distance. She touched the scratches on her face. With a layer of make-up they were barely noticeable, or so she wanted to believe, and fortunately, although she'd been getting strange looks, no one had come out and asked her where they'd come from. So far she

287

hadn't had to admit to losing the parrot.

The rabbit-hutch door hung off its top hinge, the straw inside was black and wet. Lawson turned away. He hoped that wasn't some sort of metaphor. This case felt as though it was rotting around him.

The kitchen door was ajar. Footprints interlaced across the dusty floor like A-roads on a map. He had no way of telling whether they'd appeared since SOCO had left. He heard Kate Rogers' feet crunching along behind him; heard her breath — short, nervous. At the lounge door he paused, took a deep breath before peering in and satisfying himself that no body lay there. Dotty's chalkline was all but gone. A dead bunch of flowers lay about where her heart would have been. He shuddered.

'Someone stepped on your grave?' WPC Rogers whispered.

'Don't.' Slower now, he headed up the stairs, making short work of the three-stair gap, pausing to offer a hand to the WPC.

'Thanks Raleigh but I can manage.'

'Never know how to tell whether a woman is feminist, butch or just plain bloody-minded. Safer to do the old-fashioned dance, that way you can only be told to get lost.'

'I didn't mean that.'

His face softened. 'I know.'

'Can you smell that?'

He sniffed, nodded. Citrus, he thought, with a touch of sandalwood perhaps, though he was no expert. 'Aftershave.'

'Ghost?' She tried a shaky smile.

He shook his head. 'Not likely.'

Sometimes, just sometimes, he wished he was armed. Wished he didn't have the disadvantage in these blind situations. He felt so naked here at the top of the stairs, three doors, all closed, on various sides of him. Anything could pop out, Jack-in-a-box-style. He did his Raleigh bit again, keeping Rogers tucked well behind him. This time she didn't complain.

'Crouch down,' he hissed under his breath. 'He won't be expecting that.' He hunkered down too, wishing he didn't feel such a coward, wishing he'd made things straight with Mum last night. Movement by awkward movement, he slid, almost on his belly, to the first door, the bathroom. Turning the knob meant he had to half-stand, sucking in a deep breath, he slammed the door back against the wall.

Empty.

He turned back to WPC Rogers. She had her eyes shut. 'All clear,' he whispered, then winked when she opened her eyes. 'Next one.'

Same performance.

Same result.

Now for the front bedroom. Again he crouched, turned the knob, but this time he jumped back as he slammed open the door. Nothing. Except . . . a lingering whiff of aftershave, stronger here, like someone had recently made their escape.

Lawson looked around. Wardrobes. He jerked his head at Rogers, indicating for her to stand one side while he stood the other. Together they each opened a door, stepped back an unconscious step, stared at emptiness. Lawson shrugged, looked at the window. Rogers crossed the room, peered out, shook her head. On her way back across the room she caught sight of something in the corner of her eye, stopped, put a hand to her mouth to stifle the gasp that escaped.

'What is it?' Lawson was at her side in two strides.

The parrot lay dead beside the bed, it's head neatly severed from its body.

'Poor thing.' Rogers rubbed her face. 'If I'd known that was going to happen to it, I'd have tried to catch it the other day.'

'What other day?' Lawson turned her to face him. 'You've been back here?' She nodded. 'Alone?'

She nodded again. 'I'll tell you about it

later. Meantime, what do we do with the body?'

'Bag it and take it in.' Lawson pulled a plastic bag from his pocket.

'What'll they do with it?'

'Don't know. Maybe they'll want to do a post mortem.'

'I think cause of death is fairly obvious.'

'Maybe that's what you're supposed to think.'

She threw him a doubtful smile. 'You are kidding right?'

'Right.'

'Good, 'cos can you imagine the stink if the taxpayers ever find out we use their money to put rabbits under surveillance and do post mortems on parrots?'

'Yeah.' Lawson dropped to his hands and knees, checking underneath the bed. Nothing. Above the bed was a mirror. He stared at this for a long moment before catching WPC Rogers' mock-astonished expression in the reflection. It wasn't often he thanked the Lord he was black, but today he did. At least it didn't reveal the fact that he was blushing.

'There's your ghost Mr Lawson,' she stepped around him to get to the door. 'Vaporises through the mirror when the police come a-calling.'

Had she realised how close to the truth those words were as she and Lawson left the house, she may have glanced back — and maybe caught sight of the scowling face watching them leave.

24

'Try him with mashed potato and cheese tonight.' Eleanor James shuffled in her chair in an effort to get more comfortable. 'My Danny used to love that.'

'But I'm tired.'

She laughed. Not a pleasant laugh, thought Jacob, more like something he'd expect from a witch — or a wicked stepmother. 'That's parenthood. There's potatoes in the cupboard under the kettle and cheese in the fridge. Peel and boil the potatoes, then mash them and add grated cheese. You know,' she licked her lips. 'I quite fancy cheese on toast myself. While you're out there, shove a couple of slices of bread under the grill. You could have some too, that way the main meal's over and done with.'

Blue was still sleeping. Jacob made for the kitchen. He could do with a kip right now, he'd had a disturbed night too. He yawned, stood in the doorway thinking. Potatoes.

In the cupboard under the kettle.

'I know.'

He opened the door. The smell was so foul, he closed it quickly again. Like something had died in there.

A rabbit?

Sod that for a game of soldiers. Jacob scoured the other cupboards. Nothing much. Various spices; an old packet of haricot beans; sugar set like concrete; Ready Brek. That would do! Humming to himself, Jacob set to reading the instructions on the back of the packet.

He tipped his guessed amount of milk into the cleanest pan he could find, set it on the gas. It was a long time since he'd lit gas and it made him jump as it flared up. Next he put bread under the grill for toast and grated the cheese. This was worse than being at home. At least all he'd had to do there was set the table and wash up. None of this girly cooking. Mind, he'd have to cook once he and Blue moved into Storm Mount, no one else to do it. 'That'll be different though.'

'What will?'

He jumped. Despite the cumbersome zimmer, he'd not heard Mrs J enter the kitchen.

'Oh, nothing. Just thinking aloud.'

You really must try and keep that loose tongue under control. Giving secrets to the enemy!

'Mm. That's what idleness does, makes you think. Makes lads like you think no good. I

294

should know, I've had my fair share of trouble at the hands of a teenager. Still, you'll be different. I'll do things differently this time.' Taking Worcestershire sauce from the cupboard, she heaved her bulk back to the lounge.

What the hell did that mean? Unease rumbled in his stomach again. She was saying one thing yet seemed to be meaning something else. Although this was nothing new — grown-ups seemed to have the monopoly on twisting the language to suit their needs — Jacob couldn't help feeling this was an entirely different situation to what he was used to.

He'd just stirred the Ready Brek into the milk when black smoke shot out from under the grill.

'Shit!' Jacob pulled out the grill pan. Too late. With a sigh, he dropped the cremated toast into the bin and set about taking fresh slices from the packet.

'What's going on?' Mrs J called through.

'Nothing.'

'Doesn't smell like nothing.'

'Just burnt the toast is all. Nothing to panic about.'

'Scrape it and butter it. We'll never know.'

'Eh?' Jacob banged his forehead with the heel of his hand. That was all he needed

— some other reason for her to bollock him. *Not necessarily.*

Provided he could vanish the burnt evidence into the bin, he could burn the next lot of toast and she'd never know the difference. Strike that. He'd burn and scrape her toast, he couldn't stand the taste of charcoal; his toast he'd rescue in plenty of time.

The cereal on the hob started to crackle thickly and burn.

Shit!

And he'd not started grating the cheese yet. At this rate everything would be burnt before he got his act together. Turning off the gas beneath the cereal, he scraped what still remained the right colour into a small bowl. The pan would take some scrubbing. With a quick glance round to make sure he was still alone in the kitchen, he shoved it right at the back of the cupboard he'd found it in. With any luck it would never be discovered.

He turned his toast, left hers to burn, and set about finding the grater. It was hiding at the back of the cutlery drawer, rusty and coated with a curious green substance. She wanted grated cheese, fine. He would have it very thinly sliced. With any luck she'd die of food poisoning in the night so all his troubles would be over in the morning.

The toast ready, he buttered it and sprinkled it with cheese before returning it to the grill to melt. Just got to get rid of the toast lurking in the pedal bin in case she checked. After another cursory glance around the room, he plumped for a bag hanging on the back of the kitchen door. It looked like a rubbish bag, papers and sweet wrappers mainly. He dropped the burnt toast in the bottom, hid it carefully with newspaper. She'd never know.

'Dinner's ready,' he called, piling it on a tray and making a careful journey to the lounge. 'Be prepared to be pleasantly surprised.' At least, he thought as he entered the room, Blue was pleased to see him, a big smile on his face.

Mrs J wore her customary scowl. 'Call that cheese on toast? I've seen more cheese in a British Rail sandwich.'

'That's all there was. I shared it out.'

'Next time you share things out, remember I get the most.' She snatched the plate offered and drowned the food in Worcestershire sauce.

She wouldn't know if there was arsenic in that.

Jacob giggled.

'What's funny?'

'Nothing.' He collected a small amount of

297

Ready Brek on a spoon, offered it to Blue.

'Not thinking again?'

'Me? Never!' Ignoring her frown, he started playing aeroplanes with Blue's dinner.

'And don't play with food. He'll never learn to respect you if you do things like that. That's the trouble with society these days — never know when they're well off.'

Jacob closed his ears. Grown-ups always said things like this, things that made no sense at all; things like 'children these days don't know they're born'. What the hell did that mean?

Blue seemed to like his dinner. Jacob, finally getting to his own congealing meal, wondered if maybe Mrs J didn't know a thing or two about babies after all.

★ ★ ★

He would review that opinion at three next morning when Blue awoke with a stinking nappy and stomach-ache. Couldn't have been the cheese; must have been the ancient Ready Brek or too much (or too old!) cow's milk. For two hours Jacob would pace the room, holding the baby over first one shoulder then the other, gently patting the baby's back, urging him to be quiet. Since Mrs J didn't yell up the stairs he thought he'd succeeded in his task. Had he been able to peek through the floorboards though, he would have come to quite the opposite conclusion.

* * *

Eleanor James listened to the rumpus upstairs with a twisted smile on her face. So far, so good. If things continued this way, the lad would soon be worn down, ready for her to step in and help; ready for any suggestion she may have. This was going to be easier than she thought. All it needed was a bit of discipline. That was where she'd gone wrong with Danny. Not enough discipline. Things would be different this time. Bill would have wanted that.

* * *

It was only once Blue was sleeping again, somewhat fitfully, that Jacob realised he'd missed an opportunity. He should have insisted on a doctor — or maybe even taking Blue to hospital. He could have handed him over to someone who really knew what they were doing. He'd done his best. Now, exhausted and fearful, he just wanted someone to look after *him*.

299

At 8:10 pm Sebastian Lawson was waiting in the bar of the Jolly Tar for Kate Rogers. He was on his second pint before she appeared, breathless and flushed, in the doorway.

'Sorry!' She kissed him lightly on the cheek. 'Didn't think I'd stood you up, I hope?'

'Of course not!' He hoped she was no good at reading minds. 'What would you like to drink?'

'Babysitter was late.' She draped her coat on a stool, sat on it. 'Gin and tonic, please.'

Lawson repeated Kate's request to the hovering barmaid, using the time she took to make the drink to think about what Kate had said. 'Babysitter?' he said finally, handing over the gin and tonic.

'Mm.' She took a sip, swirled her glass, watched the liquid as she spoke.

'I've got a four-year-old daughter.'

'I had no idea.'

'It's not something I talk about at work — you know how discriminating some people can be.'

'But not me?'

She smiled. 'I believe you are the last person to discriminate against another.'

'Mm.' Lawson wasn't committing himself.

'Anyway, back to my excuse for being late. Usually Mum babysits for me, but she'd got a previous arrangement I'd forgotten about so I had to ask a neighbour's daughter. She's done it before and she knows where I am if there's a problem, so everything's fine.'

He got the distinct impression she was trying to convince herself. 'Look, if you'd rather make it another — '

'No.' She smiled, looking in his eyes for almost the first time since she entered the pub. 'This is fine.'

'Let's sit down.' Since he'd arrived he'd had the feeling he was being watched. A cursory glance around revealed nothing. Maybe he'd feel better in a different position. He led the way to a table tucked in the corner beside a rather ferocious flame-effect fire. 'Have you eaten?'

She peered mischievously at him from beneath perfectly manicured brows. It was odd but he always noticed that about a woman: whether or not she was particular about her eyebrows. 'Does a Cup-a-Soup at lunchtime count?'

'No.' He wasn't pretending the stern tone.

'Then no, I haven't.' She went to take another sip. 'Oh, yes I have — I had half a fish finger that Siobhan left.'

'Well, that's it then — you've pigged out for

tonight. Your punishment is to watch me eat lasagne and chips — the best in town.'

'Oooh!' Her stomach rumbled; they both laughed.

Lawson stuck his thumbs into imaginary breast pocket. 'It seems, M'Lud, that the jury disagrees. The lady is, in fact, starving. Therefore, not only does she get lasagne and chips but I pass sentence that she has Knickerbocker Glory to finish.'

She giggled, shaking her head. 'I was right earlier — you are quite, quite mad.'

He took a sip of lager, wiped away froth with the back of his hand. 'Insanity keeps me sane.'

★　★　★

They'd eaten the first course and were taking a breather before their Knickerbocker Glories before he brought up the subject of Kate's daughter again. 'This is going to sound really corny — '

'But you're going to say it anyway.'

'Yes! You don't look old enough to have a four-year-old daughter.'

'Oh, but I am.'

Silence. She wasn't going to reveal her true age and he was chivalrous (or scared) enough not to ask.

'So, how long have you had her?'

She laughed, not just a giggle but a throw back your head sort of a laugh that made people on nearby tables stop to see what was going on. 'Four years.'

He looked abashed. 'Silly me. Look, if you don't want to talk about her — '

'I'd rather talk about you, but . . . ' she held up a hand to stop him butting in ' . . . obviously you need to sort this thing out. I had a boyfriend for a couple of years on the cusp of leaving school. I got pregnant, he legged it, end of story.'

'But it's not, you're here, a copper. It hasn't stopped you.'

'I wouldn't say that. I'm very wary of getting involved with men now. But professionally, why should it? Women use the crudest things as excuses to stop them achieving. Do you know what's behind it?'

He shook his head, not quite knowing what he was expected to say.

'Lack of self-esteem. The 'oh, I didn't manage to get to the moon because the baby needed feeding-changing-watching grow up' syndrome.'

'But not everyone wants to go to the moon.'

She gave him a withering look. 'OK, replace moon with, I don't know, winning an

Olympic gold medal or broadcasting the news or, hell, working as a doctor's receptionist. The point is, it's not the baby's fault but the mother's — and only hers in that it's her self-esteem that's low. It's easier to make excuses not to do something than it is to find the balls to get up and do it.'

'You seem to have plenty of balls.'

Another sidelong glance. 'That's my mother. She insisted my life wasn't going to change any more than it had to when Siobhan was born. Without her bullying and babysitting and nursemaiding me, I'd never have made it.'

'Nursemaiding?' Still he couldn't shake the feeling he was being watched.

'Running me a bath when she knew I was coming in, having a hot meal ready for me, doing the housework, washing, ironing, you name it, when she could have been — should have been — out finding herself a new fella.'

Lawson felt a sharp twinge of guilt. 'Your mum does all that for you?'

'Not any more. She discovered bingo about six months ago so I have to share her with that. That's where she is tonight. Do you know the awful thing?' She turned to him, deadly serious. 'When I rang her and she said she couldn't babysit because of the bingo, I felt so angry with her, that she was no longer

304

putting me first. I soon came round though, after a hot bath and a gin and tonic.' She was smiling again. Lawson found he was quite taken with her smile, the way the end of her nose tucked up when she did. 'What about you? Any kids?'

'No. But a similar type of mum. Except she hasn't let me go yet.' He went on to explain his situation.

'She sounds lonely,' Kate said when he'd finished. 'Maybe you should invite her down, spoil her.'

Guilt. 'Do you really think so?'

Kate nodded. 'I think she would really appreciate it.'

'Maybe.' He thanked the girl as she brought over their desserts. 'At least then I'd not be worrying that she's paddling around not coping with life.'

'Oh dear.'

'What?' he looked at her horrified face.

'If I'd known you were so mixed up I'd not have agreed to come out with you tonight.'

'You didn't agree — *you asked me*. And while we're on this subject, what would you say if I told you I think I know who the murderer is — but I have absolutely no idea?'

'I'd say you were about ready for your straitjacket.'

'Thanks. No, I know I know something; I

305

know I've seen something; and I know it's important but I'm damned if I can remember what it is.'

She watched him momentarily, slowly shaking her head. 'I think you're lying to me.'

'About what, precisely?'

'Not having children. You know what they say — insanity's hereditary, you get it from your kids. The way you're talking, you must have a set of sextuplets somewhere!' She stood. 'If you'll excuse me, I'm going to powder my nose.'

He watched her sashay through the thronging punters, mainly in their early twenties like themselves. A feeling he'd not often experienced was warming his body, making him feel as though he was over-heating only, fortunately, no one seemed to be noticing. Was Kate the one? Was he likely to know so soon? What was his next step?

Slowly, slowly, catchee monkey. He smiled. He remembered his dad saying that when he was trying to catch a cricket in the back garden. Not that he likened Kate Rogers to a cricket. Perish the thought!

'Good-looking mother you've got there.'

The voice was familiar. Horribly.

'Can understand why you stood me up for her. Tomorrow night though, I won't take no for an answer.'

Lawson turned to face Dungannon whose face, illuminated by the fake flames from the fire, looked like Darth Maul.

'G . . . Good evening sir. I never expected to see you in here.'

'That much, my cherub, is patently obvious. Were you any kind of detective, you'd have done your research and discovered that the Jolly Tar is my local. In fact, at this current moment in time, it is my home.' With that, and a whiff of best brandy, William Dungannon left the bar through a door marked 'Private.'

'You OK?' Kate, moments later, returned. 'You look like you've seen — '

'The ghost of Christmas past. The Big D was here, *here*!' He pointed out the exact spot. 'Told me he lived here. Told me off for standing him up.'

'Eh?'

He waved a hand. 'Doesn't matter. Long, involved story that's likely to make you think I'm a lost cause.'

'Never! 'Nother drink?'

'No.' Lawson, feeling ill now, just wanted to get home, but saw her face. 'Oh, what the hell. Just one then. At least I know who's watching me now.'

He went to the bar leaving Kate, shaking her head, to watch him go.

25

Toothpaste slipped neatly into her inside pocket. It was an unconscious move, one made by a sleepwalker, but at some level her brain had said 'that will fit in there nicely'.

It wasn't what the security guard said when she tried to pass him in the doorway.

'Would you care to empty your pockets, madam?'

Audrey Willis looked at the shining pate of the man, half a head taller than her, blocking her exit. 'No I wouldn't!'

'Then I'm afraid you'll have to come with me.'

She opened her mouth to protest but the grip on her elbow took the words away. Typical English, she thought, watching people turning away. 'Help me you buffoons!' she screeched, mentally wondering why her father's favourite word for a congregation of humans had just passed her lips. Understandably the mothers and pensioners, out at ten o'clock this morning to do their shopping, turned away.

She was directed to a door marked 'Private' beside the bakery. Once through it, she was marched down a grey passage, the air muggy and cloyed with the smell of baking bread. Strange how something so appetising can turn to something smothering in a moment of extreme pressure. The office, tucked immediately behind the bakery, was hellishly hot. Her stomach turned, her head swam, as she was offered a seat on an orange moulded plastic chair.

'Now,' the guard (obviously fancying himself as a cowboy) straddled another such orange creation and attempted a pitying smile. 'Maybe you'd like to explain what's going on.'

It was the pity that did it, she decided later; not something she took gladly from anyone. To her complete and utter humiliation, her mouth opened and a stream of banshee-like yells, several loud hiccup-like sobs and a complete river of mucus popped out.

'I'll get a female,' said the guard hot-stepping it back into the corridor.

The torrent continued. She had no tissues, she discovered, in the bag she proudly thought contained everything, nor were there any on the small desk shoved tight into the far corner of the shoebox-like office. She used her cuffs, blue chenille now glistening with snail-like trails.

'Hello, my name's Nina,' the 'female' was barely more than eighteen, with dark curly hair and a tightly fitting suit. 'What seems to be the problem?' Nina, fresh from college, had dealt with crises before: burnt hot-cross buns, over-charged customers, even someone who'd found a glass eye in a packet of cornflakes (later discovered to have become disconnected from the free toy enclosed) so this lady, sobbing waterfalls, was bound to be a walkover.

Not.

It was probably the word 'murder' that did it.

She leapt from her seat, opened the door and called 'Get the police,' to the shiny-pated guard who'd positioned himself, legs firmly apart, hands behind his back, eyes front, outside the door, the way he'd seen it done a long time ago on *The Professionals*.

★   ★   ★

Today was going to be a bastard, Lawson prophesied. He'd attempted to repair his relationship with his mother — no joy — and now he was being diverted from 'the body on the riverbank' inquiry to deal with a hysterical woman who'd shoplifted a tube of toothpaste, who, as soon as she saw his uniform, ran to

310

the back of the office and started pulling at her hair.

'Look,' he said, wearily sitting on the orange plastic chair and removing his cap. 'I don't want to be here any more than you do. How's about you tell me what's going on and we can both get back to where we came from.'

'I didn't mean to do it,' she held out the (now slightly squashed) tube of toothpaste.

'I'm sure you didn't. I don't know about you, but if I go shoplifting it's usually something expensive and totally useless.' It was then he suddenly remembered where he knew her from. 'We've met before. I spoke to you about Dotty Spangle.'

'I know. I was hoping you wouldn't recognise me.'

He smiled. 'OK. Back to the toothpaste.'

She sobbed a laugh. 'I didn't know it was there until the guard told me.'

'Maybe it jumped in when you weren't looking.'

She laughed again. 'Maybe he planted it on me.'

'That's the spirit. Now, shall we start at the beginning?'

★ ★ ★

At ten thirty, after the 'Trisha' show, Audrey was watching the adverts. One came on for butter (or 'not' butter), the one with the talking cows which normally she despised but which, this morning, reminded her that she had run out. CashSave seemed the place to go. Despite a freezing wind and ominous clouds, she'd put on her lightweight coral jacket, more suited to spring and early summer than the depths of winter. She wore it unbuttoned, just her arms folded across her chest to keep out the worst of the wind.

On her way, to keep her mind from thinking *my daughter's dead*, she mentally walked through the rooms in her house, adding items to the shopping list as she considered fit. Toothpaste. Did she need toothpaste? Maybe. She'd get a tube just in case. Hairspray. She hardly ever used it but she might need it one day — *for the funeral*.

There would have to be a funeral. What would happen to her daughter if she didn't claim her? Would she be placed in a pauper's grave with no headstone so that she, Audrey, wouldn't even be able to take flowers and apologise for being such a wuss? She'd get hairspray. And grapes. And soda crystals. And frozen chips. And then she'd wander round the store checking everything over and over just to make sure she didn't need it.

She'd got as far as the toothpaste. Choosing one brand was so difficult. They each professed to be better than their neighbour. Did she truthfully want teeth that looked as though they'd been bleached in the California sun? You betcha! It was so expensive though, still —

'Audrey?'

She whirled around. Morag Hunter, next-door neighbour.

'Hello.'

'Busy shopping, I see.' The rotund woman with the worst case of facial hair this side of *An American Werewolf in London* and breath to match sidled closer. 'Don't often see you in here.'

This was because, usually, Audrey had her wits about her and ducked into the next aisle when she saw her coming. 'No.'

'That toothpaste,' she nodded in the general direction of Audrey's right hand. 'Is very good.'

Audrey, deciding that if this was an advert for the product she wouldn't bother, put it back on the shelf. 'I was just looking.'

'How's that daughter of yours doing? Haven't seen her around lately.'

A mist started to descend on Audrey's vision. 'Really must be getting on. Nice to see you.' She hurried to the end of the aisle,

313

waited for Morag to go. Once she had, Audrey nipped back, collected a different brand of toothpaste and headed off for the checkouts. Social minefields like this could wait until another day. Only when she reached the checkout, Morag was at the next one. Without stopping to consider, Audrey headed for the door, dumping her basket and slipping the toothpaste into her pocket as she went.

★ ★ ★

Lawson nodded. 'Easily done.' He closed his notebook. 'Now, you have a huge decision to make.' She gazed uneasily at him. 'Don't worry, it's not life or death. Do you wish to pay for the toothpaste, or shall we put it back on the shelf and forget the whole thing?' It wasn't until he looked up that he realised she was sobbing again. 'What is it?'

She looked up, placed a shaking hand on his arm. 'I need to make a confession.'

Inwardly, Lawson sighed. All he needed today was another melodramatic female. Wasn't it enough that he'd already had his mother sobbing down the phone? He forced a smile. 'Go on.'

'My daughter, Tabitha, she left home — quite a while ago now and she wasn't old enough to go and I didn't report it because it was easier for me not to — '

'Whoa, whoa,' he said soothingly, trying to stem the flow. It didn't work.

'And now she's gone and got herself murdered and I don't know what's happened to the baby and I don't know what to do — '

'*Whoa!*' Lawson waited until she looked him in the eyes. 'I think we'd better continue this at the station.'

★ ★ ★

'It's not how you want your daughter to end up, is it?'

Lawson, not knowing whether she meant dead or working as a prostitute, said nothing, shook his head.

'A prostitute, I mean.'

So it was OK to be dead then? He frowned.

'We called her Tabitha.' This last with a sigh as though the name a child was christened with could protect it from evil. 'She shortened it to Tabbi. That's probably what did it.' Audrey Willis smiled bitterly at Lawson and ignored WPC Rogers sitting by the interview-room door.

'Mmm.' He wasn't sure he could see what it had done. He pressed on. 'How can you be sure the body on the riverbank is your daughter?'

'Call it mother's intuition.'

'Nothing concrete though?' He acknowledged her frown. 'No one's told you definitely it's her. You have no proof?' She shook her head. 'When did you last see your daughter?'

'Six months ago.' She frowned, two short parallel lines appeared between her eyebrows. 'It was a Wednesday. I'd just had my roots done. Usual thing — could I babysit while she went to work. She thought I believed she was working nights at the supermarket — stacking shelves. Since when did they employ half-dressed girls? Just like when she used to bunk-off school. Told the teachers she had a doctor's appointment; told me the school was shut 'cos the heating had bust. Never entered her head that the two parties might communicate over her head.'

'And did you?' Lawson sipped his lukewarm coffee.

'What?'

'Babysit?'

She shook her head. 'Told her she'd made her bed, she could lie in it.'

Lawson winced, ignored the tut that came from the WPC.

'By the time I found out, she'd been at it a year. Couldn't give it up. Got used to the

316

money. That was the one thing I couldn't give her.' Her eyes were bitter. 'At least, I could, but she wouldn't take any of Seymour's money.'

'Seymour?'

'Her stepfather. Said it was all his fault she'd taken it up in the first place.' She mopped another tear sliding down her cheek, carried on unprompted. 'Said that if she could have sex with him, she could do it with anyone.'

'Pardon?'

'She reckoned he used to go to her when I wasn't there, force himself on her.'

'But you didn't believe her?'

'Of course not. She was always jealous of him; always trying to put him off me or vice versa. That was just another ploy.' No longer able to look him in the eye, she mumbled into the crumpled tissue. 'What was I supposed to do? Give in to her or follow my heart?'

Silence. There didn't seem to be anything worth saying.

Eventually Lawson said. 'How did you find out?'

'She got pregnant. Came to me, frightened, asking for help. Can you imagine not knowing who the father of your baby was?'

At last, thought Lawson, compassion —

'So I told her what a dirty slut I thought

317

she was, gave her some of Seymour's money and told her to do what she felt she had to.'

— Not.

'I was not prepared to encourage her. She said that things would be different when the baby was born, that politics would fly out of the window when there was an actual baby.'

'And?'

'She was right. I babysat then, sometimes. Then Seymour died and I . . . went to pieces, needed her. She said,' she sobbed again. 'She said I'd made my bed so I'd have to lie in it.'

'If you weren't babysitting, then who was?'

'She had a way of attracting young kids — nothing sinister, they just liked her. Gave them a fiver for keeping an eye on Blue. Wonder Social Services never got their hands on him. Mind, I'd have stepped in permanent if that'd happened. That's what I'll have to do now,' she said, jutting her jaw with terrier-like determination. 'I take it that's where he is — with Social Services?'

Lawson looked at WPC Rogers who shrugged. 'I . . . er . . . ' he started, cleared his throat. 'That is, I'm not rightly sure. I'll find out for you.'

A baby? There's a baby alone out there somewhere?

Then he knew. Pennies dropping all over the place, like he was sitting in a slot machine. The baby wasn't alone. He knew that — and he knew where to find him.

'Does this mean you don't know where he is?'

'No,' he answered her truthfully. 'It means that I don't know if we can get immediate access to him.' He watched a shadow cross her face and carried on, not so truthfully. 'It's something to do with the trauma he's already suffered. They'll like to know he's emotionally up to another change.'

She nodded, apparently satisfied. WPC Rogers, completely in the dark, frowned.

'Well Mrs Willis,' Lawson stood. 'I think that's all for now but I'm afraid I'm going to have to warn you that, once the body's ready for viewing, we'll have to ask you to identify it.'

She nodded, made for the door.

'Just one more thing,' WPC Rogers stepped forward. 'What was Tabitha's surname?'

'Oh, Willis. She never changed it. I went back to Willis after Seymour died. I couldn't forgive him the deceit. I've never felt so betrayed.' She sat down again.

Lawson sat down again as she began to cry. He'd been right. Today was going to be a right bastard.

★ ★ ★

Kate Rogers got straight onto Social Services. Surely they'd been aware of Tabbi and her baby? No, said Sophie Sullivan who rang back after checking the records, that one obviously got away. Sometimes happened with girls that age — on the brink between girlhood and adulthood — that they slipped between the cracks. Especially when no one at home reported them missing.

And there but for the grace of God, thought Kate, go I.

26

Jacob watched Storm Mount with growing unease. A light was on in the bedroom that had been Tabbi's. He was sure he'd not left it on. He was sure it wasn't on the last time he'd looked. Switching his own light off, he sat in the darkness and watched.

And watched.

Nearly an hour had gone by when he realised that a light he hadn't previously noticed — above Tabbi's bedroom — had gone out. His stomach lurched. So Storm Mount *was* haunted! He didn't want to watch any longer but, perversely, couldn't bear not to. Blue murmured, turned in his sleep. Jacob, momentarily concerned the child may roll off the bed, looked away from the window. When he looked again, a shadow had appeared against the pale background of closed curtains. It was a big shadow but a man not a monster. (He was later to re-evaluate that opinion.) It moved slightly side to side as though, thought Jacob, completely set in 'parent' mode, it was rocking a pushchair. Briefly it turned full on towards him then gradually got smaller as it headed for the door. The light went out. Nothing.

Jacob examined his thoughts. If it wasn't a ghost but a man, who could it be?

It's the ghost of a man.

But would it have a shadow if it were a ghost? No. Vampires didn't have reflections. Stood to reason. So it was a man. But who? Who would want to live in Storm Mount?

You.

'Piss off.' Jacob spoke to the chill air. The sound of his voice, not trembling with the fear he felt, made him feel more confident. He looked back across the road. The stair light was on. Off. The hall light went on. Stayed on. The front door opened. Jacob squinted. Couldn't make out who it was. Now the shape just looked like a blob. It hunched, the flash of a match briefly lit its face. Still Jacob couldn't identify it. It closed the front door and for a moment Jacob couldn't see whether it had gone back inside or remained in the garden. Just when he thought it must have gone in for the night, he caught a movement. Leaning forward so his nose almost touched the cold glass, close enough to create a circle of condensation as he breathed, Jacob waited.

The shadow moved toward the gate, paused, stepped onto the pavement. Into the circular yellow spotlight of a streetlight.

Danny!

Oh shit!

Jacob ducked away from the window, noting as he did that Danny was headed this way. Leaping into bed, pulling Blue to him, he strained his ears. Surely Danny wasn't coming here?

Why not, it's his home.

Footsteps in the porch, a key in the front door, a whispered 'hello' in the hall. Jacob heard Danny go into the lounge, his mother's bedroom, heard the TV being turned down, heard their voices. Couldn't make out what was being said. The TV was turned up again, the door opened and closed. Footsteps in the hall, coming up the stairs, stopping outside his room.

Jacob clutched Blue so tight the baby squeaked in his sleep. Jacob giggled — out of fear more than humour. Heart beating so loudly he could barely hear anything else, Jacob closed his eyes and prayed.

He never considered there might be a God. If there was, He belonged to everyone else and not him. He must have been sent out of the room when God was handing out parents. Jacob always felt that he'd never had a fair share. So this now, praying, was a new experience. Maybe it was because he now felt he had a family — well Blue, anyway. It was being protective had brought it out of him, he guessed. Normally there was only him — and he was capable of relying on himself. Now, because he refused to run and leave Blue to fend for himself, he was vulnerable. Scared.

Please God, make Danny go away. Please make him leave us alone. And if he won't, please give me the weapons to deal with him.

Jacob wasn't sure that asking God for weapons was such a good thing but it was the only word he could think of that seemed appropriate. Eyes tight shut, he said 'Amen,' then again, louder, just to be sure he'd been heard.

The door handle turned. Jacob didn't see it as much as hear it. Even if his eyes had been open, it was too dark in the room to see the door handle. He held his breath. Waited — for the monster to leap in, slit his throat, leave him bloody and dying on the blankets.

He held his breath. Waited. He took a breath, couldn't hold it any longer. It sounded louder than he'd planned. His heart thumped harder than ever in his chest. The doorknob turned again. Jacob sent up a silent prayer, promising all kinds of things he would break as soon as he got out of this.

If you get out.

Silence.

He fancied he could hear breathing. Was it in the room or still behind the door? Blue wriggled, kicking him low in the stomach. Breath whooshed out. He gulped in another lungful. Footsteps. Definitely footsteps. Coming his way? He daren't peer, didn't want to know. Still footsteps, going away. Going away? He opened one eye as though that might help him hear better. Definitely going away.

The door next to the bedroom creaked open, then closed. Floorboards revealed movement, across the room and back again. Then the bed, groaning under pressure. A light switch. Off, presumably. Silence.

Jacob opened his other eye, stared at the black hole that was the ceiling. Danny was here! Had he come for the photos he'd left in his wardrobe — some of which Jacob now had tucked at the bottom of Blue's string bag?

Danny was in the next room. As far as Jacob saw it, he had two choices — to stay or to run.

Run!

It was tempting. Very. But — he cuddled Blue closer — how would he get the baby and the buggy and the nappies out of the house without waking everyone? Running was all very well but sometimes, he decided, you had to stay and deal with the problem. Had he but realised it, Jacob had just matured way beyond the level his father had ever attained.

The thought of staying frightened him almost as much as thinking Danny was coming to slit his throat. He knew there was no chance of sleep tonight. No chance at all. He'd stay awake all night and wait for dawn to bring its candy fingers into the room. He'd stay awake and plan what he was going to do tomorrow. James Bond would have a plan, he'd be movement-perfect before daybreak came.

So, Jacob thought, they'd have breakfast as normal, then he'd offer to go to the shop and take Blue and . . .

The next thing he knew, it was seven o'clock and Blue, hungry and thirsty, was wittering beside him.

27

Jacob turned Tabbi's mobile over in his hands. He'd found a number in her diary with 'Mom' written next to it. Why had she used the American term? he wondered. Idly he switched it on, a task that had been achieved by trial and error. He started to dial the number. With one to go, he stopped, switched off the phone. What would he say? Hello Mrs — What? — I'm a friend of your dead daughter. At present I'm looking after her son, your grandson, and I'd like your permission to continue to do so for the foreseeable.' Likely? No.

She'll set the police on you. Accuse you of abduction.

He couldn't risk that. He hid the phone back under his pillow.

Danny hadn't stirred yet as far as he knew. Blue was settled, happily gnawing on a rusk, nappy changed, PJs still on. He'd thought ringing this number was a brainwave, that it was his way out of this mess. Now he knew he'd just be digging a deeper hole. He had to face it, there was only one person he could trust here. Himself.

How long had it taken Blue to stop missing his mother, Jacob wondered idly. He didn't seem to have noticed she'd gone at all. Maybe it was because he was a baby. Jacob still missed his mother — but she'd gone when he was nine. He'd never forget, never, ever, ever. One day, when he'd done Storm Mount up and bought a flash car and saved up enough money he'd go to Spain until he found a woman who only spoke English and that would be his mother. And it would be as simple as that. He remembered Tabbi's cruel laughter when he said this to her. Maybe she was right, but he didn't want to believe so.

A solitary tear slipped free, slid down his cheek. With a grimy fist he wiped it away. Movement in the next room. Danny was up, then. Jacob cast a worried glance at Blue. Happily unaware of the tension, the baby continued to decimate his rusk. Footsteps outside the door; a knock. Jacob was suddenly transported into the terror of the night before. What was Danny capable of doing to them? What was Danny *not* capable of doing to them?

'You in there?' The voice was cigarette-gruff. 'Hello?'

Jacob didn't know what to do. Should he stay quiet and hope Danny would go away?

Don't be daft!

'H . . . hello.'

'Open the fucking door then, invite me in.'

'Door's open.'

'Open it.' The voice was now a growl.

Jacob did.

'See, I don't know what booby-traps you might have laid, telling me to walk in like that. How are you?'

Jacob, not understanding why Danny was trying to be civil, shrugged.

'It's not a difficult question is it?' Jacob shook his head. 'So how the fuck are you?'

'I'm good.' Jacob sidled closer to Blue.

Danny noticed. 'And how's the sprog?'

'Pissed off 'cos his mother's dead, what do you think?'

'Does he know?' Danny was deadly earnest. 'If so, how do you know he's pissed off?'

'Wouldn't you be?'

Danny thought momentarily. 'No. House'd be mine then. No more nagging. Heaven.' He grinned, revealing black stumps as teeth. 'You could stay, keep me company.' His grin widened.

'Couldn't do that,' Jacob didn't like the warning signs that were flashing in his brain. What was it about Danny that gave him the willies? 'I'd not be able to pay the rent and I like to pay my way.'

'Oh,' Danny stepped to within a foot of Jacob, touched his forearm. 'I'm sure we could come to some arrangement. In fact,' Danny placed his other hand on Blue's leg. The baby briefly stopped chewing to study him. 'There's a little job you could do for me right now.'

'Now?' Jacob's voice shook.

'Why not. It's time we got better acquainted if we're going to live under the same roof.'

'I . . . ' Jacob, backed against the windowsill, had nowhere to go except down. He didn't know what Danny was angling at but he knew it didn't smell right. If jumping was his only option then jumping was what he would do. He considered the steps involved; grab Blue (he couldn't leave Blue to face Danny alone); wriggle back so he was sitting on the windowsill; hug Blue to him and push back as hard as he could, praying that the glass would break and let him fall to the ground. He edged towards Blue.

'Danny?' Mrs J's voice tremeloed up the stairs. 'Danny, what are you doing?'

'Coming, Mum.' He looked at Jacob, smiled. 'We'll continue this later.' Gently pinching Blue's cheek, he left the room without a backward glance.

Jacob hugged the baby to him. 'We've got

330

to get out of here — and today. Don't know where we'll go.' Briefly he considered ringing that phone number again, but discounted the idea. 'And Storm Mount isn't the safest place to be right now.' Packing was a good idea though. He'd time it before Blue needed dealing with again to collect his few things, including the phone, and put them in Tabbi's string bag, then he'd be ready for the off as soon as he got the opportunity.

'Jacob?' Mrs J's voice again. 'Come down here.'

'Please,' he mumbled under his breath, arranging Blue on his hip and placing the bag on the buggy's seat. If he put it on the handles now he knew, from bitter experience, that the whole thing would tip up. It was hard being a mother, he'd worked that out. Another step beyond the point his father had ever reached. Jacob swore that, should he ever find a woman he wanted to marry (he didn't think it was likely, they were all such wusses) he'd treat her with a lot more respect than his father had ever shown. Dad's idea of affection was to belt his current lady friend when he got pissed on Friday night. Jacob, to his credit, had worked out this wasn't the nicest way to make a woman stay with you.

Something was cooking, he realised as he went down the stairs — bacon, eggs. His

331

mouth watered. Mrs J was waiting for him in the hall.

'Kitchen floor needs cleaning. There's grease on it.'

How can you tell? he wanted to ask. Daren't when Danny appeared in the doorway.

'Smell good?' Danny jerked his reptilian neck back towards the kitchen. 'Enjoy, sucker, 'cos that's the closest you're going to get — apart from clearing up my grease that is.'

Jacob looked to Mrs J for confirmation. She nodded. 'What can I have for breakfast?' asked Jacob.

'I'm sure there's a slice of bread or something.' She shuffled into the lounge and closed the door but not before saying, 'When you've done the kitchen floor you can start sorting the cupboards out — give us a chance to see what we've got and what we've not.'

Danny sniggered. 'Mum's a poet and she don't know it.'

'Grow up Danny!' She slammed the door.

Danny, bacon-and-egg sandwich dripping from his mouth, stepped forward. 'All yours, Sonny. I've got to go out now — but don't forget our little chat, will you? I'll catch up with you later, put you in the picture. OK?'

Jacob nodded. 'OK.' He tried to smile. Couldn't.

He waited until Danny had left before going into the kitchen. Was he expected to remove simply what Danny had added that morning — or did he have to scrape off the inches already there? He figured on the latter, found the nicest knife he could and got down onto his hands and knees.

Cleaning greasy floors was women's work. The more he scraped, the more mess he made, the less it would wipe up with the lukewarm water he aimed at it from time to time. A woman would know how to deal with this crap riding the tide across the floor. No wonder Dad insisted on women staying home while he went out and got pissed. He'd got his priorities right. At least Blue wasn't here to witness his degrading antics — Mrs J had, eventually, appeared dressed (a different nylon nightie with fewer cigarette burns) and taken him to her room. Occasionally he heard the baby giggle; a sure sign she wasn't torturing him.

He controlled the urge to throw up. One thing, this job was putting him off fried food; he'd never be able to walk into Jim's Café again. It also drove the desire from him to ever eat in this house again. How come they hadn't all died of food poisoning before now?

Shame really, would have saved him a lot of trouble if they had.

A knock at the door.

Jacob froze, visions of Danny's long, lecherous fingers insinuated themselves into his brain. This wasn't Danny though, even if he'd lost his key. The knock was firm, authoritative. 'Let me in,' it said, 'I know you're there.'

Mrs J, Blue untidily arranged in her arms, appeared at the lounge door. 'Take him and go into the shed.'

'Eh?'

'Do it.' It was a hiss, and Jacob had no doubt of what might happen to him should he disobey.

He took Blue, paused long enough to see the police uniform when Mrs J opened the door, and did as he was told. Sheds, outhouses, all the same. Cobwebs, mouse crap, damp and cold creating dead piles in dark corners, unused implements hanging from the ceiling.

And ghosts.

Jacob squeezed Blue as a child, only a few years younger, would a teddy. He giggled self-consciously. What would James Bond do here? No doubt one of Q's famous gadgets would be hidden in the nappy. Press the switch, detonate the nuclear warhead, blow the enemy to Kingdom-come. Only who was the enemy here? Jacob shook his head. The police had always been the enemy, Dad had instilled that in him. Yet he, Jacob, had already turned to them when he'd found Dotty's body; considered it when he found Tabbi's — though he'd felt he was betraying her by contacting them then — and anyway, they might think he'd something to do with it. Finding two bodies made you the main suspect, he knew that. Gave them enough evidence to lock him up forever. Dad had been locked up twice on less evidence than that, he knew. Dad had told him.

Or was Mrs J the enemy? A day ago he'd have laughed in your face if you told him that anyone over thirty had enough energy to be bad. After all, wouldn't be long till you got your old age pension, would it? Now he was faced with a woman, at least a hundred years old, who seemed to be saying one thing and meaning another. Maybe it was Danny though, pulling the strings of an ancient marionette. More likely. Jacob smiled. He was proud of that word, *marionette*. Something good Tina had done; taken him to the show on the pier in Bognor. She'd told him that fancy name for a puppet. He liked to show off and use it. Made him more educated than the other kids at school. When he went.

So, assuming there *was* a nuclear warhead in Blue's nappy, who would he aim it at? Or would he just blow the whole house out of the water and waste both of them? Tricky question. One that needed a lot of thought.

★ ★ ★

'Got visitors, Mrs James?' Lawson was in no mood for small-talk. Mother was back on side, but dictating instructions like there was no tomorrow.

She gave him a sideways look, simpered. (Was she flirting with him? He shuddered.) 'I can't imagine who'd want to come and stay with an old lady like me, Mr Lawson — '

'That's PC.' Might as well continue the way he'd started.

She looked taken aback. 'PC Lawson. I mean, what do I have to offer? Age-old memories of a time not many people understand any longer.'

My heart bleeds, thought Lawson as he looked around the room. Nothing had changed, muck, dust, rubbish everywhere.

'Anyway, this place is such a mess,' she followed his eyes. 'They'd run straight out the back door when I let them in the front.'

True, thought Lawson, very true. He stopped short when he realised he was nodding. 'Mrs James,' he decided to try the subtle route, she wasn't smart enough to work that out. 'I understand you have a woman who does for you? A cleaner?'

She smiled. False vanity. 'Yes. Well . . . I did. She doesn't come any more.'

'Her name?'

'Audrey.' He raised his eyebrows. 'Audrey Willis.'

So far, so good. 'Uh-huh. And would that be the same Audrey Willis who resides at twenty one Riverside Drive?'

'Yes.'

'Did it never seem strange to you that someone who lives in Riverside Drive might want to work as a cleaner?'

'No.' Clearly bemused, Mrs James now leaned her elbow heavily on the chair arm, supporting her jaw with the palm of her hand.

'Did she ever speak of family?'

Mrs J's eyes sparkled. Now she was back on familiar territory. 'She had a daughter. Wayward wretch. Worse than my Danny — and that's saying something,' she added, saving Lawson the trouble of thinking it. 'At least my Danny couldn't get pregnant.'

Lawson studied her face. It revealed nothing. 'Mrs James, you are aware that a second body has been found?'

'On the riverbank? Yes. Makes me glad to be old.' She looked at his questioning expression. 'They'd not give me a second look, lad. Get to my age and they let you rot in peace.'

He took a deep breath. 'Mrs James, since the discovery of the second body, have you been aware of anyone hanging around?'

'Are you saying I'm a nosey-parker?'

Yes. 'No, I'm just thinking that since you're the only one in Amber Close who's around all day, you're the most likely one to have noticed something odd.'

Flattery, my son, will get you everywhere.

'Well,' she appeared to ponder the question. 'No.'

'Not even that young lad?'

Was it his imagination or did she hesitate?

'Which young lad would that be?'

'The one you used to notice — Jacob Palmer?'

'Oh, him. I'd forgotten about him. That's old age,' she added, in case this deliberate lie should make this nice copper think her an unreliable witness. 'I remember everything else. No, he's definitely not been around.'

'I see.' He pretended to jot something in his notebook. 'What about lights — have there been any lights on at night across there? Only . . . ' he pushed on as she shook her

338

head and opened her mouth ' . . . the night the body was found on the riverbank, there were lights on at Storm Mount.'

'Oh, I . . . ' He watched her trying to rearrange her lie. 'Yes, now you come to mention it, there have been lights on at odd times.'

'Odd?'

'I don't mean odd, odd, I mean odd as in occasional.'

'I see. How occasional?'

'Mm?'

'Every night? Every other night? At the same times? Different times? All night? What?'

'I don't rightly know.' Her face brightened. 'Maybe there's one of those devices, you know, that switch lights on while you're away to make burglars think there's someone there.'

'Maybe.' Now back to the jugular. 'Since when did you have a baby here?'

'Baby?' Was it his imagination or did she go a strange shade of yellow? 'There's no baby here.'

'Oh. I only ask because there's a smashed jar in the front garden — it's had baby food in it.'

Jacob! She'd kill him, lazy git. 'Oh, is there? Maybe someone threw it there as they were passing.'

'Maybe.' He watched her relax. 'Only it's a strange thing to be carrying down the street isn't it, an empty jar of food?'

'Yes,' she agreed obediently. Her face brightened again. 'I remember! Next door's cat!'

Lawson was glad Dungannon wasn't here to drop in 'Tastes good with pureed apple does he?' or some other such inane comment. Said something for his state of mind that he was even considering what Dungannon would say. Maybe it was the threat of tonight's 'social' meeting that was playing on his mind. 'Cat?' He was proud of himself, he'd managed not to smile.

'Yes. She sometimes gives it to him — gippy tummy, you know.'

Pureed apple?

'Gippy tummy? Yes, I see. How come the jar has ended up in your garden?'

'She must have accidently thrown it over the wall.'

'Of course.' He stood. 'Well thank you Mrs James, you've been a great help.'

She simpered. He smiled grimly. He'd learnt an awful lot more than she'd told him.

★ ★ ★

Mrs J.

Jacob heard the front door close as the policeman left.

Mrs J was the enemy, not the police. Now all he had to do was find a way of vanquishing her — and creating enough evidence for the police to put her away.

★   ★   ★

Lawson strolled around the corner, wanting to see if he could see into Mrs James' back garden. He was looking for evidence of Jacob and the baby. He'd wanted to demand access to the back yard but knew that Dungannon would reprehend him severely for doing it with no good reason.

The wall was weathered brick, five foot high, but the slight downward slope of the pavement made it seem higher; made it harder for him to peer over the top. But he managed it. He smiled to himself. There, emerging from the shed like a butterfly from a chrysalis, were Jacob and Blue.

28

'He's gone.'

Jacob waited a moment or two after Mrs J's hissed message came from the back door before taking his hand from Blue's mouth. The baby smiled, blew a bubble.

'You lazy bugger,' the hissing continued. 'He saw the jar of baby food you couldn't be bothered to clear up. Told some cock-and-bull story but it threw me — he'll be onto you, you'll see, and then you'll be for it.'

Maybe that wouldn't be such a bad thing, thought Jacob, at least it would stop her moaning at him for the rest of the day.

'Are you coming in?'

'Yes, yes.' Pushing the buggy, Jacob crossed the yard, bounced the buggy over the doorstep, tipping it well back. Blue smiled again.

'He'll know I've been telling lies,' Mrs J greeted him in the lounge doorway, zimmer before her in the hall. 'He'll know you were here. He'll be back.'

Good.

'He probably knew before he came.

Coppers always do. That's what me dad says anyway.'

'Dad? Since when did you have a dad?'

'Since always. Look are you going to stand there all day? I need to get Blue some breakfast and change his nappy.' He wasn't aware, at first, where the cane came from; wasn't even sure what it was until it had belted him heavily across the left shoulder. 'What the fuck?' His screaming sent Blue off into panic-stricken howls. Jacob caught his breath. 'What the fuck . . . did you . . . do that for?'

Mrs J, breathless with effort, smiled. 'I will not be spoken to like that. My Bill would have beaten you black and blue for that. You're lucky that I can only manage one swipe at a time.' She pulled the zimmer back to let him pass. 'Where's your dad now?' As though nothing had happened, she followed him into the kitchen.

'Dunno. At home I guess.' Jacob, barely able to find the energy to speak to her, did so only because he feared another wallop.

She's quite mad. Insane!

He took another careful breath; it hurt to do it too quickly. 'Home with Tina probably. Unless he's frightened her off too.'

'Home? Where's home?' Impatient now, her voice had taken on a rasping quality.

'Not far from here.' Jacob narrowed his eyes. 'And he can get very nasty — so watch out if he ever finds out what you did to me.'

Sheer inspiration, with no truth in it whatsoever. If Dave Palmer ever found out she'd belted Jacob, he'd belt Jacob too for needing one in the first place.

'And he knows about the police?' Wary now, Mrs J took a step back.

'More than most. He reckons that no matter what they say you've done, they can't never prove it, so you shouldn't worry — just plead ignorant. That's what he does.'

Her face softened. 'You're a good boy, Jacob. Just like my Danny used to be before . . .'

'Yeah.' Jacob didn't have a clue what she was on about but decided that agreeing with her would get Blue's food prepared sooner. His face had taken on the mournful expression it wore just before collapsing into hunger-ridden wailing. On the subject of food, he didn't quite know what he was going to serve. The baby food was all gone. Blue wouldn't eat peeled tomatoes or marrowfat peas and that's all the tinned food the cupboards held. Bread? No. Cereal? Jacob looked. Weetabix — and enough milk to soften it. That would have to do.

'I'll feed him quick then nip to the shop for

some nappies — he hasn't any left.' He spoke with his back to Mrs J, mashing the Weetabix into a pulp. He scraped up some of the cereal, spooned it into the eager red mouth. Blue took his fill. Jacob stopped feeding him when Weetabix started foaming at the baby's lips.

Mrs J had watched this pantomime with quiet amusement. 'You're not going out today.'

Jacob froze, trying to control his emotions, he didn't want another bash from the cane. 'So,' he spoke softly, proud that his voice wasn't shaking with anger. 'What does Blue do for nappies?'

'You'll have to use a tea towel.'

Jacob opened his mouth but, so angry was he, nothing came out.

'Do you have a better idea?'

He shook his head. Numbly he lay Blue on the table, keeping his back to Mrs J so he wouldn't have to look at her sneering face. He plucked a tea towel from the ironing pile towering towards the ceiling.

'Fold it into a kite shape,' she instructed.

Jacob grudgingly obeyed. He wasn't daft. Tea towels as nappies was a non-starter. Blue, kicking his legs energetically, agreed, peeing enthusiastically as the cotton touched his skin. Mrs J cackled, left the room. Jacob,

345

rubbing his sore shoulder, watched her go. Maybe, if he completely lost his rag, he could get the better of her.

★ ★ ★

It took nearly an hour for Jacob to fix an acceptable nappy (he found some cotton wool in the bathroom cabinet, which padded the tea towel out a bit), rock Blue to sleep and take his anger in hand. He had to appeal to Mrs J's better nature — *Does she have one?* — if he wanted to win this battle.

'Mrs J,' he peered cautiously, having knocked and received no reply, around the door.

'What?' Eyes firmly fixed on the TV, she betrayed nothing.

'There's not even enough food. One of us is going to have to go out for supplies today.' Silence, save for the canned laughter coming from the corner.

'No baby food,' she spoke quietly, still watching the screen. 'I've told you before, when I was bringing up my Danny food didn't come in jars. He ate the same as Bill and me — only I mashed it up. Blue'll thrive on proper food, you'll see. That processed rubbish'll rot his socks. Come a day when he'll thank me.' She paused, turned to look at

Jacob. 'Anyway, you've still got to finish the kitchen floor and the cupboards. You've more than enough to occupy you today.'

'I agree,' Jacob dropped his voice, took another step into the room. 'But there isn't even much proper food. I'm sure, if I get on, I can fit in a quick shop too.'

She studied him for a long moment before nodding slowly. 'Very well.' She leant forward, took a slip of paper and a pencil from the top of a pile of newspaper. 'So, get potatoes, carrots, that kind of thing; bananas, baked beans, cereal, milk. I need some coffee — not that crappy decaf stuff the doctor's always telling me to have, need something to look forward to these days — and a slab of ginger cake. That'll just about do it.'

'Bread?' Jacob couldn't believe how easy this was going to be. Blue was asleep in his buggy, their bag of stuff was tucked underneath the stairs, Mrs J would have to give him at least a fiver which he wouldn't spend at the supermarket — he wasn't *going* to the supermarket — enough to keep them going a day or two.

'Yes, bread.'

'Nappies?' His voice, hardly daring to say the word, was little more than a whisper.

She sighed. 'Very well.' She'd have to give him a tenner.

'Excellent.'

She took the money from a handbag beside her on the chair and handed him the note.

'I'll just get Blue and I'll be off.' Had he not mentioned Blue he might have got away with it, she may not have realised he planned to take the baby.

As it was, her head turned, the cane miraculously appeared in her right hand. 'Oh no,' she hissed. 'You're not taking my insurance.' Jacob frowned. Mrs J continued. 'I'm not daft. If I let you take the money *and* the baby, I'll not see you again. Keeping Blue here means you'll return — and I know you will. You're fond of Blue, aren't you?' Jacob nodded. 'Now, run along and shop — and be back in half an hour else it'll be the very last time you see the outside world.'

She'd said it with a smile on her face but Jacob didn't doubt that she meant what she said; something to do with the cold glare in her eyes. He pushed the buggy into her room, gently stroked Blue's cheek, and left. The thought hit him as he opened the front door. Heading back into the house, he took the stairs two at a time and was delving under the pillow before he heard Mrs J's voice coming up the stairs.

'What are you doing?'

'Nothing.' He ran downstairs again. 'I'm off now.'

'Remember, no tricks,' she yelled after him as he scampered down the path.

He ran until he reached the church tower, ducked into the doorway where he was sure she wouldn't see him. Then he plucked the trophy from his pocket. Tabbi's mobile phone. This was his — and Blue's — only way out. Whatever happened — and they would probably be separated — it was up to him to ring Tabbi's mum, tell her what was happening and ask for her help. He took out her number, went to switch the phone on, froze.

'Bollocks!' He stared in disbelief at the phone. He'd forgotten to switch it off, the battery was dead. 'Bollocks!' he said again, flinging it as far away from him as he could.

★ ★ ★

'You're late,' Mrs J, eyes once more fixed on the TV screen, didn't move as he walked in.

'Shop was busy.'

'Not good enough,' now she did move, eyes only, narrowed, nasty. 'You'll have to be penalised.'

'Do what?' Jacob flung down the two carrier bags in disgust.

349

'Don't get smart with me, young man.'

'So what's to penalise when I get held up at the shops?'

'You forget,' she turned her tortoise-like head towards him. 'That I'm used to boys your age. Had one of my own once. Liked to pull the wool too, he did. Think I'm daft, don't you? Legs don't work, older than dad, she's easy to get one over on. Well I'm not — and whether you're late because the shop was busy or whether it's because you was up to some little scam of your own, you're going to be penalised. To teach you. Then you'll see who's daft.' Planting ham-like hands on the chair arms she heaved herself up, grabbed the zimmer, struggled towards him. 'Me laddo's in the shed — '

'Blue?' Jacob was aghast. 'You can't put him in the shed.'

'Oh can't I? Tell him not to bellow while you're gone and I won't need to do it again. Stop!'

Jacob, halfway out the door, did as he was bidden.

'You needn't think you're doing no knight-in-shining-armour thing either. Leave him to yell a while longer.'

'If anyone hears him they'll . . . '

Call the police? Social services?

Jacob fell silent, stepped back into the

room. That would be the best thing to happen right now. *Please God, let someone hear him and worry — that copper, the vicar, anyone. Get help.*

'You praying?'

He opened his eyes, not realising he'd shut them. 'No . . . thinking.' *God's on a coffee break, he can't hear you. Got to work this one out yourself, sunshine.*

'Well,' she stopped in front of him, grabbed his wrist with a surprisingly firm grip. 'Start thinking about your penalty while you lock the front door,' she fished down her cleavage for the key. 'You can start with the ironing. Do it in the kitchen and you'll be able to hear young 'un if he gets more upset.'

'The ironing?' Jacob's jaw threatened to get splinters from the floorboards. 'What, all of it?'

'Yes. And that's only for being a few minutes late — imagine what it'll be if you go beyond that.'

He couldn't bear to.

The kitchen was cold, and smelled of fried food and damp. His breath wisped before his nose as he pulled the ironing board from behind its curtain in the adjoining loo and took the iron from under the sink. He'd never ironed before. He'd recently been responsible for his own school uniform but, since he hardly ever went, and since it often got ripped in fights when he did, he didn't bother to do more than stuff it under the mattress before he went to sleep. This iron, he realised, was supposed to have water in it. It took a minute or two for him to work out where to put it then, while he waited for it to heat up, he snuck into the yard.

All was silent. Was that a good thing? Was Blue asleep? Or had he died of hypothermia — or asphyxiation? Opening the shed door and peering in was something he wanted to prepare himself for, but he daren't. Mrs J could be on him at any moment. He took a deep breath, forced himself to open the door and look. Blue, cheeks rosy and tramlined with dried tears, slept. His chest, in his purple all-in-one, rose and fell gently. Jacob let out the breath he hadn't realised he was holding. That was all right then. He touched Blue's hand, testing the temperature. Cold. Shucking off his jacket, he draped it over the baby and let him be. Later, if Mrs J seemed amenable, he'd wheel the buggy into the kitchen. Maybe he could stash it in the larder. He'd reached the door before he decided to do that anyway. What could she do to him? Make him scrub the carpets? Anything would be worth keeping Blue warm.

The iron was steaming by the time he'd got the still-sleeping baby ensconced in his new dwelling. The door was ajar, hiding the buggy from the hall doorway should Mrs J come and hover there. Should she wander round the kitchen, he was in shit.

Ironing was probably the hardest thing he'd ever attempted, he decided. Shirts were bloody impossible. The sleeves were OK — but the fronts and the backs! Either one was fine on its own. Do the back — perfect. But turn the garment over and try to do the fronts and you buggered up the back again. No wonder it took women all fucking day to do things like this. He could remember Dad clonking them one 'cos he thought they'd not done enough work in the house while he'd been at work. Maybe he should have tried ironing. Maybe he would've understood then.

Twenty minutes it took him to do his first shirt. Twenty five the second. And by then he was hot and very, very angry. What else was there in the basket? Tea towels. Plenty of them. He only had to do one side if he folded them ironed side up — no one would be any the wiser. Fifteen minutes it took him to do all those. Stopped counting after twenty. Why did she need so many tea towels? She couldn't have known in advance that Blue would be a house guest.

Tablecloths next; and hankies; towels? Who ironed towels? Tina never had. Jacob didn't intend to. Folding them, he put them beneath the tea towels. Just the shirts then. Fuck that! Folding them as best he could, he placed them at the bottom of the basket with everything else on top. He finished just as Blue started snuffling for attention.

29

The Jolly Tar. Not an original name for a pub, thought Lawson, taking his pint and making for the same table he'd shared with Kate the previous evening. How he wished he could transport himself back twenty four hours. He'd take her to a different pub and they'd never bump into Big D. Sod's law. Lawson's luck. Still, his optimistic voice insisted, it'll give us a chance to discuss the case properly if nothing else. Quality time at the nick was impossible, Lawson found himself feeling strangely neglected. He checked his watch. Big D was nearly twenty minutes late. Again he thought back to the previous evening, Kate had been this late. He'd just been thinking she'd stood him up when she'd arrived — and dropped the bombshell that she was a parent. And it had been a bombshell. He was ashamed of that.

He'd always considered that a woman he liked having a child already wouldn't be an issue. Only it was. He'd sat up most of the night thinking, with the aid of Jack Daniel's — not that there was much sense to be had there. He didn't want a ready-made family, didn't want the responsibility of being a father when he was still getting used to the idea of having another adult around permanently. That had shocked him though, that he was even considering getting serious with Kate when he barely knew her.

Slowly, slowly, catchee monkey, said his father's voice again.

'Started without me,' said Dungannon's voice in his ear. 'Won't take me long to catch up mind. What you on?'

'Lager.'

'Chaser?'

'No thanks,' Lawson smiled. 'Had enough of them last night.'

'Case getting on top of you?'

'No, it's not the case.'

'I see, say no more,' Dungannon threw him a sly wink before getting the drinks.

'Here, get that down your neck.' He put two pints in front of Lawson. 'Two for the price of one,' he said in reply to Lawson's raised eyebrows. 'Lodger's perk.'

'How long have you been living here?' Immediately, Dungannon's face closed and Lawson regretted asking the question. 'Sorry, I didn't mean to pry.'

'You're not,' Dungannon sighed. 'About a month, in answer to your question. Between billets, you might say.' He sipped his beer, indicating the end of that particular subject. 'How you settling in, lad?'

'OK.'

'How's your mother?'

Lawson opened his mouth to give the genuine answer then caught Dungannon's grin. 'Oh, you mean my date with Kate?' He knew he shouldn't have lied to his boss.

'The very same.'

'It was a little white lie, saying I was going out with my mother last night.'

'I'm a detective, I'd worked that out, son. Don't blame you though, given the choice of companion, I'd have plumped for her too.'

Lawson smiled. 'Thanks.'

'Mind, you've got your hands full with these two dead 'uns and two missing kids.'

'Yep — but I've located the kids, they're where I thought they were.'

'Eyeballed 'em, have you?'

'Yep. This morning.'

'So why didn't you go in all guns blazing?'

'Sophie's in charge of that side. I'm just lending the muscle.'

'Sophie Sullivan,' Dungannon stared morosely into his glass. 'Can't shake her, can I?'

'Sir,' Lawson hesitated. 'Can I ask what your problem is with her?'

'No.'

'OK. Oh, she did send a message for you . . . '

Dungannon's head snapped up. 'Did she?'

'Well, kind of. She said to ask you how Arnie was.' Lawson watched Dungannon's face closely, but he was giving nothing away.

'Uh-huh. Let's get back to the case, shall we? How we doing?'

'Both bodies, same MO, same murderer, same area, no real idea who did it.' Lawson took a mouthful of lager, wiped the froth from his upper lip on his sleeve.

'Prime suspect?'

'Interchangeable. All got impenetratable alibis.'

'Lovely!'

'Delightful.'

'And who are these suspects?'

'Main one — Danny James.'

Dungannon grunted. 'Always top of the hit parade, that one. It'd be nice to pin it on him and get him out of circulation for the rest of my career. Very nice indeed. Evidence?'

'Not a lot. Gut feeling.'

'A jury won't go for that.'

'I know.'

'Who else?' Dungannon downed the last of his second pint.

'Well, there's Margaret Dubois and Stan Rawlings and one or two others all linked

358

with The Fairweather Organisation; it could be a co-operative sort of a murder.'

'What, they all did it?' Dungannon frowned.

Lawson nodded.

'Very Agatha Christie. What about Dotty's fella — Gus, was it?'

'Nah, he fell at the first hurdle. But,' Lawson stood, collected the glasses. 'I can't help thinking I know something I can't quite remember.'

'In my experience that's a lack of alcohol. Get 'em in lad.'

'So,' Dungannon spoke as Lawson returned to the table. 'How do the two youngsters end up with Ma James?'

'Not sure. Find it odd, I have to say, that Jacob ends up in the enemy camp.'

'Have you spoken to Ma James about this?'

'Yes. She categorically denied having anyone there.'

'Surprise, surprise. Is Danny there too?'

Lawson shook his head. 'By all accounts, Danny is on holiday.'

'Which actually means he's gone to ground, is my guess. He can't move far without leaving a trail of breadcrumbs like Hansel and Gretel. Might be worth getting heavy with one or two of his cohorts. Danny James doesn't know the meaning of discreet.

In the meantime, are those kids safe there? When is Sophie planning to go in?'

'Tomorrow.'

'Seems strange to me — the delay.'

'Don't look at me, sir, I'm just doing as I'm told.'

'I'm not blaming you Lawson, believe me, I know what she can be like.'

'Mm.'

'Don't go all quiet on me — what are you thinking?'

'That thought that was floating just out of reach?'

Dungannon nodded.

'I think it's coming in to land.'

'See, lubrication's the answer. Spit it out.'

'Last time we went to Dave Palmer's there was a letter addressed to Mrs B. Harker. Didn't think anything of it. But I was going through a file earlier regarding The Fairweather Organisation. There were two contact names — one was the president, Margaret Dubois. The other was the secretary, Bettina Harker. And, the day I found Dotty's leggings in Stan Rawlings' car, there was a note pad in the glove box with the name 'Betty' and a phone number next to it.'

'I can tell by the tone of your voice that I should be getting this — but I'm afraid I'm not so you'll have to enlighten me.'

'Bettina Harker — Tina Harker?'

'Could well be. Why wasn't it followed up sooner?'

'Other stuff happened. But, if it is — '

'It opens the case up nicely again.' Dungannon smiled. 'So, after you've done your rescuing bit with Sophie tomorrow, you and Kate can pay another visit to Margaret Dubois. Is the mother worth questioning again?'

'Audrey Willis?' Lawson shook his head. 'Poor cow is shot. Wondering where her grandson is isn't helping.'

'She'll take him on?'

'Presumably.'

'Actually, I'd quite like to be involved in the raid in the morning. I'll pick you up at eight-thirty sharp. Which means,' he checked his watch, stood. 'It must be time for bed. Good night.' He headed for the door marked 'Private', paused, retraced his steps. 'If I may just say something on the subject of women — not that I profess to be an expert or anything — colleagues can make very complicated bedfellows. I'm not saying don't do it. I'm saying that if forgetting to call her by her professional title in regard to work is the simplest mistake you make, you're a very lucky man.'

Lawson watched him go. He'd misjudged

the man. Expecting a bollocking, the gentle chiding had left him wordless and limp. If Dungannon was as thoughtful about everything else as he'd been about Kate, working with him might not be such a trial after all. Maybe, in time, he'd feel free enough to solve the latest mystery. Just who the hell was Arnie?

* * *

'How many times do I need a policeman on my doorstep to qualify for a teasmade?' Margaret Dubois, all glitter eyeshadow and gold nail polish, stood, mini-skirted, on her doorstep.

'What a fetching outfit,' Dungannon sleazed, deliberately ignoring her sarcasm and eyeing her thighs. 'May we come in? Else you may find you're only eligible for the booby prize.'

'Might prefer it.'

'It includes a ride to the station,' he stepped back, waved an arm at the waiting car. 'Shall we go?'

Sighing, she let them in. 'I'm not making tea, mind . . .'

'That's fine, I only drink coffee in the morning anyway.'

She led them past a tightly shut lounge

door to the kitchen. 'You needn't get too comfortable; I'm going out shortly. And sit at the table, will you? I don't want anyone walking by and seeing you here.'

Lawson obeyed, moving a pile of newspapers across the table to make room for his elbows. 'Nice piece of pine,' he started hopefully, swiping his palm across its surface.

Dungannon, crossing to the window, snorted. 'We're not here to make small talk.' He wiped a hole in the condensationed window, peered out. 'A pathway and a stream. How quaint. Can I ask where it goes to and from?'

'From the shops at Fern Corner to the Common.'

'And it gets a lot of use?'

There's a lot of people on this estate Mr . . . ?'

'DI Dungannon. So sorry, very remiss of me not to introduce myself. And you don't want anyone seeing us here. Is that because of the job we do — or the job *you* do?' He turned his back to the window, leant against the sink.

'That's harassment,' Margaret Dubois said in a quiet but assertive voice.

'Not in my book. I'm merely respecting the height to which you've managed to scramble up your chosen tree. From this distance,' he paused to flash a Cheshire-cat smile. 'Yours appears to be a monkey puzzle.'

'Pardon?'

Lawson was glad she'd responded thus, it was on the tip of his tongue to do the same.

Dungannon steepled his fingers. 'I'm always honoured to meet someone who has a high-ranking title — particularly one so high-ranking as president. Ah,' he smiled again as she turned chalk-white. 'I see we're on the same wavelength. Contrary to anything you may have said previously, we have discovered a link between you and Bettina Harker.'

'I didn't say anything.' Her cheeks were fired with red now, her eyes blazing.

'Did you not?' He didn't wait for a reply. 'No matter, we've found one anyway. Still having trouble with the link to Tabbi Willis — but Dotty Spangle and you must have gone back a long way. She being in the organisation and you being president. I take it the vacancy wasn't advertised in the local paper? Something you inherit, isn't it?'

She dropped her eyes to the floor then looked at Lawson. He had the sudden image of a deer looking down the barrel of a hunter's gun, fearful, trapped. 'I knew Dotty, yes.'

'Goo-ood. Co-operation at last.'

Lawson thought Dungannon only needed the hypnotising eyes to be doing a bloody good impression of Kaa in the Jungle Book. And, he conceded, he was doing a bloody good impression of a bemused Mowgli.

'Had you known Dotty from school?' He became serious. 'Don't take this the wrong way,' he looked her up and down. 'But my guess is you could have been in the same class.'

'Flattery will get you everywhere, Mr Dungannon. As I'm sure you're very well aware, I'm considerably older than Dotty was.'

'Just better preserved?'

She eyed him with hostility. 'Let's just say my path was less pot-holed, my bank balance more stable.'

'But you knew her as a child?'

She nodded. 'I was in the last year of grammar school when she started.'

Lawson started scribbling in his notebook.

'So,' Dungannon stretched, moved across to the Welsh dresser on the dividing wall and pretended to peruse the collection of plates that sat on it. 'How did you become pally?'

She paused again, half-closed her eyes as though trying to work out how she should proceed. Who, or what, was she afraid of, wondered Lawson. There must be something or else why hadn't she admitted to all this sooner?

'It's curious how things work out,' she smiled tightly at Dungannon before carrying on.

At school the two girls had been enemies. 'I was supposed to be keeping an eye on her class — make sure they settled in properly — but I couldn't stand her then.'

Dotty had come from the rough end of town, only daughter of a manic-depressive mother and an alcoholic father. Her father had eventually not come home one night, was not heard of again. Strangely, it was when he'd been given up for dead that her mother became 'cured'.

Margaret's life had been completely opposite. Daddy had been a banker, Mummy a housewife. She had wanted for nothing — material — that is. Emotion, though, was not allowed. When her cat had been run over and she'd cried on seeing its stiff, sightless body, she'd been sent upstairs to her room and told not to come down again until she'd 'pulled herself together'.

'Very stiff upper lip,' she said now with a bitter smile.

Then Daddy had died. Again there was no emotion — until her mother discovered he'd left no money; that the house they lived in was mortgaged beyond the hilt; that they would lose everything, for she had no way to support the pair of them. She had a nervous breakdown.

'So, I was alone in the world with no money — and no means of getting any. What's a girl to do?'

'Become a prostitute?' suggested Dungannon.

'I'm glad you weren't my careers advisor. No, that came later.'

She'd been wandering the town one night, not drinking unless someone bought her a drink, killing the hours until, exhausted, she would crash in a shop doorway for a few hours before moving on again. ('It happened even then you know. Today doesn't have the monopoly.') Outside a pub, the Joiner's Arms, a man she had vaguely known had offered her a drink. Cold, lonely, she accepted. The pub was busy, warm and there was someone singing, well, in the far corner. She moved closer to see. Dorothy Smith or, as the legend painted on an ancient drum said, 'Dotty Spangle and her Spanglettes.'

The Spanglettes weren't up to much, something she wasted no time in telling Dotty during a break in the performance. The landlord, a grizzled ex-mariner, agreed. 'What you needs,' he croaked on a wave of tobacco-tainted breath, 'Is to get rid of them three no-goods and go solo. Go to London, the streets there is paved with gold.'

In a moment of rashness, which to this day, she couldn't explain, Margaret offered to be Dotty's agent, to do the touting for business and to find a place for them to live, since the main objection on Dotty's part seemed to be that if she got rid of the Spanglettes, she'd lose her bed on their sofa. 'I can 'elp you wiv that,' continued the landlord. 'I got a place across the street wot you can rent. Cheap, like.'

'So we did,' Margaret smiled at the memory. 'God, it was the pits. Forty seven Godolphin Terrace. Slums like you've never seen nor likely be able to imagine. Could have been Buck House as far as we were concerned — our own place. All we had to do was pay the rent.'

'Godolphin Terrace?' Dungannon frowned. 'I'm not familiar with that.'

'It was where CashSave is now,' she smiled and said quietly. 'Bless her, Dotty never wanted to leave the nerve centre.' After a thoughtful pause, she carried on.

They went up to London where they soon discovered that the streets *were* paved with gold — but only at night when it was raining and the streetlights threw off their yellow glow.

'She made a few gigs. She was good — it wasn't that — and I was a pretty good agent. Trouble is, there's so many sharks out for an easy buck — promise you this, that and the other for after you've performed, then bog off before the end of the performance. We soon got wise and asked for money up-front. Mostly they said no, but sometimes they would as long as we agreed to stay the night too.'

'And did you?' Lawson was incredulous.

'Sure. We had rent to pay. We had to prove to our mothers that we were capable of independence. We had to prove to ourselves that we could manage without men — we didn't want to end up like our mothers, chewed up and spat out.'

'And didn't you?' Lawson persisted.

She looked at him sadly 'Yes. But we couldn't admit that to anyone. Oh . . . ' she wiped away a stray tear ' . . . the arrogance of youth.'

The pull of London hadn't lasted long. Transport costs backwards and forwards added to their financial crisis. Digs in London were too expensive to even contemplate. They set up their operation in Godolphin Terrace, foregoing the singing side and getting straight down to the other. They made a packet, eventually buying the property from the landlord and ultimately acquiring the whole terrace which they sold, much later and for a very healthy sum, to the council, who promptly bulldozed it flat.

'A prostitute, though, reaches an age where the work dries up — along with her skin,' she gave a hollow laugh. 'We were lucky, we'd got money enough to last us our lifetimes. Many others *weren't* so lucky. And then I inherited the managing-directorship of The Fairweather Organisation.'

'Coincidence?' Lawson hazarded.

She frowned. 'No, always on the cards. But it was a fabulous opportunity for those women who weren't ready to be put out to pasture, just needed a hand to re-train, learn new life skills. Like Income Support, only much, much, more — if you need a comparison.'

'So,' Dungannon cracked his knuckles. 'Dotty Spangle's monthly income — the two-thousand-pound direct debit — came from the organisation?'

Ms Dubois nodded. 'It was all I could do to help her. She got involved with Gus see, stupid cow.' She shook her head. 'She was so proud of the fact she'd hooked this fella *and* had enough regular clients still prepared to sleep with her to make her feel special.'

'*That* made her feel special?' Lawson looked up in surprise.

'You forget,' she crossed the room, flicked on the kettle. 'She'd been abandoned by her father. It was the only treatment she knew from men — it was the only way she knew how to deal with them. She expected no emotional support, just money enough to help her survive.'

'But as fast as the money was going into her account, it was going out again.' Dungannon's eyes had lit up at the prospect of coffee.

'She gave it all to Gus. He said he was into stocks and shares — maybe he was, but he wasn't very good. She gave him all her money. Can you believe that — *all* her money? And he promptly lost it. Or so he said. I'm not sure he didn't put it into his account for his twilight years — maybe it's still there.'

'Couldn't you have put the money somewhere where it would stay safe until — if — she needed it?' Lawson smiled at Dungannon's face as Ms Dubois took one mug off the mug tree, tipped in a spoonful of coffee and added hot water.

'Mr Lawson, I am neither her mother nor her financial advisor. What she does — did

— with her own money was entirely down to her.'

'Do you think Gus is capable of killing?' Dungannon, overcoming his disappointment, fiddled with a plate.

'Please don't do that. Gus?' She pondered as though she'd never contemplated this possibility before. 'He'd been in some trouble, oh, a long time before he met her, but I've never seen him anything other than courteous — '

'Doesn't mean anything,' Dungannon sneered.

'Oh, I know, I know, Mr Dungannon. Believe me, the first rule of survival if you're going to become a prostitute is to learn to work out which punters are likely to kill you — and then give them a wide berth.'

'Didn't help Dotty.' Dungannon prompted again. 'Gus?'

She paused. 'No. No, he wouldn't kill her.'

'You seem very sure.'

'I am.'

'Any idea who might?'

'Do you not think I've spent hours trying to work that out?'

'Bettina Harker? Could she have done it?'

'Who?'

'Bettina Harker — secretary of the organisation.'

'Oh,' suddenly she looked very uncomfortable. 'You have been doing your homework. I don't know — and I'm being straight here. She was elected without my approval — '

'Behind your back?' Lawson gasped, scribbling quickly enough to take the gold medal should it ever become an Olympic sport.

'No, without my approval. I admit she was the most . . . appropriate . . . candidate, I just didn't like her. No reason for that either — don't know her well enough. Keep out of her way and she keeps out of mine.'

'Difficult to run a tight ship if the captain and first mate don't see eye to eye,' Dungannon observed. 'Wasn't Dotty the most likely candidate?'

'She would have been if she'd remained manless.'

'I see,' Dungannon nodded, frowned. 'But Tina's with Dave Palmer — '

'And now you see my objection. Young blood see, want things changing. I'm not old-fashioned, perish the thought, but I do have my standards.'

'Tabbi Willis,' Dungannon hoped a sudden change of tack might wrong-foot her and offer up some answers. 'Where does she fit in?'

She bit her lip, dropped her gaze.

Silence.

There were more questions than ever now, Dungannon sighed inwardly, and unfortunately he seemed to have utilised the handbrake as far as Ms Dubois was concerned.

'If it helps, I can arrest you — make you tell us what you know.'

She shrugged. 'You can do what you like, I'm saying no more here.'

Dungannon nodded at Lawson to do the honours and went to prepare the car for taking their passenger in.

30

'I take it I'm allowed my own pet solicitor.' Margaret Dubois, looking so laid back Lawson thought she'd be better suited to lying on a beach, dragged deeply on her cigarette.

'Of course,' Lawson smiled nervously. Somehow the balance seemed to have tipped. Instead of him having the edge on his own territory, he felt a tension in the air, as though Ms Dubois were a tiger waiting to pounce.

'Good.' She blew a smoke ring. 'Then I insist on having Fiona Rex.' She grinned triumphantly.

Lawson sighed. A run-in with Tyrannosaurus was the last thing he needed today. He raised a smile. 'Very well. I shall call her and we'll start this interview just as soon as she arrives. In the meantime, I'm sure the WPC ... ' he nodded to the young woman sitting by the door ' ... will be glad to provide you with coffee if you so desire.'

★ ★ ★

Finally. Lawson couldn't believe his ears — or his luck; just when he was going for a quick coffee-break. 'Dave Palmer?' He repeated when the duty sergeant told him.

'Yep. In interview room two. Get your skates on and you just might get to say hi before he's released once more.'

'Funny ha, ha. Like I'm supposed to know he's there when no one's told me!'

'And here's me thinking you attended that ESP course the other week!'

'Kate,' Lawson grabbed her arm as she passed. 'Busy?'

'Well, I wasn't — but I can always invent something!'

'Don't you start playing me up! Dave Palmer's turned up . . .'

'How?'

Lawson shrugged. 'Not the foggiest. But I need to speak to him — like, yesterday. Free to assist?'

She smiled grimly. 'Try stopping me.'

★ ★ ★

'Ain't seen Jacob for a week.' Palmer screwed up his face. 'I think.'

'This isn't actually about Jacob.' Lawson straddled the chair across the desk from him.

'And I don't know where Tina got them bruises from.'

'My, my, we do have a guilty conscience, don't we?'

Palmer gave him a sidelong glance. 'So, see, you can't keep me here. Ain't got nothing on me.'

'We just want a chat with you,' Kate Rogers smiled, placed a cup of coffee before each of them. 'We just want to know if you knew, say, Danny James?'

Palmer shook his head, caught the expression on Lawson's face, sighed, nodded. 'Yeah. I know of Danny. Not seen him for ages though.'

'Of course not.' Lawson steepled his fingers. 'Can you be more specific about the last time you *did* see him?'

'No.'

'Mr Palmer,' Kate Rogers put her pen down, looked him directly in the eye. 'You might show us the courtesy of at least *thinking* about it.'

'And you won't let me go until I do, right?'

'Something like that,' said Lawson in as pleasant a tone as he could muster.

'OK. Let me think.'

In the silence that followed, Lawson listened to his heart beating in time to the clock on the wall; tried, surreptitiously, to glance sideways at Kate who, it appeared, was trying to do the same to him.

''Bout ten days.'

'And where was this?'

'He came round the house. Said he was on to a job that was a winner and that he could cut me in.'

'And what did you say?' Lawson leaned forward.

'I said I weren't interested. Been stung by him before — don't need it, know what I mean?'

'No.'

'Well, he's not always good at remembering who's done him favours — especially when payment's due — and I ain't doing nowt for free ever again.'

'Sensible strategy,' Kate Rogers mumbled.

'Any idea what this job was?' Lawson prodded.

'Not rightly, no. Usually up to no good. I mean ... ' he tried the innocent plea ' ... even for me. I can't be getting involved with that side of things.'

'He still doing the porn then?' Lawson stood as Dungannon entered the room.

'I ... don't rightly know. Like I said, I didn't want to get involved.'

'You wouldn't be going all shy just because I've shown my pretty little face, would you?' Dungannon perched on the edge of the table.

'For the benefit of the tape, DI Dungannon has just entered the room,' Lawson said.

'Nothing like stating the obvious, lad,' Dungannon sat down and put his feet on Lawson's chair. 'Now then, what can you tell me about the death of Dotty Spangle?'

Palmer's face went through several shades before remaining a dull red. 'I ain't done that! What's the real reason you got me in here? To pin all your unsolved crimes on me?'

'Don't tempt me, Mr Palmer.' Dungannon dropped his voice. 'I believe you *did* have something to do with Dotty's death because you weren't at home that night.'

'I wasn't, you're right,' Palmer nodded slowly. 'Tina covered for me.'

'And that is because?'

'I nipped over on the ferry — did a drinks run.'

'Filled up a Transit with cheap booze and sold it on for a profit?'

'Yeah.'

'And, when you heard about Dotty, you asked Tina to lie for you because you knew that we'd think you did it.'

'Yeah.'

'And so now, because that *is* what we think, you're suddenly, conveniently, out of the country with no alibis . . . I take it you *do* have no alibis?'

'Yeah.'

'Oh dear,' Dungannon got up, started pacing the room. 'I think you may be in a teency-weency bit of trouble, Mr Palmer. My colleague and I . . . ' he nodded at Lawson ' . . . will leave you to consider your options while we catch up on some other pressing business.'

★ ★ ★

Tyrannosaurus had arrived. 'My client is innocent.'

'Of course she is. We just wanted a chat, that's all.'

Margaret Dubois, still looking very intimidating, smiled coldly. 'That isn't the way it sounded before.'

'Let's just say,' Lawson intoned. 'That things have changed subtly since we last spoke. Perhaps you would like to continue where you left off at the house?'

Tina was a family friend of Stan and Nora Rawlings and Nora's sister and brother-in-law, Mr and Mrs Flint. Floating around on the periphery of Danny's organisation, she got involved with Dave when Danny started to get heavy with her.

Audrey Willis had also 'helped' Stan Rawlings with his housework.

380

'Gets around doesn't she?' Lawson mused. 'Any particular reason? Was he somehow involved with Tabbi too?'

He'd known, admitted Ms Dubois, and had joined the pact to keep an eye on her. Not, she continued, that he saw much of her. Tabbi wasn't one for home visiting.

'There now,' Dungannon flashed a humourless smile. 'That didn't hurt did it?'

'Is that it?' Tyrannosaurus glared.

'Like I said,' Lawson tried to soothe the situation. 'Things had changed slightly by the time you arrived.'

'Then I shall take my leave and,' she turned to her client, 'if I were you, I'd get out of here before they think of some other useless questions to ask you.'

★ ★ ★

Kate and Sophie marched on one Amber Close together. Lawson, unexpectedly delayed with the continuation of his interview with Dave Palmer, had told them to carry on without him.

The front door opened before they'd hardly had time to knock.

'Mrs James,' Sophie stepped forward. 'We've come to talk to you about a young lad we've reason to believe has been staying here

— Jacob Palmer? And we also believe there may be a baby with him.'

Mrs James shook her head. 'Ain't been no baby. Lad's been here a night or two. Moved on now though.'

'Oh,' Sophie sounded surprised. 'When did he go?'

'Last evening.'

'And did he give you any idea as to where he might have been going?'

Mrs James shook her head. 'Not got a clue.'

An uneasy silence fell, along with the drizzle that fell relentlessly from the overcast sky. Finally Mrs James spoke.

'What is it you want me to say? That I can magic him out of thin air? That you can come in and look round? Well, I can do the latter if it means you'll get off my doorstep and let me get back to the telly.'

Kate sighed. If this was the reaction they were getting then there was little doubt the boy wasn't here. Missed him again. She half-turned for the gate, was surprised to hear Sophie say yes, of course they'd appreciate being able to look round, and disappearing into the gloom.

He wasn't there.

He'd been there. A T-shirt in the kitchen and an empty nappy packet in the bathroom left them in no doubt. But he wasn't there now. The policewoman and the social worker left side by side, at a loss as to what to do now.

*   *   *

Mrs J had seen them coming and sent him out into the shed. Last night she'd instructed him to pack everything into a dustbin sack and leave it by the kitchen door, ready for just such an eventuality. She wasn't daft; she'd known that it wouldn't be long now before the law got firmer. He'd managed to leave a T-shirt in the kitchen, hoped it would give them a clue that he was still around. Blue whimpered beside him.

'Won't be long,' he whispered. 'Someone'll get us out of here soon.'

*   *   *

Things were getting worse, decided Lawson. Lots. Not only had they lost the boy, they'd just received a message to say Stan Rawlings had died. And so, unless they got a medium in, his secrets had gone with him to the next life.

31

Danny closed the loft hatch after him. A four-pack to keep him company through his vigil, he sat on the windowsill at the opposite end of the rose window, peering across the road to the bedroom next to his. He'd followed the boy to the supermarket; entertained himself by dodging around ends of aisles split seconds before the boy would see him. Got him shopping for her now had she? Trying to make him into a son. Ha! He'd soon stop that.

Beside his leather trainers, grubby, cracked, hole in the right toe, was a pile of videos. White labels gave nothing away. Danny smiled. Would Jacob be gullible enough to have his head turned by the opportunity to star in a movie? Maybe, others had. Got the jitters when they realised there was no Tom Cruise to star alongside them. Naked women; perverts; no Tom Cruise. Danny took the top video in his hand, turned it over and over like a large bar of soap; he stroked the spine, gently.

The bedroom light went on across the road. Jacob, getting ready for bed, was naked to the waist. Danny watched, fascinated. He didn't want to know what other men saw in women; young lads did it for him. Since that catastrophe with Melanie all those years before. Put him right off. And he'd been right — Jacob *was* star material. The boy stood at the window, one hand on each curtain, ready to pull them shut. He paused, looked directly at Danny who, although he knew Jacob couldn't see him, ducked. He watched as the boy stood, frozen as though crucified (now there was an idea!), before his shoulders sagged. He let go the curtains, leaving them open, and turned towards the bed. He bent forward, straightened up with the crying brat in his arms. What youngster, thought Danny, spent all his time looking after a brat like that if there was nothing in it for him? In his experience, no one. So, the lad must have sinister ideas about the brat . . . a man after his own heart. Cracking open the first can of beer, Danny sat back to watch the cabaret as Jacob strutted back and forth with Blue.

★ ★ ★

She swore she'd never come here again. Swore she'd leave things well alone. At the corner of Church Lane and Amber Close she paused, checking all around her. No one in sight. No witnesses. Good. Slipping across the road, she kept to the shadows, moving on tip-toe, turning her face away from the circle of light thrown by the streetlight outside Storm Mount.

Trying to define her motivation for this adventure was something that had kept Margaret Dubois clinging to her leather sofa for most of the evening — time she knew she shouldn't waste. Since when had she worried about anyone else's welfare? Not since those early, heady days with Dotty had she cared who was in what kind of trouble. Got her in too much trouble, her conscience. She'd sworn long ago to leave people to their fates. Which was fine until the person going to get clobbered was a young lad with no one to look out for him. She'd smiled then, over her gin and tonic. Was that maternal instinct calling? At forty seven? 'Bit fucking late!' she growled.

The thinking about it, the planning, were completely different to actually performing the act. She'd not accounted for the cold for a start. Mohair and mink she may be wearing, but it was still bloody cold. And shoes. She'd not be seen dead in flatties in daylight, and here she was in trainers, a pair she couldn't even remember buying, but must have since they were stuffed at the back of her wardrobe. And her Versace jeans — blue denim tonight, not white. There *were* limits, even to this sort of caper. Now, breathlessly skulking in shadows, she realised how unfit she was. Too many fags, that was what it was.

Two lights were on at number one. The lounge and the bedroom directly above it. She ducked back as the boy crossed the window, disappeared, appeared a moment later going the other way, babe in arms, mind in a parallel universe. Waiting till the boy was briefly out of sight, she eased open the gate, trotted down the path, tripped over what turned out to be a black sack. She bit back a curse, limped the last few yards. Deciding to go straight to the spider's parlour, she tapped on the window. The TV, loud before, was suddenly silent. She could feel fear oozing through the walls. She tapped again.

This time a voice, shaky, barely audible. 'Who's there?'

'Margaret.'

'Oh!' Gasped surprise.

Margaret grimaced. Not half as surprised as she'd been when this whole crazy idea popped into her head. The narrow window to the side opened; the net curtain billowed out craving freedom like a pit pony to pasture after months underground.

'You'd better come in,' the disembodied voice continued; the sharp voice, now completely in control, that Margaret remembered so well.

'Hello.' Margaret clambered over the sill, landed in disarray on a pile of newspaper.

Mrs J laughed. 'Now I've seen everything. Lady Muck sneaking into my room at dead of night with *trainers* on her feet.'

'And thank God,' Margaret stared in disbelief around the room. 'Anything less would have brought me into contact with this contamination.'

'Not learnt no manners since you've been gone, I see.'

'Too tight to employ a cleaner?'

Mrs J narrowed her eyes. 'Just careful.'

'Don't want anyone sniffing round your no good son and finding out things you don't want them to.'

'No!'

'Eleanor, there's no need to be defensive with me — I know all there is to know. Remember?'

'Look,' Mrs J shuffled back to her chair, plonked herself down. 'I don't want you here. Tell me what brings you here then piss off.'

'Charming! Well,' Margaret closed the window, hunkered down so her head wasn't visible from outside. 'I'm here about your precious son.'

'Danny?'

'Do you have another?' Margaret raised her eyebrows, smiled into the silence. 'I thought not. Word has it that he's been up to his tricks again.'

'Word? Whose word?'

'Never you mind.'

'You always were a lying whore.'

'The words 'glass houses' and 'stones' come to mind, Eleanor. I have heard, from a reliable source — '

'The Fucking Fairweather Organisation still trying to put the world to rights, is it?'

' — that Danny owes a big favour — and he's going to use your young guest to pay it off.'

'Jacob?' Mrs J's voice dropped, her face paled.

Margaret nodded.

'No,' Mrs J shook her head. 'No. I don't believe you. Now leave. *Go!*' She hefted her cane over her shoulder like a javelin.

'Have it your way,' Margaret raised her palms in submission, pushed herself to her feet. 'But you mark my words, Danny is going to corrupt Jacob.'

Long into the night Eleanor sat, considering her unwelcome guest's words.

Long into the night, Danny sat across the road, considering the implications of the visit that had taken place at his mother's house.

★ ★ ★

The visitor had startled Jacob. Heart-thumping moments passed as he tried to pinpoint where the noises were coming from.
Downstairs.
Was it Danny again? Had he come for him this time? He could hear voices — but no deep male grunts. Who? Laying the sleeping Blue on the bed and turning off the light, he crossed to the window, catching sight only of a bulky figure clambering from Mrs J's window and half-running, half-walking down the path. His stomach lurched. Mum! Mum had come to find him, rescue him; she'd be back come morning, taking him with her.
Your mother would have taken you tonight.
He knew it was true. Sighing, he went back to bed. Sleep not possible now, he spent restless hours trying to plan for what must be the biggest escape attempt since the wooden horse.

★ ★ ★

Mother was silent. Lawson hated that. Ever since childhood she'd used that one. If he did something wrong, he only knew by the complete lack of conversation, which didn't, he told her when he reached teenagerhood, help him at all because she never explained what she was unhappy about. He could only guess — and judging by the amount and length of the silences, guessing wasn't one of his strong points. He tried again now.

'I promise,' Lawson wiped a weary hand over his brow. 'That as soon as all this is tied up you can come down. I'll have a word tomorrow about some leave.'

'But that doesn't solve my problem, does it? I know you're not eating properly, not resting properly, and I can't do anything about it.'

'It goes with the territory.'

'I know, but what I'm saying is that it didn't go with the territory when you lived here. The solution is simple: either you come back up here — or I come down there.'

'To live?' This was all he needed right now, Mother in forceful mood. She had too long to think about things, that was the trouble; no diversions in her life.

'Why not?'

'Because . . . ' What? A hundred things he couldn't say to her. 'It's not something you can decide on just like that.'

'It didn't stop you.'

True.

'But that's different, you'll leave your whole life — home, friends, culture — it's all completely different down here.'

'I don't care,' to Lawson's consternation, she started crying. 'I am *so* unhappy that I'd go to the moon if I thought it would help.'

It was Lawson's turn to fall silent. Guilt, in ladles. What was he supposed to do now?

Mother solved the dilemma. 'I think I'd better go now. Let's both think about things shall we?' The phone went dead.

Lawson sighed. Mothers were worse than wives or daughters. Where had *that* come from? He'd no experience with either. Could soon be having trouble with both. He'd seen Kate as he was leaving the station. To his shame he'd pretended not to notice her; pretended to be reading something on the noticeboard while she passed and, since she was on her way elsewhere with two others, she hadn't had the chance to stop. Naughty of him, he knew, but getting his head around this whole family thing was going to take some doing. *You've only been out with her once.*

But she was a mother, a *single* mother, and what did single mothers want? A man who was an easy touch to provide a comfortable life for her and her offspring. Deep down he didn't really believe Kate was like that — he didn't think he believed it in any case. She seemed so nice, so . . . normal. He picked up his Jack Daniel's; this was going to take some thinking about.

And then there was Tabbi Willis. Another single mother. She'd been making her way in the world — not one recommended by the government, admittedly, but she'd relied on no one save the kids she got to babysit. And she did pay them. Wrong it may have been to expect teenagers to babysit her child all night but there was a sort of fait accompli to the whole thing. Tabbi had used men in a different way — a more moral way, in his opinion. She was up-front, you knew what you were getting. A quick jump and an exchange of money. That's all. No hidden agenda, no looking back ten years down the line to see you'd been conned out of half your house, your earnings, your life. But had she really been looking for one guy she could be with? One guy to look after her and her baby? Was she just testing out any that came her way — and charging them for the pleasure? 'Sebastian Lawson,' he told himself firmly, 'You're one hell of a cynical guy.' Especially when drinking JD.

32

Tina Harker. Where to start looking? She was no longer living at Water Lane — Dave Palmer had seen to that. It seemed his best bet was the condemned building she had originally inhabited. Lawson sighed, slapped the file onto his desk. He'd have to speak to her again, no doubt about that. Her file, somewhat incomplete, revealed a darker side to her nature. Another woman out for what she could get. After a childhood spent in care- and foster-homes, she'd spent her college years in Holloway, coming out with expensive tastes — and devious ways of pandering to them. There were many gaps in her file, times when she either wasn't in Righton, wasn't documented or had been using a different name. Or she'd been sponging off some guy. Like she had Dave Palmer. But he was as bad. Got what he deserved. Bad as each other. A thought wriggled up, something that had occurred that day he and Dungannon had visited her. She'd had a black eye. Both police officers had assumed it was Palmer's handiwork. When asked, she'd shaken her head. Protecting him, was their assumption. But what if she'd wanted them to think that when, in fact, it wasn't Palmer at all? Where else would she have got a black eye from? Dotty? Was Tina capable of murder? He thought of her file again. Yes — if the price was right. Motive. He'd have to work that one out.

'Coffee?'

He jumped. Kate Rogers.

'Er, no thanks. Just got one.' He smiled thinly, picked up a cup on his desk, took a swig, forced himself not to flinch as the stone-cold liquid from yesterday slid down his throat.

'You avoiding me?' She arranged herself on the corner of his desk.

'Me?' Was it in-bred in women — this alluring pose when one was trying to play it cool?

'Yes you. I saw you making a poor job of ignoring me yesterday. Is it the thought of being responsible for a single mother that's hit the panic button?'

Thank God, he thought, I don't blush.

'Thought as much,' she stood. 'Don't deny it. I can tell by the way you can't look me in the eye. Don't worry, I'll not bother you again.'

Shit! He watched her go. That wasn't what

he wanted at all. Not at all. Why was nothing in this life ever straightforward?

'What we got?' Dungannon, nursing an oozing bacon sandwich, arranged himself on the corner of the desk Kate had just vacated. Not so alluring. Nothing so unattractive as middle-aged spread stretching shirt buttons to their limit.

'New prime suspect — Tina Harker.'

'You got there then? Thought you would eventually.' A dollop of tomato ketchup slid from the grease to land on his trousers. He whipped out an immaculately pressed handkerchief to mop it. 'Not an easy step — from Danny James to Tina Harker, I mean.'

'What do you mean, I got there in the end? You sound as though you've been waiting for me to catch up.'

'Just enjoyed watching you tussle with things, that's all. Think you've reached a sensible conclusion though.'

'I see,' Lawson, stung, leapt to his feet, scraping his chair across the tiled floor with a loud screech. 'And I suppose you're waiting for me to dot-to-dot the motive together. Well, rest assured, I'm working on it now. Just need to sharpen my pencil.'

'Touchy!' Dungannon, smiling at Lawson's retreating back, helped himself to the warm chair, dripping ketchup on Tina Harker's file and smudging it off with his pristine hankie.

'Bastard!' Lawson stormed up the corridor. 'Bastard! Bastard! Bastard!' He'd find Tina if it was the last thing he did, and the motive. He'd show Dungannon. Supercilious Son-of-a-B — Wait. What was it he'd said? Not an easy step between Danny and Tina. Was there a link? Maybe, maybe not. Good a place as any to start though.

★   ★   ★

He thought he'd got it wrong. The little house still appeared as deserted as it had the first time he'd been here, what seemed like light years ago, as he tried to track down members of The Fairweather Organisation. He wished he'd got the sixth sense that so many fictional detectives have — the one which enables them to know that a house isn't empty just because it appears that way. What Lawson possessed was a lack of knowing where else to try; Dave Palmer's place was a no-go for Tina now — if she valued her life at all. It was this lack of initiative which kept him on the doorstep, alternately ringing the bell and clattering the letterbox.

'All right, all right, all right!' A shadow lurched from the depths of the hall to distort against the patterned glass. 'All right already.

397

Give me a chance. Oh,' Tina held a towel on her wet hair. 'It's you.'

'Thought you weren't in.' Lawson stepped into the hall, followed her to the back of the house.

'Didn't stop you trying to knock the door down though.' Standing in front of the mirror in the dining room, Tina eyed him in the reflection. 'What d'you want?'

'To talk to you.' He stood in the doorway should she try to escape.

'Fire away.'

'How well did you know Dotty Spangle?'

'Who?' She rubbed her hair roughly with the towel. 'Oh, wasn't that the name of that prossie they found at Storm Mount?'

'You know damn well it was.'

'And what makes you so sure, Mr Policeman?'

'Because you're secretary of The Fair-weather Organisation and Dotty was a member.'

'So? My job's to keep the register and send out invites for our annual get-together, hardly buddy-buddy stuff.' She picked up the hair dryer sitting beside her on a Welsh dresser, switched it on, watched Lawson's face with undisguised delight as the noise denied any conversation. It took all of the five minutes she kept it on for Lawson to work out what was different about her. At first he'd thought it was merely that her hair was wet but, now it was nearly dry, he could see it was a different colour: red, in fact.

'Like it?' She switched off the dryer, fingered her hair. 'I'm off to Rio tomorrow, thought I'd change my image to fool the local constabulary.'

'Oh.'

She cackled. 'I'm joking. Surely this isn't enough to fool anyone. Just fancied a change is all.'

'Back to Dotty Spangle — '

'God, you're a bundle of fun.'

' — When did you last see her?'

'She's been dead God knows how long. What am I supposed to say?'

'The truth?'

'My version of the truth could well be different to yours.'

'Try me.'

'Like I said, I didn't know her well. I didn't know she was dead until I saw it in the paper.'

'And what did you think?'

'I was sorry. You don't think I'd put the flags out, do you?'

'That depends.'

'On what?'

Lawson shrugged.

She frowned. 'This is getting too deep for

me. I was sorry she was dead, period.'

He leaned against the door jamb, unbuttoned his coat. The house seemed unnaturally warm even on a cold day like today, a fact he put down to not being used to central heating. 'And, in your role as secretary, are there any special duties you are required to perform?'

'On a dead body?' She pulled a face.

'I meant,' he said, getting flustered. 'In the paperwork line?'

'No.' She looked confused.

'Do you contact the next name on the waiting list when a place in the organisation becomes vacant?'

'Yes.'

'And who's was the next name on your list?'

'I . . . don't remember.'

'And what about Danny James? Have you ever had more than a friendship with him?'

'I don't think that's any of your business.'

'Surprise, surprise. Maybe a voyage to the police station will jog your memory.'

'Voyage?'

'It's a little-known fact that the Righton police station is a tardis — and that once you get inside there's very little chance of you finding your way out alive.'

She eyed him curiously. 'You're mad!'

'So people tell me. So, what's it to be?'

'I'm intrigued. I'll come with you to the nick.'

He sighed. That had all turned out wrong. Next time he wouldn't be so clever.

★ ★ ★

'I thought you said she was the murderer.' Dungannon wedged him up against the wall of the corridor.

'You thought so too.'

'I *still* think so. I also think she's one very cool customer — coming in here and fronting it up. Where are you at?'

'Just about to audition for the Wizard of Oz.' He caught Dungannon's expression. 'I know, I know, I'm mad. Lack of daylight, guv, plays hell with my melanin. Add to that the fact my mother's once again on side and you'll see that I'm light-headed and free from care.'

'I see. Well,' Dungannon squeezed his shoulder, turned him back to the interview room door. 'I suggest you get your brain in gear and solve this fucking puzzle before I summon Dorothy myself and swop you for the Tin Man.'

'Sure. Er, guv?' He paused in the doorway. 'Can you just do one thing for me?'

401

Dungannon raised an eyebrow. 'Can you ring Margaret Dubois and see if she knows who was next on the waiting list for The Fairweather Organisation?' Lawson started to open the door, pulled it shut again. 'Oh! One more thing, can you get the description of the clothes Dotty was wearing the evening she died?'

'That's two things — and the answer's no. Get M'lady in there to spout about the first — '

'I think it'll take longer than I've got left on this planet to crack her.'

'Then I'm sure,' Dungannon wheeled round, grabbed a passing Kate Rogers by the shoulders and positioned her in front of Lawson. 'This young lady would be pleased to be your lacky.' He looked at his watch. 'I've got a pressing appointment with a pint.'

Ten minutes later Lawson's interview was briefly interrupted by a tap on the door. Kate Rogers, task completed, handed him a scrap of paper. 'Thanks.'

He waited until Rogers had seated herself quietly beside the door before handing the paper to Stewart to read and speaking again. 'Now we're cooking on gas. Tabbi Willis. That name ring a bell?'

'Nah. Should it?' She glared at him with the insolence of a teenage girl caught smoking behind the bike sheds.

'It was the next name on the waiting list.' He waited. Nothing. 'It's also the name . . .' he leant across the desk to look directly into Tina's eyes ' . . . the name of the girl found murdered on the riverbank.'

'Oh yeah. Remember now. Heard it on the news.'

'Coincidence, don't you think? That two dead women are linked to the organisation?'

She shrugged. 'Someone with a grudge, happens all the time.'

'Does it indeed? I think you've been watching too much telly, Ms Harker. If it is because they were linked to the organisation then Tabbi's death had to be down to someone who knew she was up for a place. That means you.'

'And Margaret.'

'Dubois? Yes, her too, but I have my reasons for believing in her innocence. No, it had to be someone who knew Tabbi was going to be offered a place — and who didn't like the idea for whatever reason. Maybe they knew someone they thought should have had that place — someone who had been waiting a long time. Maybe someone else put the squeeze on whoever murdered Tabbi. Let's say, hypothetically, that it was you.' She jumped, half-stood, slumped back into the plastic chair.

'Let's say that someone you know, who deals with iffy things, has something on you — you owe him. Maybe you're looking out for someone to fit a particular niche on his behalf. And maybe, in Tabbi, you find a way of clearing your slate. Only she won't play ball. A prostitute she may be, but only because she has a child to support. In all other ways, her outlook on life, she's a nice, moral girl.' He started pacing round the table, getting quicker as the words poured out. 'So you approach her, tell her that part of her membership of the organisation is to do whatever your friend, let's call him Danny, asks of her. Let's assume, for this hypothetical situation, that this has worked in the past, that Dotty herself was involved in just such an exercise. Did Dotty want out? Is that why she died?

'When you lay your cards on the table, Tabbi tells you to poke it. I think even you could have accepted that rejection but it's when she threatens to go to Margaret that you panic. You've got a vested interest in this deal going through. Money. Root of all evil. I remember you saying you were only staying with Dave until some money that you were expecting came through.'

'You can't prove anything.'

'Well, that's where you're wrong.' He felt all eyes in the room on him. 'Your little habit has dropped you in it, Ms Harker.'

She looked bemused.

'I thought, as soon as I saw you at your home this morning, that I recognised that top you are wearing — and yet I've never set eyes on it before. How would you describe it to me?' He turned to Stewart.

'Lacy, pink, pretty neckline . . . '

'How about, 'sexy lace top with a plunging neckline in a sort of metallic pink'?'

Stewart nodded. Tina Harker went white.

'Oh whoops, Ms Harker. I do believe you're wearing the top Dotty was last seen in — and I'm sure Forensic will back me up. How am I doing?'

'Not saying.'

'No, thought not. Still,' he clapped his hands. 'It means I can keep you here in the tardis for a while, keep you away from Danny — wouldn't want any tip-offs now, would we? WPC Rogers will show you to your accommodation. Be careful of the Daleks.'

Dungannon, who had quietly appeared in the doorway, started to applaud. 'That was some performance. Knew you'd put it all together in the end.'

'Are you telling me you were already

there?' Lawson frowned. 'Thought you were going for a pint.'

'Decided I didn't want to miss the denouement. No, I wasn't quite there — it was the recognising her top that was the master-stroke. But there is one small, niggling question. Where did the money in Margaret Dubois' account come from?'

★   ★   ★

'That's easy,' she smiled, handed them coffee. 'Audrey Willis paid me it to keep an eye on Tabbi.'

'She knew where Tabbi was?'

'No. But she knew I knew where she was, and that I was in a position to keep an eye on her.'

'So her cleaning for the neighbour was just a cover?'

'Kind of. It kept her busy — she didn't need the money. But, yes, it gave her an excuse to be here regularly without the neighbours getting suspicious.'

'So she popped in to see you for news of her daughter?'

'God no, nothing so casual. Have you any idea what that woman can be like when she starts talking? No, if I had anything to tell her, I'd put a vase of flowers in the window.

She'd pop in then. She can't help being the way she is, I know. She's lonely. She just wants people to talk to.'

Mum, thought Lawson.

Guilt.

33

It emerged as though from a dream. Escape. It was so easy he couldn't understand why he'd not thought of it before. He'd even, unintentionally, put in the groundwork. There was just one snag — Blue hadn't manifested in this escape plan. Jacob scoured the landscape from his bedroom window for an escape route. There was no conceivable way he could get Blue out unless he left the front door open. Which was no-go. If Mrs J didn't see him, Danny would from Storm Mount. And after Danny's antics the other night, Jacob had no intention of letting him anywhere near Blue. He'd have to tuck him away somewhere.

The bathroom.

Excellent idea. It has a bolt.

But to throw it he'd have to shut himself in. Time to investigate escape routes from the bathroom. Wheeling Blue, he parked him alongside the white, claw-footed bath and locked the door. He looked around. The window was small with frosted glass. He pushed it as wide open as he could, looked down. All he had to do was get down without killing himself. What would happen to Blue in that event?

Forget that. Concentrate on the job in hand.

He must have lost weight these last few days of worrying, for he slid through the window easier than he had done the kitchen window at Dad's — and that was larger than this one. A drainpipe, its paint peeling, its black covered with green, was just out of reach. If he stretched a bit further, moved his toe to the very end of the windowsill, gripped the windowframe with his nails . . . no, couldn't quite reach it.

He pulled the curtain through the window. He'd have to chance that no one would look up and notice it flapping once he'd gone. Wrapping the end of the curtain around his waist, he leant forward, launching himself at forty five degrees to the concrete below. If his foot slipped . . .

Don't think about it. Concentrate.

He had to succeed. There was no one else who knew Blue was locked in the bathroom. Although eventually, when hunger struck, it would become apparent where he was. And then there was only one person likely to attend him — Danny.

His fingers touched the drainpipe, slipped off. He stretched again. This time his palm gripped briefly but the pipe was too wide for him to get proper purchase. What to do? He looked down. The top of the back-door frame was immediately below him. Dare he abseil towards that? Did he have a choice? Already he'd gone almost too far to be able to wriggle back through the bathroom window anyway. He took a deep breath.

It was one of those moments that seem to last forever. He was conscious of every little crack in the brickwork, every speck of dirt. A spider had set up home in a crevice beneath the bathroom windowsill. Bird shit splattered down the wall. Jacob slid slowly down, his shoes scuffing the wall. He prayed no one would come into the kitchen until he was down.

No one did.

The drop between the door frame and the ground came suddenly. Time only to prepare his body for landing. Bending his knees the way he'd done so many times from trees after scrumping apples, he landed with a grunt on the concrete. Sneakers don't have very good shock absorbers; Jacob felt every last ripple shudder through his ankles, knees, body. Then he was running, crouching low, heading for the back wall.

Here another moment of worry in case anyone saw him from the house. He scrambled up, dived over the other side, not once glancing back. Straight across the road to the churchyard wall. Here he had cover. He followed the wall as it curved to accommodate the lane until he reached the junction. Climbing back over the wall, he headed for the corner shop. Now he prayed he didn't run into Danny. He'd never prayed so much as he had today.

There was one customer in the shop. Jacob watched through the window until he was sure the shopkeeper (the son, Jacob noted) had seen him, then he stepped casually inside. He didn't go to the babyfood this time. He fancied something more expensive as his swansong. Tucked in the alcove under a flight of metal stairs was a selection of videos. He'd look there. The advantage of being here was that he could keep an eye on the shopkeeper through the iron slats.

He picked up two videos, not caring which they were, laid them carefully on one of the steps. Then he thumbed through the other cases slowly, deliberately, all the time watching the shopkeeper watch him. Then, when the customer had made her purchases and the shopkeeper started over, Jacob made his move. Picking up the two videos, he ran for the door, dodging around the toiletries shelf to make it look more authentic. With the shopkeeper in hot pursuit, Jacob was out of the door and heading for the alleyway.

Deliberately he kept his pace slower than before. This time he needed to be caught. The instinct to run however, when there's footsteps behind you and you're used to being in trouble, is hard to control, but control it he did. He'd not made the first bend when the shopkeeper's arms fastened themselves around his knees and brought him, with a painful crunch, to the floor. He lay winded for a moment. His head hurt where he'd banged it and it suddenly occurred to him he could die there and no one would know what he'd been trying to do.

'Get up!' Ranjit gripped Jacob's shoulder, and pulled him to his feet. 'Come on!' He hauled him back towards the shop.

A small crowd had gathered outside and when Ranjit appeared shoving his conquest before him, they broke into whistles and applause. One held the shop door open and Jacob was pushed inside. There was no escape now. The crowd outside were blocking the door and the elderly man, the shopkeeper's father, was standing behind the counter. For the first time in his life, Jacob hoped they would call the police. That was the most important phase of his plan.

Blood dripped from his nose to the floor.

The old man pulled some tissues from a box beneath the counter and handed them to him. His head was throbbing now and his hip hurt where he'd landed on the concrete. Once again he hoped the police were on their way.

It seemed like hours later the door opened, its bell jangling. Ranjit turned round, Jacob craned to see. Relief flooded through him as he recognised the visitor. 'Thank God,' he said as Lawson stepped sternly towards him. Then Jacob collapsed in a dead faint.

* * *

He came to in the back of the police car. Even the thrill of tearing through the streets with the siren blaring didn't take the edge off his fear. Somehow he had to prove to this copper that he'd only been stealing videos to attract attention.

He studied the profile of the young policeman, PC Lawson he'd introduced himself as through the haze of Jacob's wooziness. He had a nose that came to a point a bit like a ski jump, tilted upward at the tip with a horizontal platform just before it. His chin was nondescript from this angle. His eyes couldn't be described either. Jacob decided that if he was going to be James

Bond, he'd have to brush up on his identification skills.

'Where are we going?' He suddenly realised they were going the wrong way for Mrs J's.

'To the nick. To return you to your family — after we've had a little chat, of course.'

'No!'

Lawson smiled. 'Having met your family I have to say I'd have the same response, but the law's the law. It's your Dad or going into care, I'm afraid.'

'Take me back to Mrs J's, please.'

'You like it better there, huh?'

'No. But Blue's there. I locked him in the bathroom so no one would get at him — but if Danny's worked out that I've run off, he'll kill Blue.'

And, of that, Lawson had no doubt. Without checking his mirror, he executed an emergency stop. Behind him a car braked sharply, the driver doubtless cursing. Lawson pulled a U-turn, set off with tyres squealing. 'Let's hope we get there in time.'

'I didn't want to leave him, Mister — I just couldn't think of any other way of getting help.'

'I'm not blaming you,' Lawson caught sight of the boy's frightened eyes in the rear-view mirror.

'I thought it was a good idea, going to Mrs

J's. Soon changed my mind — then she wouldn't let us leave.'

'Why?'

'Cos she's madder 'un my Aunt Fanny.'

Lawson laughed. 'Is she indeed? And how mad's that?'

'Mad enough that I had to jump out of the bathroom window to get to the corner shop to get done for shoplifting to get you to come and rescue me. Danny's watching the front of her house from Storm Mount so I couldn't even get to the phone box on the corner.'

'I see.' Lawson frowned thoughtfully. 'I think I'd better call for back-up. This could turn out to be quite a bunfight.'

34

There were no black bags on the drive. Jacob kept tucked behind Lawson, fearfully watching the upstairs curtains for clues as to occupancy. As he knocked on the door, Lawson heard sirens in the distance. Back-up wouldn't be long.

Mrs James came to the door. If she was surprised to see Jacob she didn't show it. 'Officer, how nice to see you. How can I help?'

'This young man,' Lawson put a comforting hand on Jacob's shoulder. 'Tells me he's been stopping here.'

'I . . . ' her face turned alabaster.

'And he says there's also a baby here.'

'Oh . . . '

'You'd better come in,' a voice boomed from inside.

Jacob jumped, shrank back. 'Danny!' he whispered.

'Come on in and close the door,' the voice said again.

Lawson turned and jerked his head at Jacob. 'Let's do as we're told.' From the corner of his eye he could see several officers arranging themselves in the Close. Crossing the threshold into the hall, he suddenly felt claustrophobic, even with only three players present — himself, Jacob and Mrs James with her zimmer frame. Jacob snuggled into the corner.

'Now then,' the voice continued from upstairs. 'Let's get a few things sorted out.' A figure stepped forward clutching something in his arms. Jacob and Lawson squinted. Jacob cried out.

'Blue! No!'

'Oh, Blue, yes.' Danny straightened his arms so the baby was hanging over the steep drop of the stairs.

'Now, let's just slow down son and get . . .'

'Don't you son me you patronising git.' Danny threw Blue into the air, caught him, grinned. 'I'm calling the shots. Got it?'

'Got it.' Lawson nodded in confirmation. 'What do you want?'

'Wouldn't you like to know?' Danny laughed. 'Even if you did know you wouldn't be able to provide it — not unless you're God in disguise.'

'Dropping the baby isn't going to make things better for you.' Lawson edged slightly forward.

'Oh, so now you know what I get off on, is that it? Don't drop the baby, it's bad for your digestion. You sound like my mother.' He hawked noisily, gobbed down the stairs. 'And that's what I think of her.'

Mrs J gave a muted cry and hobbled into the lounge.

'I know what you're up to,' Jacob stepped forward. 'I've got something of yours that the police will be *really* interested in. You drop Blue and I'll drop you in it.'

Lawson waved a hand at Jacob, indicating for him to follow Mrs J. If this was going to get any uglier he didn't want the boy witnessing it. Jacob resolutely ignored the PC. He was going nowhere. Blue, quiet so far, suddenly started whimpering.

'He's scared,' said Jacob. 'Please Danny, please let him go.'

'What, like this?' Danny opened his hands, let Blue go, caught him again before he dropped more than a few inches. 'Is that what you want, baby on the floor?'

'No, I mean let me come and get him. I'll give him to the police, you can have me instead and I'll give you the photos back too. That's what you want, isn't it Danny? That's what you told me before, that you had a job for me. For *me*, Danny, not for a baby. He doesn't understand what you want. I do.'

Danny laughed. 'I don't think you do — but thanks for the offer. I've changed my mind, I think a baby might be just what I need.'

'Bu — '

'Sssh!' Lawson placed a hand over Jacob's mouth. 'Let me do the talking.'

'Yeah,' Danny joined in. 'Let the big man do the talking. What you gonna do, big man? Offer to take the baby's place? I'll tell you this for nothing, I ain't interested in you.'

Lawson didn't know what to say. Any training he'd had in dealing with hostage situations hadn't involved a baby being held over a fatal drop. Thoughts whirred. There was no way he could get to the top of the stairs and grab the baby before Danny let go; there was no way of getting behind Danny and overpowering him. This was one of those puzzles he'd prefer to deal with alone in the privacy of his mind until he'd solved it and could transfer it to real life.

'Hurry up copper. What you going to do? My arms are getting tired, can't hold him here forever.'

'Give yourself up, Danny.'

'No.'

'You're not doing yourself any good.'

'And you won't do me any good if I give up.'

True.

A loud banging on the door. 'Open up!'

Lawson threw himself against Jacob, flattening the boy against the wall. Reflex, he told himself, not fear. Dungannon had just succeeded in cutting his life short by two decades. He looked up the stairs. Danny had disappeared, jolted too, no doubt, by the unexpected intrusion. Lawson opened the door.

''Bout time. Thought I'd have to get my credit card out and force the lock.' Dungannon entered, carelessly attired in flapping mac and shiny-kneed trousers. 'Heard your call. Sounded exciting. Thought I'd pop in. Where is he?'

'He was up there,' Lawson jerked his head. 'Holding the baby over the stairs. Bogged off when you politely requested entry.'

Dungannon stood, hands on hips, feet apart. 'Well, what you waiting for? Up and at him officer. Show him what you're made of. And you,' he grabbed Jacob by the scruff of the neck as he started for the stairs. 'Stay put. You're not invited this time.'

Two steps at a time, back pressed against the wall, eyes desperately searching the landing, Lawson went up. The only room with a lock on, according to Jacob, was the bathroom; the door stood open. So Danny was in a bedroom — couldn't be locked but the door could be wedged with furniture.

'Danny?' His voice shook, silently he cursed. Fine time to show his fear. It wasn't Danny who answered but Blue, whimpering softly from the front bedroom. Lawson nodded, smiled grimly. He pointed for Dungannon's benefit. His superior, two paces behind, nodded. 'After you,' he mouthed.

Lawson stood beside the door, his back to the wall, handle clutched in his sweating palm. Dungannon crossed to the other side, mouthed a count to three. Lawson turned the handle, praying his grip would hold. It did. He flung the door wide. No furniture wedging it, then — good. Lawson stepped into the room. The window was open, Danny and Blue could only have gone one way. He crossed the room, was about to peer out when the door slammed shut behind him.

'Fell for it, copper. Maybe you need to go on a refresher course.' Danny, holding Blue beneath his armpits with one hand, held a knife in the other. 'Sit on the window ledge, legs out over the sill. Go on,' he waved the knife when Lawson hesitated. 'Something else you need reminding about — the one with the weapon also has the upper hand.'

'Unless you've left the one with the brains outside the room,' boomed Dungannon. 'Am

I clear for take-off Lawson?'

'Yeah.' Lawson didn't have a clue what he was talking about.

The next few seconds were chaotic. A war cry went up from outside the bedroom, a loud thud sounded, the door shook from a large impact. Shook but didn't open. Danny stepped away from the door, a grin splitting his face into a Jack O'Lantern. He held the knife at the baby's throat.

'Tell the cavalry to back off.'

Lawson opened his mouth. Too late. Another attempt at entry was successful though not in the door-slamming-back, gun-toting way of movies; more in a splintered-door-frame, damp squib of an effort. Still, Dungannon, a red-faced Humpty Dumpty, entered at a half-jog. He cannoned into Danny, unintentionally, but with enough propulsion to send Danny and the baby in Lawson's direction. Lawson neatly side-stepped, plucked Blue from Danny's arms and watched as Danny disappeared head-first out of the window.

'Is he dead?' Like a Saint Bernard, Dungannon's tongue was hanging out.

'Dunno, guv.' Lawson stepped gingerly towards the window. He wasn't daft, he'd seen the movies where the invincible villain had grabbed the hero by the throat just when the audience thought the whole thing was done and dusted. Danny lay spreadeagled on the concrete, moaning. 'Nah, he's not dead.'

'Pity,' Dungannon turned to leave, paused at the door. 'Do something about that infant's nappy, it stinks.'

Lawson, inhaling deeply, agreed. He looked around. Where to put Blue? Jacob appeared, white-faced, in the doorway. 'Here,' Lawson handed Blue over. 'Do something with this.'

★ ★ ★

'You can take the rest of the day off,' Dungannon greeted him from the hall as he went downstairs. 'Danny's on his way to hospital. I'll follow him and twist that broken arm some, get him to confess. Mrs J has been taken in; holding a person against their will seems a pretty good place to start.'

'Yeah.' Lawson swallowed. Arrogance, he decided, could be a killer. He'd taken it upon himself to presume the boy was safe with her, not once had he considered the boy might consider it any other way. If it hadn't been for the boy's daring escape, who knows when all this may have come to light? He stepped towards the open front door, the chill air already promising to take his breath. 'Before you go, there's one last little job you can do.'

'Sure.' He stepped back to look squarely at Dungannon.

'Prise that lad from the baby. They'll have to go into care and they can't go together.'

35

Kate Rogers was descending the station steps as Lawson dragged weary legs up them. 'Tough day?'

He looked at her sympathetic face. 'Yeah.'

'Want to talk about it? I've time for a quick coffee.'

'I . . . er . . . no, I don't think so.' Ignoring her hurt expression he ploughed on. The front desk was busy. He pushed his way through, hoping none of them required his expertise. Right now, he didn't feel as though he was expert at anything. Human relationships were beyond his understanding. They were so *hard*. He couldn't imagine having feelings for anyone the way Jacob had for Blue.

It had turned his stomach inside-out having to separate them. Not because Jacob had become hysterical. No, it was worse than that. The lad had nodded sagely when Lawson told him they'd be separated. He'd handed Blue over without a murmur, gently stroking the baby's cheek before Lawson carried him to a waiting WPC. Lawson had turned at the gate to wave Jacob goodbye

— and witnessed silent tears waterfalling down his face. To need someone the way Jacob had needed Blue was something Lawson hadn't felt for a very long time. He'd been numb since his father had died. Maybe it was time to get over it, start again.

He looked after the retreating back of Kate Rogers. Should he call her back? Should he run and catch her up, go to a café away from the nick? He shook his head. With her came another set of responsibilities — and he didn't think he was up to dealing with them yet.

There was something he could do.

He hurried upstairs, grabbed the first available phone, dialled. Answerphone. 'Mum,' he tried to keep his voice level. 'Mum, if you're there pick up please. I need to talk to you. Please pick up.' Nothing. Mum, he continued in his head, I need you there; need to say I'm sorry; need you to understand where I'm coming from.

'You busy, lad?' Dungannon, firmly back in control of the situation, strode in.

'No.'

'Good, you can help me interview Tina Harker again.'

'You said I could have the rest of the day off.'

'Did I?' Dungannon looked mystified. 'Well I didn't mean it.'

You should have gone for a coffee, his father's voice said.

'Yeah.' Lawson agreed.

★ ★ ★

'Danny has told us everything.' Dungannon, puce-faced, leaned over Tina's hunched body. 'So you've nowhere left to hide, young lady.'

'He wouldn't. He promised.'

'I guess that would be before he fell out of the window. Amazing what pain can do to help the cause. The only thing I can't work out is where Dave Palmer fits into all this.'

'That's easy,' said Lawson with the confidence of sudden enlightenment. 'Dave and Danny were a team once upon a time. Danny always had a healthy regard — or should that be fear — for Dave. You decided to set this scam up with him but protected yourself from his perverse attentions by shacking up with the one person on the planet he wouldn't want to meet in a dark alley. Very clever, Ms Harker. Very, very clever.'

'Good work,' Dungannon hiked an impressed eyebrow at Lawson. 'It's nice when the jigsaw falls into place, but I do have one last question. Why did you put Dotty's leggings into Stan's car?'

'It seemed like a good idea at the time. I should have burnt them.'

Dungannon shook his head. 'Destroying the evidence would only have delayed the inevitable — we'd have got there in the end. You're set for quite a stay at Her Majesty's Pleasure. Maybe that'll take the wind out of your sails.'

Defiantly she spat in their wake as they left the room.

'Sir?' Lawson stopped in the corridor, Dungannon kept walking. 'Sir!' This time his tone commanded Dungannon to stop. 'What's going to happen to Jacob?'

'He's going back to his dad.'

'Is that wise?'

Dungannon shook his head. 'Shouldn't think so for a minute.'

'And Blue?'

'Going to live with his Gran.'

'Happy families,' muttered Lawson. 'Pity she can't have Jacob too.'

'Back to living in fairy tales are we?' Dungannon eyed him closely. 'Don't get emotionally involved with your cases, Sebastian. Concentrate on your colleagues.' He sighed, fiddled with a piece of paper on the noticeboard. 'Look, I know it's none of my business — and I know I've said this before — but you're making a huge mistake if you let Kate walk out of your life just because you can't get your head in gear. You'll live to regret it. I know things haven't been easy for you,' he raised a hand to stem Lawson's retort. 'But there comes a time when you have to move on, put it behind you, resolved or not. Some things we will never fathom. It's knowing when to let go that's the secret, not solving every little thing to the nth degree. She's a good girl. You'd make a good couple.' And with that he left, leaving Lawson standing open-mouthed.

★ ★ ★

Jacob Palmer hadn't expected much of a homecoming. He stood behind Sophie Sullivan trying to decide what to do. At intervals he peered round her to his dad's contorted face beyond. Sophie, after a pep-talk about how she would be keeping in regular contact and, if things seemed to be getting no better, she would be forced to remove Jacob from the household, squeezed Jacob's shoulder and left.

Make your decision.

I need time James, thought Jacob, don't push me.

'Fancy letting her bring you home,' Dave growled through bared teeth. 'Fucking busybody sticking her fucking nose into everybody else's business.'

'She's all right.'

Palmer carried on as though he hadn't heard him. 'And what the fuck have you to do with Tina being nicked? Why would I want you instead of her?'

'Tina's been nicked?' Jacob stared at his father. 'Why?'

Palmer barked a laugh, pushed Jacob into the house. 'Reckon she killed that Dotty tart and that other loser they found by the canal.'

'She weren't no loser!' Jacob wriggled from his father's grip. 'She was a good friend to me.'

'You knew her?'

'Yes.' Defiant.

'So you was involved then. Fucking thought so.' Dave idly clipped Jacob's ear. 'Your fault Tina got clobbered — '

'I never said nothing — '

'So you can take over her jobs in the house. Kept the place clean and tidy, I'll say that for her. 'Bout all she was good for. Bitch!'

So you were right about her after all.

'Yeah.' Agreeing seemed the best policy — for now. Jacob had no intention of staying here, he'd decided. He was out of here as soon as the opportunity revealed itself.

Keep your mouth shut, your head down — and leg it just as soon as you can.

At six his dad had sent him out for fish and chips. He could have run for it then only he knew Dad was watching him, daring him to do it. The chippy was only round the corner. He wouldn't have had a good enough head start. And anyway, the stash of money his dad kept in the freezer, the one he thought Jacob knew nothing about, had been added to since the last time Jacob had looked. This time when he ran away, he was never coming home again. He'd take the money in lieu for all the food and clothes his dad wouldn't have to provide for him. And, if he knew his dad at all, the opportunity to leave wouldn't be long in coming.

Less than three hours later Jacob was leaving the family home in Water Lane for the very last time. Dad had gone to the pub. Jacob had been banking on that. There was no way Jacob was hanging around for Dad to get back. With no woman at home to clobber he was bound to come after his son. Jacob had helped himself to the money, packed the few clothes that remained in that house, and a photo of his mother and himself taken outside the giraffe house at some zoo he couldn't remember visiting. Dad wouldn't be home yet. And when he came home, he'd have no idea where to start looking.

He'd toyed with several ideas. Spain was the obvious one but, as he didn't really have any idea where to go to get there — and anyway, he didn't have a passport — that was really a non-starter.

Tabbi's mum was another idea. Maybe she'd take pity on him, let him live alongside Blue forever. Maybe not. He daren't risk it.

Sophie Sullivan. She'd given him a card with a phone number where he could reach her any time day or night. Normally he didn't trust 'official' people, but Sophie seemed different — and that dark-skinned copper. He stopped, scrutinised himself. Was he going soft?

No, you're doing the right thing — the thing that's right for you at this moment at any rate.

Jacob nodded, James was right. Taking the card and a coin from his pocket, he went into the phone box on the corner.

★ ★ ★

Lawson pulled up outside the neat terraced house. Unsure of his welcome, he sat in the car, rehearsing a speech. He didn't know how she would react when she discovered the Big

432

D had released her address to him. Spots of rain started mingling on the windscreen with the sticky residue from the trees in the police station car park. He'd really have to park in a different space. Now or never. Pulling up his collar, he took a deep breath and headed for the front door.

Tubs sat one each side of the black painted door. Empty now, the soil was ready for next spring's blooms. He knocked lightly on the door. Why? Was he justifying the journey, banking on her not hearing him, tiptoeing away?

Coward.

The one thing his father hadn't been. According to a witness the gang that attacked had done so because he'd stepped in to stop another lad getting a beating. He probably hadn't seen the knife but, thought Lawson, he wouldn't have hesitated even so. Got him in the heart. No chance. And here, three years down the line, he, Sebastian, couldn't knock on the door of a friend. Or was she? She could only be unwelcoming though, not violent. He knocked again, this time hard enough to make the letterbox rattle.

'I'll get it!' He heard a child's voice, excited; footsteps scampering towards him. After a series of unladylike grunts, the door swung slowly open to reveal a small girl stretched to her limit to release the snib. 'Hello.'

'Hello,' he smiled at the blonde-haired child dressed in a shiny pink party frock. 'Is your mummy in?'

'Depends.' She frowned.

'On what?'

'Whether she wants to talk to you. What's your name?'

'Sebastian.'

'Wait there.' The door closed.

Moments later it opened again, this time Kate stood before him. 'Hi.'

'Hi,' he grinned. 'Some bodyguard you've got there.'

'Yeah.' She frowned. 'Did I forget to do something? Only the last time I had a doorstep visitation it was the Big D to take me back to the nick after I'd left a prisoner too long in a cell. Made me apologise.'

'Oh no, it's nothing like that. The Big D *did* send me — well kinda — he gave me your address,' he cleared his throat, shuffled back a step in case he needed to make a run for it. 'Thing is, I felt we'd got off on the wrong foot — and I'd really like to start again.'

'I see.' She smiled. 'Well that sounds acceptable to me. You'd better come in.' She stepped back. 'Oh,' she said as she closed the door behind him. 'Did I ever tell you who Arnie was?'

'No.'

'Dungannon's cat.'

THE END

We do hope that you have enjoyed reading this large print book.

Did you know that all of our titles are available for purchase?

We publish a wide range of high quality large print books including:
Romances, Mysteries, Classics
General Fiction
Non Fiction and Westerns

Special interest titles available in large print are:
The Little Oxford Dictionary
Music Book
Song Book
Hymn Book
Service Book

Also available from us courtesy of Oxford University Press:
Young Readers' Dictionary
(large print edition)
Young Readers' Thesaurus
(large print edition)

For further information or a free brochure, please contact us at:
Ulverscroft Large Print Books Ltd.,
The Green, Bradgate Road, Anstey,
Leicester, LE7 7FU, England.
Tel: (00 44) 0116 236 4325
Fax: (00 44) 0116 234 0205

SLAUGHTER HORSE

Michael Maguire

The Turf Security Division is surprised
and suspicious when playboy Wesley
Falloway's second-rate horses develop
overnight into winners. Simon Drake
investigates, but suddenly there is a new
twist — someone is out to steal General
O'Hara, the star of British bloodstock,
owned by Wesley Falloway's mother. With
a few million pounds at stake, lives are
cheap; Drake finds himself both hunter
and quarry in a murderous chase where
even his closest associates may be playing
a double game.

MERMAID'S GROUND

Alice Marlow

It's been five years since Kate Williams' beloved husband died, leaving her with two young children to raise. Now she's built a good life in one of Wiltshire's prettiest villages, and she has her dream job, as gardener at Moxham Court. For the last year, Kate has had a lover, roguishly attractive Justin Spencer, but he won't commit to more than a night here and there. When she takes in a male lodger, Jem, Kate's secretly hoping his presence will provoke a jealous reaction in Justin. What she hasn't reckoned on is exactly how attractive Jem will turn out to be.